A TREE ON FIRE

'In Albert Handley, the painter, Alan Sillitoe has given us a magnificent and memorable character.'
The Birmingham Post

'Superb Algerian interlude ... the harsh realities of the campaign are conveyed with a prose passionate with love and hate.'
Evening Standard

'There is an almost Dickensian richness in the story-telling ...'
American Publishers' Weekly

Besides Dickens, Alan Sillitoe has lately been compared to Lawrence, Silone, Camus – as formerly he was compared to such contemporary 'angry young men' as Kingsley Amis and John Braine. But comparisons are unnecessary. With this sequel to *The Death of William Posters*, Alan Sillitoe is at the peak of his powers – in a class by himself.

A TREE ON FIRE

ALAN SILLITOE

UNABRIDGED

PAN BOOKS LTD : LONDON

First published 1967 by Macmillan and Company Ltd.
This edition published 1969 by Pan Books Ltd.,
33 Tothill Street, London, S.W.1

330 02378 0

Printed in Great Britain by
Richard Clay (The Chaucer Press), Ltd., Bungay, Suffolk

PART ONE

CHAPTER ONE

WITH four-week-old Mark wrapped in his woollen shawl she went out to the upper deck. Early morning, and the liner was landlocked, grappled in stoneland near the beginning of March, white frost painted on the customs sheds under a smoky pink sky, brilliant and sharply cold, more beautiful than she'd expected, a trace of cirrus cloud, as if just scratched there by a cry from the baby and an unthinking motion of his hand. She held him upright against her shoulder, and his uneasiness subsided.

The ship had died, she thought, watching the steward move her luggage into the first-class saloon, lost its beauty and function. The grace of the sea had withdrawn from it, left dead wood, subsiding metal, a mighty ship, disembowelled of its own true spirit. She was anxious to move beyond dock cranes and sheds and dismal marshes, but stood back from the rail, an hour still to go before landing, feeling as if she'd never been to England before, a tourist about to enter a country for which no guide-book had been written. Frank had gone into the sun – or whatever he liked to call it, and the role of gun-runner to Algerian Nationalists fitted him more than most, except that here she was, landing as if she had already suffered her greatest loss because he might be dead and out of her life for ever.

Having read of a baby dying on a jet trip, she had taken the ferry from Tangier and a liner from Gibraltar. The Rock was left in cloud and rain, and green upchucking white-lipped sea, the launch packed with people ill from the squall and finally hooked to the enormous port-holed flank, so that she staggered along the gangway with Mark, luggage thrown after her. The safe ship took them in, dull luxury rocking monotonously through Biscay, enclosed among the fine yet doleful trapping of a generation ago, over the bleak Channel, three days of discomfort in balancing herself firmly to bathe the baby each evening, then sitting on the lower bunk and giving him the breast before setting him down to sleep, vivid face become tranquil, cries finished, and wind gone. In the first hour of life he looked like a rabbi, the vigorous mature face of a Jewish scholar emerging from the bluntness of Frank Dawley's fast-receding features. There was now a little more of Frank in him, but the subtleties seemed to be holding their own. By Talmudic law he was a Jew, which made her glad, though she had decided against his being circumcised in the hospital, and she was equally pleased that his father was not Jewish, proud of the rich mixture of his Saxon and Hebrew antecedents, and finally she was embarrassed at her own narrow brand of racism that, before having a child, would not have surfaced with such crudity.

Frank had gone into Algeria and never come back – not so far, anyway. During the birth her sufferings had seemed to be those of his own death, made her wonder why she had decided to bear it in Tangier instead of flying to England as she'd intended. The idea was to wait until the final possibility had beamed itself out. He'd said ten days, and she'd stayed two months beyond his point of no return. How long could one hang on? The umbilical string withered, and a new one flashed before her eyes through a smell of ether. Half conscious, she saw it, felt the final cut, and heard the first cry, senses coming back fast and clear before the great inertia of sleep. She had until now looked on her life as a long, violent, multi-scaled overture to an opera on which the curtain would never really go up. The magical lifting of it had not so far caught her eye. Yet she thought that perhaps one day it would after all lift and reveal a great new aspect of her life.

Faces passed, dazed like her own at the sudden upshoot of cranes and pink sky, calm frost, and bottle-green frog-water. The classbound world of the liner had sheltered them since Malaya and India, wherein they had dressed for dinner as if the middle of the twentieth century hadn't already passed them by. What would Frank have thought of it? She smiled at his stony nonconformity, the scorn that burned only in his eyes – as he did as he damn-well liked or

8

turned his back on it. They were middle-aged and elderly, withered dummies, formal for fear of crumbling to powder at the sudden treachery of a false move, fashion-plates from romantic pulp-stories in magazines of the thirties. To themselves, they no doubt blazed from each centre, as if a tilting safety-lamp were always about to flare up – death-faces and corpse-skins surrounding and enclosing the fire of life.

As the sun broke clearer through, smoke and fog came smelting along the outlets of the dock, revealing masts and ship-funnels just in, or about to move. Morocco was a long way from these factories, power stations, bridges. On Sundays the power slept, but she saw beyond the ratchet-faces of the English, to the features of those Moslem youths marching down the Tangier boulevard, shouting for independence in Algeria, who would never be like their fathers, because they too hoped the smoke-flags of industry might one day drift over olive-groves and carob farms, when they would also wear the masks of ratchet-faces until all nobility and peace froze out of them.

The dead wood of the unyielding ship was pleasant, no more haunting terrible gale-wail playing at black midnight through the wires and superstructure, its overture of the medieval elements about to shatter and scatter two thousand people over the tight-lipped waves. Mark slept, as if both of them were still on the voyage, an oval face already formed, lips tight to keep the soul, peace, and innocence, deliberately in. He had come out sallow and jaundiced, but the world air had tempered his skin to a normal tone. Coming through Biscay and grey humps of spume-crested sea-water as long as the boat, she'd stood one afternoon alone on the open deck, looking towards the shifting rain cliffs and the dark smudge of another ship, the baby held tight. Raindrops caught her hair, spread over glasses until she could barely see, and an impulse gripped her to lean too close, to look too far over and let her arms fall limp. Lightning shivered, a naked needle of it, piercing her infanticidal terror. The deck was empty, wet wood, chairs under cover, the ship lifting, shuddering as if to snap in spite of its liner bulk. It was nothing, they were all nothing. She would go as well, so

9

that both of them like magic would merge with the cold green nothingness of the fish-sea.

A mad malignant nothing drew her back from the rail and the hypnotic, heaving fundamental water. One nothing was as good as any other, and you were closest to death's bosom when in the deepest trough of some change. You struck the glimmer-light of nothing's deepest eyes. She sipped hot coffee in the saloon, handed Mark to the nurse for a few hours, not going on to open deck again even by herself, till now when the ship was in dock and its very wood, steel, even light-switches, had died. She had left England with a man she hardly knew, got pregnant by him, and ended up in Tangier while he went gun-running for the Algerians. So would run one version of her fate, she smiled. He had promised to come back in ten days, and certainly believed that he would, but his ideals must have got the better of him, and he had succumbed to them, unless he'd been killed crossing the invisible line of frontier that ran through the wilderness, and the baby had been fatherless even before birth. It all sounded too melodramatic – though such hard words might mean she was coming back to real earth and out of this ship.

But Dawley had vanished, and she'd never felt so much love for another person, though his love for her was such that it faded when his ideals took shape towards action. She said to him when he gone that he must not confuse ambition with fantasy. Ambition, she said to him – but to the empty blue-washed wall of her high-up terrace above Tangier – is what comes through patience, tact, and skill. Fantasy is what you strive to bring about against reason and sense. Leave it alone. Call it fantasy if you like, but enjoy it in dreams. Ambition is something to attain because at the same time it works for you. Fantasy works against you, chops across the grain of your true personality like an axe. Only if it ultimately destroys you is it worth while.

People were moving off, first-class first, which meant her, so she found her pile of luggage and joined the procession, held tightly to the rail as if the ship were still moving and she was afraid of being pitched, baby and all, too quickly down. Through the hangar-wide doorway Albert Handley stood on the quayside, talking to one of the stewards. She had written, not asking him to meet her, yet knowing he would. He wore a long brown overcoat, collar up, and a cap with a short peak. He'd offered a cigar to the steward, lit one himself, talking all the time and looking the ship's length to try and find her. But he gazed offhandedly along the wrong deck, as if further gangplanks would slide out from there and she would descend, easy to see, all alone but for the baby. He seemed too close to the earth to look in the right place. She waved. He saw her. The great doors of the shed opened, luggage and people already going in. He flapped back: 'Get off that coffin, before you start to love it. Come on, I've bribed the customs to let that pot and hashish through!'

She smiled at such rousing, had seen him only once, dead drunk at the opening of his first Bond Street show that made him catastrophically rich and famous as a painter. Being Frank's friend, he was tenuously hers, and turned out to welcome her in spite of the final-sounding quarrel when he and Frank last met.

Tall, slim, and swart, his eyes glowed with wellbeing, odours of cigar-smoke and after-shave. They neither kissed nor shook hands, but he uncovered the baby and bent close: 'You go off with my best friend, and this is what you bring back!' – grinning as they stood on the quay. 'Come on, my Rambler's waiting on the other side of that concentration-camp wire-fence. I'll run you home to Buckinghamshire if that's where you want to go. Shall I carry the heir to the Dawley millions? I expect he will end up as the bloody Emir of Khazakstan after Frank's done freebooting around, in spite of his spine-communism. What's he trying to do, anyway? Liberate colonial peoples from the gin-traps of modern imperialism? He can't tell that to me. If he was a real liberator he'd be right back here trying to liberate us from these dead tectonic chiselheads about to open your case. Look at them. Go on, look at them! Then he'd really wither up under the napalm of their blank stares.'

She was early off the boat, and three came towards her. A

pale long-lined face with bluebottle eyes, holding a notice in front of her saying what she could and could not bring into the country, asked her to read it. The baby cried, and two of the customs men frowned. The one who didn't must be a Welshman, Handley thought, or a Scot.

'Open that,' Jack Lantern said, tapping one of her cases with his notice-board. Albert bent to do so. 'Are you her husband?'

'No,' he said. 'We don't live together, either. We do it by post – registered.'

The man looked at her underwear, Moroccan slippers, a Moslem robe, filigree daggerwork from Fez. 'Can I see your passport?'

'I don't have one,' Handley said, 'on me.'

'How did you get into the country?' A faint smile, as if seeing him already marched screaming back to the ship.

'He came to meet me,' Myra said, quietening Mark. More people were spreading bewildered into the enormous shed.

'You're not allowed in here,' Jack Lantern said. 'You know that, don't you?'

'My car's outside,' Handley told them. 'I had a word with the AA man and the RAC man as I came in. They'll vouch for me.'

'How are we to know you're telling the truth?' Jack Lantern's pal put in with a sneer.

Handley made a genuine appeal. 'Would you do me a favour?'

Now they'd got him. He was begging for something, the first stage towards tears and breakdown. They lightened in feature: 'What exactly do you mean?'

'Deport me. Go on. Get me on that ship so that I can leave when it turns round, away from the servile snuffed-out porridge-faces of this pissed-off country. It goes to Australia, doesn't it? There's a bit of the Ned Kelly in me, so send me there. Not to mention a touch of the tarbrush and a lick of the didacoi. I'm an alien right enough. I don't even have one of your seed-catalogue passports. So deport me if you don't believe me, and see if I grovel and scream to stay in this senile dumping-ground.'

He picked up Myra's cases and she followed him towards the exit, expecting at any moment to be pounced on and dragged back towards some sort of aliens' pen. Albert didn't look round, his neck and face, every pore and inch of skin, fighting to keep the blood from bursting out of him: 'Frank was right. How can you start here? You can't. It'll be so desperate though, when it does start, that you'll need the training-grounds of Algeria to stand any chance at all.'

His car was parked in the sunshine, a low-slung black American station-wagon with rear red indicators as round as traffic-lights. 'I need this monster for my mob. Seven kids I've got, or did have when I last counted them, and they'll never leave me now that I've struck money. Before, I thought there was a chance they might starve to death or get run over, but now they're with me for life.' He assembled a carrycot in the back. 'I thought you might need it. It was Enid's kind thought, really. We've got a dozen or two around the house and gardens. You can keep it till he walks. A coming-home present.'

CHAPTER TWO

BECAUSE of his bellicose mood he drove slowly through the patched-up flat marshland of Essex. The radio played, the heater warmed, the baby slept after his psychic shouting at the customs. 'They couldn't touch me,' he said. 'They could deport me, they could put me inside for a bit, but I wouldn't bat an eyelid. Whatever happens boils up the old paint-pot for when the keel gets level again.'

'You wouldn't talk like that if you weren't a well-known painter,' she said, though knowing that he would.

He overtook a giant bowser full of milk-shake: 'It makes me bitter, the way they treat people. All I did was scale a wall, snap open a door, and walk under a crane to get to the ship. When I meet people I meet them, not wait behind a gate as if I know my place. If I wasn't a well-known painter I don't suppose I'd be meeting somebody like you at all, coming off a big posh liner. I was at a party last night, and bumped into a publisher – Arbuthnot by name – who's got your husband's book on his list – George Bassingfield, isn't it? – and he was raving about how superb it was. You're a woman of the world, even if you have had a baby by my best gun-humping pal!'

There was no way to stop him ripping open wounds like letters with a paper-knife. She had sent George's manuscript to the publisher he'd mentioned while still alive, and would sign the contract now that she was back in England.

She fed the baby in a pub, Handley tasting his first pint of the day at the bar, as the baby supped the milk of Myra's nowadays ample breasts in a private room upstairs. They were taken for man and wife, Handley lean, sardonic, and domineering; Myra cool, dark-haired, attentive to her baby – a couple who, being so hard to place and travelling in such a car, were thought by those who served them to have inherited vast amounts of money they could never have deserved. 'Do not define yourself. Other people can do that,' she thought, holding Mark high on her shoulder for his glass-eyed paradisial belch.

On the road again, gliding between frosty March fields to the almost silent sewing-machine engine, Myra thanked him for coming all the way down from Lincolnshire to meet her.

'Let's say it's in memory of Frank, and at the same time to show hope that he'll come back from Algeria. I only feel really generous when I'm walking in the rain to tell you the truth, not on a frosty day like this. I'd give all I've got, then, including the coat off my back. The rain makes me feel good, even when I start sneezing. It's only when the sun comes out and I've got pneumonia that I feel foul. I haven't done much in the last fortnight, so I came down to London for a break. I don't paint so easily as I used to. Success is a funny thing: can eat your guts out. But the secret of beating such an enemy is not to regard it as success, to keep on thinking of yourself as an exiled, unemployed nobody – which doesn't need much effort from me – though I suppose I was a bit brash and unnerved by it at first, as Frank no doubt told you. I've been so broody lately that Enid was glad to get rid of me. It's rough on her these days, though. In the autumn I'm hoping to go to Russia for a month if nothing goes wrong with my house and brood. Teddy Greensleaves, the man who owns the gallery, doesn't want me to. Not that I'm finally decided about it. Says they'll turn me into the tool of international communism – or some such thing – but I said it would take more than Russia to do that. I'm nobody's tool, anyway, and certainly not his. I'm an artist, which means that nobody can tell me what to do. If they advise me to do the opposite of what they want me to do in the hope that I'll go against them and so do the right thing they'll still be disappointed because they can't dream just how subtle and independent I can be.'

He roared his car along an empty hundred-yard stretch of dual carriageway, heading for the next narrow bottle-neck of the woods. 'I'll drive to Russia if I go, through Berlin and Warsaw, strap my canvases to the roof, get a bit of work done while I'm there. Might paint a couple of tractors if they stuff me with caviare.'

Myra listened: the subtleties of a rogue-elephant flatter-ing himself that he had enemies. He had. They'll get him, she thought, by making him continue to the blind end the role they had forced him into. Or maybe they wouldn't. Frank hadn't been able to make him out – though that needn't mean much, since they'd been friends for such a short time.

'What are you going to do with a baby and without Frank?' he asked.

'Get home,' she smiled. 'And ponder things for a while.'

An AA man acknowledged his car, and he gave the clenched fist salute. 'I was going to say and I talked it over with Enid, that if you'd like to come up to Lincolnshire and muck in with my mob, you're welcome. I'm having an extension built on, and I've got two big caravans in the garden. You'll find it friendly. Maybe Frank told you: we're a bit rough, but don't let that put you off. There are seven kids, a bulldog, six tom-cats and two *au pair* girls (one of them pregnant already) so you and the baby will be well looked after, fixed up in a room like the Ritz. The air's good, walks lovely, and people say good morning again now that I've stopped tapping them and stealing their rabbits and cabbages. You won't even see me from one weekend to another, because though I complain, I'm working all the time for my next show. I'll send one of the lads to fetch you if you like.'

'After a fortnight at home,' she said, 'I might feel like a change.' She couldn't force herself to say much, though her mind was full. A bomb had fallen on her life, and the pieces hadn't yet come together. Handley, for all his affluence, was rooted in the earth, a tree that died and flowered frequently but never changed colour or character, and she thought he wouldn't understand the recent fragmentation she had undergone. Yet being an artist perhaps he would, though she still couldn't begin to tell him until she could with absolute clarity begin to tell herself. Maybe the baby had completed the powerful outspreading flower of the explosion. Life before he was born seemed purifyingly simple, but now she was not only geared to her own unanswerable complexities, but also to Mark's creature-like timetable wants that occupied her till midnight and claimed her again at six in the morning. His darkening hair and Dawley-blue eyes kept her body and soul separate from each other because they dominated both. He was her life and suicide, the great divider and conqueror that would not allow her to use the fragments of her past life in order to construct a future. With husband dead and lover missing he warmed her, an organism fully alive but not yet conscious, eyes to see and lungs to shout with, the facility to eat, excrete, inexorably grow yet every day seem exactly the same. She was stunned by this ruthless parcel of give-and-take that nature had put into her arms. She could now understand how certain natives of the South Seas had never thought to connect childbirth with sexual intercourse, whereas before such an idea had seemed hilarious.

The integuments of passing landscape drifted by: layers of brown field and lead-green wood, cottages smoking like old men, a countryside at rest as if it had never worked to deserve it, peaceful, apathetic, and full of beauty. The sky was clouding, as if they were driving towards rain, a softening watery grey that made the green grass picturesquely livid by the roadside, a piebald emerald covering the pre-Raphaelite soul of England. She existed in it, felt the cool grass-air on her cheek, merely by looking at it, still familiar after her years in the country with George.

'I expect you're glad to get back,' Handley said, 'orange-juice and cheap milk.'

'There's always some reason to come back,' she answered, 'usually unimportant. I need to put my house in order – literally.'

'Then what?'

'I don't know. But I shall.'

'Come up to us for a while. There's nothing like violent change to shake perspective into place. Not that I'm suggesting our place is violent. I hate violence because there's so much in me. I love an ordered life – never having had one. I used to think that once I got money I'd achieve this peace that pisseth out understanding, but no such luck. My daughter Mandy banged at my studio door the other day. She's seventeen: "Dad, can I have a car?" When I looked at her as if my eyes were hand-grenades she pouted and said: "Only a Mini." I tried to throw her out, but she threw a fit and tipped paint on a big job I'd been working on for weeks and that I might have bought two Minis with. Then she shouted: "Do I have to go on the streets before I can get what I want, you tight-fisted rat?" That's only one thing. I could go on, but why bother? Richard – one of my sons – he's more devious. Wants to set up a magazine, devoted to pacifism and the arts – poems and things. Promised a whole issue to an intellectual assessment of my *own* work! My own son! I could have battered his skull in. But my life's bloody-well plagued. I didn't know how mean I was till I had money. But I'd be in the gutter again if I wasn't. I'm thinking of buying a shotgun and mounting guard over my cheque-books. My wife's all right, the angel in the house, so we could do twelve hours on and twelve off. As soon as the money started rolling in I began to really get into debt.

There's not a radio, furniture, books, clothes, or food shop for miles around at which I don't owe a few hundred pounds. My instinct told me this was right, for if ever the money stops rolling in I shan't be the only one to suffer. The whole economy will go under with one terrible groan. I used to live by sending out begging letters, but nowadays it's me that gets them, floods of them every morning. In fact if I get another begging letter I'll do my nut, because I suffer when I read them. Not long after my money started to roll in all my relatives came up from Leicester to say hello, poured out of their cars and hinted how I ought to give them a few bungalows for holidays in summer. They didn't notice the rural slum I was living in. I soon pushed that snipe-nosed lot off. They still drop in in ones and twos. One of the best begging letters I ever penned bounced back to me because Mandy had spent the stamp-money on sweets, so I had it mounted and framed, hung above the mantelpiece for all of them to see. Of course, then they said: "Aw, old Albert's a bit of a lad! Likes a joke," as they knocked back some more of my whisky. Money *is* a bloody curse, when you think about it. They say that a fool and his money's soon parted, but I wouldn't regard him as a fool – though I'm learning to hang on to mine just the same. I used to think that what an indigent artist needed was money, until I'd got some, when I thought that all he wanted was to be indigent. But as long as he's hard as iron it don't matter what he wants nor what he gets. It's being hard that's made me an artist, nothing else, and it's being hard that'll keep me one. When I was poor a local bigwig who bought a picture now and again asked me if I was a Catholic because I had so many kids. "You're an artist, so you have plenty of other things to do besides that." "Maybe," I told him, "but it's the Chinese you want to get at, not me. We can pack another fifty million into this country yet. Don't talk to me about the population boom. I don't mind sharing my dinner with you if you'll share yours with me." He got offended at that and humped off for good. I'm not saying they were fine days, but I was anybody's equal and still am. Many's the time I took off my watch before walking into the National Assistance Board. I was interviewed not long ago by some putty-faced pipe-smoking chubbyguts from that magazine *Monthly Upchuck of the Arts* and all he could do was try to needle me about "class", wondering when the day was going to come when my "origins" – that's his sickly word, not mine – were going to show more clearly in my work. So I asked him when his origins were going to stop showing in his stupid questions. I nearly puked over his snuff-coloured suit. The article never came out, thank God. Teddy Greensleaves was disappointed: "If you aren't careful," he said, "the critics will give you the kiss of death." "As long as it's a big kiss," I said. "Why do you keep on acting the fool, Albert? It's just that little bit *passé*, you know, to go on talking about money, and be for ever ranting against the critics." I didn't answer, because that would be playing his game.'

'Why do you?' Myra asked, drawn at last from the somnolence of his car and monologue.

'You know why? Because it's a smoke-screen behind which I can carry on my real work – without being bothered by a lot of soapy-mouthed English stupidities. Mind if I roll the window up? I shan't smoke another cigar: since I've been rich I feel the cold more. You're right, though. It's no use getting excited about it. We're all a pack of grown-up, half-educated neurasthenics. Camus came to the conclusion that, after all, the artist was a romantic. I began there. Where I am now I know exactly; but where I'm going I never shall know till I get there.'

CHAPTER THREE

IT was the sort of fine rain that would never soak you, rasping over the leaves, light enough in weight not to bend them, yet steady enough to turn the lawn soggy underfoot. Her only task in life was to resurrect the house and look after the baby. The garden, which had been totally neglected, needed unearthing like the ruins of Troy, and she had hardly made a start on it. Vegetable proliferations feeding on rich soil had climbed and coiled from fence to fence. Paths had vanished under it. Flowerbeds with stone and tile borders could not be seen. Lush on top, it was rotten underneath after seven months' absence. Frogs like small vivid leaves had come up from the river and made it their private jungle. She cleared the paths, but the rest did not matter.

Myra had darkened after the baby, and a more ample figure made her appear taller. Hair grown long made her seem plainer. She looked in the full-length bedroom mirror, a corner of the double-bed reflected at her knees and thighs. The baby slept in a heavy, antique wooden rocking-cradle set between the bed and far wall, a cradle that had been in the family for generations, passed on to her by Pam. Their grandmother, one of twelve who had slept their first months in it, had tugged and handled it from the far marches of eastern Europe – hardly any luggage, and pulling that huge heavy mahogany cradle across tracks and platforms and guarding it on the deck of a crowded rat-eaten rusting steamer from Hamburg. Mark looked safe in it, eternal, never wanting to grow up, grateful to that misty forgotten grandmother for taking so much trouble. It rocked him gently, high sides dwarfing the Dawley blood in him.

The house was a corpse, and she gave it the kiss of life – phone, gas, electricity, water. Everything shone again except the garden. The house glowed from within, warm from the baby out. Having a child alone with her, she was sometimes terrified of a disaster happening while asleep upstairs, that she would faint or die and, nobody aware of anything, and thinking she had gone to her parents in London, the baby would starve to death. The vision haunted her on deep and windy nights of spring, a penalty of winter's end, and punishment for living alone.

Her body in the mirror shone back, had reshaped well from the birth, firm and immobile as she looked at it, different now that her breasts were full, aching slightly from the weight of the next feed, marked by blue veins where they rounded towards her arms. She drew back at the touch of her own thighs and slipped the nightdress over. Down in the darkness the garden was three sides around the house. She sat on the edge of the bed.

Outside it was mist and mud, primroses beyond the leaded windows, the elaborate cave of the house. Cat, paraffin, coal-smoke from the stove where the central heating was re-engineered. Wet grass, night birds continually, a cow in labour bellowing, dunghills steaming in the nearby farm. Buds, confetti stuck on thorns for the marriage of mist, and mud under the hill of Thieving Grove. An aeroplane prowled on old-fashioned engines through low cloud. She'd read *Wuthering Heights* and *Pilgrim's Progress*. Her house was under the cat-back of the hills. She'd bought mimosa in Aylesbury, but the house odours soon killed it. The tooth-less cat, old marmalade, sat on the outside windowsill downstairs, senile and independent. There had been no sun till four in the afternoon. Where was he? Lost in the vast freezing acreage of the *bled*? Her body shuddered for him, shook as she gripped herself.

The baby was fed, changed, back to sleep by the time Mrs Harrod unlatched the gate next morning. Mark was put to bed, and she was putting herself back to a loneliness similar to when George was with her, now that he wasn't here any more. The day was cold, so she built a wood fire in the living room, heaped up logs and drew back furniture that might get scorched, smiling to realize there could be no danger of it. It was a waste of wood, for she still had work to do and could not be near it, but it was like another inhabitant of the house in which everything nevertheless was so strange. She wanted to fill the house with noise and fires and people, drench it in light and vigour. But at the moment that seemed a dream. So in her quiet way she worked to restore it to a common translucent state of ordinary comfort, oblivious to anything beyond the foundations of what had been built years before by George and herself. When perfection reigned and ruled you could venture elsewhere.

21

ALBERT HANDLEY'S house had been named The Gallery, and often he didn't know whether one might call it an art gallery, a rogues' gallery, or a shooting gallery, though mostly it was a bit of all three rolled into one mad house. It stood on a hill beyond the village, at the end of a lane that wound up from the paved road between two thick closed-off copses – a large simple house with two floors and a spacious attic, late Victorian country-nondescript that had at one time served the manager of an estate long since hammered up. The slate roof glistened in weak morning sunshine, its brick façade glowed. Two caravans stood in the large front garden, forming a sharp angle pointing away from the house like a scarp designed on Vauban's defence system. Across the path, amid a marshalling-yard of tracks and rut-marks, stood a Land-Rover and a well polished Ford Rambler. A newly built kennel beside the front door stored a bulldog that, when standing belligerently out, looked like a miniature iron bedstead about to leap. Behind the house was a long newly-erected wooden hut used as a children's playroom, and a solarium had been built near by, as well as a new fuel store. This was the house that Handley had lived in while poor, and that he preferred to stay in now that he was better off.

After his unaccustomed toil up the hill Russell Jones noted these details of the Handley locale for when he sat in his London flat to write a monthly middle-piece on Albert Handley the painter. If his rise hadn't been so sudden and from such obscurity Jones might have thought of him as an artist instead of a painter – but there, a man of his sort couldn't have everything, though it looked as if he had much of it already to judge from the various mounds of obsolescent gear scattered around the house: 'like the camp of some gypsy king who had struck it rich in middle age'. Or should he say 'Middle Ages'? He'd decide on the train going back. 'Someone who had been through the biggest supermarket in the world and collected with a free pass more than he could ever need.' If phrases came so quickly the article should be good. He'd been feeling rather stale of late, too many parties, too much drink, proved by the ache in his legs and the constriction in his lungs on his walk up from the village pub. His well-planted hair was too warm under his Moscow fur hat – he'd imagined frost and flecks of snow persisting on these northern wolds, but the worst of it had gone and his London ears proved tougher than he'd even given them credit for.

He stood to light a cigarette. Handley should be expecting him, but the house seemed deserted. At nine in the morning where were the children on their way to school? He sensed that all was not right in the kennel. By the threshold lay a gnawed unheeded bone, and for a moment he thought of swinging his camera on to it, for a possibly symbolic shot in another illustrated article which he might publish under his mother's maiden name. A piece of sacking hung over the kennel exit, and suddenly framed in its place was a wide-headed vile-toothed British bulldog. Jones didn't know whether his fur hat flew off at the sight of it or whether it wasn't released a second later as the dog sped through the air for his collar and tie.

In the far-off top-floor studio Albert stirred in his sleep. He'd worked till two, then undressed and slid into the camp-bed so as not to disturb Enid's ever-fragile slumber. It was just about warm all through, though the cold was ever poised outside to heave against and overwhelm him. Pushing his legs straight, he tried to ignore it. It sounded as if somebody had left the wireless on, and a wild drama to which no one listened played in a dark room. He couldn't believe it was morning. The noise ate into the old army blankets covering his long body. It seemed as if his great fear had at last come about, that the family had united against Eric Bloodaxe, the pride and prime of the bulldog breed, to do him that final and fatal injury together that no one had the courage to attempt single-handed. Enid kept a crowbar in the hall should he ever get out of control, but that was only for reassurance since he had so far been the gentlest of pets where the family was concerned, kept when they were poor to hold creditors at bay, maintained now that Handley was rich to ward off gutter-press journalists, professional beggars, and ill-wishers from the village. There were shouts, doors banging, vague blows, and a rending series of howls from Eric Bloodaxe. Was the ship going under at last, and water about to pour through the portholes that fate had left maliciously open? His long thin body was naked, his face irascible and swarthy as he drew on trousers and shirt, not even a mug of black coffee to sustain him on a flying rush down the stairs.

Russell Jones crouched, back to the gate, a round and raddled face inadequately protected by his uplifted arm, an angular tear hanging from the sleeve of his expensive tweed overcoat.

'Haven't you heard of the bloody telephone?' Handley shouted from the door. Eric, foam on his mouth, pulled on the extended radius of his chain, clawing the ground a few inches from Jones's camera.

Enid stood with a bar suspended over the dog's head should his chain snap. Three school-aged children grinned from the door of the nearest caravan. 'It's out of order,' she said. 'I tried to get the off-licence for more wine last night but couldn't.'

'Back!' Handley commanded, and Eric shuffled inside. 'He might have had the arse off you,' he said to Jones. 'I don't want to be responsible for that. Who are you anyway?'

Jones stood up, pale as a bottle of milk that had been left all night in the snow: 'I came to interview you. Did you receive our letter?'

'*Sunday Pulp* was it? Or *Old Nation*? I didn't think you were serious. Come in and have some breakfast. Don't mind the dog: he does his best.'

Jones swore under his breath. Like hell he was serious. He'd passed much of last night at the pub buying drinks for the customers and finding out how much was known about the Handley Kraal up on the hill. As hearsay was so much more picturesque than the truth, and rang so convincingly as to sound like the truth, he'd discovered more than ever he hoped would be possible, facts still spinning in his head because that predatory dog had all but emptied it. Fortunately, working for respectable papers in England had advantages in that whatever you wrote was accepted as the truth. Articles weren't his regular occupation, and he looked on such assignments as a holiday from the regular chore of reviewing. Not that Lincolnshire could be classed as vacation land at this or any other time of the year. What else could one do but become famous if one had been stuck in it for twenty years? Either that, or go mad, if you had anything about you, as Handley presumably had – though we'll see about that.

They went into the hall. Where a portrait of the Queen had stood when he was poor, a framed photo of Mao Tse Tung hung now that he was, by comparison, rich. Handley, though tall, had a slight stoop at the shoulder, as if he had walked great distances at some time in his life. He also, Jones noted, had the faintest beginnings of a paunch, not uncommon in a man past forty, a painter who had had half a year of fame with which to glut himself. But Jones found the atmosphere bleak, and was glad when they descended into the large warm kitchen, where Enid passed them black coffee in Denbigh-ware bowls, and thick slices of white bread and butter on wooden plates. Jones thought there was a certain austerity about the house, though nothing that an extended visit to Heal's wouldn't fix.

'What's to be the tone of your article?' Handley said, fastening the neck of his collarless shirt. 'I'm perished. Still, we'll have the central heating man in next week, then we can start to live.'

'Don't you think central heating makes people soft?' Jones said.

'You mean like the Russians?' Handley snapped. 'I've nothing against it.'

Jones was glad of the coffee. The uptilted bowl almost hid his small mouth, and wide all-knowing eyes, brown curly hair coiled aggressively above. 'Much to do with painting?' Handley went on.

'It's more of a profile – painting, of course, but a general sort of article, something very respectable on you as a man, to explain your painting.'

'High in tone, low in intent. That sort of thing?'

'You're mixing us up with another paper,' Jones laughed. 'I'll tell you when I've seen it.'

'What newspapers do you take?'

'I don't. I pick one up once a month, just to make sure I didn't need to.'

'Don't you find yourself awfully cut off?'

'From my painting?'

Enid filled his coffee-bowl without asking, and he absent-mindedly helped himself to another slab of bread and butter. 'London, for example?'

Handley reached for toothpicks. 'Is this the interview already, or are we just chatting?'

'Whatever you like,' Jones said, managing a smile. An *au pair* girl came into the room, all black ringlets and bosom, a sallow Florentine face at the stove putting on hot water for more coffee. She must be dying in this dead-end, Jones thought, though from what people in the pub said she mightn't be as bored as she looked. Probably just tired.

'Whatever I like gives me a crick in the diaphragm,' Handley said, 'so we might as well get it over with.'

Enid was cutting vegetables at the other end of the table: 'You could at least be polite now he's here.'

'I don't need your advice.' Albert said. 'It's taking me all my time not to choke. Just give me another pint of coffee and shut up.'

'You encourage these people, then insult them, go on as if they were your mother and father or something. They've got to live. Everybody has their work. You ought to control your craven emotions a bit. I know you got out of bed a bit sudden, but it's no use taking it out on him.'

Jones shrank, but soon it was plain that the more Enid spoke the more affable Handley became. 'She doesn't mean to insult you!' he said.

Her face went cold and grey, but kept its remarkable beauty. Who wouldn't become famous living with such a highly passionate handsome woman, Jones thought, who'd even allowed Handley to give her seven children? She spoke to Jones as if using language and enunciation she might once have had command of, but had lost after her marriage to Handley: 'There are some people to whom being an out-and-out bastard gives strength. Oh, I don't mean the weedy or puffy sort who never have the strength to be real bastards anyway, like you. But I mean the man who, not strong in the beginning, like Albert, soon finds himself becoming so when he gets money, and the *urge to be a swine gets into his blood.*'

Jones felt as if he had been struck in the face. He was ready to leave. Albert had also gone white at this whipcrack from Enid so early in the morning, a time when he found it extremely difficult to take such insults. He grasped Jones by the arm: 'Let's go to my studio. I'll raise the drawbridge and drop the portcullis, boil oil, and sharpen spears. There's brandy up there.'

'I think I'll leave,' Jones stammered, hurt to the core. What kind of family was this, that took a total stranger to its quarrelling heart and clawed him to death?

'Don't go,' Handley said, concerned for him. 'I can't let you come all this way for nothing. Enid's got a bomb on her shoulders this morning though, and I don't like shrapnel.' They walked across the hall and towards the stairfoot. 'I'll buy a new overcoat if you aren't insured, or don't get danger-money. I'm sure editors are as mean as any other gaffer.'

They went in silence to the first floor, Russell Jones taking note of what regions of the house he was privileged to go through, trying to fix the many noises muffling from behind various closed doors. Handley's studio was an enlarged attic, skylight windows showing grey clouds drifting overhead. It was bitterly cold, though Handley took off shirt and trousers, standing naked to put on underwear and dress properly. 'You'll excuse me,' he said to embarrassed Jones, 'but I'd die otherwise.' Shirt, trousers, and two pullovers went on, then a waistcoat and jacket, followed by a heavy woollen scarf, a cap, and pair of mittens. 'Sit down while I light this pot-bellied stove. It's as cold as Stalingrad up here.'

Jones thought how strange it was that rough language from Handley had frightening barbaric undertones about it, while the same words from his London friends seemed neither uncivilized nor out of place. He watched him break an orange-box in pieces, rake out cold ash, and pull a lump of coal into cobbles with his bare hands. With such habits where did the subtlety come from to be found in many of his paintings? He looked around the room: apart from the bed were two large old-fashioned kitchen tables covered with the usual painter's bric-a-brac – queer-shaped stones and pieces of wood Handley had picked up on his walks, odd drawing-pads, pictures from magazines, heaps of books, horseshoe, magnifying glass, cigarette lighter. Along one wall was a record-player, heart of a stereophonic system. The record on the turntable was Mozart's *Coronation Mass*.

Under the skylight a large half-finished picture stood on an easel. Shelves were filled mostly with modern novels, books on country life and natural history. On a low table were bottles of brandy and beer, a packet of cigarettes, and a box of Havana cigars. In an opposite corner was a small sink heaped with glasses and cups. What struck Jones with great force, and what he held his eyes from until the last, was the newly cured skin of an outsize fox pegged neatly on the frame of an old door – leaning beside the now closed door they had entered by. He only took his eyes from it to look at the presumably new painting from Handley's brush.

Handley was making feverish work at the fire, which was now on the point of springing into strong life. 'Whenever I'm painting I want to sleep. I want to sleep more than I want to paint whenever I pick up that brush, but somehow I paint, I work at it. I don't go mad like any old Jack Spatula puttying away, mind you, but I think I'm right in saying it's sleep that drives me along.'

In the painting he had used the shape of the fox pinned on the door, a fox motif, the spreadeagled vulpine set in an aureole of colours, a fox in the rising sun flaring over the sea. From subtlety and delicate feeling at the centre, the form and colours had been made to expand, reaching a brilliance and panache Jones had never seen before – a great spending of the daywake above the grey blue line of the Lincolnshire sea, and in the bottom left corner a man humping home from an all-night fish or poach with a moon in his net. Observing Handley's face as he knelt by the stone brought the word 'Byzantine' to mind.

Handley took off his jacket and cap, poured two glasses of brandy. 'A man from the *Daily Retch* came up a month ago, and needled me about being rich. He got ratty on the way out so I gave him what for. You should have seen the article: they really set the dogs on me. I don't care about being rich. We're rich, it's true, compared to a year ago. But the stuff we lose or get nicked. If only I was rich enough to look after my things and lose nothing. Still, I wouldn't be an artist then. Cheers!'

'Cheers!' Brandy after coffee brought his tone of confidence to exactly the right pitch. Handley stood before the picture, eyes glowing: 'I'll have to do it again. Nothing's ever quite right. Never was.'

'Do you manage to work all day and every day?' Jones asked.

'There are certain questions I can't answer.' Handley said, wrenching open a bottle of turps. 'If I was a journalist I'd ask people the sort of question they only put to themselves in the pitch-black at four in the morning.'

'I'm interested in how different painters work.'

Handley leant over and nudged him sharply with his elbow, an exaggerated wink and leer. 'So you're a bit of a *voyeur*, are you? Eh? Dirty old bastard! Still, don't be ashamed of it. Do go on. Ask me something else.'

'I'll be quite happy,' said Jones, 'if you just talk.'

'I'll bet you will. But I'm not frightened of hanging myself. I was born in Wolverhampton. The old man had a builder's yard. Left school at fourteen and worked for him, slaved, I should say. Nothing ragged-trousered about me: had no trousers at all most of the time. Never work for your father. The old bastard owned a row of slum houses, and we never knew it till he'd croaked. Six brothers, and we sold up the lot. Got forty pounds apiece after the lawyers had done. I'd left home by then, came up from London to collect it. Boozed it all up in three days, then joined the artillery. The war had just started, and I thought I'd get stuck into fascism. Knew all about it from fourteen because I read a lot and heard what was going on. Stuck on the Lincolnshire coast, bored to death so started painting, reading, demobbed, married, writing begging letters. A bad life with seven kids to keep, but there was no other way. Anything else?'

Jones found it difficult to believe that this lank man of forty had been able to paint such pictures. Rough and bordering on the primitive, they had yet a certain beauty almost belied by the rancorous striding bully in front of him. 'What about politics?' he asked mildly.

'Politics?' Handley sat in the other armchair. 'I left off that sort of thing as soon as I felt they were necessary, as soon as I understood them and realized I had nothing left to learn. I'll only take an interest in politics where there's a civil war. In the meantime, let who will rule. If they want to indulge in that kind of self and mutual destruction it's up to them. I've got too much work to do, and leave that sort of thing to people like Frank Dawley, who's more fitted for it than me. He's in Algeria somewhere, taking pot-shots at the French. At least I hope so: I wouldn't like him to die on me, though I would feel better if he was taking pot-shots at some of the British I know.' He poured some more brandy: 'Let's drink to good old Frank.'

'Certainly. To Frank,' – whoever he was, but it was good brandy, anyway. 'Don't you think the artist *should* take an interest in politics, Mr Handley?'

'If you start mistering me I'll shut up and sulk,' he laughed. 'Like the rest of the world I'm a split personality when it comes to art and politics: I can't hear the glories of Mozart's *Coronation Mass* without catching an echo of the *Ça ira* in the background, the sublime about to be pushed aside – temporarily, of course – by the clogs and sandals of the proletariat. So don't ask me for an opinion, old rum-chum. Two of my lads are up to their necks in this Ban-the-Bomb stunt, so I'm involved to that extent.'

Like many people who drank a lot Jones got drunk too quickly. By the third large brandy his brain lost its usual middling sharpness, and the soporific warmth of the stove made his eyes heavy. 'Aren't there any political causes you help?'

Handley lit a cigar. 'That depends. I do send money to certain organizations – if they look like causing enough trouble. That's the only thing. So few of 'em do. It's throwing away good money. Maybe something'll turn up one day. You see, I have a system. I've invested five thousand pounds in industrial shares, and what dividends I get go into any trouble-making or revolutionary organization aimed at disrupting the system we live under. You can't be more apolitical than that, can you? Invest in the system in order to destroy it. Not that I think it'll ever be destroyed, mind you, but if I thought it would last for ever I'd not paint another thing. Maybe I'd be happy if I just lived on an ice-floe that never stopped drifting, painting until it melted under me and I took to the boat to find another ice-floe.'

Jones grinned. There were times when he seemed like one of us after all. 'What if there were no boat?'

'I'd sink.'

'Would you mind?'

'Not all that much. I've got a couple of heavy quick-firing ambush-guns defending this house, well-placed and concealed, a fine field of fire organized mainly, I must admit, by my son Richard, and my brother John, who've studied such matters. The cellars are stocked with food – self-perpetuating flour, expanding water – all that sort of thing.'

'Don't you find yourself a bit cut off from reality?'

'Closer. How much closer to eternal reality can you get – an artist with a machine-gun waiting for the end of the world? I drink strong tea and walk through fields, fight with a cat-and-dog family, stand alone on the strand at Mablethorpe and watch the steamroller waves updrumming for me as I run back over the dunes dropping my

31

notebook which they hobble-gobble, and cursing them as they spit defeated in my face. What do you mean, not normal? Do you think I should work in a factory? Hump shit around a farmyard? Paint fashionable nose-picking pictures that'll reproduce nicely in the posh magazines? Get hooked. I'd rather listen to the wind and flirt with chaos.'

'Do you often fall in love?'

Handley smiled. 'What do *you* think?'

'I don't know. I'm asking you, really.'

'No, I'm asking you.'

'I might say "yes",' Russell said.

'You might be wrong. If I said "often" you'd say I was sentimental. If I said "rarely" you'd say I was cold. It's hard to answer with a simple yes or no. But I do fall in love from time to time.' He reached to the table and opened a book so that a photograph of his daughter Mandy fell out. Jones picked it up. 'I'm in love with her at the moment,' said Handley, snapping it back between the covers before Jones could twig the similarity of feature. 'But I don't see what it has to do with me as a painter.'

'I was just curious.'

'Anything else?' Handley wanted to know.

'What about theories?'

He closed one eye, and farted. 'Theories?'

'Regarding art – painting.'

'*You* can fart as well – if you want to. Liberty Hall. I know it's catching. A theory is only a way of explaining how your art died. I never use 'em.'

Jones was exasperated, needed a break. 'Do you mind if I go to your john?'

'Down the stairs and second on the right.' Handley wondered how someone like Russell Jones had already become acquainted with his brother John.

He was at the door: 'It's all right. I'll find it.' Handley shrugged, turned to his painting. The head-down fox was falling back to earth after its trip to the sky, a visit to the foxgods who forthwith sent him speeding to the nether world, his life one long and agonizing vacillation between air and fire, space and boiling rock, vulpine trap into which he had by chance of birth been driven. The blazing circular limits of the sun surrounded his existence, and yet at the same time the eternal powerhouse of his drive showed him as the lit-up centre of Handley's wide-scope world immediately forgotten as he plunged back in.

The stairs were narrow, but Jones found his way to the wider landing of the lower floor. A girl was pushing a sweeping brush ineffectually around dark corners. He thought of trying to kiss her, but his nerve for it wasn't in the right place this morning. Opening the second door without hesitation, he found it didn't give into a lavatory at all, but a normal-sized blind-drawn room flooded by brilliant electric light. Much space was taken by racks of wireless receivers and transmitters, wavemeters and goniometers, speakers and microphones. At a table beside it sat a bald, middle-aged man wearing earphones and with hands busy at a morse key. On being suddenly disturbed he sprang up, careful to unplug the earphones, lifted a heavy service revolver and set its spout towards Jones. 'Get out!' he cried hoarsely, 'Get out!' – an unforgettable picture.

The door had closed behind Jones who, being so certain he was in the right room, had advanced a good way into it before realizing the mistake which now seemed set for ludicrous and terrible proportions as this pop-eyed sallow-faced maniac came for him.

The door seemed to have locked itself: 'I can't get out. I can't.' Though unaccustomed to shouting, Jones did so now. It somehow humanized him, reduced the tension in the room to one of ordinary pathetic impotence, and at the panic-pitched sound of it the man who threatened him put down the gun, and a charming smile spread over his face.

The door knocked Jones in the back, and he stepped aside, forgetting the painful jolt in anticipation of the next surprise assault. The great menace was still the man with the earphones hanging round his neck like a stethoscope. He gave a fixed and fearful smile as if, having come from Italy to some *bruto* northern court in the Middle Ages, he was demonstrating it as a new invention for the human face

– a subtle yet novel expression that could be used by anyone not absolutely perishing of melancholy, and that was now sweeping the Mediterranean world.

'John,' Handley said, 'sit down and get back to work.' Smile drained, John revealed a mature and gentle face, brown sensitive eyes, and a tan as if he either suffered with his liver or spent much time out of doors. He wore a grey finely-cut suit, well-polished shoes, collar and tie. Beside his morse-key was a gold fob-watch, and a writing-pad two-thirds covered by pencilled block-capitals. The opposite wall was racked with books, and one by the door was laid with a map of North Africa. Jones noted all this with a trained eye, while Handley explained: 'You said to me "Do you mind if I go to your John?" Well, this is my brother John, and I admit I was mystified, but I thought you'd been talking to people in the pub last night and knew about him. You were my guest so I couldn't come the "Am I my brother's keeper?" lark. John, this is Russell Jones, a journalist who's come to interview me.'

John mumbled a greeting, showing a nature basically shy, if at times unpredictably violent. 'He lives in this room with his radio gear, has in fact ever since he came home from the Jap prison-camp in 1945. He was in the army – signals – had a commission, which I was brother enough never to hold against him.'

'I didn't mean to turn on you,' John said. 'I feel rather bewildered if I'm disturbed. It doesn't happen often, I might say, which I suppose makes me react more noticeably than I need to when it does.' He spoke gently, and now that the shock was wearing off Jones felt that here at least was one member of the Handley household with whom he might have something in common – even if he was a raving lunatic.

'Mind you, he never does make contact,' Handley said in a kindly voice. 'Do you, John?'

His eyes gleamed, as if his whole life had been a disappointment, yet as if this continual state contained the seeds of hope. 'Not yet, Albert. I keep on trying, though. Perhaps I just never get on the right wavelength at the right time, or maybe I'm asleep at the moment when I might be making contact. I get lots of false hope, and false messages even – as if somebody else engaged in the same thing is always trying to thwart me from making contact even though it may at the same time stop him doing so. It's a dog-eat-dog world up in the ether, I suspect, all sorts of imps and birds and atmospherics trying to foil me, so that I'm sure the devil himself has a hand in it. The whole sky, from earth to stars and even beyond, is where my signals criss-cross, so you can imagine the scope I have, the space, the great, grandiloquent marvellous space! Oh, of course, I get plenty of ordinary messages, but they don't count. I can send messages too, to ships or Moscow, but it's not the same. I want to make contact with someone I've had in mind for a long time.'

Sweat ran down his leathery face as he felt for a case and took out a cigarette, a normally courteous man who, because he did not offer one, must have forgotten they were in the room. 'It's no easy task,' he smiled, 'but I feel that someone has to make the attempt, and I seem to have been cut out for it. As I go on trying in my mundane methodical fashion I also dream about the time when I will finally make contact. I can't tell you how the thought of it thrills and sustains me. It's as if the whole light of the world will go on, when my signals and those signals meet in the ether, and the great love of the universe illumines every face, when I ask the only question and an answer comes through at last, as it is bound to do. Still, I sometimes have to admit that it's a lonely life. I hardly ever leave this room, for who knows that in the few minutes I'm away, it wouldn't have been the time and opportunity for me to make the first contact? My eyes often ache, my hand often falters, and a touch of despair forces me into sleep when I should be awake, but I go on, losing count of time, listening to all the signals and waiting for the propitious time to send out my own words in order to make the great meeting. I suppose you find this uninteresting?'

Jones caught the dark threat of his question and replied that no, just the opposite, the idea seemed rather a thrilling one. What he wanted to know, but hadn't the courage to ask, was what he was trying to make contact *with*.

'Someone,' John continued, as if reading his query, 'once stumbled into this room and had the temerity to ask what or with whom I was trying to make contact. But the world is full of such people, fools and doubters who want to drag all spiritual people like myself down to hell, tempters and demons continually hoping to annihilate one, who know plainly in their very bones what it is one must always strive to make contact with, but who can't bear the sight and sound of anyone trying, and so attempt in all ways to destroy them and their faith. I fought with him desperately, for he nearly overcame me with his strength and valour – until I got him outside and threw him down the stairs.'

'I remember,' said Handley. 'It was the window-cleaner.'

'Don't you think he deserved it?' John demanded.

Jones leaned against the door, arms folded. 'Yes, I suppose I do.'

'Aren't you sure? Are you one of them? Once upon a time I was interested in politics, and met quite a few of your sort. Maybe I'll be interested in them again one day. In fact I'm sure I shall be, after I've made contact. But let me tell you, because I remember it clearly and can never forget it, when I was in the prison camp at Singapore, not long after we were captured by the Japanese devils, some of us formed a left-wing group, all from the ranks except me. In those hell conditions we kept ourselves alive by talks and meetings, and managed to produce a sort of newspaper, in opposition to the British officers as well as the Japanese. Naturally, the officers got to know that we left-wingers were giving secret lectures on militarism and the class-war, in which we condemned their incompetence and cowardice. Do you know what they did? The Japanese had quite rightly ordered them to work with the rest of the men on building-sites, but in order that they would not persevere with this order the CO did a deal. He betrayed us, and agreed to keep them informed of any future suchlike activities, if he and his brother officers were not forced to work the same as the ordinary men. Out of those groups I was the only one who, by accident, came home alive. Shall I strip and show you my scars? Is it any wonder that I'm trying to make contact?'

Jones felt the blood draining out of himself. He was not so much horrified at the story, as at the effect on John while he was telling it. Handley stood at his brother's side, an arm over his shoulder: 'Get some sleep, John. Have a bit of rest. I'll send Enid up with some soup.'

'I'll have the soup,' John said, calm and forceful again, 'but I'll go on working for a while.'

The morse-key was rattling feverishly as they went quietly out. 'At one time,' Handley said when Jones came back from the lavatory, 'I thought we'd have to have him certified, but he's quietened down a bit since then. He went through such unimaginable horrors in those prison camps that it almost finished him off. But he came to live with me, and bought that wireless stuff with his gratuity. Gets a pension still. The rest of the family wouldn't have him, he was so much off his head. But I never thought so. He's on some search, you know, Johnny is. He's doing some of it for me, maybe for all of us – in this house. We believe in him. He's the man in the boat whose spirit's kept this place afloat for years.'

'But that anecdote about the prison camp,' Jones said, 'is it true?'

They went upstairs, back to the studio, and Handley turned at the top step: 'Is that the only question you've got? You were privileged to see your John just now, though I don't imagine it means much to you. There's only one story in John's life, and that's it.'

Handley moved to the other side of the studio table and lit a cigar. He offered one, but Russell Jones took out a large curved pipe, so Albert pushed a tin of tobacco towards him. 'Try this Spanish stuff. Teddy Greensleaves brought it back from the Canary Islands.'

It was dry and flaky, and Handley had put two cuts of apple in to keep it moist. One of these small pieces was inadvertently packed into the huge space of Russell's pipe bowl, and before Handley could tell him, it was being lit, and a fragrant smell of burning fruit filled the room. Russell glanced uneasily, but continued puffing.

'I think you took a chunk of my apple,' Handley said, 'moistener, you know.' Russell looked as if he'd been poisoned, but didn't know which of them had done it, then apologized and picked it out, dropping it like a dead black-cock in the ash-tray.

Handley put it back in his tin. 'How do I know,' he said, 'what sort of an article you're going to write?' He prised up a skylight window and ledged it. Clean air rushed in, cold and ruthless, though sweet to Handley once the scarf was back round his neck.

'You don't, really,' Russell smiled.

'I have to take it on trust?' Handley yawned, and at the sight and sound of it Russell felt an impulse to do the same, but fought it off in order not to appear imitative or weak. 'I'm afraid you do, really.'

'Really?' He slammed the window, frame dropping as if to smash. 'Fresh air's the bane of my baleful life. Shakes the cobwebs. Makes me hate people. But listen : no lies. Do you hear? No lies, or I'll come down to London and pull the tripes out of you.'

Russell smiled. That sort is ruthless, Handley thought, born and bred to it. But I'm ruthless as well. The trouble is that my ruthlessness makes me suffer. Nevertheless, mine wins in the end because it has a soul burning somewhere inside it. 'You can smile,' he said, 'but I've seen the way you scumpots and editors treat people who are trying to do real work. Not that you can really do them harm, but by God you do your best. The toffee-nosed posh papers are the worst of all, because those who write for them once fancied themselves a bit as well.'

'You're quite wrong,' Russell said, standing up to fasten his overcoat. 'Your work is much better than it was, so why do you have to make these unnecessary and insulting state-ments? Your personality isn't that bad.'

'I'm so bad that even breeding couldn't make me perfect. But don't patronize me. Just try and get close to the truth if you must scribble your impressions.'

'I use a typewriter. I wanted to invite you down to the pub for lunch.'

'If you don't get out I'll set the dog on you. I've nothing against you, personally. It's just that everything you stand for sticks in my craw. Still, I'll show you out. I suppose we must part on reasonable terms.'

The village clock struck eleven, a distant booming carried on the wind as they stood by the front door and shook hands.

CHAPTER FIVE

THE mellow and subtle mood of many days had broken. He was poisoned but not dead, halfway between ashes and honey. What man could stand up to it? They hit you with vilification, thumped you with praise, and any day you might die of heart bruise. He could add nothing to the canvas, threw down his brush. Treat them civilly and you felt like a collaborator with the Germans who deserved to be shot or have your hair shorn. If you insulted them you betrayed your own easy and generous nature. It was no easy matter. Perhaps there was some clever and not unnatural balance between the two which his psyche had not yet struck (or was that merely the final proof that he wanted to cooperate with them?) which would put them in their place while leaving his self-respect unsoiled. Fortunately such questions were an aberration on the endless world of his work that he was king of and could walk across at will, that dominated all waking and sleeping hours as if life and sanity depended on it. Reaching beyond the end of what he had never seen any other artist do, he was out in the wilderness, crawling through fire with an unquiet soul.

He walked down, along the corridor to Richard's room. It seemed amiable and light compared to his own cave hemmed in by cloud and canvases. A large space was taken up by a table covered by conjoined sheets of the Ordnance Survey quarter-inch map of England and Wales. On the walls were maps in enlarged detail, special tracings of atomic establishments and bomber bases drawn up by some draughtsman who knew his business well. 'What's the situation in our civil war?' Handley wanted to know, lighting a cigar.

Richard's fingers went over the intricate formation of coloured pins and labels, as if he were blind and the battle situation were set out in braille. Above an opposite notice board hung a huge Algerian FLN banner which Mandy had been pressed into painting during the long nights of last snowbound winter. 'It's confused,' he said, 'but at the moment, on balance, we seem to be losing.'

He was tall and swart, with black curly hair and a Roman nose, high cheek-bones, sallow below the eyes – which were quick to see through the hugely complex patterns that led to the main chance, a skill developed during twenty years learning how to deal with a father like Handley who never had one thought or action similar to any that had gone before. In that sense, Richard was dominated by his father, yet it had trained him to dominate everyone else. He wore a camel-hair sweater and smoked a home-rolled cigarette.

'You'd better stop losing,' Handley said.

'After the A-flash over London and Liverpool, government troops are hounding all guerrillas into the Midlands. I don't like the look of it.'

'Break it off then,' Handley said. 'Melt 'em away and pull back through the Marches. Re-form in Wales. The Black Mountains'll make a good base – plenty of blokes to draw on from the valleys. Good lads, them Taffies. Promise 'em self-government when it's all over.'

Richard began to argue, the only way to find out what was on his father's mind. 'I'd thought of that, but . . .'

'Got a better plan?'

'What about some in the Lakes and Devon?'

'No good. Keep 'em together at the moment. Wales is big enough. They'll be too busy cleaning up to bother with us for a while. Then, but all in good time, we can come back, take Shrewsbury, and make for the Black Country. Like fish in water. Move in with the spring tides, with the people.

They'll rise for the bait, don't worry. If not, we'll suck our rings and drop dead.'

Richard was moving the pins, and Handley bent over the map with a feeling of satisfaction. 'Sent off the plans of the secret bases yet to Moscow?'

'Last week. Rolled them in a bundle of *New Statesman*s. Printed matter, unregistered, surface mail – to make sure they'll get there.'

'Send another batch then, this week.'

'All right,' Richard said. The telephone rang, and he listened.

'Well?'

'They're liquidating the Coventry group. Regular army.'

He straightened up from the map, threw his cigar out of the window. 'What did I tell you? Get them to melt, turn into carol-singers or poppy-sellers. I'll call in this afternoon when I'm back from the pub. Maybe you'll have better news.'

'Father, there's just one thing. Adam and I found a beautiful old printing-press in Louth. We can get it for fifteen pounds, then go ahead with the magazine. It'll cost fifty pounds an issue if we set it up ourselves.'

He thought for a moment. They'll be the ruin of me, if I'm not too stingy with them. And the same if I am. 'Win that civil war to my satisfaction, and I'll do it.'

'That'll take weeks. We could print some subversive leaflets in the meantime. I know a way to get them handed round factories in Nottingham. Also at Scunthorpe.'

He took half a dozen ten-pound notes from his pocket and, in mint-condition, they swallowed down on to the Thames valley. 'Get the press, then, and we'll see how it goes.' Richard stood back to consider the overall situation. Handley's head showed in again. 'Shove the poetry out of your mind for a bit – do you hear me? – and get them fucking Welshmen up from the valleys.'

'Yes, father.'

He walked aimlessly around the garden. Furrows under-foot were muddy, ridges of salt-loam beaten in by sea-wind, this part of the garden scarred by miniature craters where cabbages had been ripped out from mother earth. It smelt good, felt soft and rich, tender to his elastic-sided boots hardly meant for the treading of such intense soil. The fruit-trees – apple, plum, pear – were empty and withered. He felt dead, snuffed out by too much winter and isolation, as if his soul were drifting and he was unable to pull it back under control. Let it drift, he thought, let me go, idle and blind, stricken and numb. I don't mind floating like a brainless fool: the quicker I get to the end and die, the sooner I'm born again. I don't believe in death, at least not in life, not for me. But oblivion is breathing close unless something happens.

Hoping to throw off such thoughts, he went in for dinner. Enid put veal and salad before him. 'That journalist didn't seem in a very good mood when he left. Walked down the hill as if he had an eagle on his back. He didn't even talk to Mandy, and that's rare.'

He cut up his meat, appetite good. 'I gave him what for. He wanted to draw me out, so I let him overdraw me. That's the only way.'

'Is it?' she said, setting her own plate down. They'd fallen in love when she was seventeen and he nineteen, in those far-off days on the Lincolnshire coast, and Enid was well pregnant at the marriage, soft-faced and big-bellied, earnestly looking at him, and he shy with a wide-open smile at being dragged into something that made him the butt of his mates' jokes while also marking him down for some special unspoken respect. She had a slim straight nose, small chin, full mouth. Her light-blue eyes had a slight slant, upper and lower lids never far apart, Tartar almost in shape, one of those rare English faces that looked as if they had come from central Asia, then full smooth cheeks and fair hair, a face on which the troubles of life do not fall too hard, though Enid had been familiar with every one. Loving Handley, she wasn't even aware of having 'put up' with him, which may have contributed to Handley's youthfulness, while hers was certainly rooted in it. Her long bound-up hair was as pale as when they'd met, and her skin had an unchanging attractive pallor, in spite of bitter Lincolnshire winters and the never-ending work of seven children. Handley loved her also, and in some way they had never stopped being afraid of each other, but during their quarrels they loathed each other so profoundly that it couldn't even be said that they were in love any more.

'Why go out of your way to make enemies?' she said. 'If you try not to make them you'll still have more than you can handle. You're not sly enough. You let these people make mincemeat of you. They've only got to stick a pin in and you jump a mile. And they always get what they came for, whether it's the posh papers or the gutter press. At your age you should know better.'

He spread butter over black rye-bread. 'At thirty I'd have been as cunning as hell, and was, but what's the point any more? I'm getting old enough not to bother about disguising my feelings.'

'Too famous, you mean. It's gone to your head.'

The house was stonily quiet, children at school, others either asleep or set on various pastimes. A cow moaned from the neighbouring field. 'Whose side are you on?'

Whenever they argued it was as if a third and impartial person were present, taking down all that they said to each other – as if they would be ultimately judged on this. She stood up to change his plate. 'See what I mean? Yours, but you're too locked in your fame to know it.'

'Fame!' He spat. 'I don't have any.'

'You do.'

'I ignore it.'

'You don't. You can't. I wish you did, but they've got you.'

'So what? Is my work any the worse for it?' He hated the word 'work' and knew that she knew it, and had made him use it, by angering him on this touchy subject. Art was not work, since it was something you were not forced to do in order to earn a living.

'Not yet it isn't,' she said.

'It won't be. When I'm working I'm completely myself.'

'And when you're not working,' she went on, eyes gleaming because a real quarrel was coming up, 'we've all got to live with you.'

'You mean *you* have. Why don't we keep personal relationships out of this?'

'You can't live without them, that's why.'

He ate his bread and Stilton, cut up an apple. 'Stalemate. Let's pack it in. Divide the spoils and go our different ways.'

She sat down and looked straight at him, a bad sign, portent of saying something unforgivable and bitter. 'If you want to give in, you can. But I won't surrender to all this muck you've dropped into. If you want to go, go. Kill yourself. If you left me you'd never paint another stroke, and if you don't believe me, try it. We've suffered too much to fly apart just when the going gets difficult. It might have been possible before, but not now, not any more.'

'I don't want to leave you, but what gives you the idea that you're my strength and mainstay?'

'Because I am, though not any more than you are mine, I admit. You've got me, but you've also got your freedom. I don't ask questions when you go to London for weeks at a time, so if you can't manage in those limits you wouldn't exist in any others.'

She boiled his coffee, poured it out. 'We've got such a bond, Albert. It would be a pity if you smashed it. We've burned in this love and torment since we were almost kids, grown up while our own kids were growing up. If I were sentimental I might call a lot of it suffering, but there was too much love for that. It's made me hard as well, but in a way that makes me sure of myself, and the more sure I am of myself the more I know that being together is the only thing that matters. We've never killed each other in a rotten married way. We've been very big about it, right above the rest of the world, and it can't be shown to anyone else, or passed on, but we own it far more than this piece of property we've bought. It's valuable and unique. It used to be the suffering that ennobles, but now it's the sort that degrades. So ruin it if you like with your black heart. You can destroy your part of it, but not mine. My part of it's out of your hands. And it's safe in mine.'

'I wasn't serious about ending it. Stop this talk.'

'I shan't. You were thinking it. You've often hinted it. If you want to run off with some girl for a dead and comfortable life, it's up to you, but I'd never forgive you your lack of backbone in doing it.'

He smashed his fist on the table, shaking half his coffee out. 'You've said enough. Stop it. You're poisoning it. I can't stand to have my love killed. The ancient feminine wrecker is on the move again!'

She stood by the sink, hands shaking, turned on a tap to stop them. Water ran out uselessly. 'I've said all I want, but if you think I was raving like a lunatic, and that what I've said doesn't mean anything, you're a fool.'

'You open your mouth, and kill things. It's disgusting.'

'Go on. I'll never stop you. Why don't you just go outside and throw up that rotten bile that's choking you? Just because some tuppenny journalist has been twisting you around his little finger you have to come in and vent your spleen on me. Not, I notice, until after you've had your dinner. Oh no! Food usually sweetens people, but it makes you bilious and sour. I won't put up with your tantrums. You're not dealing with those spineless people from London who only say "What a genius!" but never see you as you really are.'

'So that's it! Jealous, are we? Jealousy brings out the spite, and all the things you weren't quick enough to get out in our other quarrels but remembered afterwards when you brooded on them. Jealous! I thought you were bigger than that, sweeter and bigger, more intelligent, perhaps. But no.'

'Life's full of disappointments for the poor of spirit,' she mocked.

'Turn that tap off. You're wasting water.'

'I'm not the gallery owner. You don't have to act the knowing peasant with me!' But she turned it off, and wiped up his coffee mess. He snatched the rag, and threw it like a dead cat into the sink. 'You're going right to the bottom,' she said. 'One move and down you go, right into the mud. And once you're there you're like an alligator that rips at any living thing.'

They stood at each end of the kitchen. 'You can't run my life,' he said. 'You never could and you never will.'

'It's not worth running. Keep your life and foul it up in your own way. But leave mine alone. I want it for myself, out of what's been good between us.'

'Have it, then. I'm making you a present of it, tie it up in an old chocolate-box with blue ribbon. I'll get the undertaker to make you a coffin, bury it with a bloody prayer-book, send it to the bottom, all your love and ideals. You can have them, mine as well, when they take a turn for the worse like this.'

He didn't see her hand shift. A full dinner-plate seemed to cut off the top of his head, stutter and break on the door-post behind. 'I don't want this sort of marriage,' she raved. 'It's nearly twenty-five years, and I've not put up with this. It's low. It's ignoble.'

He staggered, eyes closed, a wetness above the left eye. The salt of blood stuck like a leaf on his palate. 'I know,' he said. 'We had fine instincts, but you want to alter all that, crush it, destroy it.' He spoke calmly, a ribbon of blood on his face. 'You can't do such a thing to me. I'm even more in the real world than you are.' Keep away from it, he said to himself, a precipice in front of him, don't throw anything. Smile. For Christ's sake lick away the blood and smile, or it's over for ever. Twenty years in jail and only bars to paint.

'You're weak,' she cried, 'bone weak. Your whole life's been built up on weakness. You can't pit your will against the ordinary hard life of the everyday world.'

His hands pressed on to the heavy kitchen table. 'That's what you always wanted, me going out to work every morning and bringing money in on Friday night, a nice steady husband with a nice steady job, an aspirin-wife and crispin-haired kids, a bungalow and little car. I've long suspected this.'

'It's not true. I mean weak in a better way than that. The way I mean is just not in your consciousness. You don't *know*. You're of poor material. You never could understand, because you're idle, unreliable, a liar . . .'

He reached her with clenched fist, brought it at her, then emptied the sink of dishes, a demon scattering all the confetti of Sheffield and the Potteries at wall and window. 'Go on,' she cried. 'What else can you do? This is the end, though, the end, I tell you.'

He spun like a windmill. Chairs shook and toppled, the table flew, drawers skimmed and blocked off the door. Deafness and blindness, the awful force of his own movements crushed him, caught him up so that he couldn't stop. 'I'll never forgive you,' she wept. 'Never. Never.'

'You've got absolutely what you wanted at last,' he said, sitting on the floor. 'Are you satisfied?'

'We're done,' she said, in tears. 'Finished.'

'Finished,' he said. 'That's it, then.'

'I can't take this again.'

'You won't have to. All your so-called love isn't worth it. Nobody's going to possess me in that way.'

'Nobody wants to, if only you could understand. You'd better go then. Let's get it over with.'

'I'm not leaving like a bloody lodger.'

'Neither am I,' she said. 'It's my house, remember. You got it in my name. You were too weak to get it for yourself. "I won't be a property-owner," you said. So I'm not going.'

'Neither am I, I won't be thrown out.'

'It's my house,' she exulted.

'Get the police then, you turncoat bourgeoise slut. You'd stoop to anything.'

From a sitting position his long thin body ricocheted across the room and caught her uplifted wrist. 'Let go, or you'll break it.'

She put the plate in the sink. 'I'll never give in,' she said. 'Not even if you crawl.'

The idea of it made him laugh, brought a spark of humour into his black day. 'That's what you've wanted all your life, but there's less chance of it now than there ever was, and there was none then.' He drew back, in danger being so close, though not of blows flying. He refused all temptation to inspect his aching cut, or touch the congealing blood.

47

'I want nothing from you,' she said, holding a hand over one eye. 'If I'd ever wanted anything we wouldn't have been together two minutes.'

'But you've had plenty. I'm the sort of person who doesn't even know when he is giving.'

Her voice was quieter, more even in tone. 'Not knowing when you give is the same as not giving.'

'You can wrap those bloody semantic floorcloths around your aphoristic neck.' He couldn't hold back, in for the kill when he didn't want to kill, didn't need to, and when there was nothing to kill. She stayed quiet, knowing it had to stop, her own impetus gone. Choler sharpened his face, staring for a reply that never came.

The door opened, pushed the table a few inches into the room, and when he snapped around Mandy stood by the pot dresser – the only furniture still upright, apart from her parents. 'You two been arguing again?'

He was angered by her buxom insolence, long auburn hair and wide sensual mouth ruined by lipstick. 'What do you want?'

'Nothing, except a couple of quid to go to the pictures. I'll go schizoid with boredom if I stay here.'

'Get this room straight first,' he said.

'Clear up your own mess. I'm not a skivvy.'

Enid's voice rang out. 'Don't talk to your father like that.'

'I'll clean it up when I come back,' she said. 'What about Maria and Catalina?'

'Probably hiding in the cellars,' Handley grinned.

'All I want,' said Mandy, 'is approximately three hundred quid for a secondhand Mini. That's not much to ask for, is it?'

'I've told you approximately three hundred times the answer's no. You cost me fifty quid for an abortion last year, and that was enough pin-money for a while.' But even while talking he took pound notes from his pocket, as if held up at gunpoint. 'Get going. Don't let me see you before teatime.'

'I wish you two would settle your differences in a civilized way,' she said, unable to move. 'I hate it when you do this to each other. I suppose it's the only way you can show love, but it gets me down. I'll set the furniture on its legs, but don't expect me to clean the blood up.'

Handley's fist struck the dresser, seemed to break every bone, even those in his toes. 'I'll murder you when you come back!' he roared, his grey face through the door she'd nipped out of.

'You asked for that,' Enid said righteously, pulling the table upright. 'You've never hit them yet, and you see what happens when you try?'

'I bloody-well miss,' he said, numbed by the pain. 'By God, the fat little trollop had better not come back too soon. My hand's finished. I'll never be able to paint again. What shall I tell Teddy? I'm ruined. And it's no laughing matter. I can't move it. Look.' The back of it was blue and swollen, a short, dark cut in one place. He leaned it against the cool wall and pressed hard.

'Do a bit of work,' she said, 'and forget it.' Bleak sunlight planted itself through the window. He swept smashed plates into a dustpan, rubble chuting musically into the plastic waste-bucket. Taking up the broken chair he opened the window and threw it out on to the quagmire garden. 'That's that,' he said, as if after an hour's good work.

'That's that,' she said, enraged. 'But it isn't.'

'I wouldn't want it to be, either,' he said, lighting two cigarettes and passing her one. 'I wouldn't want all this to be for nothing. As forty-year-old Romeo said to his dear Juliet across the Sunday dinner-table. "What did you expect?" – before dodging the loaded teapot. They were in love though, I suppose, bless 'em.' He dropped his cigarette into the sink, and slid an arm around her. 'Every word we say is true,' he said, 'between us. But it doesn't matter. It can't touch my love, nor yours.' She said nothing, no bitterness left, words crushed as they kissed, unable to withdraw from the black infesting lust.

CHAPTER SIX

MANDY fastened her leather coat and ran down the muddy lane. When far enough from the house she walked, and took out the four notes her father had pushed at her, enough to get to Boston and back, and buy a meal for herself and Ralph. It was just after two by her watch, solid gold that Handley had bought in London and swore cost forty quid – though she knew he'd doubled the price on his way back just to impress her.

Since his success she'd wondered which was worse, being the daughter of a famous artist, or of a bone-idle penniless no-good. Certainly his fame hadn't got her the Mini she craved and thought it should have. Before, men used to give her money, buy her drinks and meals, now they expected her to pay for them, because her father was supposed to be rich and lavish. Nobody had done a thing for her this last year. It was as if she'd lost her purpose in life. All the force and wiles seriously expended piecemeal on other men now became one long ploy against her father, though, of course, in this relationship she could never play that final card of sexual attraction that she often had with others.

It rained in the village, and still needed forty minutes for a bus to the station. With a souped-up Mini she could reach Boston in thirty, while this way it was a day trip. Who would imagine that when your own father had seven thousand pounds in his current account (she'd been through his papers and seen his bank statements) he'd be so mean as to refuse you a secondhand Mini for a measly three hundred? What was he expecting to do with such a fortune? Shoot himself and leave it to a dog's home? He was harder than nails. When she'd got pregnant last year, hoping he'd set her and Ralph up in a new house, since they would have to get married, he'd thrown a fit and made her have an abortion, and on top of it all met Ralph and punched him in the face for what he was supposed to have done, but actually hadn't because another man had done it. So Ralph was chary of venturing up that neck of the country now, and she had to traipse all the way down to dismal Boston for a glimpse of him. What could you do with such a father? He was too knowing to do you any good at all. He'd never considered what damage an abortion did to you psychologically, especially at a time when all she'd wanted was to settle down with Ralph in a nice house and really have a kid if that was the price she had to pay for it. I can't stay in a house like The Gallery all my life, she thought, with such terrible black upchucks going on all the time. Not that I really wanted to get married, for Jack Christ's sake. Trust Dad to see through that one and get me off the hook. A trick that came today and went tomorrow. But what do I want to do with my life? I'm eighteen already and might be dead before I'm twenty-two. It's all right reading Huxley and Lawrence (and those dirty books Dad brought back from Paris – he'd cut my throat if he knew I'd got at them as well) and brooding in my room over their slow-winded lies, but I suppose one day I'd better make up my mind and do something. Dad's always on at me to get a job, and so I'd like to if one had any interest in it, but not like I did for six months in that estate-agent's office, typing cards all day with particulars of houses on them to stick in the window, with Mr Awful-Fearnshaw trying to get his hands up my thighs.

Thank God for bus-shelters, anyway. He isn't good for much else. I suppose the highest I can hope for is to be either a nurse, or a teacher, but I don't want to be anything yet, except something good and worthwhile when I do, so that I can be of use to somebody in the world. I've got my School Cert, so I can get my A levels and go to University, because I know that's what Dad would really like.

Miss Bigwell stopped in her new A40: 'Want a lift?'

'I'm going to Louth,' Mandy said, ready to take anything to get out of the rain and sit between four wheels. Always prone to dislike someone before she could possibly grow to like them. Mandy made an exception for Miss Bigwell, for whom she had a vague admiration. In the old days, that is to say two or three years ago, half-frozen in her winter mittens, she sometimes made her way to Miss Bigwell's cottage at the end of the village with a book of raffle-tickets hoping to sell a few at a shilling each for a painting of her father's. Because Miss Bigwell usually bought half a dozen and at the same time never won a picture (no one did) she was careful not to go there too often.

· Pulling into second gear, her car shot from the bus-stop. 'Why on a day like this? It's pouring mackerel. Boyfriend, I suppose. I'm off to see my brother Joe – not well again.'

Miss Bigwell was said to have a private income, in order to explain how she lived well and did no work. The reason people called it private was that few of them knew where it came from, though Handley said she was the only daughter of the Coningsby Bigwells. There was little he didn't know about the rich families of the county, for he had tapped them all at one time or another. She and her brother Joe had sold all the land when the old man finally croaked and invested the money in the holiday-making industry of Skegness. She was a big shrewd woman of about sixty, with a moon-face and glasses, whom you might have thought rather common if she didn't have money and a few of the ways that go with it. Like every local person she couldn't resist pumping Mandy about how her father felt now that he was famous. It never ceased to amaze Mandy that local people almost respected him, while to her he was the same old stingy bastard he'd always been. Her aim in getting away from the family was simply to reach some state in life where there was so much money that it ceased to have either meaning or importance. Lack of it had always cramped her natural zest for living – and so it was more vital in her life than it ought to have been. When she was a child in school the headmistress had said hands high those who want to pay two shillings for a Christmas party. Mandy shot hers up because it was all her father could afford anyway. But no one else moved because they knew what was coming: hands high those who want to spend five shillings for a *real* party – as if this price included champagne, the sheep! A wheatfield fluttered, naturally. When they subsided she said let's see again, (laughter already) those who even now want the cheap rate of two shillings. I still said yes, to everybody's surprise. Imagine thinking I'd change my mind just because I was all on my own! The headmistress went, then came back with a beautifully bound hymn-book inscribed from her, which she was giving me for my 'independent spirit'. I said thank you. What else could I say? She must have made about five pounds profit on that party, so what was a miserly hymn-book to her? Yet if she gave me something it ought to have been more than a book I never opened and couldn't even sell to the girls. So I went through all that for him, and he won't even buy me a car now that he's rolling in it.

Once in the car and it stopped raining she wished she'd waited for a bus instead of putting up with Alice Bigwell's endless ramblings about the best way of making compostheaps. She pumped on concerning slops and vegetation and manure and proportions of water, (nothing after all except complex euphemisms for common shit) building it up and putting it to bed, taking temperatures and saying how long it took to become soil. Mandy wondered whether she hadn't an incurable and repulsive obsession with birth and cannibalism, and whether she didn't serve the stuff up as a first course to any starving and unsuspecting traveller who knocked at her door for a bite of bread and cheese. Nothing would surprise her from the people around here. Though born in the place, she didn't really *belong*, for her father had come from Leicester (where they still went occasionally to visit hordes of the family) and didn't have an occupation like everyone else round about. He'd always been either a malingering no-good on the scrounge or, as lately, a celebrity with a murky past they were so ready to forget that it would surely be thrown up in his face with real fury if ever he went back to scrounging. And with the confidence of people who had lived for generations in one place, they realized how possible this was.

Because there was no saying when his suddenly acquired fortune would vanish, Mandy wanted to get out before it did. She couldn't believe that from now on he'd be able to earn good money doing something or other in the world of

53

art. He could turn his hand to many things, but being pig-headed, would never do anything his integrity told him was wrong. Otherwise why had they lived a desperate existence for so many years? To deviate from such principles would turn it into an awful waste, and though she realized how much of a pity this would be, at the same time she didn't want to go on living in the greater uncertainty that unexpected affluence had created. She was the daughter of a true artist in that she wanted the sort of settled life her upbringing had denied her the means of acquiring. And having the same determination as her father she would go to great lengths to get it, in the course of it justifying the inversion of the common maxim to say that the sins of the children are visited on the parents.

Sun flooded the coastal meadows with light, dust jumping from her train seat when she fell on to it for a better view of the fields embossed in green and yellow. Comfort was beauty, and she was always passing both. When you liked the landscape but had no feeling for the people set there, it was a place where you could live with pleasure but not grow up in, which at eighteen was a good reason to get out even though it broke your heart. The fact that her parents lived here would make it easier.

She met Ralph by the Stump. 'I'd have waited all day and all night,' he said, as if she'd been hurrying for his benefit. 'Time never drags when I'm expecting you.'

'I wish I knew when you were being sarcastic and when you weren't.'

'That's easy,' he laughed, as they walked arm in arm towards the bridge. 'I never am. Bitter, disappointed, perhaps, but only a fool is sarcastic.'

Ralph had long ago made up his mind never to do any farming, and so was locked in an internecine conflict with his father who was determined that he should – who wished he'd never encouraged him to go to Cambridge, though in fact there'd been no choice. After getting his degree in English Ralph set out with fifty pounds on a trip round the world. His father drove him as far as Grantham, and shook hands with a grin that expected to see him back in a few days. Ralph felt this, but strode off south along the Great North Road in anticipation of his first real lift. Tall, ruddy-cheeked, a gleam in his eye that had not yet received its baptism of worldly irony as had his father's, he travelled fast and reached Yugoslavia in a week. He there discovered a profitable frontier trade in foreign currency and so made enough money to live on the Dalmatian coast for a few weeks before resuming his advance through Greece and Turkey. In Ankara he translated letters for a business firm, then bought an old Italian motor-bike to ride across Iraq and Persia. He wore jeans and checked shirt, with a sheep-skin coat for the mountains, and a pipe of cheap local chok-ing tobacco was gripped in his teeth as he bumped at fifteen miles an hour over boulder roads. In place of his ruddiness came a sallow tan, permanently stamped when he became ill in Baluchistan with a violent form of liver-fluke. He lay for weeks on a rope bed in a remote khan, gaunt and bearded, raving at the cannonball lodged in his stomach. A junior consular official of the same age walked in one day as the worst of his fevers and cramps were leaving. He was taken to a salubrious Dak bungalow, and lived there on bacon and tinned carrots until fit to ride east again – which he did against the advice of the consul with so little grace that they afterwards marked him in their common memories as one of those northerners whose taciturnity is only a mask for a cretinous disposition.

The guts of his motor-bike dropped out above the high gorge of the Indus, and he picked it up bodily and threw it hundreds of feet towards the water, so that it narrowly missed a floating raft on which some family had spread their pots and tents.

Weeks later he reached Bangkok, and at Cook's found three dozen letters from his parents begging him to come home. In one sense he was heading there, but not in the way they expected. They filled him with rage, then pro-foundly depressed him. He was getting out of their clutches at last. The fact that they'd done so little for him since he was born except send him to live with moronic relations was beginning to make them feel guilty, and so they didn't want to lose him – which made him feel free and happy as he tore the letters up.

In Saigon he got work with the American 'advisers' typing inexplicable orders for the replacement of lethal supplies to the South Vietnamese army – in those early days. His genial and generous employers said his job could only be temporary, until he was politically 'cleared' by an organization in Washington. For some reason he was not 'cleared', and regretfully told that he must go. He picked up his pipes and tobacco, helped himself to the contents of an unguarded cash-box, and walked out at six o'clock one evening. Two minutes later a tri-shaw loaded with TNT was pushed into the main door of the building, and no one inside escaped death or injury.

He was pulled from his mosquito-net next morning and questioned by American detectives, but he was too innocent for any blame to be laid on him. The astuteness that enabled him to see what was going on in South Vietnam also persuaded him to keep his mouth shut when speaking to people or being interviewed, as he was now, by two intelligent numskulls. He answered slowly and reasonably, as if to comprehend yet stay out of trouble merely showed an absence of passion. While talking he dimly sensed that he would acquire this passion only when he had lost both these talents. He was blessed with the good sense of a young man with a conventional upbringing suddenly out on a limb and doing something unusual – he reflected while travelling deck-class to Hong Kong. The rusting steamer slid through oily blue water under a sun that blistered down for six days. After a few hours he found it necessary to escape from the overcrowded decks, and the only way to do this was by taking refuge in himself. He knew what the boat must look like from shore or passing ship, having seen one once going down the Saigon river – a dilapidated steamer of four thousand tons whose decks, funnels, and superstructure were completely hidden by human beings. Nothing else could be seen, not an air-vent, porthole, or derrick.

He gave English lessons in Hong Kong and caught a

mild venereal disease from one of his earnest and beautiful slit-skirted pupils who only wanted to learn phrases of endearment for her work with those American advisers recuperating from their assistance to South Vietnam. He regretted that the lessons had taken such a practical turn, but was able to get his ailment cured in Japan, the next stop on his world tour, where he got respectable work lecturing on English literature at certain universities. He waited there for a visa that would allow him to pass through America on his way home, the whole journey having taken a year out of his life.

Leaning over the parapet of the bridge with Mandy he still hadn't sorted out his impressions, even though a year had passed and he had reached the ripe age of twenty-five. The sheer built-up sides of the river had been left mildewed by the outgone tide, its water licking fitfully way out in the sand of Boston Deeps. Traffic stifled the air with fumes and thunder, and a coastal barge worked itself towards a quay downstream. Mandy had forgotten the fight with her father at home, being with Ralph and trying to talk to him, break her way through into that set face gazing along the river.

'I told you we shouldn't see each other again,' he said, without turning round.

'You were waiting for me.'

'I happened to be here.'

She looked at him, glad he was turned away so that she could do so without starting a fight. 'If you can stand it, I can. If you think you're going to make me talk about love you're mistaken. It doesn't make me happy to go on like this, but it seems to satisfy you. I suppose hanging around for weeks is the only way you'll make up your mind.'

His long sallow face became indignant at her accuracy. 'You're talking a lot of rubbish as usual. You'll be threatening to put your head in the gas-oven next, if I'm not careful and don't humour you.'

'You're marvellous when you say things like that,' she laughed. 'I feel you really mean it, so it's the only time you look properly alive – except when we're making love.'

'It's a pity you're so young,' he said. 'Otherwise you'd

have walked off instead of laughing.' He was determined to get his own way, but was so strong in it that she never knew what it was. Neither, in fact, did he, and the force of this subterranean desire was sapping his life before he had even started to live. His trip around the world had thrown him so basically off balance that he was unable to make up his mind concerning a career, or even on taking another trip round the world, which he often wanted to do.

They went into a fish-bar, but neither was hungry. She split open the batter and ate some of the white flesh. Ralph drank thirstily at his cup of rotten tea. 'Will you still come away with me?'

'Yes,' she said readily. 'But I wouldn't mind knowing where.'

'Neither would I. The old man wants me to go to agricultural college and learn the trade of raping the earth. But it's not in me, though I toyed with the idea just to please him.'

'It doesn't sound your style.'

'What is my style?'

'Not that.'

He pushed his plate away. 'A lot of help you are.'

'As much as you want me to be. You're afraid of me helping you in case it should show that I love you. But I don't anyway. Never have, never will, and never could.' She stood up and fastened her coat. He took her elbow and opened the door, her shoulder against his chest as they went through.

They walked into the country invigorated by a forceful moist breeze coming from the sea. 'What I really want to do,' he said with an enthusiasm that irritated her, 'is to get a house in Lincolnshire and fill it with books. Live on my own, I think, perhaps work as a teacher at some local school. It's the only thing that appeals to me at the moment.'

It amazed and distressed her that he might after all know what he wanted, and that this might well be it. The life he drew appealed to her as well, and for this reason it seemed horrible, decadent, corrupting, a way of dying before you really started to live. She listened to him talking about gardens, dogs, a couple of guns to go shooting now and again, the rubbish-bin of his father's already fulfilled and deadened desires. He'd furnish the house from auctions at market-towns round about so as to get beautiful antique furniture. She knew that if he really set his heart on it his ageing daddy might buy him a house simply to get rid of him.

'That trip round the world knocked holes in you,' she said.

'It showed me what I wanted.'

'When you know that you're finished.' They walked quickly, open country on either side, keeping well in to avoid traffic.

'That sounds like another of your father's sayings,' he said. 'I like his paintings, but I don't like the way he justifies them.'

'If you want to be with it,' she said, 'stop knowing what you want. Dad couldn't have told me that.'

'I'd still like to have one of his pictures, anyway,' he said. She'd once taken him to the studio to see Handley's work, about the time all the fuss had started. When he said he'd like to have one for his own room, she'd retorted that he should have thought of that a year ago when he could have chosen anything for a few quid.

'I thought you were set on having a house? You can't have both.' Perhaps, he thought, but realized that it would be morally wrong, if not actually degenerate, not to try and get all he wanted while still young enough to remember what it was he had wanted in the first place.

'I could,' he suggested, 'if you persuaded him to give me one. He hates my guts after what happened last year, but I don't think he'd bear a grudge all his life.'

She laughed, showing her fine even teeth, before a cigarette went between her lips. 'He wouldn't give a pencil stroke away any more.'

He cupped his large hands and passed a light over. They were pale and smooth after the long recuperation from his trip, for he hadn't even helped on his father's farm, she thought, since coming back. 'He's got a trunk full of note-books that he's written ideas in for the last twenty years. An American university offered him a fat sum for them, but he wouldn't part. Keeping them for a rainy day, I suppose.'

'Why don't you just walk out with a painting for me?'

Grey clouds were torn into shreds by invisible dogs of wind. 'I hope we hit Wainfleet before it rains,' she said. 'I get a bus from there. Still, it's better doing this than moping around Boston. The only time you talk is when we're walking. Your words are like tadpoles: they have to grow legs before they jump out.' She waited for him to retaliate, but he became morose, which was his way of self-control. 'What makes you so eager to get at the old man's painting? You haven't even seen the latest.'

'I want to stick one on my wall for as long as I can stand it, and try and get to know something about you.'

'There's no connection between them and me. It'd prob-ably send you absolutely off your bonce.'

'It's a good idea though. Don't you think so?'

'It gives us something to talk about,' she said. 'I thought you'd have known plenty about me. We've had it often enough.'

'You've been reading too much Lawrence, I suppose. That sort of thing actually stops you getting to know somebody, blinds you to everything about a person. But to have one of your father's pictures on my wall would really tell me something.'

'What a love-affair ours is!' she said. 'You've burned me out at eighteen! I can get you one of my father's paintings any time, but I expect I'd go to prison for it. He'd put his whole family behind bars if it'd interfered with his work. You've no idea what he's like. Ruthless isn't the word. He'd track us to the end of the world to recover a fading sketch in a penny notebook if he knew he might never have a chance of looking at it again. Give him a hundred for it, and that's another matter.'

'You're exaggerating.'

'Not altogether. I could walk out with one, but I won't. If

you want one that badly you'd better break in and steal it, but it'll be difficult. We've got alarm-wires on the gate and a bull-dog near the front door. Then there's Uncle John who's completely insane and sits awake all night listening to his radio with a loaded revolver nearby in case anybody comes to take him away.'

'I hadn't seriously considered it.'

'That's the only way,' she said. 'The trouble about dreams is that they cause so much trouble.' They sat on a gate to enjoy a temporary burst of sun, his arms around her shoulders. She leaned comfortably close. 'And if Richard and Adam got hold of you they'd be delighted to practise karate on one of the landed gentry. I can see it all.'

'I'll bet you damned well can.'

The kiss lasted till they lost balance and nearly fell off the gate. The surest way to make him do something was tease him about it. He knew it, too, but didn't want to resist his fate unnaturally – while wanting to seem as if meeting it of his own free will. 'You want the date and the time?' he grinned. 'I'm not so stupid as to tell you that.'

'Life gets more exciting every day,' she said, on the last mile towards Wainfleet, rain pouring on to them when they were too happy to worry about it any more.

CHAPTER SEVEN

AFTER dusk light was abundant, as if they lived next door to a power station and tapped it free. More than anything else, they must have light. Once put on, a bulb was left blazing even in the smallest and most useless hall or cupboard, one-, two-, three-hundred-watt incandescences in every room – a thousand watts to the kitchen, another thousand to Albert's studio, and what Uncle John consumed on his spiritual searches through the ether nobody could even guess. There was a uniting family passion for light when the world around them was dark. If Albert opened a door by mistake, and in passing noticed there was no light within, he absent-mindedly flicked down the switch so that from then on the light would permanently blaze in a renewed self-created aura. The lit-up house was visible from far and wide, planted firmly on a high ridge backing against the sky.

Only Enid remarked, but just once, on the superabundance of light, and the possible waste of it. They were walking home after an hour at the pub, and from a bend in the lane four uncurtained windows were flooding the approaches with a sickly phosphorescence. Albert's studio lights were eating at the sky above. The caravans were illuminated. Side windows shone from either flank of the house. 'Anybody would think you were afraid of burglars,' she said.

'I've always liked light, I don't know why. If there were a power failure I'd die.'

'I suppose you need something to light up the black pits of your soul,' she said.

From the right window came the full-blast noise of Shostakovich's *Seventh Symphony*, and from the left the rhythms and phrases of Uncle John's ecstatic morse sounds mixed sublimely with the music, killed by it as the wind veered. Opening the gate, they trod carefully over power-lines supplying the caravans. 'It's good to have light,' he said. 'I can beat the moon. Get down, Eric,' he said to the welcoming dog, 'you bloody fool, get back.'

'I don't see what good it is,' she said, 'it might let you see every inch of the house inside, but once you're in you can't see at all beyond the windows. If you want to see outside you've got to switch 'em off.'

They went into the kitchen that was so clean not even the smell of cleanliness remained. Enid put on the kettle for tea and a hot-water bottle. Handley sat at the table, forgetting to take his cap off, and looking as if about to set off for the night-shift. 'Perhaps I'm religious,' he quipped, 'being afraid of the dark.'

'Well,' she said, 'you haven't grown up, and that's a fact.'

'There's plenty of time for that when I'm dead. I'm in no hurry. Grown-up, mature people are ten-a-penny. They're all over the place, like flies in summer, strong-faced vacuous venomous pipe-smokers and happy savers and careful drivers. Don't talk to me about the lumpen living-dead. Put them in a room with a strong light and they'd start to confess. Me, I'd ask 'em to turn it up a bit. Even take off my dark glasses to show good faith. Still, we can put a forty-watt bulb in your room if you ever want to escape and get back to reality.'

'You've made your point,' she said. 'Do you want milk or lemon in your tea?'

'Both.'

'Milk or lemon?'

'Lemon, then.'

The house at next morning's breakfast fell into silence when papers and magazines were brought in, and the quiet concentration at the altars of soft-brained reading-matter began. Mandy looked up before turning a page and noticed her mother staring with unmixed loathing and malevolence at her father. She walked quietly out of the room with her particular newspaper, wondering what cloudburst they were in for now, and before closing the door she reached back and turned the radio full blast to some church service, thus drowning the door slam and her rush upstairs.

Windows were steamed from breakfast cooking, masking a thin continuous drizzle outside. On such days cold rain wedged them into the house, or shunting quietly from one caravan to another. A rush to the Rambler or Land-Rover, and a quick acceleration down the mud-flooding lane was the farthest anyone would get on such a day, to the village shop where they weren't allowed to dawdle, but were served before other people because of the enormous bills they ran up with such thoughtlessness.

Maria dipped her bread in coffee. Brought up in a staid Milan family, it was as if she had now been pitched into a brood of Sicilian peasants who had won on the lottery, or killed grandma and inherited her secret wealth. The employment agency was a villain who had misrepresented the job to her – 'a modern house belonging to an elderly child-less couple on the northern outskirts of London.' Handley had met her at Heathrow late one night, and the northern outskirts proved to be five hours away, ending in a pandemonium scream of rage and fear when she finally stepped from the Rambler into six inches of pure Lincolnshire mud as a wilful dawn light was breaking over the hills.

Enid did not look malignantly at Albert but merely hard, and he was so busy in a dash to kill the religious heat of the radio's breath that he didn't notice it till sitting down again. She threw the magazine at him, one corner splaying across the open butter dish. 'Read that.'

'What? That bit about stately homes?'

'Open it. You'll see.'

He knew what it must be. 'I'll read it out loud. Listen, everybody. An article about me, and don't double up till I've finished.'

'Get on with it,' she snapped.

The reproductions of his work were superb and should have been left unexplained, but accompanying them was an inflated view by Russell Jones on Handley at Work, and Handley at Home, Handley the half-mad inspired painter, the uneducated gypsy-like creature running amok with paint-brushes in a house without books, that was guarded by a pair of good old English bulldogs. After this drunken rubbish came a few sentences on how he actually worked, undeniably accurate, but then more personal detail reappeared, and this was obviously the cause of Enid's dangerous set stare.

His female admirers were mentioned – to which Handley had presumably admitted – for, Jones wrote, when the photo of a pretty girl fell from his wallet Handley said with a smile that it happened to be of a girl with whom he was in love at the moment. A few general smears and critical sentences rounded off the article so beautifully printed and laid out.

'What a laugh it is,' said Richard. 'They've got you, Dad. You might as well sit back and enjoy it.'

He tried to explain. Adam slid a mug of tea across, at which he sipped now and again. 'It was a photo of Mandy. I saw his eyes pop, so thought I'd have a bit of fun. You know how irresistible it is. I don't see how I can be blamed.'

Enid felt nothing but shame – not, she retorted, that she could ever be insulted by that dirty magazine, but because Handley had been so intent on having his senseless stupid fun that he hadn't considered her feelings at all. They'd had this out before, often, but whenever journalists came crawling to the door, especially from *posh* papers, he just slobbered all over them like an adolescent instead of acting like a grown man, spewed out everything like a clown instead of behaving with dignity and sense. If you didn't know how to handle them, why let them in at all? Slam the door in their faces and they'd think none the worse of you. And now your naïveté has led to this, a little weasel of the intellectual gutter smirking his foulness into a so-called reputable magazine.

'That's enough,' Handley said, standing up again. 'I know all about it now. I'll get that jumped-up fretwork little bastard. I'll make a wax figure and stick pins in it. I'll burn his effigy on bonfire night. I'll go down to London and pummel his putty head on every pavement in Knightsbridge.'

Adam and Richard cheered. Uncle John continued his silent reading of the newspaper, looking perhaps for some cryptogrammatical clue that would send him on another frantic and exhilarating search across the far-and-wide ether.

'Wipe your mouth,' Enid said, 'there's foam on it.'

'I'll write a letter to the Editor. I'll sue them. I'll go to the Press Council about it.' She leaned towards him and shouted four words, as if they were the final message from a beleaguered and capitulating city before the defenders blew themselves up on the powder magazine: 'WILL-YOU-NEVER-LEARN?'

Richard took her arm: 'Mother, please, don't get so upset.'

She snapped him away. 'I'm supposed to be living in a house where your father is openly carrying on as if he had a harem.'

'As long as it's not true,' Handley said desperately, wrathful and hurt by any attack on his wife's dignity.

65

'It would be better if it were. But now you want to make things worse by trying to do something about it. You're deliberately ruining our world. Go on, though, smash it up. That's what they want you to do. They'll applaud you. The clown is performing again. A letter from you, and they'd gladly put it in, giving that interviewer the last crushing word of course.'

He felt emptied, blistered, pilloried. She was right – perhaps. A free spirit was abroad, and they were out to pull you down to the general level of nonentity that never thought to question anything. Woe betide any poor and stupid bastard who recognizes himself as a free spirit, because once you did you weren't free any more.

'All right,' he said. 'I'll do nothing. You're right, though it chokes me to say so. By driving me to say it, you've jumped on to their side.'

'That's your last word, is it?'

'It is.'

'Is it?'

'Yes, it is. I'll bump into him at a party some time, and then we'll see.'

Richard pinned her down at the wrist. Nevertheless the full black pot of scalding tea capsized and ran over the table.

CHAPTER EIGHT

CODE and cipher manuals brought out of the army, marked CONFIDENTIAL and NOT TO BE TAKEN AWAY and TOP SECRET were stacked by the long-range communications receiver. Though useless and out-of-date, continual study enabled him to break any code piercing his earphones. A few nights of concentration and he worked them into plain language. There were no secrets he could not tap, useless commonplaces for the most part, yet they might one day yield a precise solution to the whole pattern of his life that he could fall down before and worship.

The set had not been switched on. He smoked a cigarette. It seemed a dead part of the week for exploring ether. It was no use trying to make contact with God or any other king of the universe with such misery in the house, Enid and Albert battling vindictively out of natures generous and broad-living. Tear-marks still on his cheeks, it shocked him that when prosperity entered by the front door peace packed its bags and left by one of the windows. An undeclared war went on continually. If they would acknowledge it, peace could be made, but when he spoke in all gentleness they'd claim to be happy, kiss and cuddle in front of everyone to prove it. They couldn't bear to have their problems brought to the surface and solved, he thought. Nobody knew why they fought, blamed success, money, or the invidious snooping of newspapermen, but these symptoms, he knew, only concealed the disease, like bushes on fire surrounding a plantation of foul fungus. Sometimes Albert and Enid did try to discuss their troubles, but the soul was involved, and so words from the human mouth were not enough to isolate and cure it. He sat long hours at his desk and wept for them because they were beyond his help. He was always hoping to save them, head in hands and tears falling as if attuned to some divine heart-rending music, waiting for it to end and the magic oracle to speak from some far-off spot of the universe. His world, their world, the whole world seemed to be in his hands, the strain of it heavy, fetching forth the tears, breaking his spirit time and time again, yet leaving him with renewed faith, a strengthened conviction that he would find a solution and be everybody's saviour – by which method he might therefore be his own.

Handley came in and sat on the spare stool. 'Any news of Frank Dawley?'

'Not yet,' John said.

'Let me know when it gets interesting down there. I'll have that new aerial fixed in next week, then perhaps we'll have better luck.'

When Handley left, he switched on, out of despair and away from it, electricity easing its weasel way through the whole superheterodyne system of valves and condensers and impedances. The magic eye came alive, green growing deeper and more vivid as if lid, pupil, and retina had been lifted off the middle Polyphemus eye of God's forehead, and was there for him to stare into. He searched and listened, when noise swelled into the earphones.

Handley got into the Rambler, knocked over a dustbin on a quick three-point turn, slid down the muddy lane like a barge, and sank between a line of bare-branched elms. He laughed, not really upset by the events of the morning. The god of the family had roared and scorched his hair, but that was all. Rain stopped as he wheeled on to the paved camber through the misty village. A few mid-morning light-bulbs glowed in cottage windows, and a group of men were making their way to the pub from work. He turned right for Catham and climbed a steep hill as if to roar into the sky, but he levelled at the top and went at seventy along the narrow lane.

Steaming fields beyond the hedges were humped and rich after winter, smells of earth and moisture reaching him through open windows. It was good to get away from the pointless bloody savagery of that house, that fogbound ship without lifeboats, and liable any minute to sink or go up in flames. A band of faint smoke stood up straight from a farmhouse chimney, and when his eyes came back to the road a large jack-rabbit slipped from hedge to hedge.

He stopped the car on Bluestone Ridge, tasting silence of the indeterminate season, spring emerging from a brittle rat-trap of winter. Air was clearing over Catham and the flattish patchwork of fields by the coast, and he imagined slugbreakers coming in on slow rebounds from the vast level sea, flaking phosphorous breaking on shrub and gravel, as he had seen it so many times when walking on empty bereft beaches without a shilling in his pocket, wait-ing till dusk before starting the twenty miles home if he didn't get a lift, back to Enid and the kids with their reasonable wants and he unable to do much about them.

Buds were sharpening on hawthorn hedges, and when the wind stopped drifting it was almost warm. Below a wood on the opposite hillside a tractor crawled along the furrows, breaking silence, undisturbing under the clouds. Every so often he felt it was time to make a change in his life, yet he distrusted this as the promptings of chaos. To swing violently on to another course was certain to kill your work for a while, and at the moment it was going well. He was deep in the industry of it, and only questioned it after some heart-shaking quarrel at home that set him to wonder whether he was living in the best possible way for his work. Such quarrels fragmented his confidence, and that was always bad. Yet without such threats, he smiled in the sweet headclearing air, the very force behind his work would rot.

He joined the main road and dropped two hundred feet towards Catham where it was raining again, a steady drift of fine spray against slate roofs and cobbled streets. It was almost as quiet as the countryside when he drove under the railway-bridge towards newer houses sprawled on the far side of town. She was in, he saw, even before turning into the crescent. Smoke came from the chimneypots, and her Hillman Minx stood outside. He could smell the sea as he stood to lock his car, grains of wet sand crossing the flats from Toddle Fen. There'd been no thought of coming to see her, yet in fleeing from home he'd landed without thought on her doorstep.

He hurried up the gravel, a tall figure bending from wind hitting the back of his head. Curtains flicked at the window, and the fancy glass panelling of the door swung open before a hand came out of his pocket to knock.

'Hello, Albert!'

He stepped by her into the hall: bookcase, holding *Principles of Banking*, *Practical Knowledge for All*, *Complete Ornithology* and a few deadbeat thrillers. Then an umbrella-stand, mirror and coat-rack. 'I thought you'd be out, so I came to see you.'

Her laugh stayed. 'As long as you aren't disappointed.'

'I can't tell yet.' He pulled her to him, tall and buxom, long brown hair falling away. 'Breadwinner in?'

Her brown eyes opened wide. 'He's gone birdwatching.

Heard of some wild geese mating near the Wash. Went out at four this morning – instead of going to the bank.'

'I hope they take their time over it.' Sitting by the coal fire in the living room she asked how things were at home. 'Wonderful,' he said. 'I couldn't betray my wife if everything weren't perfect between us. That's why I haven't been to see you lately. Too many rows.'

She was thirty-eight, a schoolteacher, strictly career woman and to hell with her husband when it came to a sweet knock or two on the side. Handley had met her in the bank on a Saturday morning, dropped one of his chequebooks, and who could ever say whether it was accident or design? If a handkerchief's the only thing a man'll pick up that a woman drops, he thought, a cheque-book's the only thing a woman will remind a man that he's dropped, whether it's her husband or no. He stood on the bank step admiring the beautiful seventeenth-century houses round about like a tourist from the Home Counties. She tapped his shoulder: 'You seem to have dropped this.'

'So I have,' he smiled familiarly. 'How would I have got through the weekend without it? *I* only found it this morning, and was getting used to affluence already.' Large brown eyes looked back at him, lips opened in a smile to reveal teeth that went well with ear-rings and fur coat. Mrs Joan Quickie in his mind's eye, until she gave her real name.

'If you did find it,' she said, though not too certain of his seriousness, 'don't you think it would be a good idea to give it back?'

The chill autumn went through to his glum face: 'Would you like to come for a drink with me so that I can think about it?' – offering her a cigarette while she made up her mind.

'No,' she said.

'Then let's talk standing here. I'm very much attracted to you. Handley's my name. I always am to someone who wants me to go straight. As a matter of fact I took it from the pocket of an old suit this morning before sending it to the cleaners. Did you think I'd really knocked it off?'

'Not altogether,' she said.

'Let's walk along. We're nearly at the Queen's Head. Good fire in there. You were coming out of the manager's office. Been to get an overdraft?'

'The bank manager's my husband,' she laughed, walking a few steps.

'I've never known a bank manager to have such a personable wife,' he said.

'You live and learn,' she said as they went in for a drink.

'Now and again,' he responded, taking her arm.

Her name, after all, was Joan, but Mallinson, though she was quick enough when it came to the point, which it did when he thought to call.

'I'm glad to see you, though I don't suppose I should say so to someone like you. Where have you been this last month?'

He took off his jacket and stood by the shelf. 'Painting. Finished a few things.' The morning papers were thrown over the padded velvet sofa. 'I saw that article,' she said. 'I don't suppose your wife felt too good about it.'

'Let's not talk about that. Is there any coffee?'

'I'll get some.' Before she could move he held her to him. 'You had a quarrel,' she said, a teasing smile.

'Not exactly. The pots didn't fly.' He took off her glasses and set them on the shelf.

'But *you* did,' she said, 'here.'

'Shut up, and let me love you. I know you're a happily married woman, but I'm a happily married man, so it's not sinful.' The day lay quiet over the house and whole road, keeping the world silent for them. Only the antique clock wrung out its bomb ticks from the shelf above. His hands were up under the back of her sweater, flattening between shoulder-blades, while her mouth writhed around his face, opened over his moustache and lips. 'Come and see me more often,' she said. 'You can always phone to check whether it's all right.'

He pressed her full breasts against him. 'Tell me that when I'm about to leave' – clearing his throat. Her mouth stopped him talking, an ether mask going over his windpipe and set for the silence and blackout of love. 'Let's go upstairs.'

He forgot his lust to the extent of noticing the bedroom furniture: the bad taste opulence of wardrobes and dressing-tables marked His and Hers (how can he suspect anything with those staring at him on coming to bed every night?) and orange eiderdown and low head-boarded bed, round piano-stools with powderpuff tops, and white sheep's-wool mats that, when barefoot, made you look as though you had no feet. The odour of bedroom cold lingered through sudden gasfire heat.

Her sweater came up and over, face flushed as if at the sight of what Handley could see. It was no love match, for she was like the sea, and Handley the little boy with his finger in the polder-hole. He wanted to take it easy, slowly, woo her, but the rush was on her, and therefore him. It's not that when we're in bed I try to make her come, he'd sometimes reflected after it was finished, so much as me trying to hold myself back. It was good, sweet, the whole point of the world, but like that, in complete abandon, would last thirty seconds before his explosion while hers was still a low rumble in the distance, a few spots of sail or seagull wing on the far horizon of a becalmed and enchanted sea. While loving her as both deserved, hand under buttocks and one around neck, kisses fronting between them, he breathed the cool air hard, counted up to ten, felt his impossible drilltip about to explode into a million diamonds deep in her, so tried to think of all the villages in Lincolnshire beginning with the letter N, and when that ran out tried to think of the names of individual seas in the world, stations on the railway up from London, every tree he knew, all spring flowers. He occasionally distrusted such a millstone system, yet it held them back from a headlong rush till they reached the calms and shallows, out of which he became an uninhibited savage and she a fishwife who came with ease and speed, Eddystone in a storm-blind sea, she upswamping as if to put out that top light with a hiss of fire and water, and a groan of triumphant chaos.

Handley wondered when he could decently get up and

look for a cigarette. He kissed her and risked it, his long trouserless legs stretched white over the orange bedside. She pulled him back. 'How can you be in such a hurry when it was so good?' But her voice was calm, and she smiled in the dim light. In spite of all hurry, she'd drawn the curtains and locked the door, and he wondered whether in the opposite house they weren't curious as to who had died. If someone came over and politely asked he wouldn't be able to tell them at the moment.

He gave her a cigarette, flicked the lighter near her face. 'I lead a dull life,' she said, 'as a schoolteacher in a small Lincolnshire town.'

'You were born here.'

'What difference does that make?' The better they found it the more discontented she felt afterwards. So where will it ever end? he wondered.

'You work hard. Why complain?'

'I am complaining, though.'

'I suppose you'd like us to go away together, drop everything and fly south to a romantic life in London or Majorca? I'm not twenty any more. I don't even love you.'

'But I love you.'

'You're lucky then. I wish to God I did, a piece of forked lightning come down from heaven and blasted me in two, one part glued to stay and the other wanting to go with some woman to the far side of the moon and rot there in a vile state of love. Fine. Randy and dandy, swoony and loony, a leper between the sun and moon. I say no thanks to it, until it hits me, and then I'll have no say in it at all. When I'm not in love I can paint great pictures as big as a wall, but if I was in love I'd paint bloody miniatures and choke on them, or do futile pieces of wire-sculpture that I'd fall down in and strangle to death.'

'How about that coffee?' he said, putting an arm round her when they got downstairs. 'Perhaps I'm dead inside, a wood-yard of seasoned timber nobody wants.'

'You're not,' she said. 'But let's go away for a few days, to London or the South coast. We can make good excuses, and it would be so wonderful.'

'It might well be. But I don't like life in small doses – a teaspoonful three times a day. I don't imagine you do, either. It's bad for the system. When it happens it must be all or nothing, but with me it hasn't happened yet. Oh yes, you're charming, you're beautiful, you're passionate, all the things I like, but there's something missing, and neither of us can risk saying what it is. Maybe the pinch of shit in a vat of cream that makes the best yoghourt. Who knows?'

'You do,' she said.

'I know I do.' She went to make coffee. Of course he did. It had happened before, and if he thought it might never happen again he'd drive his car at a hundred into the nearest tree. She came back with a tray : milk, coffee, delicate cups, sugar in lumps, biscuits. 'I hope your husband takes his time,' he said, 'wandering around those marshes in his salt-and-pepper drag.'

Low in the armchair, her legs showed up well. 'He'll be in for lunch.'

'So you read that article?' He'd held the question back, not wanting to spoil their time together.

She put her glasses on, her brown eyes half closed behind them. 'I did.'

Handley drank the scalding coffee in one gulp. 'He made it all up. Oh well, I'll bump into him. Nobody's going to smear me from the safety of their newspapers and not get it back between the eyes. I'll rip that chuckle out of his blackheads.'

'It was certainly a nasty piece,' she said, though laughing. He looked into her eyes, his narrow forehead and chisel-nose, thin determined mouth, dark dry hair spread short and thick around his gypsy-like skull. She couldn't imagine where he came from, but hoped that in all his bitter sharpness he'd come straight to her and stay there. He was lost in the vast spaces of his own isolation, wandering between the heat and cold of a continental climate, unconnected to her or anyone in the world, and she wanted to take care of him and manage his life, though in this she would find her own destruction, wall against wall, because there was nothing in him that could ever be looked after. Filled with the latest in modern psychology, she thought he might have been too savagely weaned as a baby, that he mightn't have been fed regularly, or that he had somehow survived in spite of no care at all, not even nurtured by a wolf, that neither breast nor bottle were ever put to him unless he screamed down the whole sky first, stars, sun, and moon, until the dust of hunger went into him and cut him off, the dust and flour of desolation making crusts that fed him through some form of bleak survival, placing him now beyond anyone but the she-wolf of the tundra, ice and sun, quartz crystals and pine-trees. Out of this came his painting, from a man in the middle of great earth-spaces who could not move one foot in any direction.

'There's a bit of suicide in all of us,' he said, 'but only the smallest bit in me.'

'I think you do have a hard time living with the world,' she said. He had taken away her desire, and she was angry at herself for letting him, falling into his trap. She wanted to get him away from a wife who did not understand him, who was alien to such an artist. It might have been all right while he was unknown, but now it would strangle him. To live in the same way as an important and famous painter as you had while struggling to become one was disastrous. She could show him how to take his place in the world of great and talented men, and she thought herself quite capable of doing this.

'As long as I can live with myself,' he said, 'which is all a painter needs.'

She poured more coffee. 'You have to live with the world, as well as yourself.'

'Which world, though?'

'There's only one world for you – the one that buys your paintings. What other can there be?'

'That's the question,' he retorted. 'An artist makes his own world, through himself. He doesn't go into one ready-made for him. He only started painting to get out of *that* one. If I was only half a man and half a painter I might not think so, but I have a bigger opinion of myself than any-body can imagine, and even had when I was unknown and struggling. Some people would like me to accept their world because they see themselves the highest common denominators of it, and the fact that I don't is a poke in the eye to them. My heart just won't let me take up with this big world you're talking about, as you and they would like me to do. It's got nothing for me, and maybe I've got nothing for it, but at least I have plenty of ideas and work to do and needn't concern myself with it.'

'Why do you complain when they attack you?'

'I don't. They attacked my wife. And there's nothing I can do about it, so I'm just letting off steam. Still, I'd like to punch that drunkard's nose. He wouldn't be able to get away with such a thing in my ideal, anarchistic, self-regulating society without getting beaten up for it.'

They gave up talking for kissing. Intellectual discussion, he said, always made him randy. There seemed nothing she could do with him in any case, which made her passion quick to return, though this time one point behind his.

CHAPTER NINE

RALPH steered his Land-Rover into the depths of a wood, tyres crushing over wet sawdust and wood-chippings of one clearing, and bumping towards another. Mud deepened so much beyond that he decided not to risk it, sat inside studying his large-scale map with the engine still running, memorizing details of the terrain between this point and the Handley house so that he would not have to open it outside and see its beautifully decorated paper buckling and warping in the rain, a thought that tightened his lips with revulsion. Beyond the western edge of the wood were three fields to cross, the last rising twenty feet and crowned by a spinney of oak-trees. From such height and cover he could observe the house in all its detail, especially the side giving access to Handley's studio.

He put on his cap, fastened the pegs of his duffel-coat, and climbed out. Mud parted around his feet, but once off the track dead twigs and leaves made it seem more solid. Primroses had deepened in the rain, speckled a whole yellowing bank like flag-day badges on the lapels of a football crowd. Bluebells and arum lilies sagged and were flattened by water. Other flower heads littered, but he'd scorned to notice them after the age of sixteen. To do so was a stage of adolescence, to swoon and rapturize over wild flowers, and all the false crap of Lawrence and Powys and Williamson, the 'I am a wild beast and proud of it but still very sensitive school because my father was a bastard to my mother' or 'the cream of my generation was killed in Flanders or Libya' – as they sat in warm cottages or Hampstead flats. Thank God that sort of thing is dead, he thought, which meant to say he hoped it was and was convinced it ought to be but was by no means sure, England being England and all the things it was.

He kept well in to the hedge, clumps of soil that looked solid enough in the lee of it now collapsing muddily underfoot, till his boots were so heavily caked that it was impossible to move and he had to pull off the earth with his hands. After a few minutes the same coagulation had built up so high under his boots that he almost overbalanced and hoped for drier weather on the chosen night so that his retreat would be easy and quick.

From the edge of the spinney he looked across four hundred yards of field at Handley's residence, heard the misty depressing snap of a canine voice shifting towards him as if it had already picked up his scent. Through binoculars he saw it sniffing between caravans in the yard. After dark it was chained up, which was useful, but he'd carry a pound of best steak on the night just in case. Yet it barked continually at nothing, as his previous nocturnal scoutings had shown, so when he was actually climbing up no one would wonder what was disturbing it.

The village clock struck eleven. He ate a bar of chocolate. The house would be crawling with parents, six children, two *au pair* girls, a mad uncle, and a man-eating bulldog; though if he kept his nerve and moved like a bat he could shin his way up the tree, leap to the windowsill, and take the final floor by a nearby drainpipe. Once in Handley's studio he could lower a picture on a piece of cord, and collect it on the ground after his own descent. It was easy to spell it out like this, but he knew something was wrong, that more was needed than a ball of string and a full moon, a tight lip and a sure grip as he entered that rotten domain. Without a dry night, the painting would be ruined, and if that happened there'd be nothing left to live for, except Mandy, and she wasn't enough, otherwise he wouldn't be planning to steal it in the first place.

Sweet-papers and beer-cans were scattered from previous hours of observation. His theory for committing the perfect crime was that you must carry it out with all possible speed, which meant scrupulous attention to the actual details of break in, though beyond that sphere of action one could be as careless as one's temperament demanded, in which case a few sweet-papers were neither here nor there. An amateur could get away with murder – as it were – whereas the adept was always liable to betray himself over some clue he'd been too careful to eradicate. A motiveless job was the safest. If even he did not know why he wanted to steal the best painting in Handley's studio, how then were the police to find out his motive? And if they couldn't deduce a motive for the so-called crime then there was no reason why he should ever be tracked down. If he got clear of the house, he was away for good. Whoever could rationalize the various stages of a crime had a fair chance of never being detected. So it sometimes worried him that he hadn't yet concretely pinned down his reasons for wanting to acquire the picture. Those he had outlined to Mandy had been little more than a legpull. If he simply needed to get his hands on a great picture in order to indulge in a lifetime of private viewing then why didn't he go to Amsterdam and steal Rembrandt's *Night Watch* from the Rijksmuseum? He daydreamed through the mechanics of such an operation, which would involve getting it in a taxi to the docks or on a porter's barrow, then sweating with apprehension as clumsy workers levered it on to the boat. All limbs shook when he saw it slipping in a nightmarish vision from their hands into the slimy bed-green water. I'd better roll it up while in the museum, even if it cracks slightly here and there. But he relinquished the idea, and immediately felt better. A latest Handley would suffice, an easier job because he didn't live far away and had the use of a Land-Rover. Such a chance came rarely, and the more he dwelt on it the more did his fear of actually stealing it increase. Such marvellous bouts of fear continually sweeping through him must mean there was little chance of his resisting what he had first broached with Mandy as a joke, and that when he came to cross the field and climb that tree all fear would go, and leave him free, cool, and swift as he soundlessly scaled that wall to a dangerous height before forcing the window.

It was hopeless, but he would do it, and succeed because he knew it was hopeless and because he had absolutely no control over whether he did it or not. He sat for hours in the tree-fork trying every optic combination of the binoculars to bring that house a foot closer across the field, the house which contained two things he wanted most in his life. He'd been there once with Mandy and, having those dull louche-brown eyes of a born reconnoitrer, remembered everything. Framed by field, sky, fences, and trees, he saw again into the rooms and stairways as if the walls were glass, recollecting the positions of doors, locks, and windows. He knew the direction of Uncle John's radio room, and where everyone slept, each secret nook of the worn-out worm-eaten labyrinth.

He reached into his pocket and took a long drink of brandy, careless of precarious balance, hoping to stave off an ulcerous hunger. An unfurled hedgehog came from a grassy bank and walked at leisure across the path, eyes calm under spiny impregnable defences. Ralph considered it put on a fine front against those it had no wish to be bothered with, an anti-social bore in the hedgehog world, when no one in his right mind could wish to be otherwise in any sort of world.

A single block of enlarged vision beyond the twin funnels of his binoculars scanned the multitudinous bricks of the great wall, broken only by the high elm leading to the side window of Handley's studio. His will centred on it as he examined all possible angles and limits of that huge flank, always drawn back to the window until it seemed that if he spread his arms and gave one great foot-thrust from the fork of the tree he would fly across the deceptively narrow expanse of field and land in a few seconds by the window he so much wanted to go in by.

Lowering the glasses, it was as impossibly far off as ever. It didn't worry him. Subtlety and solitude ruled out any shocks from life, and he smiled at the pleasures of continual observation, that nevertheless gave no results and got him no closer to what in such a desperate key he wanted to get his hands on. It was a game, and the course was an un-stoppable zombie-like action leading to a double and satis-fying jackpot. He smoked a pipe to comfort himself under the drizzle and raindrops from higher branches, which might have been torture to anyone less fundamentally pre-occupied.

When he next allowed his focus to drift up to Handley's window he saw that it was slightly open, a pleasant surprise, because he felt as if it had suddenly become more human. It had. A head fixed there had a sort of machine where the eyes should have been, and with a shock he realized that they were more powerful binoculars than the infantry glasses of his father's slung round his neck. By some in-vidious mechanism of auto-attraction both sets of glasses seemed unable to cease observing the other, and this situa-tion was painful to Ralph, because he'd been at it longer and could only be the cause of this unexpected retaliation. He wanted to smile, wave, and nonchalantly slip his glasses back in their case, but they seemed glued to his eyes, his arms frozen at the joints, and he would have been set in that pose all day if Handley's window had not slammed shut. He imagined he'd heard the noise of it, though he couldn't remember having actually seen the face rip aside even though he'd been fixed on it to the end.

Half in and half out of an overcoat, Handley ran at great speed across the yard, disappeared for a moment between the caravans, then seemed to go head first through the window of his Rambler. A few seconds later it dropped out of sight like a submarine.

Embarrassing questions stung his face like ants, and all the answers pointed to the fact that he'd better get out of the wood. He threw the empty bottle into a bush, and the ten-foot jump folded him like a joiner's ruler, but he straightened and looked for a hollow tree-hole in which to hide his binoculars, where they would stay dry and safe till he returned for them in a few days.

When they were stowed, and the tree noted by pointing the bottleneck towards it from the far side of the path, he walked leisurely back to his car. Studying the map in its dry cabin, it was obvious which way Handley would go to bar his exit to the metalled road. And yet, perhaps when he dashed out so wildly to his car just now he'd only gone down to the village for a drink, and not because he'd seen him perched in the tree. But his paranoid senses told him that such an assumption was the dangerous road to normality, and that evasive tactics were necessary. To avoid Handley's obvious manoeuvre, his best plan was not to turn back but to continue through the wood, in spite of the quagmire, and take the bridle track running through Waller's farm, which would eventually bring him to a road miles out of harm's way, so that while Handley was waiting in useless fury at the southern exit he would be through Catham and halfway to Boston.

After appalling difficulties in the mud, tackled with such noble restraint that he actually enjoyed them, he drove along the last stretch of hedgebound track before the paved road. Turning a bend on the last hundred yards his way was completely blocked by the longside view of a black twenty-foot station-waggon. Handley himself stood by it, smoking a long thin cigar to calm his impatience, and on first seeing the Land-Rover – which he thought for a moment might be Waller's who also had one and who wore a cap the same style as Ralph's – he felt a pang of disappointment, which then turned to joy at having an intensely complex plan worked out in a few seconds triumphantly succeed.

Being so neatly trapped made Ralph reflect that maybe older people were more devious after all, and had developed greater reserves of cunning in the extra time that one still had to suffer through. This reflection showed on his face in a cold look of neutrality, an unexpected meeting with someone he tried not to know.

Handley walked up to his cab. 'Where are your binoculars?'

'What binoculars?'

'Eyes. Glass eyes. Spy rings.' He looked inside but they weren't to be seen.

'I haven't any,' said Ralph.

'You've been spying on my house for the last two hours. My sons were watching you, and I saw you as well. Get down.'

The sudden closing of the trap in a ten-to-one chance had unnerved Ralph. He wanted to stay in the protection of his car, but Handley came back from his own with a long heavy monkey-wrench. 'If you don't get down, I'll smash your headlights.'

He lifted the spanner, and only a quick strangled cry from Ralph stopped it splintering the glass.

'All right,' Handley said, when he stood before him on the path. 'If you don't stop chasing Mandy I'll break every bone in your body. You've no right or reason to sit like a batman in that wood for days with your binoculars trained on us. I'd think you were casing the joint if I thought there was anything worth nicking. But next time I see you spying you'll be for it. I've got enough witnesses to peg you down. It's called loitering with intent to commit a felony, and don't think that because I'm an artist and an anarchist I wouldn't call the police and have you put away. I could have done it any time this morning, and they'd have been on to you while you were still stuck up that tree hoping for a sight of Mandy, and you'd have been in the loony-bin already. All that stopped me was the thought that it might upset her, and no man in his right senses would want to do that, which makes me wonder how straight in the head you are if you're supposed to have any regard for her at all.'

Ralph heard him, and did not hear. The words registered, but did not hurt. Paranoia absorbed his tirade, and vanity took the bite out of it. Handley didn't like him, because he was almost as invulnerable as he was himself, with that firm jaw, penetrating brown eyes and a pride that, because it didn't fit the final uncertainty of them, was flawed in a grave way.

'Is that all?' he wanted to know.

'Yes, but it's only the end if you make sure I've seen the last of you.'

There was no apology, explanation or voice of regret. He climbed into his Land-Rover in silence, started the engine as Handley, face pounding with rage, backed his car into the road and drove off.

CHAPTER TEN

THE pint of coffee went cold as he paced his studio, but he swigged it off straight as if it were beer. It's no use thinking about the state of the world when you lift that pot and wield your paint-brush at the great white canvas bigger than you are tall. In all ways vast, it dazzles you with off-white pallor, limited by the clear borders of a giant oblong, ambitious to become a tabloid of colours that mean something to every eye but only all to mine, my third Polyphemus peeper with the black patch off, opening into me and burning like magic its green and red rays over that canvas. I paint, and the world pours into the neck of an egg-timer, distilled sand in the bag of myself drowning out through that fragile lit-up funnel on to the sandless desert of my canvas.

I forget all else and others when the feeling for this big one is building up and over me like a pot-seed culled from the far side of the sun and peppered in front so that my nose unknowingly breathes it in. Empty for weeks and never waiting, but living in the acceptable torment of domestic war until now I'm waking, walking, set to paint in the land of the dead. For I'm dead when painting, a corpse because nobody in the land of the living can get at me, paint best when I'm that sort of corpse, temporarily dead, self-induced deathly dead so that colours can pour in and I'm set for a trance like throwing a switch during those days or weeks, and in that trance I'm flying.

A time of inner torment is slowly building up from part of my submerged everyday life so that it's almost unnoticed. Then as if at some pre-set signal the anguish stops, and I die, begin to paint a picture. It lasts some days or maybe more, and I die because while painting I'm not aware of my existence, become a vampire, half dead, a foot in the grave and one in life, wondering whether I'll live to finish it, whether the world will end before I can – a stake to be driven in my heart to finally finish both me and this painting off.

I'm so sure of myself I don't even hurry when priming the canvas, hours, days, and weeks are insects crushed under my boots as they vanish into the land of the living. Forked lightning of way back and a sharp distance forward don't flash by in a shocking and temporary junction but stay locked in me, shake hands in my brain and declare peace in my heart as they travel through me hand-in-hand like two filaments meeting to light me up, mixing energy in my hands to paint by day and night. I don't call it anything or even think about it, because to explain at such a time is to destroy, refute, negate, spit at the stars, and belch at the sun when it comes from behind the clouds.

The biggest colour began as green, fields, oases, valleys, seaweed, and estuary, life-perpetuation, love in the environs of Venice and Voronezh, vile green effluvia falling from bomb-canisters lobbed on paddy-fields, lodged in ditches where green men were fighting or burning (a change of colour here towards yellow, orange, saffron robes of Buddhist monks firing modern and complex artillery with deadly precision from fortified pagodas) or flashpanning out over hamlets from which men have fled but women and children cannot. Green gas yellowing over green fields to destroy all seeds and shoots of life. A leg goes green, gangrene, dead-green and livid, jealousy of green by those who are dead for the living flowers of people unconscious in life but full of work and struggle. Iron and steel go green in that humid green forest, blistering enmouldering green, emerald of defeat for the iron merchants and industrial strong whose chewing-gum tastes of spite and who try to belt down the guerrilla men and women of the coming world. The green hand lopped by the sinewy arm of a rice-man who cometh for the whole lot to eject them into the green and boiling sea, is carried off by a green snake into a part of the forest-world no one can penetrate. The green mould from far away is rotten, the diseased soul trying to transplant itself on their earth, but the homegrown home-green forest of the sovietcongo partisans hides them in ambush and makes them invincible. Green is my fear, green is my friend, and on they go fighting with no end possible except the ultimate friendships of green because green will be my peace in which to paint the colours of mine or somebody's soul.

Grey is a sky, a bird, turning into a dive-bomber I shot at in the war, now an airliner, a vanguard whale of a hundred people lifted into that grey cloud and through into the far-off corner blue of dome-sky, a hundred souls divided between four great engines bursting with primal power, making one co-ordinated soul of ascent and hoped-for descent. Grey is machinery, machines in a factory, each with its stream of sud-bile sizzling over metal and shavings, grey flour caked in years of grease, I've worked in long enough to know, like and dislike of long ago, remember how those grey faces turn pink or pallid on stepping into open air, as if that putty-colour was only in the noise of grey machines. Christ, what haven't I done in my two-score paltry years, walked or crawled through every colour I can think of or make up. Take red, a rust-red blood on newspaper deadened with age in a green copse, dark brown, as if somebody had been wounded and spilled himself on print before stagger-ing for help. The red blood left had been shone on by warm sun, dried, left by the green summer bush till going orange

85

like the saffron of those Buddhist monks and composition returns to life, out of suicide which was only a trick to frighten it back into the cosmic order striven for. Blood on that mantrap, for evil be to him who poaches, and a shock of steel teeth grabs him round the waist when he walks towards a patch of cowslips all yellow and bright. You had no business here, you know, but neither had yellow, yet in it goes, over red, green and grey, blue and bile, throw my semen on the canvas and paint a magic eye in it, mark of generations and regeneration, showing the third eye, the cosmological squirt and squint in bile and blue and grey and green, far-seeing and deep-sighted as you step inside and look at it from foot and window-distance among work and colour there already.

The grand design comes up and gets my throat, starting with skeleton fabric, working from each rim and edging in, fix the middle and moving out, creating this engine with universal gears, forests and fields, sealine and winking sun, moon and magic eye, flanking fanbelt cogwheeling the existence of all men and making me momentarily wonder whether I'll ever paint another picture after this, but knowing that I will before forgetting such an insane question and setting to.

Red is the thing I can't get away from, blood-red and blind red, dazzling crimson and falsehood carmine streaking down the back of a shorthorn cow in one of the top corners, and vermilion merging to rust-red down the back of a man riding it. Red and rust, all forms of shamblemark making horrorpitch in various set places easing from the blues and greens of oblivion. That's fine maybe, but what I'm always shying off is brown, the baking earth-cracked paper brown, meaningless cloaca brown unless perhaps it means the final unfeeling melting back into underneath with which I never can be bothered. I spit on my hands and leave such a vein, this pit-seam in my lowest galleries, turn my headlamp up and go on to red again and rust if temptation gets my throat and won't let go. A hundred subtleties make big crude things, but even they can be refined, splayed, and coaxed back into their subtle coats, yet this time grander still and more exactly what I wanted and will deem worth while.

Out of the forest, down from the mountains, back towards animals and men, yellow of butterflies meeting in valleys and vineyards of abundance, coming like smoke from farmhouse chimneys, bridging the banks of the lazuli river and patching the gardens among ox-blood and olive, emerald, and Baltic-blue. Tributary streams burn quicksilver down the hillsides, a waterfall at one point verging to yellowy brown as it filters through soil and rocks and all this is the big eye of a cow under the chiselwedge of a slaughterer, the enormous bovine peephole of the world of Albert Handley's painting growing day by day under my fungus hand and furtive eye.

The other eye is green, already done and gone, dead and finished with, a jungle holding its own, backed up by the men who make their own guns (or steal them, which is more my line), wear tyre sandals, grit rice between their teeth and call it a meal. When in doubt say yes, do it, walk, but best is never to be in doubt, like them, unless from caution, when weigh it in your hands before throwing it like a hand-grenade at the feet of whoever is coming forward without seeing you. Fight shy of the stiltmen of Spital Hill, because a demon has breathed on them, a tatterfoal haunting the lower slopes, lurking for unwary travellers that pass at night, facing a shaggy foal that leaps right out and hugs them to death in mist and darkness. A grey-black tatterfoal lurked at the exit to his abundant valley behind primeval cowland Lincolnshire before ditches were dug, its eyes so wide they must be blind, but deepening nostrils beamed on unwary people gloated with meat and knowledge staggering safe out of cottages but never to return, having laughed at legends but never taken them as warning, the wandering wild tatterfoal still and silent as a milestone on a mud road until it got you in the night and put the lights of that valley out of your eyes forever in death by hugger-mugger, as you swirled for eternity through the colours of that rainbow and some that the rainbow had never thought of, a painful spectrum paying you out for the sins of your art and the indiscretions of an occasionally unpalatable palette.

Mount your painting like a horse and ride it away, or better, let it carry you, control the uncontrollable so that the uncontrolled can control you. The burden of the spirit is a sack of flour that you need to live on. But the sack gets filled as you tread those fields of yellow corn and are born again, borne on the wings of Pegasus, no longer the shaggy tatterfoal of myth and nightmare from the quaint tales of old and scatty Lincolnshire.

In one far corner the sun turned blue, raylight merging with the sea that was always humid, made to appear limitless, and phosphorescent. The oxy-acetylene stars joined this enlivening universe, beneath which there had to be sea, for otherwise there would be no life. And so had the sun, because both were the soul of blue, the twin lifedip of electricity. Sweat bled and blood perspired in a land beyond all tarns and towers, hummocks and nipple-hills. The barbed wire had bled him white, but his own land had been claimed out by the brute force and iron in the soul of a born survivor, and the bridge of jungle rope from himself to the canvas, slim and dangerously swaying yet somehow eternally secure, was used by the jungle men cast off from himself who crossed it with grace and depth, colours on their backs as they flattened themselves on to the empty desert plains of the canvas to escape the devastation–guns of self-criticism and turned into a humanized landscape at last. Then the devil in him churned it up, goodness of evil that soon came closer to what he'd intended in the beginning when the work of transference was once more complete.

To crawl from the forest and slime of your work, fly above it and levitate by the engines of imagination, sit in that plane-seat and fasten your safety-belt when the dark-haired blue-eyed beautiful steward-goddess looks at you with a brain-scorching gaze that furnishes the energy of all joints and muscles, makes them move with you unaware of it. The earth of your painting is left behind, and trying to forget the fear of the plane floor shaking beneath you unclip the safety-belt and look out of the window at the colours and contours and inhabitants of the work you are making. It doesn't exactly tally to the map spread on your knee, but that is usual and as it should be. Out of a nearby cloud come the unapproachable hooves of nightmare, but the plane veers and you look instead at the close configuration of ash-grey mountaintops, eyes at the end of binoculars, cocktail-sticks searching out the individual valleys of desolate beauty balanced by their inhabitants of men and animals. Eyes wilt and tire, fold back into you, and soon you become frightened at being so far above the earth with nothing to stop you bouldering down if the energy of one engine baulked against its supergravitational task. He sweated against death, spinning into the colours of creation and never waking up, every minute expecting it in the hope that it wouldn't come. The journey went on, as dangerous as autumn when it won't become winter, till suddenly the engines fluttered and the beautiful dark-haired woman stood at the door, and the descent was smooth coming down, down, a quiet and gentle drift towards the canvas once more in human proportion and set on its easel before him.

He stayed in his studio at night, strip-lighting dazzling the air brighter than day and throwing over the canvas a metallized glaze that, if the actual colour, could only have been done by a man in the last stages of kidney disease. The stopgap night of Lincolnshire blackened outside, and when he switched off the lights, opened a window and looked out in his shirt-sleeves the silence was profound and complete, not even a dog barking, or a cow shaking its mangy spirit free. It was mild June, smell of foxglove and late cowslips, the demise of spring, and a cool drift of fresh air threw a few heavy drops of rain against the leaves of an alder-tree below.

Colours mixed, and before him were two canvases, one for day and one for night, bloodland and deepgreen forest that never came out of the swamp of fecundity boiling on pot and sleeplessness; butterflies and bovine eyes with world on the wing and in retina, the viable inexplicable shapes and colours, themes and highlit pictures of the land and spirit where he had no maps to follow, all came out of his blue-cooled ice-drawn soul-filled heart. Drugs and pot, I'm high all the time on the powders of my own brain, the tadpole blood of my veins – except when I'm not and am low in the swamps of life. I'm free-wheeling over this great plateau, neither young nor old, clock-smashed, calendar-burned and picking my teeth with the compass-needle after chewing flintlock lilies and limestone daisies.

He came out of the valley of life and death to look at it, green bulbs and bridges, windows into the green where the decomposed has been resurrected and composed, limited by other shapes and colours, log-brown trees across the green where the valley is blocked, branching out till finally a way is open into green, at night and in the morning an ochred sky striking terror and respect into the unruly inhabitants of Handley's world. Worship is possible, the mutterings and blank stare of animal-men and women who can't go mad because they do not believe in the past or the future. They have struck an eternal expression that was never seen before, yet is recognized as a universal truth now that it is set down plainly for everybody to see. He pulled it back with him out of the unknown desert-emptinesses that he'd stumbled into and taken the courage to cross. All of last year's notebooks, sketches, cartoons had possessed these faces, gradually emerging from the subliminal slime and sand of his awkward, pertinacious vision.

One goes on for months, moody, will-less, unable to paint anything big and solid, then suddenly the tomb of oblivion is opened, the great boulder falls away (a little pull perhaps is all that's necessary) and in you go, cartwheeling and energetic, frenetically possessed, haggard and unshaven as you catch its treasure rolling towards you.

CHAPTER ELEVEN

GEORGE BASSINGFIELD's publishers owned a massive house in Belgravia and used it, not too frequently, for parties and receptions. Tonight they gave one of those long and lavish midweek parties which, because everyone could afford to stay in bed next day, made it seem like Saturday night. So it was a good party, though Handley wasn't yet drowned in the mood and booze of it, and in fact had no intention of becoming so. He had learned, since enmeshing himself in the so-called cultural life of London, that soberness was the best weapon when faced with an excess of drunken bonhomie. Unable to paint except in his own pure and right senses, he could not insult people unless in that mind either. If an insult wasn't creative it served no purpose. He preferred that people would leave him alone, would not approach him with fatuous and catty remarks that, when sober, they would only make in their articles.

Wearing a dark-grey suit, he moved about the large room looking for Myra. He was hungry, and one whisky put him at last into a good mood. Lady Ritmeester was involved with a group of men whose faces he half knew, and she took his arm as he tried to get by. 'Here's Handley. Let's ask him!'

'What?' he smiled. 'Are you inviting me to become a social being?'

Her piled hair was phosphorescent, clamped into place by a blue and gilded fish. 'Good Lord, no!'

'You haven't even kissed me, and we can never be friends until we're over that little obstacle.'

'Now look, Albert, Kenneth here says that those who take no interest in political matters fit very well into a declining society.'

'I don't take an interest myself,' Kenneth said with a fat chuckle, 'so I'm not prejudiced.'

Not you, thought Albert. 'An interest in politics is only valuable in a declining society. Then you might get enough blood and brains out of it to make a revolution. If you see what I mean.'

Lady Ritmeester yelped joyously as if someone had stepped on her tail. 'I thought painters weren't very revolutionary people?'

'Some are, some aren't,' Kenneth put in. 'Don't you think so, Raymond?'

'More or less,' said Raymond, who didn't know what they were talking about.

'I didn't think *you* were,' Lady Ritmeester said to Handley, as if a look from her beautiful eyes would bring him back on to the true path.

'I wouldn't stand *you* up against a wall, Lady Ritmeester, and that's a fact.'

John looked at Malcolm, as if wondering whether they should throw this boor out before the American cultural attaché arrived.

'I'm a revolutionary by faith,' he said, 'though perhaps not by conviction, living in England, if you know what I mean, which lacks the imagination or energy to be revolutionary.'

This seemed more of an insult than his last remark to Lady Ritmeester. Mark and John linked arms and walked off, while only Kenneth was goodnatured about it: 'You mustn't mention the word energy at a party.'

'Energy's a relative thing,' Handley said, mocking himself with his own pomposity. 'I once knew a man who worked double-shifts in a factory, sixteen hours every single day, for three months. Then he took a week off to go to the Isle of Wight. On the station platform he dropped a box of matches and when he bent down he never got up again. That particular movement had never been in his job. All the chaps remembered the way he died, and from then on he was the man who never even had the energy to pick up a box of matches.'

'I'm so glad you're telling us how spineless the workers are, Albert.'

'Imagine bending down to pick up your lap-dog,' Handley said to her, 'and pegging out that way.'

'This conversation's too morbid for me,' Lady Ritmeester said, turning to another group and hoping to cut the ground from everyone's feet except her own.

He moved towards the wall, where huge blown-up pictures of George Bassingfield, Myra's late and never-lamented husband looked down from beyond the grave at this strange company drinking homage to his book. Broad forehead, dark smouldering eyes, and bushy moustache gave him the slightly old-fashioned appearance of a works foreman who had volunteered for the First World War and perished on the Somme – probably because the enlargement had been blown up from a snapshot. It was a very English face, of a man who saw and felt everything but had been unable to express anything, except that such a malaise had driven him to write what was by all accounts a quite marvellous book. Copies were stacked on a card-table by the door, and Handley flipped through one while Myra was talking to her dead husband's publisher. A year ago she'd met Frank Dawley at Handley's first show. They'd decided to go away together, she leaving her husband whose photograph now looked down so mournfully and proud. On the evening she was to leave him for good George got in his high-powered car intending to run into them and kill both on their way to the bus-stop. By some split-second mishap in his desperate and foolhardy brain he had killed himself, injured Frank, and missed Myra altogether.

The publisher, Larry, was regretting George's untimely death. 'On the showing of this book he had a lot to give the world. He was a poet, really, who'd have knocked Rachel Carson right out of the picture on this line of writing.'

She looked far from easy, for the party called all the life-changing events of the last year before her. Yet self-control increased her confidence, and set up in her a beauty that Albert had never seen before. Like many men of unstable temperament he tended to fall in love only with unhappy women, but Myra's misfortunes had inspired her beyond such a state, for which transition he had a respect and tenderness he tried never to let her see.

The publisher was a tall dark middle-aged man wearing

sweat-shirt, jeans, and sneakers, who tried to inveigle authors into his net by looking young, being with it, and getting rich. When Myra introduced him to Handley he gave a radiantly shy smile and asked if they could publish his autobiography.

'I haven't written it yet,' Handley said, still holding Myra's hand, which she'd given him by way of greeting. 'My life's so dull nobody'd be interested. Artists lead dull lives, otherwise how would they feed their imagination?'

Larry gave a great laugh. 'There, you see? He says something like that, and wants us to believe he'd write a dull book. We'd give five hundred pounds on signature.'

'If you gave me that much money I'd never write the book,' Handley said. 'I'm a painter, not a thief. Everyone I meet tries to get me to give up painting. Maybe I'm good, after all.' Larry asked if he had any more of those long thin cigars he was smoking, on the principle that if you want to charm someone get them to do you a favour. Albert opened his tin. 'You offer me five hundred pounds one minute and beg a cigar off me the next. I don't know what the publishing world is coming to. I suppose you'll have a knighthood soon.'

'I'll tell you what, then,' said Larry, 'why don't you do a series of book-jackets for us?' Relishing the cigar, he mentioned an artist who'd also done some, whom he considered to be Handley's superior because all the critics applauded him, but whom Handley thought was the lowest kind of paint-smearer – obscene, bloody, and perverse. When he said so, Larry gave up and moved away, so that Handley received his first silent compliment of the evening.

He released Myra's hand. 'It's over two months since I saw you. Thanks for getting them to send an invitation.'

'They were delighted, as you saw.'

'I didn't much like leaving you alone in your cold house when I drove you back from the ship.'

'Everything's all right. The baby's fine. He's with my sister in Hampstead.'

'Everything?' he said. She smiled, and it delighted him to see that life had for once ennobled someone. To say there was a bond between them would be too accurate for it to be helpful.

'There's no news of Frank,' she said. 'It's over five months.'

'I suppose he's learned how to fix a bomb in a car and connect the contacts to the ignition. That's all they seem to be doing these days in Algeria. When I first saw you to-night I thought you'd had news, you looked so radiant.'

'He must still be in the desert,' she said, 'if he's anywhere at all.' She didn't like to talk about it, and had argued with herself for hours as to whether she should have Albert invited to the party. It was bad enough to think about it on waking for hours in the middle of the night, but to talk of it with a friend who also knew Frank brought back the desperate ache in her heart and stomach, and it was difficult not to be stricken with tears. 'I can't wait for him to come back. I'm really unable to dwell on that part of it.'

It was possible that Frank would not come back, he thought. His life wasn't worth much, having thrown it into such a desert. There was less chance of him returning than even she thought in her most pessimistic moments, though when speculation joined them, as now, he was wrong, be-cause her hopes were often in a worse plight than that.

'As I said before,' he smiled, so that not even she could disbelieve him, 'we'll soon see Frank. And who knows, the time might not be too far off.' Death isn't the end of all idealists, he thought. Some live to tell the tale. They must. In her wildest moments she had imagined him coming out of it, a sudden turning up at the house that blinded her with all the happiness she'd ever dreamed about. But the swing into oblivion was more bitter. Hope and optimism were a sin to be paid for by the further sin of despair. Both were the deadly enemies of suffering mankind. Handley was trying to comfort her, when the only accurate opinion on the matter was total silence, to push it out of her mind and trust that such policy would never lead to indifference.

'I'd rather talk about other people,' she said. The party was gathering force. Someone fell down near the door, a crash of glass as he went. A prominent critic gave a half-hearted cheer, as if it were a shadow-faced novelist from the north about to indulge in another blackout.

'My trouble,' he said, 'is that my daughter Mandy's got herself in love with a farmer's son who's a bit of a layabout. Not that I mind that. I'm one myself, but he's a bit of a nut as well. I caught him last week spying out the house with binoculars, trying to see how Mandy lives, I suppose, when she's in the sanctity of the home.'

'He seems moonstruck,' she smiled.

'I suppose I must give his binoculars back, because when he saw I was on to him he hid them, and made his getaway. I found them, so when he came back for them later he'd be unlucky. The people I get landed with. Still, I did a painting this last week that I'd have given my right arm for a couple of years ago. I don't know what anybody else'll think, but it's left me all of a sweat.'

'I'd like to see it,' she said.

'Any time. I'm going back tomorrow. Come up with me.'

'What about Mark?'

'Bring him. My kids'll be all over him. You'll have a comfortable journey in the car. I'll pick you up at your sister's at twelve.'

She was tempted. 'Are you sure?'

'I've got to see Teddy Greensleaves for an hour. After that I'll call on you.'

She decided: 'All right.'

'I'm the happiest man in the world,' he said.

'Wasn't that the village Frank lived in?'

'That's it. I'll tell you all about it. He won't mind.' She was even clinging to that. 'It's marvellous, Lincolnshire. You'll like it.'

She didn't hear. 'I've finished with this party. Can we go to supper?' He collected her coat, sensed the inner fight to assuage her suffering. 'We'll go to the Blue Dumpling. It's quiet there, plenty of space.'

'Anywhere,' she said. 'Where's your car?'

'In a garage. We'll get a taxi.' She clung to his arm as they went through the hall. Someone greeted her, wanted to talk, but they walked on.

Outside, in the half-light, Albert recognized Russell

Jones. From a happy and forgiving mood at the beginning of the party, Myra's torment had now suffused acid into his blood and brought back his morose bitterness. He disengaged his arm – 'See you in ten minutes' – walked over and gripped Jones's wrist.

'Remember me?'

Jones greeted him with the friendliness of a journalist who imagines that no artist could have any success if it weren't for them. 'Albert! How are you? I thought you might be here, and decided to look out for you.'

'I'll bet you fucking well did,' Handley said, half dragging him around the corner where it was dark. He slammed him against a wall. 'What have you got to say for yourself?'

'What the devil do you mean? Let go. Let go, for God's sake.' Handley saw that Jones was absolutely unaware how spiteful and slanderous his article had been. If you felt innocent you were innocent – and so such people escaped death by guilty conscience or hanging. Handley's faith in the ultimate goodness of human nature was shaken once more. He'd never expected otherwise, and he relaxed his grip, though still enraged at the idea of vainly hoping someone like Jones could realize that by any standards he'd done wrong. 'That article you wrote about me, remember it?'

'Of course. It was a jolly good one.'

His fierce moustached face jutted out as if he were about to fight a battle with his head. 'You said I had mistresses, was carrying on with God knows how many women, when you knew I was happily married with a wife and seven kids. Many people saw the lousy injustice of it. My lawyer said it was actionable, but I didn't want to make you more notorious than you are by skinning you of every penny, you drunken high-living word-spinning scumpot.'

'It wasn't meant to be taken in that way at all,' Jones said, unabashed as he straightened his jacket.

'My bloody lawyer didn't think so,' Handley raised his fist. 'You bastards print what you like, foul up people's lives and don't even know it, never mind expect to pay for it when the time comes.'

Jones tried to push by, but the way was blocked. 'Tell me honestly, what did you have against me that you'd write something like that? I'm just a bit curious about such an aberration of human nature.'

'I wrote the truth. That's what people want.'

'I wish I had your editor here as well.' So did Jones. 'He allowed it to be printed, though I suppose he'd just smile and say it was nothing but the truth as well?'

'If it wasn't the truth,' Jones said, 'who was the woman you were with just now? Isn't she one of your mistresses?'

Handley was afraid to strike. There were some people you couldn't hit, unless you wanted all the pride sucked out of your marrow. And once you began, you didn't stop till they were half-dead. He raised his screwed up fist and drew it back, saw the first sign of life in Jones's eyes when they lit up with panic. Then he smashed his fist with all the human force he could muster – right into the wall behind Jones's head. The pain nearly split him in two, but it was the only way to take the boiling power out of his body and yet save him from the humiliation of smashing Russell Jones. He held bruised knuckles to his pale, frightened face. 'Your mug should have been like this,' – lifted his good hand: 'And I can still do it. But the respect I've got for myself is bigger than the loathing I've got for you. I might as well try to knock that wall down as think I can bash some humanity into such a drunken pimp.'

He left him shaken against the wall. As long as you knew you couldn't win you could not humiliate yourself, and so they could not hurt you. You kept your faith, while reserving a special category for these innocents of the devil who did not even know when they were doing harm.

CHAPTER TWELVE

WHILE Eric Bloodaxe gorged on four pounds of shin-of-beef in the black of the morning, Ralph climbed up the wall with a chisel between his teeth and broke into Handley's studio. Tall, well-built, lantern-jawed Ralph, pale in bone and fibre, jaundiced skin from his jaunt around the world, and brown eyes that had taken in too much of it, skimmed up by the drainpipe as if he were also hollow inside and weighing no more than a paper figure of himself. Green sweat of the night shone on him, and hot breath came from his slightly open, eager mouth. Action speaks louder than thought, he said as, wearing his old thornproofs and a cap, he pulled flatly up the wall that, though his enemy, he prayed would be his friend for the next few minutes. He'd also prayed while making the dog his friend during the break-in. Make friends with your enemies, and then defeat them, he smiled, as he slipped his sharp chisel under the latch. What else is an honest man to do whose only aim in life is to marry Handley's daughter?

He unclipped the huge painting, spread it on the floor and rolled it up like a sheet of old lino. Stale cigar-smoke lay heavy, and the thought of kindling the whole studio into a fire made his heart race, but because Mandy was sleeping below, any conflagration he might cause, no matter how wild and orange when seen from the edge of the wood where he'd stand and watch it, might take her sweet face and nubile body away from him for ever. And since he was only indulging in this felony as a roundabout way of winning her, where would be the sense in that? Such a scene moistened his eyes, and muttering that he must get on, get on, get on and act, he took a length of string from his pocket and tied it round the painting.

It had somehow been too easy, and therefore disappointing. His torch flashed around the room. Should he write a message in red paint across the wall, take out all the light-bulbs, slash the stocks of canvas, mix Handley's drink in their bottles along the shelf? A multiplicity of ideas staggered and paralysed him, and deciding that ideas only killed action he opened the door and moved silently downstairs.

Light blinded him, and he switched off his torch so as to save the battery. All doors were closed, no snores coming from the sound sleepers. Silence was heavy in the whole house, the deadest hour of the twenty-four when nobody was awake unless ill or mad. Halfway along the corridor, he wondered if he should try the door of Mandy's room. A goodnight in her bed would be pleasant while robbing the house she lived in. She'd let him out by the front door, so that he'd lose the peril of a sheer descent down the wall with his half-hundredweight of rolled-up masterpiece.

But he didn't know which door led to her room. He wanted to retreat. The glittering light was bad for his confidence, the white metal of the cruel strip-lighting that seemed to mark every few feet of the long ceiling above. He looked for a fusebox, and when it dawned on him that there weren't any, or in this illuminated madhouse were too cunningly hidden, he asked himself what he was doing in such a long and mercilessly exposed corridor, when he'd merely meant to break in Handley's studio and flee with a painting. There was no answer except a heavy and inexplicable sense of having failed in his expedition and of now wanting to give in after so much success to the delicious experience of sitting on the carpet and weeping until someone found him and phoned the police, or threw him to the bulldog at the end of its meat-feast. Light wilted him, took his will away, so that life wasn't worth living, and he hadn't the strength to walk from its powerful pernicious illumination. This house of light was a prison. Did no one ever switch them off? Were they so rich or sane as not to mind? Mandy had told him about every occupant of the house, but they had become total strangers again due to this passion for light, a startling factor that she hadn't thought to mention. If Handley suddenly appeared he would grovel and ask forgiveness – but he was two hundred miles away.

Such light seemed the greatest enemy of mankind. A door-latch clicked, and a baldheaded man of middle height, dressed in pyjamas and holding a writing-pad came up the corridor towards him as if knowing he was there, and merely wanting him to sign a paper before going back to a peaceful sleep. At the sight of another face the malignant and brilliant light lost its influence, and Ralph smiled, recognizing the man as Handley's brother and trying to draw back snatches of his psychotic history related at odd times by Mandy.

Ralph greeted him with his perfect nocturnal confidence. 'I have a message for you.'

John's eyes brightened at this figure he'd not seen before on his ramblings to and from the lavatory. The effort to hide his surprise and write the message robbed him of speech. 'I'm on the same job as you,' Ralph said. 'The world is nowhere to be seen at night. That's your message. Send it to all stations.' He turned and walked quietly up the stairs.

He took a luggage-strap from his pocket and looped it around the painting, a roll so huge and long that when fastened to his back it looked like a stake to which he had tied himself before some ritual auto-execution. He climbed out of the window and descended safely. Mud jacked-up the sides of his boots as he ran across the field with his burden, wanting to be home before the loathsome day arrived, the dazzling light that turned his flesh so pale that his mother continually complained of how unwell he seemed, though when he came in late at night she would find nothing strange in his complexion. Wind beat against the outer limits of the wood, but deep within it never reached, and the darkness was warm as he walked the narrow path stooping under the nagging weight of his shoulder-roll.

He bumped along the wood track, then south along narrow lanes, flicking headlights at each bend or turn. Luminous lines of day would soon appear across the flat-lands and sea to his left, a flank attack pouring light over him alone, swamping him in molten sunless steel. The main road was wide open, and he drove hard down with a dawn sweat on his cheeks, the smell of wet cloud and grass out of the open window, nothing to see except the inexorable swing of the world spurring him on.

The cocks greeted him like the false dawn, for it was still more dark than light when he drove directly into the open barn, leapt down and pulled his bundle from the back. It fell in the mud, but he hauled it quickly across to the house. The night's work had been planned, worked out for months and fearfully sweated over and, enraptured by the idea of possible success, he had often lain on his bed half-conscious, blinds pulled down, unable to stop the shivering of his arms and legs. A tree grew by his parents' house also, and on several dark nights he'd taken a log of wood up and out again to show his limbs what they would have to do on the real job.

As he lifted the painting up the staircase his mother called him. She slept between one and four o'clock during the night, and for as long as he could remember she had not been to bed with his father. Refusing to take pills she read herself to sleep, and returned to her book on waking three hours later. He left his roll outside and went in, stepping warily across the room as if expecting to be shot as a Peeping Tom who had inexplicably changed at last to a man of action.

'I knew you were out,' she said. His room was above, so that she could hear every sound. 'Where have you been?' She lay in a double bed, a sidelight shining on an open book, face half in shadow. He kissed her lightly, as was customary and expected, bending over awkwardly so that he knocked her spectacles to the floor. She was forty-five, and not a handsome woman, but anaemic and strong, and who would often remind him, after affectionate feelings that she could not always resist, that she had nearly lost her life in bringing him into the world. But her affection pulled the shutters down over his consciousness, dazed and shattered him. He needed it so much that he couldn't stand it, and only afterwards when his consciousness returned would he put his arm around her shyly – a time when her love for him had vanished and she felt repulsion at his touch because he reminded her of his father whom she hated.

He picked up her spectacles. 'I spent the evening in Boston with friends. We had something to drink and forgot the time. I had a marvellous drive back.'

'I thought you might have been with that Handley girl.'

'I didn't know you knew about her.'

'I saw you together once, but you didn't see me. Miss

Bigwell told me a few things. She seems a common vicious little slut.'

Such terrible slander made it difficult for him to defend Mandy. 'She's all right,' he said. Also it was the first time she'd mentioned any of his friends by name, and though angry, he was at the same time pleased to think she took some interest in him after all.

She shifted her weight across the bed. 'So you have been with her tonight?' Their few arguments had always taken place at night, now he came to think of it. 'There are some good families around here, good Lincolnshire families, with nice young women among them, and I think it's about time you settled yourself in a career so that you could see your way to marrying one of them.'

'I don't see why you should be so concerned about me,' he said.

'I want you to do some of the right things in your life before you ruin it,' she rapped, 'instead of ruining it before you do the right things.' He remembered the story of a younger brother of her father's, who went to Oxford and gassed himself at twenty-one. When his trunk came home they found it filled with gold sovereigns and pornographic books. He was immortalized eternally as a misguided young devil who should never have been born, but who nevertheless had broken his mother's heart when he died. 'According to Annie Bigwell that Handley girl is a disgrace, the things she's been up to in her short lifetime. She wants horsewhipping. And her parents must be the lowest form of rubbish to let her carry on so.'

'I don't believe it,' he said. But it was useless to argue. Mandy had told him, indeed, that Annie Bigmouth Bigwell was a ferocious old dike who had once tried to lure her into bed, and whom she had bitten for her trouble – which explained the stories she would spread about her. There was no point in repeating this to his mother, for what she couldn't understand simply did not exist.

'It takes a long time to convince a fool,' she said. 'You'll ruin yourself on her. This country's full of nice people. I thought you liked Jennifer Snow? Don't you?'

He knew there was no arguing with your own mother. You could only agree, and ignore her. 'There are lots of *creatures*, all horse and no woman. I don't want them.'

'Well,' she said, 'I'd stay away from Mandy Handley if I were you. Her family's rotten. A pack of beggars.'

'Her father's a talented artist.'

'Oh yes, I saw the papers. He should be quietly put into some asylum, doing such fraudulent pictures. I don't suppose he's ever painted a horse in his life. Not capable, I should think. If I had a painting of his in my house I'd burn it. It's a disgrace that he should deceive people so.'

'They're very good by any standards,' he said, leaning uncomfortably, wanting to leave, but not able to while she was in this distraught attacking state.

'Anyway, it's very distressing to receive a letter from a man like that. It came a few days ago, but I've not known whether or not to tell you about it.'

He pressed his hands on to her dressing-table to stop himself trembling or falling. 'What did he want?'

She was agitated, and he could only feel sorry for anyone receiving a letter from a man who was, after all, the lowest form of brute in spite of his talent. 'He wrote about you. Said you were to stop pestering his daughter, which I suppose means this Mandy creature.'

He smiled at hearing her name from his mother's lips, even in disapproval, for it brought the softening aura of her beauty right against him. 'It does.'

'I don't know why you smile. It was an ugly letter. He also called you a thief. Said you might try to break in and steal his paintings. He must be absolutely insane.'

'I must go now, mother. I'm awfully tired.'

'Yes,' she said, 'I suppose you had better go and get some sleep,' – the word 'sleep' contemptuously spoken, as if it were opium or marijuana that she'd never thought a child of hers would need. As he closed the door and went with a heavier step than usual to his room, she picked up her book hoping, in spite of everything set against it, that he might after all be changing his habits, and that his daily life would begin instead of end with the dawn.

He wasn't conscious of total victory until closed in his room, with drawn curtains and light switched on. The largest and best room of the house, it was an act of spoliation after his return from Cambridge in order to make him feel more welcome. While on his world tour it stayed empty to lure him back, and this constant pampering by his parents (who when he was with them didn't seem to care whether he lived or died) drove him into a frantic melancholy. But at the moment he appreciated their kindness because, after moving table and chairs to the window enough space was left to flatten Handley's canvas on the floor. He stood a chair-leg at each corner, holding it down like an unrolled map of some complex world with one layer of earth peeled off. It frightened him, the enormity of what he'd done. He flicked off the light and ran up a blind. His window looked eastwards over flat and saturated fields. The dawn was like pale lead, a long red knife-edged streak slit across it from end to end as if someone from a land of blood beyond were trying to prise the sky in two. The day would pour in like a bursting dam, and when you gave in to the dawn you were marked like a wounded animal, to be hunted down by the sundogs of the day.

Shirt, trousers, underwear went on to the floor. One had to sleep, and what was wrong with the day? Hide by the day in sleep, and those who slept at night could never get you. He had nothing against Handley when he was safe in his own room, and he stood naked, morosely conning the reasons why he had acquired the picture considering that in many ways he liked him. He was buoyant and *bruto* and had a crude sort of wit. There was no denying that. But at the same time he'd been a hard-bitten old-fashioned patriarchal beast when he'd wanted to marry Mandy, had forced her into the nastiness of an abortion, which accounted for her wild behaviour so that county baggages like old Miss Bigwell broadcast her exaggerated sins all over the place. He took his old Scout knife from a drawer.

The cowman sloshed across the yard in his waders, and the main gate squeaked as if it trapped a demon when pulled open. A tractor coughed out the cockcrow and cattle moans. Ralph stepped around the painting, slowly between the anchoring chairs, a widershins at its disordered colourful soul, his naked faint shadow shimmering the desk and divan bed, the long thorn of knife hovering around the heart of Handley's work. If I tear it, will it scream? Shall I cut it to shreds and drop it bit by bit down the lavatory during the next three months, or bury it under the barn floor at midnight with a storm-lamp glimmering on the rafters? Shall I wedge it in a trunk and send it by rail to a non-existent inhabitant of Thurso or Wick? I could burn it, but I don't go by cremation – or by creation as Mrs Axeby, a farm labourer's wife, put it: 'When one of my relations died who had got on in Boston he asked to be created, not buried ordinary like the rest of us. What sort of finish-off is that?' No, I certainly shan't 'create' it.

He pulled pyjamas from under the pillow and got into them, slipped on his dressing-gown. What made life rich was the urges you did not give in to. He spent many a fertile hour brooding on them – brewing up even finer urges that he did give in to. The knife went back in its case. He sat at his desk and picked up a pen. 'If you give me your daughter's hand in marriage I will send it back safe and sound. You know what I mean. But if you squeak about it to anyone beyond your family, I will cut it into little strips, and then into little squares, and mix it with my father's linseed cake that he feeds his cattle with. I am not a man to be trifled with, as you may so far have thought. If you do not hurry I shall be only too glad to give in to my atavistic rage – after which I will fly to the ends of the earth. Yet somehow I don't think that will be necessary, if we are sensible enough to open diplomatic negotiations immediately.'

He slept through the day as if it were night, intending to post the letter when he woke in the darkening balm of evening.

CHAPTER THIRTEEN

WHEN he picked up the menu to order she noticed his damaged hand. He'd been pale and silent in the taxi, as if gritting his teeth for some reason. 'Did you fight with that man?'

'You know who it was?'

'I thought he was a friend you were being particularly jovial with.'

'It was Russell Jones. I've no secrets from you.'

She understood. 'I meant to ask you whether it caused much of an upset. It was a pretty bad thing to write.'

'There wasn't too much trouble. But I still had to have a word with him.'

'You need something over it,' she said. 'It might fester.'

'If it does it'll teach me not to shoot my mouth off. Enid's right. It would have festered, though, if I had hit him.'

'Didn't you?'

'I hit the wall. Come on, what would you like to start with? I fancy a bit of salmon, myself. The sight of a swine like that makes me gluttonous. I was only hungry up to then. Gluttony's a good feeling now and again: it means you haven't lost your will to live. You can't let me down by ordering a grapefruit. Have some fish, then a steak, and we'll wash it down with champagne. I'll do the ordering, and you just sit quiet. You aren't living alone while you're out having a meal with me!'

She spread her napkin. 'I'm used to it though, and it makes me afraid. I'm getting into a routine of coping with solitude, and I actually like it. It's the first time in my life I've lived alone, and when you invite me to Lincolnshire I become cautious of leaving. It's like a disease that you don't want to lose because it gives you a sense of self-importance, and that's a vital thing for me right now. In your own house nobody else's spirit competes for the psychic space you need to feed on. Sometimes I don't think I'll be able to live with anyone again. Don't be afraid,' she smiled, 'it hasn't altered my love for Frank. It deepens it in a strange sort of way.'

The Scotch salmon lay like thin paper over their plates. 'We'll drink to Frank Dawley,' he said.

'I wonder whether he's drinking champagne right now?'

'Don't wonder,' he said. 'To Frank.'

She held her glass up.

Instead of squeezing his lemon on the fish he pressed it over his knuckles and rubbed them, replacing the dull ache by sharp antiseptic stabs. 'There's plenty of time to be alone when you're in the grave,' he said. 'You can't live alone while you're alive. I suppose the baby will change that even if Frank doesn't come back for a while.'

'It's not so bad,' she said. 'You're more aware of yourself. Maybe after a while your personality would dissolve into a sort of low-grade insanity, but for a time you feel in greater control of yourself than you ever have. I think an individual can only exist if she's living alone, though you're not really allowed to live alone, unless you make a great effort. As long as you still feel lonely. Those who live alone, and don't, have a dangerous kink in them, I suspect. When I stop feeling lonely, I'll stop living alone.'

'It's twisty,' he said, 'but still not convincing.'

'Here's to the big painting you told me about.'

He lifted his glass and winked: 'Cheers.'

'Will you be able to drive back with your hand in that state?'

'And paint with it,' he said. 'I'm always damaging my hands so as to be aware I've got them. It shows I love my work, at least. I feel in good form tonight, which stopped me punching Russell Jones the way he deserved.'

She cut into her steak. 'I suppose all journalists are pretty bad. That's just the way they are.'

'Some have honour,' he said. 'Some don't. It's been my luck to meet one who didn't.'

'You know,' she said after a while, 'I still feel rather guilty about Frank. I was so shattered when George died, even though I didn't love him in the least, so that I didn't give

Frank what love I really had for him. If I had, he might not have gone into Algeria.'

His laugh shocked her. 'I'd never deny anybody's guilt, or argue against it. It's a precious thing that stops you going mad, the most precious thing some people have, just as real hatred stops you getting cancer. Still, I don't think you knew Frank. Hundreds of years of suppressed idealism suddenly came up in him. He's like a savage who finds an engine and takes it to pieces, sees exactly how it works all on his own, nobody telling him. He's got the key to the universe. Or his universe, at any rate. Nobody could have stopped Frank. If he'd been an artist I'd say you should have argued him out of it, because no artist has the right to go and fight for the oppressed peoples, etc., unless he's seen the enemy rape his wife and burn his house, in which case he's got the same rights as any other man. But Frank was an ordinary man, must have felt before he went like I did years ago when I sensed some talent for painting. Nobody could have made me give it up, just as it would have been impossible for you or anybody else to make Frank forget his ideas. Love can't do everything, sweetheart! It's a good job it can't, or the world would become desperate and degenerate in a day.'

She listened, handicapped when it came to replying. My love, my love, a pendulum swinging between bitterness and terror, telling the time till he comes back, moving across fields of primroses, wood-anemones, lesser celandines, violets, red campions, moths and seasons pulling me down. 'It's nothing,' she said, 'to how long some people have had to wait. You hear about it and shake your head and say how sad, but never realize it's like this.'

He called for another bottle of champagne, became troubled and soddened, mellow and complex, the longer they stayed at the table. The intensity reminded him of endless nights sat with John when first back from Singapore. He forgot Myra in telling her about him. As a shell-shock case John had always thought he would die at the end of the day. He'd go to bed, after suitable goodbyes to everyone, which made them raw and edgy, with a copy of the Bible, a tin of corned beef, a candle, writing-paper, and envelopes. When they fixed him up with his radio equipment, he recovered a flimsy sort of sanity. They lured the corned beef away from him one night and made a stew next day.

'You must meet him when you come and see us.'

'They're waiting to close,' she said. 'Are you trying to drown my sorrows in talk or drink?' She held his hand, and he wanted to draw it away, unable to bear the warmth and softness of it, knowing that her reasons for putting it there were not the same as his reasons for wanting to take it away.

'Both,' he said, looking directly at her. She met his gaze and smiled, drew her hand away as if she'd not known his was there when she put it in that direction. He called the waiter. 'I'll get a taxi and take you up to your sister's.'

'Are you sure you want to bother? It's out of your way.'

'I'll enjoy the ride,' he said.

Wearing the same formal suit as on the previous night he left the hotel early and walked across Berkeley Square, streets deserted but for the occasional delivery van. The underground garage was like an air-raid shelter. An attendant pointed to his washed and fuelled car, its nose set towards the exit. It disgusted him the way they lavished so many 'sirs'. Such treatment turned him sour – which seemed to increase their deference. He once told one attendant not to call him sir, but from then on he ceased to be helpful, and actually disliked him for reminding him of his unconscious servility. If you have money people try to take away your self-respect, believing that no one has a right to both.

After a long breakfast with Teddy Greensleaves, haggling over conditions for a big autumn show, he filtered his car up Baker Street and steered north towards Hampstead. Traffic not too bad. Smaller fry shifted aside for his Minicrusher. It was cloudy here, but maybe blue above patchwork fields and closed-in woods. He'd enjoy a sunny ride to the freshets of Wash and Humber with Myra, only hoping no great disaster had smitten his hearth and home. A myriad of little ones no doubt had locusted there to chew up his peace of mind for a few days, but that was to be expected. He was in the mood for work, to sing and fly over the off-white canvas world, and once settling Myra into the family bosom he would set to and hope for the whistling best. The black gloom of last night was blown away by the brisk wind of morning. He pulled to the kerb near Hampstead station to look up Myra's street in the *A to Z*.

Someone tapped the window, drawing his eyes from complicated street angles. 'You can't park here.'

Handley waved the ill-printed map, and without winding down the window shaped out an obscene word before drifting calmly off. One might momentarily think that, with his cap, he was driving the car for his employer, yet his sharp face of authority and ownership was immediately confounding. Prejudices went to pieces against the barbs of Handley's classlessness, which disconcerted most of the English he bumped into. He was so remotely old-fashioned, and at the same time so in advance of most other people that he had few friends. Living without the topo-marks of convention gave a strength and a naivety hard to penetrate, an unbreakable wall of social will that was necessary for life in England.

Myra was waiting in the hall, Mark in his carrycot on the kitchen table. 'Would you like some coffee before we go?'

'We can have a jug on the road,' he said, picking up her case.

He did a calm unhurried ton on the outside lane of the M1. They seemed reluctant to talk after the openness of last night's supper, almost as if we'd been to bed together, he thought, and to say as much to himself was showing the black side of his nature swelling up from the sewer depths with vindictive suddenness. In his civilized mind he'd never think such words, but sometimes they caught him unawares, and weren't to be ignored, for their springs often hid some secret truth he'd otherwise never have known among the shallow verbiage of normal daydreams.

Mrs Harrod was tidying the bedrooms, but left her

vacuum-cleaner to look at the baby, the downcurved mouth of her round face reshaped by a smile: 'He'll soon be sitting up,' she said, holding a finger to him, a wonder in her voice as if such a development was the first time it had miraculously happened. Mark looked at her, full of love it seemed to Albert, who sat in the kitchen while Myra made coffee.

Leaving Mark with Mrs Harrod, she showed him the house, feeling pleased that it belonged to her. He was the first person to see it since George died, and it was only now, after a promenade through the living room where George's books still lined the walls, then to his study bordered by shelves and files of maps, around the garden whose lawns and plots had merged under the unifying heaps of the months, and up into the untouched uninhabited flat over the garage in which George's mother had died, that she realized the value of what was totally hers. 'It may be wrong to own property, but I'm glad to have this house. I can shut myself off, and feel free, and it's a good place to wait in.'

They stood on the lawn, by the garage door. 'There's nothing wrong in owning your own place,' he said, 'as long as you don't exploit people by letting rooms and living off the rent. I'd always wanted to stop shelling out to a landlord, and the first thing I did on getting money was to buy the house we live in.'

When Mrs Harrod left, she insisted on making lunch, though he needed little prompting to accept. 'I'm not expected till midnight,' he said, 'and if you read the map we'll get across the country in no time.'

There was steak in the refrigerator, lettuce and potatoes in a box under the sink, and Albert went to the car for the bottle of champagne he'd been taking to Enid. He could give her the headscarf intended for Mandy, and give Mandy the necklace meant for Freda, and give Freda the Charlie Parker LP bought for the *au pair* girls, and the *au pair* girls would have to wait for their loot till he made another trip south or into Boston. Though creased by such manifold responsibilities he blessed them now as he set champagne on the table and saw the pleasure on Myra's face at such delicate foresight. 'I didn't know when we'd need it,' he said, 'but I saw us parked in some desolate lay-by while you fed the baby. Since we're drinking it here I can sling the paper cups, or use them some time to make sketches on if I'm stuck for paper!'

She went upstairs to feed Mark and change her clothes, came down wearing a white cotton blouse and dark skirt. While they were eating, the champagne dry enough to make a pleasurable meal, the air darkened and large pieces of rain flaked against the window. He frowned at it: 'I was hoping for a sunny ride.'

'Perhaps it's only local,' she said, 'or it won't last long.'

'We'll have a smoke after coffee, then go. I'll switch on the heater and play soft music. If I could I'd draw the curtains and drive blind – radar-driving, switch on and go to sleep, with a bell to wake me after a hundred and umpteen miles. There was an article in that magazine *Jerry-car*. A good bit of steak, this.'

'We've done nothing but eat since we met yesterday.'

'Never mind,' he said, 'we'll go long walks over the wolds with Enid. We often set out for the day, sometimes walking as far as the coast and taking a taxi back.'

The pitch and splash of rain increased, till he thought the outside world might be an aquarium, and fish would appear at the window, opening their hobgobble mouths, and waiting for the glass to break. Myra switched on the lights. There would be a storm whose force would press her to stay in the house, unable to leave unless the sky was blue and empty. Wet leaves brushed and slopped in the wind in a way they hadn't when George was here because the trees were regularly pruned. Her neglect had changed the character of the house. Surrounding noises differed as well as interior settings of furniture. It took on her own temperament. Never in love with George, it needed a long time to forget his thick presence. Life was long and grief short, but in this case it didn't seem so because, having met Frank just before George died, a low-grade grief for the six-year habit of George was enduring at the same time as her wait for Frank that might turn out to be a greater and more terrifying grief if he never came back. To end George's nagging unnecessary memory maybe she should sell the house and go elsewhere, though now when the blue light bumped at the French windows she couldn't bear to leave it, remembering so much while there, that she was torn between wanting to lock all doors and windows on herself, and going out of it never to come back.

Thunder bullied and brawled, and she thought how comfortable a place it was in a storm, with such proportions and furnishing that she hoped the never-ending furore would become part of normal life, because its spreading calmness subjected all memories to the nullifying elements of the present. To become so purely herself, memory gone, future unimportant, was a rare and luxurious rest.

Handley noticed her mood, and didn't speak. The controlled calm of last night that struck glamour in her face had gone, replaced by excitement which he put down to the heavy atmosphere that the storm was trying to break up. He disliked such storms, felt they cut open parts of himself that he wanted to keep hidden. They tormented him, and he walked around the room while Myra went to the kitchen for coffee. He wished they hadn't stopped for lunch, had gone speeding along roads where thunder and lightning would hardly have been noticed, and not turned out to be so clearly responsible for something that he would only blame himself for.

When she set the coffeepot on the table he put his arms around her. She gave herself with such an open passion that he knew there could be no love in it for him, which vivid truth caused a black sadness that drove his embraces wild. She received it gladly, as telling herself also that this affair of the moment had no love that could ever prove embarrassing to them both.

Her body had been waiting for someone to hold and meet her kisses, and the lessening psychic force generated by the storm had enabled it to take place. He wanted to break away, but his body caught him in a trap that he'd made and hoped for since meeting her from the ship three months ago. Now that she was forcing him to it he could only accept it under some vague conditions of love that he'd never ceased to believe in. But he kissed her closed eyes softly, a hand on her face, tenderly because her gentle need had turned its privilege on him.

'Come up to the bedroom,' she said. He stood alone for a few minutes, smoking a cigarette, boyishly agitated. It was impossible. I'm falling in love with her, but she's in love with somebody else, and always will be. He wasn't capable of walking away. Too abrupt and brutal. Even his lust had vanished. God knows, I shouldn't have brought in that champagne that's launching a bloody strange ship. He heard the toilet go upstairs, water in the cistern drowning the noise of outside rain. He poured more coffee, slewed it down half-cold. Here am I, full of admiration for my friend Dawley, and while he in the prime of his guts gets on with his life's slaughtering work I'm making love to Myra. Maybe the kickback will show me what my ideals are really worth, though to know might strip off my illusions, and nobody deserves a fate like that. A door clicked and, shedding his boots, he walked up. Lying in bed, she turned to him. The room was dark, blue air beyond, rain locked out but trying to wear through the glass, its noise drumming away all words inside him.

They were startled later by a loud knock at the door. She smiled at his alarm: 'It's the grocery order. He'll leave it in the garage.'

He sat up nevertheless. 'We'd better go. It's four, and there are a few miles to flatten before Lincolnshire.'

The sheets covered her. 'Get dressed, then I'll come down and heat some more coffee.' He put on his underwear, kept his back to her, though knew she wasn't looking at him. She wanted to get dressed with him out of the room, and this touch of modesty drove him to make love again, which she accepted with the same quick passion as before.

She came into the living room as if nothing had happened, almost as if she hadn't seen him for a few days. He didn't even have the heart to grin, knowing exactly where he stood and hoping that some time he would be able to go on from there, yet not wanting to because she loved a person whom he respected too much to betray. They drank hot coffee in silence, until he said: 'Shall we start?' In Lincolnshire for a few days, he would at least be able to see her. 'The storm's letting up now.'

'Do you think we can?'

'Why not?' He lit a cigar. 'We can stick to our arrangement.'

'We'd better not. I want to be alone. I hope you don't mind.'

'Of course I do. But do as you want.' At least it meant so much that she couldn't now go with him. He moved to kiss her at the door, and she offered him her cheek, which he touched with his hand, and walked to his car parked on the road.

On the long drive he reproached himself for what he didn't do and say that might have persuaded her to come with him. Even at forty, one made the same mistakes as a youth in love for the first time. One could go through it a hundred times and learn nothing. Only a nonentity could believe otherwise. But as hours stretched into darkness and headlights flooded the road he was glad it had ended like this, when there'd been no real wish for it to begin. Full of regret and turmoil till he saw her again, he nevertheless couldn't really doubt that this was the end, whether he wanted it to be or not. The soft flush of engine-noise carried him to his studio and the large new picture, which took his mind back to colours and shapes and images flooding him for another piece of work that would keep him civilized and abstracted, as far as the family would be concerned, for the next fortnight.

He drew up to a pub beyond Sleaford for a pint of mild and a meat pie, his first stop, as if fleeing before Frank Dawley's wrath, who'd magically known of his afternoon's work though clambed and parched in some wild region of Algeria. He wished Frank had not vanished with such idealistic thoroughness, wanted to see him now, take him to the house and show the new big picture which he knew would interest him. I'll dedicate it to him, dead or alive.

Both he and Myra will like it, because its range and breadth fit him perfectly. The meat pie was so foul it deranged his hunger. He called the woman because he needed more cigars, having to bellow it into her ear to swamp a television speaker racketing above his head. Some radio maniac had fixed them through the pub, even installed a speaker in the lavatory.

'I can hear you,' she said. 'You needn't shout.'

'Do you always have it on that loud, you vile old Lincolnshire hot-slot?'

'What?'

'I said have you got a cigar?'

'Are you blind? They're over there. I don't know.' She came down a ladder, all varicose veins and stocking-tops, a lovable Lincolnshire lollipop a long way past it, he surmised, but still full of salt. She shoved two boxes at him: 'Do you want one for seven-and-six, or one at one-and-four?'

He passed two florins. 'Give me four bob's worth of the small ones. I'm rich, but not a millionaire.'

'I don't want to know about your private life. I've got enough trouble of my own. Some people are the end, the absolute bloody rhubarb-end. They buy a pint of beer and expect five years psycho-analysis thrown in. I'm fed up with it, I am. Feeding chickens all day and drudging around here at opening times.' She passed him four cigars. He slid one back, trying to wring at least one bit of honesty out of the day. 'Four bob's worth is only three.'

She pondered this. 'So it is. Are you trying to be funny?' He lit a cigar and finished his drink, shouting 'Goodnight, missis!' – so loud that even the man reading the news seemed to lift an eyebrow as he walked out.

Lincolnshire was the county of silence and peace, especially when it was dark, of sandy coast and rolling wolds, and lowlands so waterlogged that he had secret plans in his drawer for a prefabricated fifty-foot fibreglass skull-hulled ark that could be put together in half an hour if the sky looked threatening. Which was why he'd chosen high land to live on. From three miles every light blazed, not a window thriftily blocked, no door closed or spotlight doused, a flared-up nomad camp in a land where all other houses had only twenty-watt bulbs, barely sufficient to stop those who lived in them bumping into the wainscot or treading on a mouse. He liked to see a living house with every eye wide open, lost sight of it entering the village and turning the narrow lane, less bumpy under the wheels at his speed, bushes on either side scratching the windows. Now that Myra wasn't with him his entrance to the yard seemed so tame that he felt unfocused and irritable, his mind scratching over all that could have gone wrong during the two days he'd been away.

'Did you have a good time?' Enid said, arms around him for a kiss.

Mandy looked up from her Pan novel by the stove: 'I wish you two wouldn't slop so much.' Handley gave Enid her headscarf and threw the necklace to Mandy, which was neatly caught. He noticed that she actually smiled. 'I went to that party last night,' he said, 'and saw Teddy this morning. Made me have lunch with him, and I didn't get away till four. What a life those ponces lead. The same routine day in and day out. Anyway, I'll have a good show this autumn. We'll be rolling in it, especially after that recent stuff.'

'You can buy me a car, then,' Mandy said.

'That's what you think, you fat little chuff. There'll be no more cars here except mine, and I sometimes think that that's one too many. Good God, I'm not in the house five minutes before I'm pestered for a car. It wouldn't be a bad idea if I went back to begging letters.'

Enid put down a bowl of chicken soup and he ate hungrily. 'There's no going back to that,' she said. 'We can't go back in this house.'

'You say it like a threat.'

'Don't start,' Mandy said. 'I can't stand it.'

He finished his meal in silence, and went up to take refuge in his studio, the place he needed to be, where he could sit and smoke in peace surrounded by his work. He knocked on John's door and went in. He was in bed, lying on his back and staring at the ceiling, hands by his side as if someone had given the order to go to sleep. The radio was switched off, his desk in shadow, earphones on a hook and gun, presumably, in the drawer.

Albert set a tin by the bed. 'I got your favourite cigarettes in town.'

'That's very kind of you, Albert.'

'Feeling well?'

John's eyes relaxed and he turned with a smile: 'All right, but I'm afraid there was some bad news today from Algeria. Reception was good from French army stations, and I broke their codes. Some of it was even in plain language they were in such a hurry to get it out. The trees were on fire. They're burning down the trees.'

Handley's pale face leaned over. 'What else?'

'Not much. I expect you're thinking of your friend, but he may not be in this particular part. It's bad news, though.'

'Are you sure?'

He turned to the wall, ready for sleep. 'I set up the new aerial system, and it came clear as a bell. I'll get back to it tomorrow. Guerrillas are attacking a base in the South. It's not finished yet by any means. There are many trees on fire.'

'I know,' said Handley. 'I bloody well know. Thank you, John. Sleep well.'

He took the stairs slowly, opened his studio door and lit it up. But he didn't bloody well know. Nobody knew. In the middle of a long great storm the ability to know was replaced by the necessity to act. It was chaos that decided what you could and would do, so that all you had to do was prepare for it, unless you were an artist, in which case every form of storm was already in you – everything.

He looked for confirmation of this to his recent painting, slid his eyes from wall to wall, over door and ceiling, under the bed. There were sketches, the skin of a dead fox, a map of Lincolnshire falling into strips, windows of blackness through which nothing could be seen. He leaned on the table, and looked again in a calm and clockwise fashion. Sickness muffled his sight after the vast day he'd gone through, senses losing the edges of their definition. Yet even under his tiredness he knew that everything was in place, stones, paints, pencils, horseshoes, cigars, knives.

Bursting open the door he launched himself downstairs, entered the living room with an insane look on his face, though not too far gone to notice the way everyone was frightened at what they saw.

'The painting,' he said. 'Where is it?'

Enid poured him some black coffee. 'What painting?'

'Somebody took it out of my studio.'

'Nobody's been in there. It stayed locked all the time you were away. Only you had the key.'

He sat down. 'It's gone. No, it can't be. I suppose it's in the house, but who'd move it from my room?'

Back upstairs he saw that the window had been forced. 'We'll phone the police,' Enid said. 'They'll soon get it back.'

'No, I can't do that. Let me think. I want to be alone.'

'Who'd rob an artist of his work?' she wondered.

'Who would?' he said. His hands trembled, he felt drained of all energy, as if he knew with horrifying accuracy and truth what it was like at last to be an old man. The heart was ripped from his autumn show, and if he didn't get it back he'd never be able to repeat what he had done. Someone had poleaxed him, and he felt himself withering at the thought that there was a person in the world who wanted to do such a thing, a malevolence that for gain or spite would rip the living heart from you because they were unable to wait till you were dead. But since I'm an artist whatever bad happens must be turned into something good if I'm to survive and win. I'll find who took it, and break whatever backbone is responsible before I'll let anyone set fire to the tree I've grown into.

PART TWO

CHAPTER FOURTEEN

A TREE was burning on a hillside, a single tree in a waste of sand and ash. They knew it well, had used it as a landmark when counter-moving for the last three days to outwit a French motorized patrol from the west. The tree had been dead for a long time but clung to the red friable substance halfway between dry sand and bitter soil, scrubbed and bitten clean by passing camels, picked at by nomads for tea-fires after dusk. No one could say when it had last borne leaves.

Plane-jelly hit the ground nearby, jumped at the tree like a monster with bared teeth, spreading out to send a black-reddish pall of oil and eucalyptus into the air above. It was a lollipop in flames, expanding like an orange candy-floss fixed in the earth's tight fist. It burned in a circle of fire, and the longer Frank watched, the more surprised he was that the tree should take so long to be consumed. From a plane it would be visible for dozens of miles, a stationary puffball down on the grey brown earth. The peeled emaciated tree would not burn through, as if it were made of iron and waiting to melt, mocking the fire which clung to it for not being hot enough to do its job. Now and again, a tiff of wind thinned the smoke, and the white claws of its outer branches were seen, though many were missing because they had already dropped to the ground.

The bomb had struck earth like the bark of a dog. He'd heard the plane coming and lay dead in the cleft of sand. There'd been nothing for the pilot to see, and he hoped it was slung out to lighten his plane after being hit by gunfire further east, or that he was simply unloading from high spirits before going back to his aerodrome. The coppery flames of the tree cleared away much of the smoke, immolation so total that the reason why the plane dropped the bomb became unimportant, though it was necessary to know it in order to lay a guideline for the preservation of their group. Everything must be accurately deduced, so that they could rationalize and plan. Each day, half day, rest, thought, had to be set into the complexities of these shifting sands, clouds, winds. But the tree fixed his eyes, its scorching fire clearing out the caverns of his mind the short time he looked at it.

It seemed as if some hidden reserves of resinous sap were feeding the flames, sent them bristling high and forcefully, as if the only hope of the tree to keep its upright shape was to succour the fire that was sure to destroy it. When the quick of the tree was reached, the flame turned white, spilling pyrotechnic fire for a few seconds. Then the whole tree burned black and smoky once more, and two of the strongest branches fell into it.

It was only now that he noticed a man in the tree, having missed him in the confusion of the first shock. He was halfway up, astride the main branch forking left, arms held around the trunk and head pressed against it. The bomb was so close that the impact must have killed him. He supposed now that the pilot had seen him move, that the man heard the plane and ran up the tree for safety. For some, a chicken in every pot, for others a bomb on every human being to keep the chicken in every pot for themselves. It was a cruel blighting expense of spirit. As soon as people take to the hills or the wilderness, God pulls out of them. You've no business in the hills as far as God is concerned: if you aren't prepared to stay in the valleys and suffer, He won't look after you. He tried to spit, but the permanent condition of his choked throat spared no saliva to put out the vision of the burning man. What sins was he booked for, to end in such a way? The smoke plumed to vanishing point not too far up, a shaky impermanent stalagmite, the only movement of Nature for hundreds of miles, all that remained of a war between man-made chemicals and an earth-succoured tree. His binoculars showed the body falling into the base of the smoke.

When you light a match in such heat, the flame is invisible, and if you aren't careful, you burn your fingers on it. With all smoke gone, a blue trunk appeared, air shimmering around it where the flame was active. They waited thirty minutes to give the plane time to come back and fly away again. New rules were conceived every day. They would not even talk, as if it might hear them with its complex spikes of homing and radar devices. In this life, there was no hope, no luck, only meticulous plotting and the certainty of what had already happened. Before survival had become an obsession they had foolishly thrown away half their force in a fight when the rest of them were lucky to have broken free, but now it had become a profession, a way of breathing, that had flattened them into the earth even before the plane was heard. He pressed hard into the grit and sand, though his body felt airless and light, fought to get deep into the earth as if to relieve the fever of thirst in him, and escape the danger clamped at his spine like a grappling-hook. If he could not cover himself in grit and dust, it was only because it wasn't deep enough. Walking, walking, walking, you seemed to hold down firmly in your body all the incurable diseases of the world, and when you have to stop and stay flat, you imagine they have got you at last, each one disjointing and attacking the longer you lie there.

The tree was a black stump that had died long before the fire beat at it, whose white bones had given up through old age, only to suffer this cremation before being blown off the face of the earth by the crepitating slick winds of the Sahara that met in battle with all-battering gusts rolling down from the Atlas. But it seemed as if the stump would last, that the fire would not reach its marrow. He'd seen trees similarly blasted in a grove near Aflou, a meeting of milestone stumps gathered to discuss what to do now that they had lost the distance-marks on their faces. Yet, an anaemic green shoot always grew from part of the sheltered base. It was hard to understand why they were so bent on survival, though looking at them, it seemed that it was not in their power to ask such a question.

He had been frightened by Algeria before getting used to it. The excess of space had no limits, as much because he was unfamiliar with the geography, as that it was really vast. At dusk, the sun went down as if setting into a sea, with the far-off humps of camels drowning in it, or the shipwreck of some oasis foundering at an inexplicable low tide by a mirage of mountains. In dangerous areas, during the weeks of great walks they had done, they marched by night, following a pocket compass, sometimes an Arab guide. The silence made them afraid to talk, and after some hours, it seemed as if it had destroyed their voices, Frank being resigned to never talking again and thinking it wouldn't be so hard an affliction as long as he could hear and see.

The fear narrowed him down, became part of growth and helped him to see his lonely stature against an enormous land-mass that was so big in fact and imagination (which fear welded together), that it also eliminated all idea of time. At first, he looked at his watch often during the day, but now it was constantly running down. Only Shelley had any check on what minutes passed from the first red spread in the east to the final blue and gold bath in the opposite direction. In the wilderness, the man who measured time was a god, until the mainspring of his watch finally packed in.

They burrowed against the scorching shale-troughs several times a day. The valley was a wide, long depression, running south-west to north-east, pointing like a javelin towards the Kabylie mountains where most of the fighting was going on, and where the guerrilla front of the FLN had friendly bridgeheads backing into the sea. From one of them, Shelley hoped to get on to an Egyptian arms ship one dark night and be floated out to Morocco or Alexandria. From Tangier again, or Libya, he would come back on the same run with another load of guns. As for Frank, here he was and here he would stay while the fighting lasted, looking on his commitment as the great oceanic end of the line for him, the wide spaces of the world that he must allow himself to be swallowed by if he was to do any good in it.

Their line of march was neither along the bed of the valley nor by one of the level crests on either side, but took the more difficult line that invisibly ran halfway up from the *oued* bottom, so that their brown garb, painfully threading the scorching rocks and thorn bushes of a never-varying contour-line, was least likely to be seen by any plane coming on them before its warning noise scraped out of the sky.

Keeping so still in the body-worn crevasse, where each grain of sand was a live ant pricking his skin, his joints froze, and arms and legs, so that at one point he felt panic turning over in his depths, ready to surface and drive him to madness. He held on, limbs dying one by one, knowing that if someone were to stick needles in him at this moment he would not feel it, that the points would go through dead flesh and his face would stay pressed against scorching rock without a tremor passing the mouth. To lie dead wasn't always so difficult, but now under the dead eye of the furnaced midday sun spreading its diamond heat across the whole ashen and stony plateau, his sweat poured out like insects breaking from every surface and running over any space between skin and cloth, columns advancing and criss-crossing in all places inaccessible. He tried to pinpoint each fresh spring, but failed because there were so many. When a river of sweat flicked on to his neck, it seemed to have some mysterious signalling system that caused another to spring from the calf of his leg, as if all outbreaks and sweat-heads were working to a co-ordinated system too subtle and complex for the human brain to pick through. Yet there seemed no purpose in it except to drive him mad, so he gripped his teeth and eventually quietened himself by saying that to succeed in such a project as to send him mad was so minor an achievement for the spending of so much force and plotting that it was not worth succumbing to.

The tree burned, a black stump surrounded by air of fire, but there had been no man on it. His trunk existed only, in the warmth, as if all the moisture of his body had run out into the grit and sand of his refuge and he couldn't under-stand why a wispy column of vapour wasn't lifting from the hole he had made. The air sucked it up, and he was dry, tinderous, dismembered, separated by yards it seemed from his dead limbs. He was glad there had been no man on the tree, that it must have been a piece of trunk falling into intense, almost solid smoke, a vision of his bodiless eyes.

The noise of an aeroplane scraped out of the sky. It came low, low-winged and propelled, slow and straight. There was nothing it could see except smoke and emptiness, a stilled sea of lava and rock, and grey sand-patches frozen suddenly as earth. The pilot wasn't air-conditioned either, as he must have yawned and looked, then swung back towards Tiaret, climbing as if to get nearer the sun where it would be cooler.

Out of the half-sleep of stupefying sun and exhaustion, his instinct was to rub his legs into life, but his hands wouldn't move. They lacked food, water, but above all he craved salt, and in his walking visions the sea was a flat metallic shimmer stretching from north to south, a line never more than a few miles ahead, and he increased its reality by wading in it, pushing into the shallow watery salt and lifting it up and over his head like sheets of silk, and in this way he felt better and the false sea became less distinct. Yet any way he turned, the horizon remained, with slothful fishing-boats that had no one aboard lifting and falling a short way out.

By his side was a bag of ammunition and food, and a plastic container whose water tasted as if it had been run through iron filings in the factory, for the smell was almost the same as that which met him on going in each morning less than two years ago. The wells were deep and the water rotten, but his stomach had sealed itself against bacteria after the first crucifying bout in the Monts des Ksours. He rubbed his hands together, and the ache of life came back into his legs. Lifting his head, he saw Mokhtar and Idris standing in front, Ahmed and Shelley further down the slope, Mohamed behind. He'd been alone, flattening every second into an infinity of isolation, and he was almost surprised to see other people as he got up and swung his arms and lifted his legs to bring the dismembered pieces back to his torso.

'It gets worse every time,' Shelley said, lighting a pipeful of his precious tobacco to show how bad it was. He pushed his lower lip out with his tongue and tried to spit because it didn't taste good in the thirst and heat. 'Two hundred miles as the Mig flies and we'll be in friendly territory. High mountains and running streams. Winter sports when it snows. We'll freeze to death then, and see how we like it.'

'It's friendly enough here,' Frank said, picking up his rifle. The lorry with the best guns and ammunition, bales of literature and maps, Chinese grenades known as 'the rice harvest', had been left in the Monts des Ksours, where the FLN was trying to tie down as many French brigades as possible to ease pressure on the Kabylie, keep a route open to Morocco, and threaten all roads from Colomb-Bechar. Nobody could say that they hadn't done their bit with that load. The four FLN soldiers had orders to escort them to the Kabylie, and cause as much damage on the way without getting killed.

'Nothing like spending summer in the mountains,' Shelley went on. 'Used to go the Catskills with mother, where my old daddy had a big house for us, while he was walking out some dame in Boston. We kept the house after the divorce. Mother skinned him, pretty well.'

'Nice tales for the camp-fire,' Frank said. 'All I want is a shave and drink of water.' Shelley seemed untouched by the trek, had a personality so strong that it would not adjust to the dominating sky and landscape, danger and lack of provisions. Every face had thinned to the bone, stubbled grey on Dawley, all eyes of whatever colour unable to shake themselves out of a fixed stare on the long stages of the march. Frank felt the sky entering his bones. All extra flesh had vanished, leaving only aching muscle to carry him, as if he had turned into the big ants he sometimes saw; a desert insect when naked, thin and brown, strong and indefinitely living. They once stripped by a muddy pool, brown ants with shaggy heads, thin limbs, and bellies firm, rushing into the magnesium filth. Ahmed missed a horned viper and, hoping anything else had fled, they went on bathing, men worn into ants, which was how Frank felt for much of the walking day. He was only a man on coming out of sleep in the morning, when he didn't have to wonder for any time at all where exactly in the world he was.

They moved another ten miles before darkness, a line of ants, each fifty yards apart, Mokhtar, the tall intellectual Nubian-Moroccan, in front; Shelley, the ever-suspicious next in line. Frank Dawley was the last man, with a full view of them filing down to the scorching dull silver of a salt lake. There was no beauty in their route, only monotony and desolation, and though now and again such adjectives made him smile, they soon lost meaning, for it was land to cross, not question or define, and the endlessness of it emptied him of all response. You took the easy way by giving your total physical being to it, he thought, so that only the unusual was beautiful, something that shocked and pierced your heart, the purple and lugubrious cold dawn striking your eyes as soon as they dared to open at the mounting pressure of it, the great rose-hipped escarpment on emerging from a twisting and narrow cleft, the sight of a hyena suddenly setting into flight from its frozen position, so that you who were also unexpected might have been a form of beauty for it. He once thought beauty ended with the eyes, struck them and that was all before you turned away, but now it only began with the eyes, and your whole body and life responded to it so completely that often you could pass through a hundred similar beauties in a day and remain unmoved, on the surface, until you tried to close your eyes in the darkness, when the delayed-action shock of the day eventually drugged you into sleep. It was beauty, and not beauty, and only the shifting mind treated you to it at the moment of its choosing.

Purple and lugubrious dawn flattened into monotone day. The great rose-hipped escarpment turned grey, was climbed and left behind. Mokhar shot the hyena and roasted its flesh for supper. A land so big could hide you like jungle if you followed certain rules. There was no condition of life in which rules were not necessary. If there was, he had yet to find it. When the unexpected vanished, its beauty was gone, because you were totally drawn back into the flattened, staring eyes of the walk, of the oblivion of racked sleep.

Under this land there was water, oil, manganese, copper, bauxite – materials that one day would put roads and railways where they walked at fifteen or twenty miles between sunstroke and moonbeam. They wanted ice-factories and water-pumps, power stations and fish-pools, cotton-farms and air-conditioned mills, soil labs and canning-plants: then one might live here and think it beautiful if someone had written poems to tell you it was so, and you had the leisure and comfort to realize that they were right as you drove through it at forty miles an hour to meet its charms halfway.

They ambled like dead men, seeking refuge from the stony midday sun, no longer knowing that they walked. Land was like alcohol; he walked, and walking was like drinking. He drank it on waking, and went all day from sundown to blackout wallowing in it until he dropped from exhaustion and total inebriation, happy and not caring if he ever woke again. Trudging all day over the flat stale beer of the stony plain, brandy of hills, mouth shut tight because it seeped in continually through eyes, ears, nose, and anus, the drink of land and the never-ending gutterbout of topography, a blinding weekend of landbooze that went on for months. Such drink killed one with thirst, that was the only trouble, but it gave you the required lift, the lighting-up time of the brain in the flaring magnetic dayflash of the desert.

The valley widened, dry at the bottom, coming from nowhere, ending nowhere, all to no purpose, until Mokhtar fell flat on his belly, and Frank was about to do the same, thinking that his sharp ears registered a plane and that they were in for another half-hour's insane steaming among the gravel and clinkers, when he saw him breaking lumps of grey crystal from the rock and pushing it in his mouth.

Frank filled his pockets for a taste later, when his craving for salt came back. 'We might make the mountains in ten days,' Shelley said, 'running streams, a bit more to eat.'

Mokhtar was walking again. Conversation of a few mundane sentences could take a whole day to shake itself out.

Shelley was an optimist of the hard-headed sort, cheerful from the deathbed of his blighted hopes. 'Did you ever see a tree on fire before? I saw a whole forest burning once in the States,' Shelley went on, 'a million trees. But never one burned like this.'

Frank was engulfed by the memory of it, and for once the land lost its dominance. 'What did you do?'

'Got in my Lincoln and headed right away, back to the highway and town.' Frank was silent. When a million burn, what can you save? When one burns you can only watch. The energy of your desire to help must coincide with the moral streak. He rubbed salt along his cracked lips as he walked, fifty paces behind Mokhtar, shaking the gravel from his sandals. He'd torn another piece from his blanket and wrapped it around his feet, but it had come loose and flapped when his legs moved forward. He bent down and tugged it right out, stuffing it in his shirt pocket. He had no real desire to get to the streams and mountains of the Kabylie, wanted to stay in the wide open wilderness, fight if there was a chance, play hide-and-seek at least, hunt if possible, and when at bay turn to break out or destroy, stay in this great outside flank of the prize being struggled for until such time as the French gave in and every member of the FLN joined the march on Algiers, which might not be long in coming, since the split between people and army was deep enough for plenty of premature and treacherous hope. But before then, there'd be negotiations, breakdown of talks. Then, more discussions, and a final betrayal when the country was handed over to the wrong men – or maybe the right ones. For himself, he didn't mind if they stayed here for good. Whoever they met was friendly and helped them, though glad, of course, to see the back of them in case the French descended and began torturing in the hope of finding in which direction they had gone. North, east, south, and west – that is the land which I like best. The ideal guerrilla can send an arm and a leg one way, and an arm and a leg the other, a limb for all four points of the compass, while the head levitates up in the air to make sure they reunite in a prearranged spot later, preferably when it is dark and behind the back of a paratrooper.

One pain did not kill another, they lived side by side, swapping sensations like goods in a free economy recently collapsed, and there was no limit to what the body and heart could take. They fed together in mutual support, becoming one monster that dominated the life you had chosen to lead, all the time trying to tell you how wrong it was, that the only life to follow was one in which you made no choices, avoided all suffering and turmoil, so that what agonies did strike at you would be acceptable to the world because they were chosen by fate and not by your own godless self. He hoped Myra understood what his mind had been incapable of formulating before he chose to leave her and help a country labouring under barbarous torments and oppression. It filtered through to him with often marvellous though fragmentary precision. He had seen enough to know he'd been right, but that all he could do and had done would not draw the final result nearer by one minute, yet he had been right to follow a positive and interior voice for the first time in his life that clarified its demands by reasons he understood and that could not be gainsaid by any cynicism he now and again dragged up to fight it with. Nothing had been escaped from, only entered into. The freedom of the wide-open wilderness had no meaning, was a myth, non-existent, outdated, a paradise of false ideas. It pushed you deeper into the prison of yourself. In order to survive it, you were locked and barred, and shackled, and accepted it utterly. You were stripped, hardened, tempered. The wilderness hammered the world into you like an iron rivet. Everything beyond your eyes – conical shale-sided hills bordering the gravel-valley they were threading – was clear in all its detail, perfectly understood, but you were the imprisoned man who could only master it by leaving it behind, crossing the same thing again, hiding in another bowl or valley, sleeping beyond a further horizon of the same landscape and pissing there when there was piss in you, the land that pushed you deep into yourself in order to give you the spiritual stamina for traversing the country from which you had come and to which you had still to go, while eventually, the prison of strength crumbled around you. He did not hope or expect to die there, but in his prison of sun and volcanic rock he felt strong, able to do safely what he had come for.

He had always seen himself as a strong man of the factory, able to handle huge machines, lug hub-boxes and iron castings from trolley to bench. But at the beginning of this voyage he had been as weak as if he'd penned all his life in an office. The unfamiliar landscape doubled each mile, and the heat became worse as they crawled over arid, unpopulated land, following the invisible line on Shelley's worn-out map, numerous memorized zigzags between one sandmark and the next. His endurance was as good as the others, but not being in their minds, he imagined it bothered them less. Shelley seemed untouched by it, perhaps because he one day expected to reach the coast and get out of the country, which was only fair, since Frank had forced him into Algeria at the point of a gun. He had been silent, except to converse with the Algerians, his thin and rocky face piqued at the way things had turned out, though not openly hostile to Frank when he had all reason to be. Not satisfied with delivering arms, Frank wanted to go right in, and could only do so with Shelley, who knew the land and language. But, in any case, they were cut off from Morocco – Frank argued. 'And you know it as well as I do.' Shelley did, but would not reply, and from then on Frank was ready in case Shelley tried to kill him, but after so many days had burned out over them, he realized that Shelley did not at all mind the long march back, even though it would take months from his life. Under the abstracted look and grizzled half-grey hair was the brain of a nonchalant, easy-going man whose idealism and sense of purpose seemed so much nearer the bone than that which had impelled Frank to set out on this ideological adventure. Shelley resented nothing, not even his passport given up at the frontier village in Morocco – because he had four more in his pocket to be used when necessary. With his fluent Arabic, he had planned the hard route in detail with FLN Intelligence in the Monts des Ksours, and checked each day's stage of it with Mokhtar before setting out on another inch over the map, not even a pencil line to show where they had come from in case they were taken and it fell into the hands of the French. His tall, thin figure walked ahead, caught by a set of ideas that had replaced a burned-out childhood; ideas that seemed to suit him far better than if he had retained the golden aura of some far-off blissful infancy. In one sense, his ideals made up for a manhood he could never have attained, and gave him a far bigger personality than if he had.

Frank saw now how naïve he had been to imagine that a man of intelligence and scholarship might not have the stamina for a trip like this; saw in fact, that accompanying him turned out to be a way of proving himself. It had taken the brawn from his middle height, and he hadn't bothered to cut his hair since Tangier, in spite of the heat. His blue-grey eyes had sunk deeper, and his cheekbones were high and more prominent, yellowish under fair hair that carried on from the denser growth below. He didn't want to know what he looked like, but felt his face had been eaten away, that there were only eyes, mouth, and nose which served the body as various instruments of a conning-tower head. In the wilderness, you shared the consciousness of those with whom you happened to be, walked along with common nullities, sank to shallow levels of the same uniting thought, paradoxically joined by being alone. As the day went on, sun moving with micrometer slowness down white-blue sky, Frank veered from collective preoccupations nearer to his own geologic levels of introspection and escape, all-absorbed and zombie-like on his walk as he drew on deeper spiritual reserves to get his body over the last few miles, not able to propel himself even slowly on the joined enthusiasms that had set them going in the morning.

The slaghills of Nottinghamshire multiplied a thousand times as far as the eye could see, humps and pyramids of grey dust and shale covering the plain, not so geometrically pure and satisfying as those in the wayback of home but something to draw in the breath at and wonder if this was to be your last sight of earth. A small, sharp stone worked between his toes, and he knelt to extract it. He disliked the encumbrance of the rifle near the worn-out ending of the day, but it had to be carried, more as a burden of self-discipline than for the use to which it might some time be put in spitting out the unseen bullets of ambush, though the bomb-jelly of fire was likely to get him, he felt, before he could draw its clumsiness up to his shoulder and fire. It was good in attack, but would you ever have the chance to defend yourself with it? Mokhtar carried a revolver, Shelley a small machine-gun resembling a Sten. He walked on with it, quick to set his fifty paces from the man behind. A dog-wind worried, swirling fine dust into clothes and faces, as if somewhere a giant egg-timer had been smashed and its contents were dispersing over this terrible extent of wind-swept land. His only impulse was to talk against the irritation of it, but he couldn't walk with the man in front, or open his mouth in case it choked him. There was a thin, ululating piping of the wind, a weird demonic tune whose insistence beat on the eyes and brain to make you want to lie down and sleep, a surface dust disturbing the earth without killing visibility. The sun could be seen, dimmed and ringed, able to stifle but not scorch, and those in front lost their clear desert definitions and became blurred, laboured figures bending forward, safe at least from patrols or planes. Grit stung his eyes, and his throat turned to rock, blocked by one of those shale hillocks that reminded him of Nottingham slagheaps. It was no use stopping, lying down to let it pass, because it spun in this dust-bowl and would bury you, never pass. You had to pass it, fight your way to sky and clear land. It was the worst day so far, a lingering torment of desolation. No conscripts fighting for a lost cause could undergo this. Mokhtar imparts faith to nomads and wanderers, talks to lop-eyed, underfed people of hamlets and encampments, tin-towns, and cave-villages. They listen and agree, laugh and shake our hands, look longingly at the guns, take pamphlets even if they cannot read and hide them as soon as we have gone. Can you create a dust-commune in this unhallowed spot on which the unmerciful clappers of heaven have ceased to open? Yet there was water underneath it all, and if the peasants worked by the sweat of their breaking backs for another twenty years, maybe they could buy the machinery to extract it.

It became as deep as snow, black snow, hot snow, filling all the inlets of his sandals, grating on to the fingers that gripped his rifle, swirled in circles as if they were beating at last towards the centre of it, the blackest eye of the earthly death that was to draw them in and through. The sun was out of sight and they pulled close so as not to lose each other in obscurity. Shadowy black buffs were nearer on either side as if they had strayed into a sinister cul-de-sac, but Frank noticed that less dust was blowing. They climbed over drifts or waded it.

Shelley stumbled. The gap widened ahead. Beyond, milk-white cloud filled the sky. The only relief was change – either danger or speculation. The brain had died, perished in dust and the effort to choke through. Thought was coming back, but the thin whistle of the wind went on as if warning them of impending earthquake, and grit flew in ordinary contemptible rolls. They gathered under a rock, sheltered from the immediate dust-storm but baking in its oven.

Frank wondered how he looked, so observed them, and at the sight of each other they too wondered how close they were to dying of thirst, wandering destitute paupers of the desert supposed to be battleworthy guerrilla soldiers ready at a moment for ambush or stab-in-the-back. 'Come on,' Frank said to Shelley, 'now that we're really in a bad way, recite us the *Communist Manifesto*!'

His boots were off, purple scabs and iodine feet. 'Oh, you irrepressible bastard. Always ready with a joke when the sky falls in and the earth knocks you in the crotch.'

'Recite it in Arabic,' Frank said, 'if you like. I'll get the gist of it. We're all brothers after all. This rest is killing me. I've got the strength to walk but not to uncork my bottle for a swig. Are you all right?'

'The same as you.'

Ahmed took a handful of beans from his pack, passed them under each face before eating some himself. Frank took one, donkey-food, chewed through the sugary straw-like covering and sucked at the hard beans inside. His stomach gripped them with tigerish hunger.

'They've sent us out as bait,' Shelley said, 'but we'll surprise them by getting this long march over. Honourable bait, however. It's all in the game and the book. Somebody's got to do it, and I'd have accepted it out of my own will and wiles. They want to keep the wilderness alive – and they do. I don't think we're the first lot.'

'You wouldn't trust your own brother,' Frank said.

'Him least of all. I'd trust everyone else.'

'If we're bait it's for the shite-hawks and dust. We got that French truck, but burst all the tyres with our own fire and smashed the steering. Then the planes nearly got us, or would have if we hadn't rabbited south for two days and nights.'

'The game is to trust them completely,' Shelley said, 'and to distrust them completely. It exercises the mind. I'm a realistic idealist. I do it with the FLN, *and* the French. We'll never forgive each other when we all wake up.'

Three hours before dusk. How can the mind live when you must learn to walk without hoping to get anywhere, never a point or picture set at or beyond the horizon on which you can visualize and feed? Not even the shape of a hut or well, the outline of a tree-cleft or hillock, not a cloud that kept form and colour. It was easy. He would match it with what life had been like when he was in the factory where he'd worked twelve years, except that now the landmarks were unknown and unimaginable so that one could hope, whereas then they had been fitted into place by three generations of family which engendered nothing but despair. He'd grown old in that life, knew it all, with wife and two children and the whole mass of housing-estate inhabitants to smoke out his giant idealisms. He'd woken up, and the joy of it was in his head, thrust him young again so that the pain of it went only to his feet and half-starved body. The crossing of the frontier had been survived and, even better, surveyed. At first, he'd been like a manipulated dead man, forgetting ideals while obeying orders, marauding and killing when the rare possibility arose. He could not think, carried a brain blacked out except for cunning and the long control of his body lurking in ambush. At the time he seemed to observe everything from a plane of normal spiritual reflection, but he had been an ant-zombie in the transition from a life in which he had grown old to a new life in which he had not yet learned to live, needing the nimble rock-scrambling feet of a goat, the locked forgotten loins of a hermit, the narrowed barely-surviving guts of an ant, the heart and brain of a newborn man who now wanted to be on his own. And even this was given to him in the never-ending march.

A huge overhanging rock made a lean-to, and they formed a circle, while Ahmed and Idris drew a smoke fire and poured water into a kettle. The strong aroma of brittle mint revived them. Frank climbed a rock and looked at the vermilion earth as far as the horizon, where the sun had almost set. The whole sky was bruised and dark, as if the sun were slowly descending right on to them, seeping invisibly down into the earth they camped on. It grew redder as he looked, then fell black in the space of a few minutes, so pitch that an inexperienced man might not have found his way back to the camp.

A glass of scalding tea was put into his hands. The fire was out, last smoke drifting, mixing with the sweet smell of mint from each glass. They fed on a mess of chickpeas and rancid mutton, biscuits, and dates. 'It didn't bother me to see the tree burn,' Shelley said, 'but it sure surprised me to find it there in the first place. Must be water not far under it.'

He'd forgotten the tree, and it burned again, blindingly over his eyes, flashing and sparking through the all-enveloping blanket of his exhaustion. He could hear it falling to pieces, cosmically destroyed now that no roaring bomb-spilling plane interfered with his pure vision of recollection. He took the bolt out of his rifle, spread the materials of a cleaning-tin at his feet – rag, pull-through, phial of oil, a mechanical action by which he hoped to shake off the white light of the tree. He didn't know whether it made a good or

bad memory. Wholly good, or wholly bad, it had not yet
played itself out, but the nagging uncertainty of its portent
palled on him. His hands and feet were cold, but the sheltering rock held off the worst raging bitterness of the night,
now a few dozen degrees down on the fetid dustfire of the
day. They were busy, making guns to slick in all parts as
good as new, knowing that the first hour of the next march
would blemish them once more. Ahmed, Idris, and
Mohamed had said their prayers towards Mecca. Mokhtar
grinned, did not believe in it, and Frank was glad, since it
took the insult out of his own grin. Shelley, having per-
formed the ablutions on his gun, passed his flashlight over
the map. One day maybe I'll tell Myra what the Israelites
felt on their way out of Egypt. They, too, had to fight a war
before taking over the promised land.

'Did you ever think you'd be a soldier,' Shelley said,
mocking the loving care he was showing his rifle, though
he'd lavished even more consideration on his own.

'I'm a communist first,' Frank said. 'It's not the same
thing as you mean.'

'Tell that to the Mecca boys.'

'Mokhtar's a communist. You remember?' A few weeks
ago, Mokhtar had assembled the score or so people at a
village along the route and lectured them on the coming
liberation, throwing in some choice bait on land-reform and
common ownership, according to the running translation
Shelley made in Frank's ear. One old man lifted a blunder-
buss, which looked as if it would blast dangerously but not
quite kill. Frank sprang and the gun fell without exploding.
The man was covered by them, while Mokhtar went on
with his talk, grinning and full of good nature. He agreed
to forgive the man who had wanted to kill him, providing
he repented before them and promised to work for the
benefit of the revolution. The man, who looked to Frank as
if he wasn't fit to do much work for anything, agreed, glad
to get off so easily. Mokhtar wasn't satisfied, wanted the
verdict of the whole village, which, after an hour's discussion, considered that Mokhtar was just and good, and that
his judgement should stand. Mokhtar was pleased. 'In that

case the man must accompany my soldiers to the next village, in order to show his faith in us.' They set off before dusk, and two days later, Mokhtar killed him while he was asleep.

'Are you as good as he is?' said Shelley.

'I am,' said Frank. 'And so are you, I suppose. The lion of Judah, he breaks every chain, but I wouldn't be surprised if it wasn't Mokhtar's turn one day.'

'One bark at a time,' Shelley said. 'That's all every dog gets that has his day. Not that I'm an animal lover.'

'If you don't trust Mokhtar why don't you peel off?'

Frank rolled his one cigarette of the day, hoping that the small bag of tobacco would last until more might come along. Shelley smoked a long shallow-bowled pipe. 'My life depends on him. I wouldn't survive for a week in this land on my own. I'd get my throat cut at the first village I stumbled into and crowed for a drop of water. It's a thin lifeline we've got.'

'You've got,' said Frank. 'You're right not to light off.' He kicked a stone, and it rolled down the slope, dragging several others with it, leaving silence but for their own soft speech.

'All I remember about my childhood,' said Shelley, 'is snow. Long winters and snow. In the books about such days the writers tell us how warm it was, and how long the summer lasted.'

Frank pulled the blanket closer to his shoulders. 'I can't stand the tune of this bloody wind. It's pulling like a knife at my tripes. I remember summers as well, though, because we had six weeks out of school. It was when I grew up that the snow fell. It was OK in the factory, where I was in with the right sort of blokes. But even when I was a kid I'd had ideas as to what the world should be like and how it should be run, and after so long I could stand it no longer, came up against a dead-end, a brick wall that I had to get through.'

'And now you're through it,' Shelley said, 'into the sand-pit, gave up wife, kids, and country because you were burning with a subconscious desire to help the world's under-dogs? Drop dead.'

Shelley's pipe rattled against the stones. Being an expensive one, it didn't break. Frank's fist drew back from a real blow. By the time Mokhtar opened his eyes, Shelley had re-lit his pipe, stood up, and walked into the darkness. He didn't go far. 'I was seeing how you'd react to the arguments I try to beat down my own spirit with. One hears often that no man is an island, and does not live by bread alone, and all that crap, but if that's true, what the hell is there? All my life I've been trying to prove that I can live alone, without man and without God, and to make it easier for me I've dedicated myself to the cause of helping people towards the togetherness of socialism.'

Frank laughed. 'Still, what you're trying to do is the main thing. What makes you do it shouldn't be much worry. There's no world happening outside of this one. This is the world, the only one and I'm glad it is. I wouldn't like another one moaning around, because this bugger we're on takes all I've got.'

'An individual can only exist if he's lonely,' Shelley said. 'In a socialist society, with so much social activity, you can really be lonely. You can then become more completely an individual than ever.'

'It only sounds convincing in the dark dust-storm of the night,' Frank said. The raw cold and his own exhaustion fixed him tight so that he leaned back, using his arm for a pillow, his last sight that of Shelley's thin light moving across a small area of the map, backwards and forwards over the route they were to take, before he split his consciousness between day and night and lost touch with the world he lived in.

CHAPTER FIFTEEN

THE dome-shaped mud roofs were hard to pick out from more than a few hundred yards away. A grove of sickly palm-trees surrounding a mud-banked pond of clear water showed its existence to Frank's binoculars. Veiled women looked at them as they entered, black hoods, black veils, eyes so black and rounded with expression that he saw brief pictures of the nearby bleak landscape in them. Hard earth divided the houses, blank walls whose livelier backs faced the water, and children played on those that had weakened and fallen in like eggshells. They seemed built to hide people rather than shelter them, and it seemed a strange way of living after so long from such inventions when the only shelter had been cave, or rock, or the occasional nomad's tent.

He felt unsure of his legs on flat solid soil stamped down by the village. The remaining grey ash of the desert ate more fiercely into his sandals, scraping his feet as if there was sandpaper even inside the eyeholes of each buckle, down through the cloth to his skin which seemed suddenly weaker, near to earth so free of gravel. Flies were bigger and fiercer, flew at his face and settled as if he didn't have the habit of bashing them off. He did, they came back only to drop dead when he caught them, one so full that he had blood on his face for the first time, which he wiped away with a rag. These people, living in such poverty and dirt with no will nor ability nor hope, were enough to make him believe it was impossible to do anything about it, that it wasn't worth fighting for, but he knew that what despair there was inside was only a wastepipe through which any uselessness that besets the mind is emptied. You can always crawl into your self-contained and tastefully furnished hole, he thought, and say what's the use as you tuck into a big dinner. All we can do is fight to get the war over, and then see what can be done for this country and these people. Children stared at their single file of ragbags and scarecrows. The men of the village had clean robes on, patched but complete, not lousy and tattered as their clothes were. After weeks of cliffs and mountains, the solidity of terrain that took all strength before allowing you to pass through it, he felt he could push even the most solid houses down with one good shove. Sunlight lifted its guillotine blade of midday as they bent low and entered the poorest house of the village. The room was empty but for a blanket which

Mokhtar, standing in the middle, was already peeling back and pointing to a hole they were to climb down. Frank followed in his turn, descended a swaying rope-ladder that he thought would unhinge and slither him into a fall of countless feet, though the rope might be attached to the supports of the house itself. His feet touched bottom, and once his eyes fully opened in the paraffin lamps he saw they were in a large hewn-out room, walls as smooth as the baked mud of the houses above. It was cool but airless, and he wanted to climb the ladder and get in the sun again. His clothes turned heavy, a layer of paste on his body. A faint song of morse came from the other end of the room, and was drowned now and again by a wind that moaned from ventilation chimneys. There were other people in the room, and Mokhtar was talking to a new voice nearby, a man who wore khaki trousers and a newly-washed shirt, had a broad forehead, short black hair, a prominent nose, and a thick-lipped smile, smoked a cigarette, and wore a ring on his left hand with a large opal stone in the middle. There was a trestle-table but no chairs. Some men slept by another exit, leaning against piles of ammunition-boxes and a rack of machine-guns. The table was thick with maps, and piled with sheets of yellow paper. He felt easy now that he could see. The youth working at the radio sat crosslegged on the floor, earphones on his knee, as if waiting for someone to replace them by a plate of food. Being in a human room and surrounded by houses made his stomach constrict as if he hadn't eaten for days, but he fought it down, for to take in details of the room seemed more important than a passing hunger, as if to notice everything was to take possession of it. He did not know how long they would stay, and his interest was increased by a contempt for this comfortable secret headquarters which controlled – most of the time at least – thousands of square miles of mute and void land, the unalloyed mercury of the sun's strength and a few scoops of muddy water never easy to find.

He sat on the floor with the others, regretted not having pushed a book into his pocket on leaving Tangier. So far he hadn't felt this lack, because there'd been nothing to wait for, only to walk towards, and then the immediate descent into sleep at night straight after food. He walked to the table. The man in khaki was writing. 'He wants us to stay a few days on his turf,' Shelley said. 'We're close to the N1 road, all pretty and paved down to Ghardaia, and he thinks we might pull off a lorry. Won't say what's in it – if anything. Just to show our strength.'

'As long as he's not throwing us away, and I don't suppose he is.'

'It's not that kind of war.'

Frank laughed. 'Every war is that kind of war.'

'We've got no say in this one,' Shelley said. 'But it's organized, the old one-two: uproar in the east, strike in the west. Pull out of the west and get chased. Then the grand slam in the north. They're so subtle it makes my nose itch.'

'Are we the ones to get chased?'

'We're not, but get your mummy rags on: we're going to be buried for two days. We're the uproar in the east. But don't get worried.'

'I won't. I just like to know.' He didn't know anything yet. It was impossible to know, because it might never take place, and plans could be changed to some different work. You could think, but need never worry, and all that your face might show was the accumulated bile of not taking part in anything that made sense until you became too numbed and exhausted to care. 'You'd better let the others know.'

'Mokhtar's doing it.' The wireless-operator disconnected batteries and aerial. Frank had seen him before, or a similar shadow far back in Lincolnshire, the visage of Handley's mad brother who sprang up and levelled a sweating gun at him. The figure of this man he'd never really known blocked out the present cellar he'd dropped into, took on uncanny featureless power as it played his memory and suddenly overwhelmed him. The face smiled, huge and important, though not so close as to be intimidating, not so distinct as to be told off as either good or evil, but a peculiar memory to roll over the earth at such a time. Or had it only come to him because he was underground? 'Don't talk for a while,' Shelley said. 'The cats are upstairs.'

A scout car stopped in the village. Frank's hunger came back. He disliked this tomb that was too deep to leap from and slip away unseen. Twenty people in it were petrified, as if ready for an archaeologist to break in with pick and flashlight and claim a great find. The FLN officer had given Shelley a tin of English tobacco, and he pressed in the steel tooth to cut away the foil of covering. A pudding-sweet smell hissed out, and for some minutes he didn't know why it stirred him so pleasantly. It touched off a memory of freedom and happiness, being more than ten years ago when he was full of youth and living a life forgotten but now re-created in every sense by this smell of newly-opened tobacco. He was puzzled, had a great yearning to be in that life, reverse the sun and moon, and live as part of it again. Yet he couldn't remember when he'd ever been happy. With half-closed eyes he counted back ten years, to a time as he had considered it then of extreme discontent working as an advertising copywriter on Madison Avenue at a job he hated because it fed the very roots of evil in a society he now wanted to destroy.

It irritated him that this unexpected whiff of desire for something lost should turn out to have been tutelage and desperation. Do you have to die before finding out what is real and what is not? he wondered, putting the cap back on the tin.

The truck left, and he woke Frank. 'They'll be feeding us soon.' Mokhtar talked French so that both understood: 'There's a system in this area. If the troops in the scout car throw any weight or hurt people to get information, we send a signal, and in the ambush try to kill everyone on it. If it causes no damage, it runs unharmed through the ambush, which it cannot see. No one suffers. It's an unwritten treaty we have with the French, because conscripts don't want to die for what they don't believe in. It's a safe zone and we're supposed to leave the road in peace, though our side will end that policy soon, because though it may be locally agreeable to the French, it's not ruthless enough for us. We already have a new headquarters.' They would open up the area to flame and spoil, sending a wave through all contiguous *wilayets*. Maybe the base zones in the Kabylie were crumbling, though the French would find it more expensive to move around this territory in force.

A veiled woman came with a large round tray, and he was given food in an earthenware dish, beans, mutton, mint tea, and bread. The radio was tuned in again to the French Army. Apparently, the scout car had gone its way in peace. *Salaam aleikum!* He wanted to get out of this hole, but he ate slowly, chewing the stringy tasteless mutton and sipping tea through his bread. 'What's the possibility of sending an airmail letter to England,' he asked Mokhtar, 'or a postcard?'

He went to find out. Frank wanted Myra to hear that he was alive, though she might not be interested in knowing it. He remembered the promise in Tangier to come back in ten days, wait with her for the baby to be born and settle down in the never-never-land of love and loyalty with the undamped fire burning the marrow of his backbone to bitter ash. And to suffer so meant dragging the other in for company, the laws of love and disappointment meshing into a poisonous stranglehold. Myra hadn't come with him, so she had nothing to reproach him for, and he could not reproach her, either, if he went back and found her ensconced in her English dream-house with two more kids and some other man.

He had come here to escape, he had come here to find, to escape what he had come to find, to find what he had come to escape, to do it unquestioningly, to move, shoot, blow the guts from his fellow-men, shift, make the break and mend the rift that had been in him from birth. Godless and beleaguered in a brown land that only lit up and changed colour according to the motion of sun and moon, he above all wanted to live at peace, but desired it so strongly that he could only achieve it on his own terms. To settle for less would be the game of half a man, a twisted fly-blown nothing-soul that was on the world only to one day die. It might be different if you believed in heaven, but there were no dreams in heaven and therefore no point in seeking it.

To kill meant to empty yourself of all that was good; to go into the desert meant emptying oneself of all that was bad in order that what should have been there in the first place could then enter. Life had so far trained him to deal with the world in simple and mechanical terms, as if his thought were based on a philosophical system thousands of years dead but that had entered into common use again at the time of his birth. Desert trek and loneliness brought reflection: all things to all men, it fitted tightly into aphorisms, often platitudes, wasn't the reasoned essays of someone who had been used all his life to logical pondering before committing himself only to rational courses of action. And if the psychic shuffledown after such travelling left him in the same state as before he started then so much the better, because he hadn't been after all evil, for if he had it would have been impossible to begin a search in the first place.

He was given a dish of dates and raisins, a smile under the veil as he thanked her in Arabic. When plagued by a question he could not answer, such as what was he doing in a cellar under a house in the middle of the wilderness, he could only reply that it was his fate or destiny. So much was unanswerable because one didn't at the moment understand one's purpose in life. Having entered into it in response to an ideal of helping oppressed people (which seemed now to have meant walking into the unknown), he had at the same time become far too complex to accept that as a satisfactory answer to his question. Three months ago it might have appeared convincing enough for the question to leave him alone, but now his total preoccupation with it caused it, by fading into the background, to take him over completely.

Mokhtar returned: 'They'll try and get your letter off in a week by courier over the Tunisian border, but at the moment our postal arrangements are erratic!' He added that they were to leave at darkness on the first twenty miles north, towards a five-day rendezvous ending in the southeast. They bedded down to snatch a few hours oblivion beforehand. At five o'clock, a plane flew low and dropped all its bombs. Half fell on the village. Still asleep, the earth was pulled from under him like a blanket, and he jumped up, head into clouds of fire. Flame shook its blue and yellow wings, bloody and shot through with dust. Two paraffin lamps had spread over the ammunition boxes, and they were trying to drag them out of the flame. Rubble was pouring from a crack in the wall and a wooden support had split. He cursed at the bad dream, hoping to fall back into peaceful sleep. Paraffin smells choked him. The room felt as if it were sinking deeper into the earth, gently and hardly noticed, as if like a crippled submarine they would never be able to surface from it. It was this feeling that stopped him rushing in panic towards the ladder on a desperate scramble to find air and daylight. The ice of hopelessness made him look around to see what he could do. A chain was formed to get the wireless operator and his equipment through the debris.

He gripped the burning handle of an ammunition box and dug his heels in to heave it clear. He knew nothing else except wanting to let go, pull away and nurse the seared flesh that made him grit his teeth to stop the tears blinding him. During the worst of it, he rehearsed his run to the clear painless air of freedom with such vividness that the box had moved a yard before unquenchable reality burned itself back. But others were helping. He ripped his hand free and flattened himself on the box, clothes rolling out the fire. Shelley threw a blanket, and they pressed on it, the room still sinking, a pressure on the head, soil, and air weighing Frank down. As he worked he waited for the last enormous explosion to shatter them all. It never left his mind, the thump that would blow his eardrums out and let in the fishes. His father as a younger man than he had been trapped in a coal-mine explosion, flattened in a cavity for twenty hours, expecting the roof to crush down before his mates could get through and pull him out. 'But you know what I did, Frank? You know what I did? You won't believe it. I lay there and did nothing. Not a bloody thing. And because I did nothing, I thought nothing. I just lay there with my eyes open doing nothing and thinking nothing. They expected to find me either dead or raving mad. But when the lads dragged me clear, I stood up, brushed myself down and wobbled home. The twenty hours didn't go too badly, and I had to pull myself up sharp a time or two. But I didn't think at all – no pictures in my mind, a sort of sleeping while I was wide awake. It was a very funny do. But I'll never forget it. Not as long as I live.' He'd heard the story till he was bored to death with it, but the memory filled his mind now. That feeling of the room sinking was suffocation. He moved, electrifying himself, beating out other flames, until they were all stamped out. They ripped off the lids.

The air was easier. Paraffin gas, and burned paint smells had thinned. Most of the men had climbed out. The room had stopped sinking. Frank thought there would still be a climb of a hundred feet to get free, but a few rungs up the ladder he saw daylight, a crazy paving of pure jagged glass through earthen slabs, bricks, and pieces of wood. He forced open his scorched hand. 'Help me,' he said to Shelley. 'Hold it there, for God's sake, and keep it flat.' There's no point in going into the desert unless you intend coming out of it. Some of those born in it were pulled from collapsed houses and laid on clear ground. White flags were spread on the rubble. An old man dipped a fist into the open belly of a donkey and smeared a broad red cross on a sheet. The animal's legs still kicked. Tears had mixed with dust and made a paste over Frank's face. 'Let go, now,' he said. 'I'll get some rag on it.'

Machine-guns were set among the houses in case the plane came back. 'They ain't got an unofficial treaty any-more,' Shelley said. 'On jobs like this they send one plane, saying he unloaded his bombs because he didn't have enough gas to carry him home. It was an accident. Two planes would be a deliberate raid, but there aren't any accidents in a war like this. We'll get them, though.'

Beyond the houses falling dust was turning the water grey. People lined it, dipping pots to bring comfort to the wounded. A child was led by with a crushed arm. They put up with this, he thought, didn't lynch us for it, didn't choke the lot of us. They tore with hands at a heap of bricks, and a young woman crawled out, naked to the waist, holding a baby. She slapped the face and its eyes opened. He expected her to smile, but she laid it on the ground and clawed at the rubble, pulling out an elaborate, dented teapot. Holding that and the baby, she ran screaming towards the water. 'If that plane comes back,' Shelley said, 'we'll be finished off, no matter how many machine-guns go at him.'

He opened the breach of his rifle and a cartridge jumped out. 'I know why I'm here. I was asking questions a couple of hours ago, but I know one big answer to keep me going. I knew then, but I know more now. They can't do this all the time and get away with it.' He wiped the cartridge on his shirt, and slid it back, setting the safety-catch.

'When a patrol is ambushed,' Shelley said, 'and somebody killed, they do this as a sort of punishment. It's normal. Everything's normal.'

'I know,' Frank said, but he felt responsible and melancholy. The trap closed around your neck, the bag over your head, and you had to battle a way out of it, get free by more skill and fighting, fire your gun at the crucial moment when all patience is eaten out of you in order to avenge this, and then the need for vengeance comes again on one side or the other, except that you, yourself, must keep on calling it war, war of liberation, for the victory of socialism, for justice, for freedom of the people. You worked with those at the bottom in order to be reborn. Bill Posters coming secretly into their country (Bill Posters who'd never allow himself to be prosecuted or persecuted), to fight for them and help them, but making them suffer the more he fought so that they would be with him and you right from whatever depths of themselves they had been able to keep a hold on. You put self-respect on their shoulders, and they staggered bloody and shattered under it, but did not throw it off.

A pall of dust and flies lifted above the rubble when bricks from the street were thrown on to it. To know is to love, he told himself. You don't love until you know everybody, everything. It was cool, but they would bury the dead in the morning. The people had been persuaded to stay in the village in the belief that they would not be stricken again. The wounded were hidden in the cool of the houses, away from preparations for burial and the shrillness of the mourners. A man had been trained in France as a doctor, and with two women as nurses, he saved what he could. A few small planes in the public service could make this village fit to live in, but at the moment, there was nothing. He felt helpless, and would be glad to get out of it. Disinfectant, fertilizers, medicines, radio-sets, ropes, ladders, spades – to want this was nothing. Concealed in a camouflaged shelter, on the edge of the village and untouched in the raid, was a Peugeot station-wagon, fully primed and ready to go, in which a receiver-transmitter set was installed, loaded with food, water, medicines, Very pistols, guns, and ammunition, in case the secret headquarters should need to move quickly, a possession that they tapped and looked on with pride, so that even in their terrible destitution, they were not without hope.

They walked north, close together, a quarter-moon giving out light. The riverbed was dry stones, loose and slippy under weights that seemed heavier and more onerous than yesterday, after the meal and daytime rest. He opened and closed his hand, splitting burned flesh under the bandages, swinging his arm when the pain was too great to bear. Where do you come from, Dawley? I don't know. Where do you? Nottingham, the same as you. But that's the past, and the only good thing about the past is that it's finished with. Why did you ask? Just to make sure. Where do you think we're going? North. That's down, or is it up? My hand's giving me gippo. Forget it. The only way to do that is for you to shut your claptrap desert mouth. I can't. I like talking. Where else in the wide world would you like to be now? On my own two feet, which means just here. I'd be a real two-timing split personality if I wanted to be other than where I was. That's a fair way of putting it. You're going to get your head shot off. It'll cure this hand then, like nothing else will. There are more important things to think about than death. That moon up there will tell you that. Or ought to. It was never my idea to come all this way to let death worry me. You won't say that when God puts in the boot. Drop dead, He wears sandals. Don't get excited. I'm not. It's always possible, isn't it, that you are? So was being born. Just get back to your gammy hand. The same to you.

The *oued* ran roughly north, and Mokhtar had a large-scale map as well as the guide – which meant that serious planning had taken place. He picked out the Pole Star, almost overhead. The rattle of feet and gun-slings seemed to fill every crevice of the hills. The ululations of a hyena had followed them from the village. Its voice was of a deliberate luring melancholy, crying out for them to stop and wait, to take it with them wherever they were going instead of heartlessly leaving it to spend a lifetime pitching its voice in competition with that of the continual wind which was bound to outlive it. They climbed a slope, zig-zagging so as not to slip back, a groaning of collective heavy breath as they crawled to the crescent-shaped skyline of the col.

Across the plain, they saw an orange pinhead of fire. The horizon beyond was in darkness. He lay on the stones, plans winding like cold rivulets through his head. At such time, while waiting to move, expose oneself to bullets and flame, he lay as still as if already killed by them, except for the intense eyes trying to drag detail closer from the darkness or distance, flat and quiet and nevertheless expecting the world to open its arms in welcoming approval, lay as if all his senses were coming firmly and surely back at last after a long illness, the malady of the trek draining away and leaving him a clear smile at the cunning ideas of action pitted into the common ring. Fire would combust on the hillside and attract the patrol. Then, in utter stealth, making a half-circle towards the camp from which it had departed, they would attack those remaining there. When they had been finished off, they would meet the returning other half of the patrol coming back in haste to see what was the matter – and finish that off, also.

It seemed infallible and classic. Afterwards, they would retreat the way they had come, but veer south-east to avoid the village bombed over them in the afternoon. 'They won't spill out,' said Shelley, 'not for night fighting.'

'They might.' Frank laid down his rifle to look for wood.

'My old man boasted all his life about a night attack in the Argonne Wood in 1918. He lost his whole battalion capturing four shell-holes, and got a string of medals for it. He's retired from the Army now, after a lifetime of service. Always wanted me to go in the Army, but they threw me out of military college, which broke the old man's heart, as my family said, and I never thought it'd be so easy, because that had always been my sole aim in life. They play right into your hands, parents.'

'That way they really cut you up,' Frank said, ripping at a tinderous bush with hand and boot. 'Best to keep away from them, then there'll always be a bit of love left between you. You should start a guerrilla war in the Deep South, and if the Yanks send the Army to put it down, you might get a chance of shooting your old man between the eyes – if it means that much.'

Shelley spat. 'You're a real barrack-room lawyer. I liked it better when you were a taciturn Limey who didn't know his own mind.'

'When was that? There never was such a time. I'll bet we get them out of that post. They'll think it's a group of nomads over here, and come to check up.'

Fires were lit below the col, on the blind side from the camp, so that only smoke and a glow would be visible to their observant eyes. They would imagine that whoever it was hadn't yet seen them, and would come out to make a surprise round-up of the fires.

'It's a tightrope,' Shelley said. 'There are six of us, seven with the guide, which is too few to pull it off. Mokhtar's forgetting the basic principles, and I don't like it one flat bit.'

So as to move quickly in the dark and not lose contact they tied a length of string from hand to hand. The moon had flowed behind the hills. Even if they don't fall for it, we

can make a surprise raid and vanish, and if they don't check
on the fires, they won't come out and pursue us. If they do
come for the fires, it means we're not outnumbered, since
we've split them. Divide the mind, a decision one side that
you could never make, and on the other something that
went fatally wrong, because it was too easy. That way was
madness and defeat. When you sharpened the mind to its
perfect logic, it was always too late to withdraw from plans
whose contemplation made them perfect and so could not
be abandoned to the anarchy of futile speculation. Three
fires cracked into flame, sere branches bunching and falling
apart, then shooting up again, sparking and bursting
around their faces. They stood a few minutes among swirling smoke, then drew back as upshooting flames strangled
it.

They descended the slope, convicts chained by the dark
string of an idea that could only snap through panic or
disaster. Voices were curbed, even thoughts, as they slid
through the darkness and flanked away from the treacherous
pull of the heart which would have led to a premature
clash with any group snared towards the smoke. The situation was spun out of nothing, a needle of fire, a shadowy
trick, and as far as Frank could see, it might be only a
nomad camp they were approaching to blow the middle out
of.

They paused, still visible to each other. He loathed silence, the dangerous voiceless steppe over which all the stars
of the universe were poised like a planetarium, the white
blood of the Milky Way fixed in that atrophied spurt towards the ultimate back-end of creation. Each star was a
spyhole through a great black wall laid over the sky; above,
it was all dazzling phosphorescent light that shone through
these pinpricks. The cool wind blew at his shirt and shook
his matted hair. With relief, he heard the jackal blowing its
heartbreak back in the hills. If it was a nomad camp there'd
be a place at the fire, a dish of beans, and tea. Then more
walking, machinery, marching, counter-marching, involved
trigonometrical exercises through the Djebel Amour, the
barren mountains of love parsimoniously decked with alfa

and shrubs that hardly sustained the life in your boots. Myra must be back in England, and he pictured her in bed with a baby in its nearby cot, breathing through the hours of similar silence wherein he went over the rocks and stones in darkness. Sensing danger, he felt alone, not belonging to the other six as they belonged to him and to each other, but a man trapped by extreme isolation, caught under the stars and fixed like a fly on the steppe which seemed of absolute immensity now that they'd been an hour on it. They were descending slightly, and he wondered if ever peace would come so that he could see the hills with the good eyes of someone who is not hunted. They were a band of men marked down, and since they were in a land where other groups roamed, they had not yet been identified and cordoned off. They struck, grabbed, ran, hid, sweating and starving in the lonely darkness, but so far, the precise military tactics of the French had not pinned them down and scorched their rage and rags off the face of the earth. Napalm and flamethrower, the cruel and wicked kiss of the sun-god was out to get them, but this great land gave them cover, and the people of similar faith somehow found them food. Such hard living settled his regard for Myra and brought on a great longing to see his child, because it seemed that they'd probably given him up for ever – whether or not he might one day go back again. This comfortless, stark knowledge had strengthened him at the time of his greatest despair when traversing the sandwaste and pure dust of the blinding dunes, a week after crossing from Morocco. With little water and no food they staggered for days over the blinding sand and grit of Satan's earth, scorched and bleeding from mouth and rectum, scabbed and tortured as they held on to rifles and submachine-guns, insane and sick, followed by huge birds waiting for them to finally drop. It was the only way to survive the hedgehog fort-zone of Colomb-Bechar, throw themselves into the worst land of the earth. Remembering it made this stony, mountainous, scrub-wilderness seem like paradise.

Both fires were visible, a dying glow from their own, the other constant as if continually built on. At the halfway point they moved in silence and slow motion, the guide covering them a few yards to the left and keeping a sharp watch to avoid any investigating party. The night was as big as the land, endless, and it needed to be, he thought, for all they had to do. At a signal, they lay flat, no stone disturbed. The noise of boots came so close that Frank thought they would be walked on, used like stepping-stones across some shallow stream. His ear to the ground, he heard their weight, heavily built and laden, not too extended, fearing nothing because they were being as cautious as they knew how, though grunting and baulking over the unexpected distance.

Mokhtar stood up. Frank walked slow, quiet, hunched. Several universes had passed over their heads but nothing had altered. Space, stars, apprehensions were the same. They quickened, keeping a single file. A Very light went over the hills from the outgoing party, a thin luminous snake vanishing into some black window of the sky as if to do its worst on the inhabitants within. A reply shell curved from the point they were approaching. Mokhtar must be happy, he thought, sensing his smile of satisfaction, forehead creased with anxiety at evidence that his plan of vengeance was halfway coming to pass.

The fire on the hills was out, and no doubt the soldiers imagined they'd been sighted and so were extending their line for the round-up. Pitch night seemed like day to Mokhtar, for he had fixed the now darkened camp in his deepset eyes for so long that he knew exactly where it was. They closed up and followed him like cats to the leeward side from which a raid would be least expected, and which was also the best direction for a retreat, since another line of broken hills sloped up out of the plain a few miles away. The pinpricked skullcap of the sky held darkness firmly over them, and with sensibility and care they picked a way blind to the far flank of the entrenchment.

A stone rampart had been thrown round a low rise of ground. Mokhtar went forward on his belly like an alligator, loaded with grenades. The others spread a few yards apart, flattened, waiting. He considered that you hadn't really experienced the wilderness unless you'd been completely alone in it, hunting and hunted in the dark middle of the night, full of uncertainty about your own self but clear on the universal laws that sent you there. The wind searched out your marrow to blow it dry and empty. He pushed forward the safety-catch, no more safety from this second on, the mechanism easy and silent, William Posters strikes again, black heart and white heart, blue brain and red, roulette-wheel spinning behind those bleeding milksop stars.

A line of sound rumbled from the hills, then a ripple of ammunition paying its own way as battle was joined with jackals and phantoms. The humping burst of a grenade carried back, and all attention in the camp was on that side. A flare issued from the hills, momentarily hung like a grey jellyfish, an unwanted diminishing moon bursting into a dazzling chandelier as if a state reception were to be held beneath it. It threw a faint light over them, and he made out the dim shadows of Shelley and Mokhtar. When the flare died and scattered its ash the night was so intense that Mokhtar, not at the closest range for throwing bombs, stood up to full height and urged them to get nearer, looking as if he would walk into the camp and shake hands with the first man he met. The Lion of Judah, he breaks every chain. Once it used to be: Kiss the hand you cannot sever.

Men were bending over the fire, some slept, and four sentries were outlined faintly in a renewed glimmer of starlight. The pain raged in his hand as if all blood were rushing there in the final tensed wait, and only the rifle lying heavily on the open palm stopped it actually jumping.

A ribbon of machine-gun fire came from the hills and, using this as a signal, Mokhtar stood again. Five of them windmilled two bombs each to the middle of the camp and fell flat before the collective roar. Frank lifted his head after the earth cracked, and while stones and gravel and death-screams raged in the chaos, he joined the rapid fire into the smoke ruin of the camp on which three rifles and three light machine-guns now played. Shelley sent a magazine bursting at the antennae, hoping to wreck the signals unit. There was an impression around Frank as he knelt for better aim at the stunned, slow-moving figures, that bees were being thrown through the air at fantastic speed. His ear burned, then turned cold as he loaded, fired, and re-loaded and slotted in another clip. 'They've got me,' he thought, still firing and in plain view. Sweat and a more copious liquid dropped on to his shirt at the shoulder. Shelley's gun leapt free, and he fell back into cover. Frank steeled himself to run forward, but wanted a general rush. He smiled at such impotence. It's all at once, or none at all, for no one man can clean up that butcher's shop. He flattened, worked towards the left: 'You all right?'

'My hand's gone. It's knocked right out.' A stone splinter caught his cheek. Steel hooks were pulling up the ground from left to right. The Lion of Judah launched his last grenade and the machine-gun stopped its multiple biting. Ahmed lay still. Dust in his mouth tasted like iron shavings and, thrown by some explosion in himself, he ran towards the parapet. Flames crawled up the tent, and his course was fixed on it, insects biting the air around him. He took cover, and Mokhtar crashed by his side: 'Allons y!'

They moved back through shattering stones, while Idris and Mohamed covered them from the front. I hope they think there are more than six of us, that we're holding off in the hope that they'll show the white clout. But we're finished, the ragtags of the wide open spaces: Ahmed killed, Shelley's hand paralysed, my face bloody and fit only to show its paint-side to the moon: and the guide is unarmed, which leaves four of us to make for those lovely, endearing blister-hills.

He carried Shelley's gun. 'Bury me with it,' he said, 'so that I can shoot the jackals when they come in to rip my meat, if there's anything left on my bones by then. I'll never see the deep, blue sea from the highest pass of the Kabylie Mountains – after the fashion of Xenophon and his ten thousand nits.'

'We did damage,' Frank said. 'Or Mokhtar did.' Out of the fire, there were no more boiling bullets to sneak up your backbone, or go ping at the neck. They ran, shots following.

'It lasted ten blind minutes,' Shelley said, tearfully.

'Twenty,' Frank insisted, his breath rasping. 'Your watch stopped. It's one o'clock.'

'We've got four hours then to get into the hills and bury ourselves, if tomorrow isn't going to be our last day on this earth that we hoped to make so bright and marvellous.'

'They'll pick up our tracks.'

'They might on God's earth, but this is the devil's.' They stopped to swallow water. A heavy lorry roared, blazing headlights set for the camp. 'Helicopters in the morning.'

'Let them come,' Frank said bitterly. 'It'll be a relief.'

They ran, and in three hours were stumbling over the rocks of a defile. The guide was an old man, brown cloth turned round his head, the gentle, half-idiotic, smiling face of one who had grazed goats and camels all his life on these slopes and knew every curve and twist of the range. They came to a valley and crossed it at right angles, crawled and cursed at the boulders.

He walked asleep, senses anywhere but where his body was. It felt as if the grazing bullet had left him bald, the wind flickering across to restart the fires of pain. There was nothing to his body but lungs and legs, engines and wheels, hands for rudders, eyes for a compass, a machine made only to transport the body without which his senses would vanish into a grave of blackness. All it could do was show him the charnel-houses of the moon and the sherbet-gardens of the sun. His body was the four-pronged cog-wheel of his retreat, out of the desert, into the desert, a retreat and at the same time an orderly advance given importance by the visions which his body carried, exuded from the pores of his sweating tormented skin.

A depression in the earth held a lake of sand which they waded through, ankle-deep, waist-deep, salt and grit blowing against all wounds and eyes. The rhythm of his legs pushed it back into the machine which he could ignore. He was climbing a great tree with many convenient branches, clothed with numerous twigs of small green leaves. It reached high, and his legs and arms took him up with the speed and ease of an orang-utang that had been born and bred in that particular tree. The wind blew cool and leaves rustled. Soon he was a few branches above the surrounding trees and able to look out of his own tree-angle at the forest ceiling that went on for ever. There was nothing to see but this gentle green undulating ocean of giant treetops, a vast extent of emerald as if, were he to launch himself surreptitiously from the end of the branch and start walking, he would find them solid enough to support him, a new earth made from the tops of massed trees. But where and in what direction would he go? It was the same wherever he looked, so he climbed higher, hoping to reach the highest branch and twigs, as if this would give him a different view, some clue at least concerning the direction he should go in. Arms and legs carried him upwards pleasantly enough, so that he could imagine no better way of using his life's strength. Once he thought of going down again to the undergrowth of the forest, but the idea almost brought the vomit into his mouth, in a way that alarmed him. After years he reached the top, wiped sweat from his forehead and looked at the perfectly flat green sea of treetops hundreds of feet below. He saw himself flying, arms outstretched as he drifted down and over it, but arms not moving and head held back, legs together, gliding perfectly in a wide arc between the sun in a blue sky and the plain of treetops. The thought made him dizzy, but he felt great pleasure even at contemplating such a flight, and when it beckoned him he spread his arms and took a long breath of the cool air to give strength and force back the vomit and flex his heels for the leap.

Mokhtar gripped his forearm. 'You were about to fall.' They had reached the summit, sky faintly blue to the east, and for a moment stood grunting and still, bent over like apes, faces and clothes as grey as the rock. The old man led them down and when almost at the bottom of the narrow valley turned into a cleft concealed by a huge boulder. They passed, one at a time, squeezing their bodies between smooth slabs of rock only a foot apart. It led through a damp, narrow corridor that opened slightly to a ledge with enough space for them to lie on. From a rock water trickled, clear and icy, and Mokhtar unhooked a mug and set it underneath so that it filled in a few minutes.

He lay flat, eyes pinned open by stars in a sky that was turning grey. They had made it. I understand you, he said, fixing them in his stare, and they became flatter, closer, lost the mystic phosphorescence in the dawn. They needed the night to flower in, to bleed themselves white for. The dawn flattened them into a sheet of paper so that the sun could burn them up. He lay calm, wide awake while the others slept, looking at the softening stars as if he'd never seen them before, or as if he'd just been born. Three months in the desert and he'd lost his identity. Killing didn't give him one, and neither did being hunted. They were part of it though, joined by this long cool examination of the stars fading above the parallel cliffs as if they would never come back. The clarity of the grey rock and the stars made him feel as if he were dying, the sky turning blue and powdery the more his eyes tried to penetrate it. He was afraid of dying, but only when he thought of going to sleep. The blank exhaustion left him heavy and boneless, yet without the need of immediate rest and like watching the minute-hand of a clock move he pressed the sky across its colour from black of night to the day's pale blue. He belonged nowhere, basked in the disembodied serenity that comes only after driving the mind and body to their limits. But the body and mind had, after all, driven you, driven themselves which were you, completed you by their movement. He belonged here, emptied even of ideas that had sent him to this particular hiding-spot in the mountains of love and desolation, and being emptied of them at such a time meant that he was fulfilling them. A man of extremes loses his identity, but a man of the middle way is referred to by the two extremes which hedge him in. Starving, riddled with exhaustion like a disease, he belonged nowhere except where he was, and saw no limit to the world that he lived in. Down in the hidden basin of the hills he could see nowhere except upwards. 'Flesh into heaven, and bones into hell. The soul falls apart.' He wrote the words across the patch of sky as if to send them somewhere as a telegram.

People who feel that the full life is not sufficient end up in the desert, if they fight hard enough to get there. The greater the fight to reach it, the more bitterly scorched is the earth that you left behind. It forces you to search the bottom of the heart, where you reach sand, stones, rock, and slate, the geologic ages of your own private earth – scorched earth and sun, frost and scorpions, salt water and bitter thorns that fester your hands at a single touch. Once in the desert you have to cross it, forget what sent you there and for what spiritual loot and lot, or what you might find on the other side, but survive in it, live in it, and move over it. The salt of the earth comes out of the desert. The great spirit rests in the wilderness – Sinai, Sahara, Takla Makan. You choose the desert, or reject it, but you reject it before you get to the point of choosing it. If chosen it is because there is no other way, because the longer way would be through death, and no one would choose that when there is no chance of resurrection, so you take the short-cut through the desert because a chance of survival is easier to believe in than the possibility of salvation.

A huge black-winged bird skimmed over the blue corridor of sky, and flew away as if falling to earth. Water was dripping into a cup. He reached and drank some, then replaced it. Falling drops of water were the only sound. There is no greater silence than that which opens around you when you are exhausted, worn to the bone. I must live, he said, I must live, and the regular fall of the waterdrops smoothed his consciousness away.

CHAPTER SIXTEEN

HEAVY rotor-blades thumped, as if the helicopter were descending because the clear blue burning air no longer had the density to support it. They lay, hidden under ledges of rock, like loaves thrown at random into an oven. He felt fresh from some sleep and food, and all the good water he could drink, and wondered why the four who were there didn't open fire at the huge precise monster, force it to burst and crumble on to the rocky land, so that those inside who wanted to bomb and spray them with a fire as if they were animals would instead be pinned on the bloody end of wrath as they tried to escape from metal and burning fabric. But the consensus was that they should sweat in their hideout till the pimping angel of Satan passed over without claiming them. But if by some fluke it suspected their presence and landed to look, they would be killed before they could scramble clear.

Shelley denied this: 'They have to get in here first, and our good shepherd knows a way out. Take 'em a year and twenty thousand men to throw a trapnet over the whole range. Even then they might not get us in the end. As long as we don't move during the day, and go quietly by night.'

A shadow passed under the sun, darkened the glaring slate. 'I'd like to look at it. I don't believe in anything I can't see.'

'They've got machine-gunners on board. Poke your head up and we'll sell you to a circus, if we can keep you alive: the man without head, hands, or feet.'

'Drop dead yourself.'

'Willingly. It's a flying platform. In some places they carry Alsatian dogs. When the helicopter lands twenty rush out, and God doesn't help those who get in their way: children, women, people in the fields, even a man with a gun – when he's not right out of it. Hard to get the dogs back, in spite of good training. They seem to vanish, go black in the night. There are no unmixed blessings, no secret weapons, just a nightmare humiliating grind. It'll be the same scuffle when it's finished, though you can't let that blunt your finer feelings while it's still on, otherwise you are not a man, and will never become a saint or commissar.'

Engine-sound weakened far out along the valley. Safe for a while. He saw nothing, suspected nothing. Heavy machine-gun fire thumped back, a man and goats being spread all over the rocks. Its chatter and the damage it did seemed utterly insignificant in such great spaces. It ceased far away, the motor noise squashed like a fly against the hot wall of the sun. The raw, tender graze along his temple no longer throbbed to the beat of pistons or gunfire. He winked at the sky – grey edges and pale blue middle. Their refuge was an oasis never to be forgotten while they were in it.

Shelley blew a trail of ants from his shattered hand. To-night, so the promise went, they would enter a village where an Italian doctor lived, who helped the FLN and asked no questions. Flesh had been honed from Shelley's face, turned grey since yesterday and left his eyes helpless and bitter, a new phase for him. He read his holiest of bibles, Mao Tse Tung's treatise on protracted warfare, drew maps of imaginary tracts of land on the endpapers with his fountain pen, and with pencil and rubber carried out intricate exercises to make plainer precepts of the great man that he had read many times. His best hand was shattered, a finger smashed and the back a blue hump of broken veins and bone, a map left in the rain whose river delta ran its colours into the mangrove of uncontrollable terrain. He sat in one place, and Frank took water and food to him. 'At least I've still got my legs and eyes,' Shelley said.

'And one arm,' said Frank. 'We'll get you seen to.'

Frank left, and Shelley flipped through the book on his knee, print which anthologized the intellectual passion of his mind: when forced into a passive disposition through some false march, a guerrilla unit must try to get itself out – quickly. How this is done depends on the circumstances, but the ability to move away must always be given first consideration. Those who learn to retreat and not flee, move and not be seen, secretly join other groups to attack in force when the enemy is weak, retreat and not scatter after having defeated him so as to avoid giving battle to reinforcements which will nearly always outnumber you, disperse unseen after memorizing complex arrangements to meet again, will become invincible and survive continual attacks. But to retreat and not flee you must be aware of the point you are heading for, otherwise you lay yourself open to defeat. Since there is no God in heaven to watch over you or to destroy you, you must take care of yourself and make cause together for the common good. In retreat know where you are retreating to, then the advantage lies with you and the initiative is but one step away. Make sure everyone is assigned clearly defined tasks, topographical limits of manoeuvre, times and places for re-assembly, foolproof means of communication. Rigidity, inertia, self-satisfaction, temptation to sloth, lead to passivity, panic, loss, either the living death of shame and slavery or complete annihilation. Those whose conditions of life you are trying to change will help you and suffer with you if you have a passionate and convincing answer to everything. You must be known to be everywhere by the enemy when he is not there or is weak: and nowhere when he is there and is strong. His weakness is your strength. His strength is your opportunity to weaken him and thereby grow strong yourself. If he is well supplied, then you must live off him and pull him down. Unless the strong can be made to fall, the world will stagnate, people will wither in the spirit and succumb entirely to the unchanging forces of nature. Evil is no mystifying concept. It is the inability to change for the good. It is being slothful among bad conditions of life, and preaching that the acceptance of present suffering makes the adventure of change unnecessary, thereby implying that suffering is sufficient adventure for the soul. One must prove that it is not – by making it possible for the weak to inherit the earth and become strong, and to use their newly-won strength in order to help those still weak in the world, which is no less than the fight for eternal justice, a uniting of mankind to give everyone equality and food and dignity that will enable them to become individuals in a universal sense. The tree must purify and burn, shed its leaves in the fires of insurrection. Trees catch fire, incendiarized by napalm. Those who look on it as an antidote to the upsurging ant-spilling poor of the world can brew it to their heart's content, but wherever it falls another tree goes up in flames and spreads its light for the so-far unconvinced to witness, to stop wavering and join. Whoever makes it, distributes it, drops it, is destroying his own soul. The art of retreat is foreign to them, skill and cunning far away. Their intelligence is sealed off, the limits of their humanity inexorably narrow, and the seeds of their own annihilation gradually emerge from the vile fungus of reaction into which they sank when faced with newly-moving forces of the earth.

In order to mislead, decoy and confuse the enemy there should be continual use of stratagems, such as making a ploy in the east but attacking from the west, appearing now in the south and now in the north, hit-and-run attacks, and night actions in which the attackers, though weaker, must always gain because the ways of retreat are infinite and cover is perfect even over open ground. And yet such infallible-sounding advice is nothing until applied by the malleability of the mind and the courage of the human body. One may lecture and discuss, but the endurance of those who fire the gun and run in the night is what counts.

Frank had climbed up and out of their hiding-place, and the grey edges to the sky disappeared when he reached the highest point of the rock-wall. It was fiery blue, butane gas burning from the holy pivot of the sun. The flat of the valley was small in area, enclosed by jagged sides down which the helicopter hadn't descended low enough to pick out their hiding-place. Machine-gun fire riveted the western end, as if a real fight were going on. It was rumoured that Boumedienne, the military brains behind the FLN, had come into the area to enliven it. Mokhtar might know what their part was to be, or he might not.

Nothing ever came of going into the desert to avoid your fellow-men. You go there to find them, find yourself, by seeking one to find many. Revolutions are initiated by those who, in order to inspire themselves, have to prove to the wretched of the earth that they, too, can be inspired. It is a search by those who want to prove to themselves and the world that they are not spiritually dead, but such effort changes everything. In their crude simplicity they may not see themselves as the makers of a new world, because such striving begins without philosophy, and there is no name in the beginning for what is to become a prime mover of people. Some may give it a name in order to control it, but this is necessary if the wretched of the earth are to become collectively strong and not be defeated by genocidal maniacs.

He lay watching for an hour before seeing a figure descend the opposite slope and walk directly across the dry riverbed towards him. In all the time there had been no shepherd nor nomad, not a friend nor enemy, and no animal life but the noise of insects and the flurry of an escaping scorpion, the sliding flight of a bird. The dry day seemed to eat up all life in its eternal oven. He sweated and stayed flat, binoculars trained, gun ready.

It was a young man wearing a blue silk shirt and khaki trousers, open jacket and brown laced shoes. He smiled, as if out for a walk on the edge of the town. Frank showed himself when he was twenty yards off, but the man, thin, of medium height, gold teeth flashing, walked on with no surprise. Leaflets flapped from his pockets. A row of pens and biros were spread like medals along his chest, and he lifted his hand in greeting. 'I have information,' he said in French.

He came sweating down the slope, and his jaundiced face was both freckled and rashed where smallpox had eaten over it. Frank picked a leaflet about to fall from his pocket, holding the gun level with the other hand towards the centre of his back. The man slid down over loose stones towards the waiting gun of Idris, who greeted him Moslem fashion and led the way into the hideout. Frank stayed on watch. A lizard warmed itself among the quiet rocks. Others came out as he lay still. One went over his wrist. A scorpion ran, and a horned viper curled itself up some feet away, as if after a long journey, and he stoned it to death. In the rocks he became a rock himself, because movement would betray as much as shade or colour. You must outdo a lizard in patience for a war like this. Who knows how it will turn out, in spite of such extremist patience? – 'extremist' being what you are labelled by those incapable of changing their ways of life, or of believing that people can change the world instead of the world changing them. He cannot expect his extremism not to be tempered later by those whom he helps to power. It is no use snivelling that a god has failed when a few of those who were weak turn into rats after you have made them strong. You move on to help others but do not lose faith. A god only fails you if you are less than a god. Strength in yourself takes time to grow. Tame the wild grit and put it to work. If you learn how to suffer, thank the earth and those who walk over it for teaching you.

The string signalled at his ankle and he went down, found them listening to the young man who had walked in from nowhere. Shelley pressed his teeth together to stop the noise that shook his whole face to tears. He held a loaded revolver high in his left hand for practice, but the bad had already infected the good with its pain and weakness and he dropped it in despair. Mokhtar was talking to the young man and the guide, moving his thick finger on the French military map. The leaflet crinkled in Frank's pocket, and he held it up to read. Shelley put down his gun and went to the water store. 'You should see this!' Frank called, laughing without wondering first whether it would be safe to do so. The leaflet told of some café-brothel of Laghouat and was meant for the eyes of French soldiers, complete with prices for the various levels of delight – clean, well-*reglemented* and safe. The young man handed them to passing convoys and incoming drafts, patrols returning from a hard slog to this staging post of rest and culture.

Shelley read it. 'Yeh, it's bad news. A sweet chick of Nubia heard it from the lips of an orgiastic *poilu*. Two brigades left this morning to clean up the area. One is spreading from the Laghouat–Aflou road, and the other's fanning out from the Géryville area. A nice little trap, complete with planes, guns, and bunsen-burners. There are a few of us in the bag. We were supposed to be massing for a raid on Laghouat – though I don't think they knew it. So we break out to the south and gather somewhere else, east of Laghouat maybe, to go in as soon as that brigade leaves, which means we might filter through the thick of them at night, and hit them in the rear if they scoot back to relieve Laghouat. The permutations are endless, but not so that you can't sort them out if you have half a brain.'

'How's your hand?'

'Improving. I don't feel the ants any more. I want to find a doctor. I'll leave you for a sweet while. When it's fixed, I'll hit the trail again.'

'It might be safer to stick with us. Have it fixed and drag along. We don't want the French to nick you. Got to pull you out in one piece.'

Shelley smiled, his eyes feverish, and teeth set. 'Don't worry. I'm an American journalist come over the Tunisian frontier to report on the situation. Working for the magazine *New People*. All my papers are in order. Take no chances. They won't like it, a left-wing mag, but at least they won't stand me up against a wall, or roast me over a slow fire.'

'I'm glad you're organized.'

'You're no good dead. Not that I'm wailing over a smack on the hand by a bullet, or cringing for the Purple Heart. Just a brief statement of principles.'

'They won't leave you behind,' Frank said, wryly. 'And we'll mend your hand. How do we get out, though?'

Shelley picked up the revolver again and levelled it shakily at the rockface. 'We climb to six thousand feet, then go north-east, up and down peaks till we cross the Laghouat–Aflou road. We start in half an hour. We'll meet no tanks so high up, but we'll have to crawl on our bellies because of planes and helicopters. The French must think there are thousands of us in this area, but I'd be surprised if there are more than a hundred.'

CHAPTER SEVENTEEN

FROM a distance the grey and orange flank of the mountain looked unassailable except with the gear of an alpine expedition. They took the hard route out, the long march, the half-possible. To look down made him dizzy, to look up promised a premature death by exhaustion – which was better, he thought, scrambling up a few more feet, than a bullet up your arse or the red cock on your shoulders. Tilt your head back and the wall moves towards your eyes. The wall went into the sky and would swing down unless you threw yourself off to avoid it. So you kept them fixed in front, and since you couldn't hold back the machine of your legs, you kept your senses locked where they could not distract or destroy you.

Below the eastern drop of the land lay a cloud of dust and smoke. It looked flat and low from where they were, with a noise as if a forest were hidden beneath, and all trees in it were falling down to the crack of their rending trunks and the dull brush of enormous treetops. 'Bazookas,' Shelley said. 'Grenade rifles. It's a privilege to fight such a well-equipped army.'

'I'm not proud,' said Frank. 'I'd rather be hounded by thugs with sticks and us have the rifles. When do we get to that six-thousand-foot mark? I've forgotten my barometer. On a useless stunt like this, I begin to forget who my friends are.'

'Delirium,' Shelley said.

'I let it have free rein. Then it goes away. I'd like to roam the world in a freebooting tank, guns firing in all directions – at friends who try to help me and enemies who try to destroy me – because there doesn't seem much difference at a time like this.'

They lay on the rocks for a short rest out of the hour. 'The trouble with you is that you're irrevocably unavoidably rotten. Maybe it's because you're English, I don't know. I love you like a brother, but I can't honestly see you getting a job in the cabinet when they form the Free Government of Reconstruction!'

'I know,' Frank said. 'It makes me sad. I cry myself to sleep about it every night. Maybe I'm rotten, but I'm burning it out of me. A few charred corners are left, that's all.'

The file moved, seven now that the young man joined them rather than risk walking alone through the French brigades. Shelley talked to him. He'd polished shoes, run errands, carried kit and luggage, lost a bus-conductor's job because he hadn't kept his hands out of the fare-bag. The café work was all right. He lived, was wiry and surprisingly strong, useful in a hundred ways. The Frenchwoman who owned it couldn't know what accurate information he dispensed to those in the street who saw that it reached the relevant people. Often he passed it on himself, trekking the hills with pockets of nuts and figs. He could read French, write his name, recognize the different tanks and aeroplanes, the various guns and weapons, explained to him boastfully by French soldiers who thought they had stumbled on a queer idiot who played up to their cause. In a world of enemies, you can make friends easily, and do much damage before being caught. His smile was too frank and continuous to be quite sane. The brothelized obscenities mouthed out of loyalty to his job and the mistress of the house, the leaflets thrown at great risk on to the backs of speeding trucks, made him known all over this part of the country. When he appeared in the midst of a battalion about to embark on a fisherman's hunt, a bundle of newspapers under his arm recording successful encounters with the FLN, and predicting a final sure end to the rebellion, they drove him away or, goodnaturedly, advised him to go home. Some would even buy his papers, and then he would walk off with a sulphurous, appealing grin, running a little, jumping, then a quick stroll until he came across a friendly shepherd who would fork up the nearest outflanking ranges to spread verbal messages over the cordoned area, to warn any who did not already know what was coming. He couldn't think back to how such work began. Nothing definite had pulled him in. Even his loathing, being intermittent, formed no basis for his consistent and intelligent action. Yet he was an easygoing rebel rather than a zealous revolutionary, and perhaps for this reason was able to make a surer contribution to the common war, since his personality fitted him perfectly for this part.

Shelley retailed it to Frank. 'He'll vanish in the night, or some time when we're through the thick of it.'

From the height of the mountain they saw into an adjacent valley. Two trucks were set across the end of it like a

172

barricade. Ants moved out, filtering between brushwood. Shelley adjusted the centre-wheel: 'They'll need alpine troops to flush us from this. They used them in the Kabylie, but lost too many. We set up the avalanche, and rolled 'em down again. They pulled 'em out quick. There will be trucks in the next valley as well. We'll go all night and lie flat tomorrow. I've got to get this hand fixed.'

His eyes were points of grey light, ready for the uncontrollable madness of pain. Frank wondered how he could stand it. The hand was blue, swollen enormously, and part of it turned pink and was beginning to split. 'We'll tell Mokhtar.'

'What can he do? In a few days, we'll find someone to hack it off. That's all I want.'

'Let's go down to the French. I'll take you. We'll make up a good story,' Frank said. He put a hand on Shelley's arm. 'Even a field-dressing would help.' They had nothing except food, water, guns, and ammunition.

'Forget it,' Shelley said. 'What's gangrene between friends? The devil's bite.'

Pain was contagious, his jovial madness catching, the violent shaking of his hand unnerving. Feeling sorry didn't help, so he tried not to. This was impossible, for it burned into him also. To share it was only to double it, not halve it, but he shared it nevertheless. It would neither help nor cure, as if sympathy were only a way of bearing other people's troubles without lessening their pain.

An enchanting fairyland of mountains lay all around them at dusk, under a few bars of purple cloud, the javelins of insurrection subtly out of reach except for those who climbed such heights. They were suspended, self-assured, outstanding, turning blue and pale against the whitening sky around and above, for there was no land higher. A cool breeze ran gently against them, the javelins thickening and growing into iron-purple. The mountain rock-tables were unevenly spread, reddening, a mad abandoned stone-age restaurant that a tribe of giants had fled from after a last vast angry supper. The cliffs were precipitous, so that he could not understand how they had humped their bodies up to the summit they stood on. Ravines and gullies divided them to the north-east, and the sloping sun beamed itself on the trackless direction they still had to take. The tables looked flat, but they were spread with boulders, indentations, cover, declivities. They found a pool among stunted bushes. He pulled out his hand, and it was covered with leeches, festoons of abundance drawing hungrily on the rich bonanza of his blood. With the free hand he found a cigarette and lit it from Shelley's pipe. 'You'd better make haste,' Shelley said, 'or there'll be nothing left of you. It's the first time they've fed on good rich yeoman blood coursing with the loam and foam of England.'

'There's little of that left.' They dropped off, or burst. 'Dip your hand in. They cure everything, as well as the fits and miseries. Take the black blood out of your soul, and the life out of your heart. Nature's remedy for life, meaning death.' The old man filled his goatskin, scooping water into a mug and straining it through a rag, now and gain throwing aside a mash of leeches to make their way back to the source of life.

'I'm not drinking that,' Frank said. Whether sweet, pure, magnesium or brackish, the water never lost its fulsome taste of the old goat in whose skin it was carried. He'd suffered the pains of dysentery and the blisters of desert-mouth, and unknown ailments that merely nagged at the stomach till he had spots and freckles in front of his eyes so that when he slept he seemed to have lost half his weight and when he walked he swore he'd doubled it.

The fairyland blackened, became a province of coal while the sky kept its pale blue. Ebony tables and cuttings flowed away, showing outcrops that weren't noticed when the sun was higher. 'I wish they were padded with two feet of snow,' Shelley said. 'We'd freeze to death, but what else could anyone wish for? I dream of it while I'm walking. I'm up to my waist in snow. If I concentrate I can smell it, blue and bitter, menthol and juniper berries, New England snow, toboggan-sledding in the Hampshires. What do you fix your mind on, Frank?'

'Whatever's in front of my eyes. If I can't stand that,

there's a black wall I can conjure up. Or I see Myra and her house in England, but that means I've got my tenth wind and am travelling well. Or I theorize on where we're going and what we're part of, making up tactical exercises that are so optimistic they make me laugh. I dream of having a book to read when we stop. I'm print-starved. When I get somewhere where there's print I'll read anything, though maybe I'll be so choosy by then, I'll read very little. I wish that youth had brought some of his newspapers, at least. Still, I think of the books I've read, make them up again and watch words passing in front of my eyes on an endless tape.'

They went on, through deep snow for Shelley, blank walls of the crowding night for Frank. They grumbled, grunted, staggered, no rest because every inch of distance had to be put behind them while it was dark. The half-moon rose and gave them a few hours of shadow, each figure with a mocking, moving twin imitating every slide and footstep, weaving clowns vitiating the bile he wanted to spit at them, but which always stuck in his throat. An icy wind blew against the graze on his head, so that it itched and chafed, as if healing from what salt was in the air. When he once pressed it the burn was like pulp and he drew back his hand, vowing to leave it alone.

When they stopped, they shivered, were glad to stand and move on. A wild dog of the mountains took up its night noise and filled the sky with a long undulating never-broken wail, the binding sound a dog in the wilderness could make yet would never help you to find it. You'd need a whole nation of soldiers to catch a few hundred dogs if they were dispersed, not ten to one, but a thousand to one. It spoke on the wind as if it were a microphone, and he thought it might be the same dog heard every night from the Moroccan frontier, a huge, wild, soulful dog following their stench and footsteps. He'd never so much as seen its silhouette, Anubis of the sand and stone, mountains and saltmarsh, a unique tree-climbing dog that, at the smell of an aeroplane in the wind, leapt down and ran, its four long legs rattling over rock and gravel before the flame-bomb exploded in the tree and an oily uprushing fire sent its death-breath after him.

What's it got to do with me? Its refugee howl runs up my back like danger and flame, but all the same it makes comforting company on the long marches of the night in which you need a soul of stone, a moonstone lit enough to show the way, to lead and beckon you, push and guide. If I saw that dog I'd want to take aim and get its hot flea-blown carcase hugging the dust, but in this sort of day and night I'd bring a thousand bullets down on us. But if I give a second thought, always worth more than the first, I wouldn't want to floor its anarchy and freedom even though I'm halfway frightened at its soulful howl from the dog-Posters world tracking me into this great self-induced desert of death. I can talk to myself, I can talk, talk myself into the grave of survival, yet that dog tells me that survival is no grave but a state of blessedness to travel for, instead of staying behind and howling alone like him.

He walked easily, no effort to get him forward at the quick goat-like progress dictated by Mokhtar and the guide, who travelled together like four shadows ahead. He let the baying of the dog lull him, turned its noise into music and speech as he watched his own shadow continually in motion before the moon's suffering light. They traversed the long hog's back of the range, slowly descending. The guide suddenly led them on a roundabout way down the steep northern slope, so that they could cross where the valley was narrow and danger least.

Before leaving the heights, they gathered fuel and crushed it almost solid, making a high mound of it. Then rocks were piled on top till the wood was covered in the shape of a huge beehive. They left a small space at the bottom in which to place a slip of paper and so ignite the inside bracken. Frank struck the match; it would burn all night and much of the next day, smoke escaping through the interstices of the loosely joined stones, a smouldering beacon to draw French troops to a vacated area.

They went down unobserved. In the valley there was no moon. They heard the first explosions of the night, saw humps of blue light opening and closing further down the range, several kilometres away. 'They're approaching this cutting so as to close it by morning,' Mokhtar said. But unfortunately for them as an army the hob-nailed boots of their guns and mortars were heard from far away, giving the moonstruck phantoms or false reports time to disappear. An idle stone rolling by chance down the slope and gathering a few more on the way was enough to establish an ambush or night attack for which the FLN irregulars were both dreaded and famous. Frank couldn't understand why the French conscripts put up with this sort of war, though there'd been plenty of desertions in the Kabylie to have the army worried. Men and sometimes officers had come over to the FLN with arms, information, and even a will to help in the fight. Mokhtar had boasted about it one night in a rare mood of speech. 'As it is,' he speculated, 'they'll waste enough bombs on that smoke we left behind to raze Paris, and send at least a company to clear the emptiness around it.'

They climbed up another flank of a thousand metres. When the sky was blue but the sun had not yet risen, a great shadow lay to the north, as if from clouds when the sun was overhead. It was the sparsely-treed area covering the hills near Aflou which, in the dim light, seemed cooler and more thickly forested than it was, a good place of refuge.

'I know what you're thinking,' Shelley said.

'You're wrong. It's so ideal it's a death-trap.'

'You say and do the right things. What does it feel like, coming from the purest bastard race on earth?'

'It'll be light soon,' Frank said. 'A big fat sun scorching our noses and elbows for the next fifteen hours.'

'It's not that,' Shelley said, 'but it's this pain I don't like. Thirty-six hours I've felt it, which feels like all my life. I reckon we're all full of pain ready to be tapped. Just needs a bullet or a knife to spark it off.'

Frank spat out a mouthful of goatwater. 'What have you got against pure bastard races like the English? Sometimes, I think you're just one of those white Anglo-Saxon

Protestant Americans fighting for the freedom of subject races – as long as they're reasonably pure. I don't understand it, you white Anglo-Saxon Freedom Fighter. You're a WASFF – a WASP with no roof to his mouth. I've read all that Jack London–Hemingway crap, and spewed over it.'

'So have I. Leave me to it and let's get on.' He looked back at him, but could find no confirmation in Frank's straight-looking eyes that he was dying. Frank knew he couldn't, would not give him this leap of satisfaction, found it better to control the outward expressions of his heart when he did not want what his eyes saw to overwhelm it.

A track ran along the dry, flat bed of the valley. While holes were dug among the rocks on either side, the newspaper-seller pulled down a bush and smoothed all trace of them out of the dust, then put the finishing touches to their burials. They lay under the rocks, loopholes opening towards the track, sweating, choking, killing scorpions that came in dozens to disturb their agony. The youth found a hiding-place, and by full daylight this part of the valley seemed as deserted and empty as the rest.

His mind reached its limits. They had nailed up the coffin but he stayed alive. Childhood and adolescent horrors came back, as they should at a time like this, otherwise how could you trust them? And how could they be of any use to you? They can't all have been for nothing, meaningless, those parts you suffered and those you loved. Every man was a coffin until his rifle or machine-gun joined the chorus of others, the new gunchurch of the revolution spitting out their cleansing hymns. He counted six helicopters, man-made tin-plated dragonflies spluttering a hundred feet up, prayed for one to land before their guns so that they could kill the dozen troops on board before they began to disembark, run out like spiders and pull it to pieces. Mokhtar had drawn diagrams showing petrol-tanks and vital parts, and Frank was as familiar with ways of destroying helicopters as he had one time known how to preserve and lengthen the life of his own motor-car when he worked in the factory. He also found it necessary to believe and ponder on the fact that the art of camouflage meant not only to melt against the sheltering land, but equally to withdraw your consciousness out of the atmosphere. If an approaching patrol has no visual hope of seeing you, some member of it will, nevertheless, sense that you are there. Your psyche is as tangible as your body, your ego as plain as iron, and unless you can master these, then the most skilful disguise can betray you. Perfect camouflage is an exercise in self-negation, an utter wiping-out of yourself, a withdrawal into non-existence, so that you can't in any way be alive to others. The only light to be kept alert is that of the eyes, so that when the ring of your ambush is perfect, the united trigger can be drawn with unexpected and shattering effect. From a state of sublime withdrawal you must leap to a state of active egotism, which means death to all who face the ray of it. Thus the span of spiritual experience is in this way wider, before the final limit chops you off in death.

They waited five hours. Shelley did not know how long he was groaning. Frank was awake, staring at the road and willing a car, lorry, tank to come along, anything with engine and wheels on which they could take Shelley to a doctor. He'd seen it before, his grandfather die, and a man at work die after being struck by falling girders, remembered the look of utter and painful consciousness on both before the breathing diminished and stopped. He'd imagined that people died quickly, or went slowly but surely under the sleep of drugs, but this state of know-all consciousness both of the world they loved and the blackness they were going to was the most disturbing thing he'd seen, and signs of it were already in Shelley's eyes. Mokhtar knew it too, and for once the demands of war and survival coincided with the need for mercy towards one of their wounded. Frank had under-estimated Mokhtar, had kept his eyes open and gun ready in case he should think to make a quick finish of Shelley if he dragged too much on their progress. But Shelley had shown such great and undeniable courage by keeping up with their race, that the Lion of Judah had decided on the way of compassion.

They felt a signal, and heard the engine. The young man

would make no sign if more than one vehicle appeared, for they could not take on a convoy. Handbills still flapping from his pocket, he ran into the middle of the track, waving his arms. It was a desert jeep, with three soldiers in it. The driver dropped gear, its noise change roaring along the flanks of the valley, shouting at him to get out of the way. He stood firm, flapping his papers with an idiot grin of welcome. The driver braked and skidded, and the man was knocked slightly as he stepped aside and fell flat into the dust to save his life, which was immediately extinguished by the only burst of bullets that one soldier of the jeep had time and inclination to fire. Mokhtar, Idris, Mohamed, and Frank, two on either side, pressed their triggers at the same time.

They dragged the bodies behind the rocks, and swept dust over the tracks and pools of blood. Frank put on a soldier's jacket and cap, and did the same for Shelley. He turned from the dead young men, his heart bursting. He was familiar with the dead, but the more he saw, the more depressed he was. He supposed the war would go on until one side or another lost heart, felt the shadow only of so much useless death, instead of pure energy-giving rage at the stony manifestation of another row of corpses. Slogans, ideals, and beliefs weakened when you pulled the warm bodies towards the holes you had lain in while waiting to kill them, with their tortured human faces and limbs still jumping. He took all field-dressings from their packs before heaping on the stones.

They squeezed in, and Frank turned the jeep around and drove back the way it had come. The guide directed him towards a gap between two mountains. A plane flew high over the loose stones, a bird with an engine stuck in its craw that would not molest them because they were no longer bandits on the run from the great clean-up, but part of it, as the pennant flapping on the car plainly showed. This was treachery, if you like, though Frank could not revel in the moral satisfaction he would have got from it because of Shelley's ash-coloured face in the mirror.

'We'll be out of it tonight,' he called.

'Out of what?' Shelley's lips moved, his eyes shone, but from a face immobilized in every pore by the unyielding grip of pain. Frank smiled as if they were on an excursion looking for a beach or oasis pool where they might drink cool beer and swim.

'If I sleep more than eight hours,' – Shelley's thin face magically threw off all sign of the blackening blood beating like a drum in his mangled hand – 'my stomach begins to ache.'

They laughed. Unreality. 'That's hunger,' Frank said.

'Or conscience. I don't think I was born to sleep.' On second thoughts, he added: 'Not yet, anyway,' – which saved Frank the hypocrisy of deciding not to contradict him.

CHAPTER EIGHTEEN

THEY went forward all day, met the sun head-on in the morning, had it pushing them from behind in the afternoon towards another great door of darkness. Ahmed had been killed, the newspaper-seller had died, and the guide had returned to his village because he was no longer familiar with the territory they were in. They were five: Mokhtar, Frank, Mohamed, Idris, and Shelley, and it did not occur to Frank how lucky they had so far been in escaping all interception.

The hills covered with scrub and trees, marked as forest on the map, closed over them at the end of the day. A thicker patch concealed them, and they laid branches over the truck. A stream had water running along its bed, and he could not believe it, until the taste went down his throat. Some rations had been taken from the truck, tins of paté, sardines and chocolate. Shelley could not eat. After a mouthful, he vomited. They hoped to find morphine in the cab, but there was none. He was unrecognizable, mouth black and torn from the grind of teeth, eyes unable to open. He felt them to be a great distance from him, a horseshoe of shadows, each a thousand needle-points trying to force his eyes open and prick them, collectively to push him so that he lost balance and sat down.

Frank lifted him. He was saturated, as if he'd been taken from a bath of scalding water. Shelley roared. There was more pain in his legs than the injured arm.

'Put him down,' Mokhtar said.

Frank wanted to drive full pelt to the nearest town, find an army doctor, any doctor, even if it meant getting captured, then shot or twenty years in prison. 'Give me some help with him.'

Shelley didn't want to go, and staggered to his feet. 'Leave me alone.'

Frank held him nevertheless, knowing he'd no right to make such decisions of life and death for him. If he wanted to die rather than become a prisoner, then he must be respected. Fortunately, it was easy to know what his true wish was.

'When we left Ahmed,' Mokhtar said, 'he was wounded, not dead. I could have saved him, but I had to save all of us. I saw him badly wounded, but not dead. If we get a doctor for Shelley, we are all caught.'

'Isn't there an FLN doctor?'

'Not near. We can reach one tomorrow, beyond the road, if we travel all night.' It meant the big risk of headlights until they ran out of petrol. Frank broke up French cigarettes and packed the tobacco into Shelley's pipe, but he couldn't hold it in his teeth. He drove, not yet in the darkest stomach of the night, straight as he could in a north-easterly direction between the trees, torment for Shelley who cried out continually for them to stop. He drove quickly along a smooth track for ten kilometres before turning off, then went back to lights in crossing rocky, thinly-forested country.

When the moon came up, they travelled by it, eyes aching at the shapes they tried to see, at the boulders missed and flanking by. Part of the forest had been hit by bombs. This war was vicious to trees and men. It was like a ruined tree-city in the moonlight, blasted by lightning and as if already blackened by time, the arboreal remains of a vanished civilization whose houses had been in the trees. Thinning trunks had been weighed and broken by the heavy fire of their top branches which had laid a thin waste of grey moonshone ash over the ground between. Maybe it was a gallows city blasted by the righteous sun. A soft wind blew ash towards him. It eddied and circled. It was warm, and when he walked a few steps, it burned his feet. Not all the trees had been destroyed. Brown and green streaks still patched some of the black boles. At one a red eye of fire smouldered. It took weeks for flame to retreat from a tree, yet it never totally destroyed it, either. Such wilderness trees always grew again, unless their roots had been absolutely blasted from the earth. It was weird, this scorched wood, reminded him of a ruined city that the inhabitants would one day come back to. Where the moon shone, the birds would return. Its leaves would return. Its leaves would grow greener than before, trunks less beautiful, but branches stronger.

He climbed back, and drove on. Why had the wood been napalmed? Perhaps if he had looked closer he would have seen blackened corpses, the flesh still red within, but undeniably dead forever. He had, as they say, blood on his own hands, but he didn't wish it away, though it seemed to widen the haunting nightmare moonshot visage of the wood he was not glad to have left behind. He couldn't regret what had taken so many years to bring about. He disliked the idea of destiny yet sometimes found it a useful word. There were too many burning trees for it not to lift up from the pool of his mind. Why was he in Algeria? Was it not destiny, that he had rationalized and decided on before taking the deliberate step? What had come first: a desire to help Algeria, or a desire to liberate himself? He could no longer blame these questions on a false sensibility whose only purpose was to break his resolution. Since they came, they were real. He asked so few questions that he was bound to respect them. He was almost grateful to them, though saw the danger of them becoming ends in themselves, questions that needed no answering, as if they were friends whose presence alone was comforting enough. His love for people was causing the death of people, but he could not look on himself as a murderer, because he was no pacifist. As soon as he stepped into Algeria, it was a matter of kill or be killed, and he could not stand idly by. He had been offered money for bringing in the guns and ammunition, but had not taken it. He had wanted to fight so that those considered the exploited and downtrodden could stand up to the so-called master races of Europe. But now it had become a fight for survival – such was their feeling as they ran from trap to trap, killing nevertheless, but fleeing undeniably. He had imagined something more deadly, more numerous, more dangerous, yet he wasn't a man to let his imagination hold him up to the ransom of disappointment. That would have been a blow at his pride, and foolish anyway. Perhaps a dozen groups such as theirs had caused the three brigades to be launched into these mountains, and so were drawn from the Kabylie where the main front was said to be in danger. The French had half a million men deployed in Algeria, which was one good reason for him to be here.

They crossed the main road at midnight. He changed into low gear and, lights full on, climbed the bank. It was wide, and he had an impulse to swing the jeep and go roaring at full speed down the length to get help for Shelley. The lights of a convoy flickered in the distance. Scout cars would reach their crossing-point in a few minutes, and in any case, if he turned along the road, even in the direction where it was dark, he knew that Mokhtar's revolver would press into the back of his neck. He dipped his lights, and went gently down the opposite slope. Shelley was moaning continually in his unconsciousness.

He drove by the moon again, met a regular track to the doctor's village and worked by patient navigation along its faint continual curves. They reached the outskirts just before dawn, and at the same time ran out of petrol.

Mokhtar and Idris went to make sure that no French were in the village, leaving them to darkness and the quiet of the night.

'Listen,' Shelley said, 'use the material in the haversack. You'll need it. And the money, everything.'

It was impossible to clap him on the shoulder and laugh. He sat in the back with him, and it was like being close to a fire. His head was a live coal. 'We'll get a doctor now. We're here. It's all right, at long bloody last.'

'Are there any lights?'

He put his arm around him: 'Hang on. Hang on.' Burning sweat went right through to his skin. He was a man dying of pneumonia. There'd be nothing in this village, and Shelley must have known it, too.

'The sea.'

Frank leaned close. 'What?'

'The sea. I shan't see it.'

'Ah! We'll all see it one day, I'm sure of that.'

'Maricarmen. Write to say I'm OK.'

He'd talked of her; his anarchist girlfriend in Barcelona, last heard of in prison. 'We want a doctor, first. They're taking a hell of a time getting him. It'll be light soon.' The cold dawn wind shelled the soul of its husks, howled around the high plain, the meeting place of south and north winds, sand and gravel, drowning even the wolfish moaning of village dogs, impatient for the warmth of the sun. Blue above the peaks changed to orange, a faint line, and no one to strike it down, nothing to do but welcome it wryly, then turn your back on it while it bled itself to death and rose up white to the top of the sky, to work out its day-long revenge.

Shadows crowded after Mokhtar. They could go forward. Frank let off the brake, and twenty men pushed the car into the village. The sea was in the light of the dawn. Shelley looked beyond to the prison of outside that forced him back into a prison of pain which seemed to be the underground dungeon in which he really lived, a deep prison with a small window through which he could visualize the fawn sea, with a long, high, single mountainous wave of fawn that would never break. Something had frozen it, fixed it against that sky, had looked down from a sky of ice and snow and pinned that high wave on the fawn sea in a never-breaking position. He felt that when this ruthless, impossible pain stopped, he would melt it, turn it to liquid fire that would only flow over himself. Someone dropped a black cloth over him, and he fought free to look again on the fawn sea and the unbreakable wave. The water should shine and move, and he considered he had a right to expect it, but not at this moment to get it. The pain played tricks on him, so it was natural that the world should, too. If the wave broke, he would drown. It became olive-green, white cloud at the top. The black cloth fell over him again, and he saw no more sea. It drew back from the light of the dawn and turned into day.

When the car stuck, they pulled stones away, and when a rut was too deep, they filled the hole in, until it was surrounded by low mud houses, and a few score curious people. When Shelley was laid flat and comfortable inside, they took the car to pieces.

An old man, hale and strong, came out of a house and walked through the crowd with a bundle under his arm. When he looked at them, they drew back. Mokhtar grinned, and watched. It was daylight, and the dogs could sleep. The old man sat cross-legged by the jeep and unfolded the leaves of old sacking. Inside was a long hacksaw and a pack of blades, greased and shining. Four men jacked up the car and took off the wheels, one by one, propping the chassis with stones. The old man sawed through steel posts that held on the hood and top, while other carefully designated demolishers unscrewed everything that it was possible to unscrew. They took out the battery, removed lamps, disconnected bumpers, doors, seats. A human chain stored and hid the priceless material. Tyres were taken from the wheels and cut into four pieces. The old man sawed indefatigably. The divided tools did their work, passed around so that the whole village contributed.

Shelley lay on the bare floor, wracked and worn with pain that had long since turned into a fight against death. He struggled, eyes closed, arms and legs paralysed. 'I got you into this,' Frank said. 'I made you come at the point of a gun. All you wanted was to go back to Tangier and organize another shipment. That would have done more good for the cause.' One sharp beam of daylight penetrated from the back of the room, enough, too much. They'd been wrong. There was no doctor here. He'd been taken by the French two days ago. In any case, it was too late. The world had its black side, set up obstacles, sheer walls in the night that you could not see. You moved. They moved with you, around you, dodged you. When you couldn't get away, you dug a grave, the only escape being into a more permanent and impenetrable blackness. Shelley had found it.

A younger man spread the canvas top on the ground. Others stood back from the main audience and called out advice. Put one sheet on another and roll it all up together. This was obviously what he should do, but now he didn't want to do it. He stopped smiling, folded each piece into quarters like a sheet of paper, placed one on top of the other, and carried them away under his arms.

The truck had been disembowelled: engine set apart from the chassis, surrounded by nuts and bolts freed with spanners from the tool-kit. A stain of oil spread on the hard earth. Most had been drained still warm into a large tin which had once held brine and olives. Frank watched them take it to pieces, trying to escape his tears. It was a slaughter-house: they cut, sawed, chopped, pulled, and nothing cried out, because, though beautifully made and capable of great power, it had never been alive. Yet you had to feel sorry for it, this machine that man had made. It would have been a laughable scene at any other time, vandals tearing to pieces something they could never make – especially in a country like England where they *were* made – in some quiet side-street on a Sunday afternoon. But it was serious here and necessary. War was wasteful and provided loot for the indigent who had nothing. Tinsmiths, blacksmiths, and cobblers craved material, and one wrecked car or lorry provided them with it. Each village and oasis had its turn. A crashed twin-engined transport plane by the highway vanished in the night. Vast territorial departments of Southern Algeria were shod on tyres. Nuts, bolts, wire, strips of aluminium, hinges, rubber, screws, found their way by camelback to the distant *souks* of Siwa, Timbuctu, Fort Lamy, and Tammanrasset. War had burned and crashed around for so long that there was no shortage of certain things, though little came their way on which to build up permanent stability.

He bent down and saw that he was dead.

A few spare limbs and scattered gobbets of the engine remained to be cleared away, sand and gravel sprinkled over the ground to conceal oilstains and metal-dust. It was a time of rejoicing, as if they'd killed the dragon, or drawn in a bumper harvest of scorpion flowers. Planes flew over, but no one was afraid, for the area had been 'pacified' a month ago, meaning that the FLN were free to come back, which the enemy believed impossible since the terrorized inhabitants would not dare to let them. So the planes flew mercifully to the south-west, to smoulder and machine-gun, rocket and carpet-bomb the area they had just vacated.

He lay on the floor inside and let the tears come from him, a pouring out of sorrow and loneliness, heartache and despair. Shelley had known Myra. He was his last link with the world, perhaps with himself. His grief was total and inexpressible. 'He was a brave man,' Mokhtar said. 'A Lion of Judah. I never saw one so brave or skilful. He was wise, a man of books, an American. We've lost him when we needed him most.' Frank stood up. He's lost a machine, a piece of machinery that fearlessly sights and fires a gun, reads a map, marches, and understands that raving brainchild, that fool-proof invention of Marxism and Algerian nationalism. As long as Mokhtar realizes what's been lost – that's all Shelley would want.

A woman washed him and he was carried on a litter to a hole that had been dug by a path leading to their own cemetery. They left a pile of stone on top so that dogs could not drag his flesh out. Those who die are in heaven or in hell, Frank thought, only as long as you remember them. It's a small place they go to for a while, a lodgement in your memory. After that, if there is any afterwards, they are finished for ever. A million worms can't keep together the body and soul that the person once had, even though the body might be said to live on in those million worms. In any case, for the one who dies it is total blackness. We all know that, or ought to. Who would want his soul distributed among a million worms? It doesn't give each of those worms a soul, unless the soul was built in a million segments that had each been a worm before they became your soul.

He could not feel alive, craved oblivion, did not want to be finally left behind by his friend. He looked through what remained of him; an address-book, three passports (the American one was made out in his own name of Shelley Jones, the French for Jean-Jacques Goulet, and one British for John Rowland Hill), a wallet with five one-hundred-dollar bills in the back, a photo of Maricarmen feeding the pigeons in the Plaza de Cataluña in Barcelona, a photo of his mother, and some address-cards. There were two pipes, a copy of Mao Tse Tung's *On Guerrilla Warfare*, a map of Algeria and a few pencils. He made a bundle and put them into his own bag. Then he fell asleep for the last few hours of daylight, and shed tears in dreams that, when he woke, he could not remember.

CHAPTER NINETEEN

THREE French brigades were busy in the Djebel trying to destroy those bands that continually attacked and vanished, harassed and withdrew, but who mostly in the end slipped through their cordons towards the desert. They regrouped outside, marched for the main-base, and moved only at night, lying miraculously concealed during the day in undisturbed hills where no one thought they could possibly be. As they approached the weakened base, revolutionary co-ordination began to work. Mokhtar's group had become twenty and made contact with other bands to left and right. After dark, an hour was spent rubbing way all trace of the daylight hideouts; two hours before dawn were taken by preparing holes and camouflage for the next day's concealment – thus giving only six hours' march out of the twenty-four, and those during darkness. Daytime helicopter patrols saw nothing. Land reconnaissances passed close, but the FLN refrained from ambush, unwilling to betray themselves and upset the delicate mechanism of their attack. To the French, the area was dead. It was pacified. The few indigenous inhabitants knew what was happening and kept silent.

Frank walked along, part of the gathering mass, a man in a dream, with nothing to justify his shape as a human being except the tangled thoughts in his head. He ate little, drank little, knew when it was time to scramble from his tomb and time to get down and dig another. He felt that sooner or later during a long journey there comes a point when the questions that assail you like hailstones have to be answered. The outside world that he had lived in could no longer answer them, which was the one good reason why he had left it. He stood alone, and though many answers came, he found none of them convincing, neither from the left hand nor the right hand. They merely served to block the question-holes inside you, instead of healing them up forever – so that others could grow in their place. In this country, question-holes turned into bullet-holes. Though he did not want perfection, and knew that everything would end up being 'more or less', the answers stopped coming. They had come to Shelley who, seeming more intelligent and complex, was able to accept the rough answers because that was the only way he could go on living. But my brain is clumsy and more simple, he thought, so I can't adapt myself to what isn't perfect and precise and what, therefore, isn't necessarily more true, because I don't have the subtlety to accept something rough-hewn and make it complex out of my own reasoning. I'd be happier if I did, and there'd be far more answers to the few questions I ask, so many that I'd even be able to pick and choose!

A true answer should contain within it a decision and the seeds of action. One such answer – whether true or false – had brought him here, and it had turned out good because, while acknowledging the unalterable and universal principles of the situation, it would also lead to a further spiritual leap into the depths of his life. This he felt strongly enough for it to be true. One answer usually leads to other answers. You could go through life leapfrogging over questions until your death, and the question you might then be moved to ask would not matter – assuming you had time to ask it. It was a case of whether the question was more important, or the answer. Was anyone ever so naive as to imagine you could have both, that questions could contain their own answers, or answers their own questions? Some people had a knack of striding rough-shod from one answer to another, never mind the bloody question, but others took years working towards the perfect question whose answer would solve all their problems, before discovering, in a flash of destructive inspiration, that there could be no complete and final answer. So they left off questions altogether and spiritually died.

After going on for so long with the nagging of half-buried questions you suddenly realize that you have had the answers for a long time. Then, after a while, you find they are not the answers you want and that you did wrong in accepting them so glibly. They are false, in spite of the struggle you went through to obtain them. So you have to set out once more on the long march and the deep search. And that's where matters stand, whether you like it or not.

A march of four nights brought them north of the base. Planes landed and took off from the airfield on a north-south axis, lifting over their heads. Two glittering lines of runway headlights channelled traffic in and out. From the point of view of retreat it would have been sensible to attack from the south-west, since they could then have spread into uninhabited country that, nevertheless, possessed a scattering of wells and water-holes. But they would have forfeited the advantage of attacking from high ground. This problem had been foreseen, and in order to help them in their imperfect line of retreat several neighbouring villages would, on the night of the attack, pass into the hands of the FLN and so keep open a route to the south-*east*, which led to equally wide-open spaces and a similar number of water-wells. Food-stores and hiding-places had been organized in that direction. All this pre-supposed that they would not capture the base. At this elated stage they thought there was a good chance of doing so. This would not only bring back the three brigades from the Djebel in a hurry but would also cause troops to be pulled out of the Grandes Kabylies. At the same time, negotiations concerning the future of Algeria were taking place, and this attack, timed to begin after dusk, might speed them on to the advantage of the Algerian Provisional Government. Main and subsidiary roads leading from the town and oasis were blocked by mines, and traffic using these routes, either to get out or to counter-attack, would be ambushed and dispersed. Reinforcements for the base would, likewise, incur losses. If the garrison wanted to move out, it could only do so to the south, and certain groups were waiting there to harass them. If they did break through, they would find no succour in that direction.

To comprehend perfectly all details of a complex plan, and at the same time to know that he was taking part in it, filled him with a transcendental joy and gave meaning to his existence. He was again united with the only part of the world that mattered. It was a similar experience, certainly as real and perhaps more valuable, to when he was first set on a machine in the factory fifteen years ago. The great lathe was fixed before him, and when the tool-setter showed the blueprint of what was to be made on it and then produced one as an example, he understood the plan, the object, and its purpose in the lorry-engine for which it was due. He was making something useful, and there was no deeper satis-faction, until he chafed at the fact that there was an even greater pattern to strive for and fit his life into.

He lay apart from the others, looking at the sparkling star-carpets overhead, smoking cigarettes plundered from the truck they had taken in an effort to get Shelley to a doctor. I am for progress, progress at any price, but when the world is socialist – then what? Yet I can't say: 'Then what?' until all the world *is* socialist or socialized. And since it will probably take more than my life and lifetime, what's the point of asking: 'Then what?' Perhaps there is a point, and that when socialism is achieved (if that's the word), we'll be free in our spare time to indulge in private mysticism: Zen masters, Zen commissars, Zen Stakhanovites. Even collective mysticism. When the state has withered away we can be mystical for part of the day, and material the other – of the world yet not in it; in the world yet not of it. East and West meet in the east and meet in the west. Unless you want to know what you will feel like after what you are fighting for has come about, you won't begin to fight for it.

The present drew him back, words for Myra, lines of poetry and rigmarole about her and the child, what his love for them meant and ought to mean, words repeated continually in his mind as he walked along, until what had been clear and perfect phrases became garbled by too much repetition, the order even of words uncertain, so that the message he strove to get into his own mind no longer existed, and his body and soul were locked in the effort of climbing and descending, a weird wild pulsing at the heart which blotted out everything, and only the stars were clear when he managed to look up, as if they would give breath to help the receding vision come back to him.

Mokhtar's group moved towards the scintillating edge of the aerodrome. Hand-grenades were given out. A large transport-plane rumbled low as they descended from stone to stone. The cold of the hills left him. He did not even sweat, felt dry and warm, wide awake, careful, and half-afraid. He was coming back to life, and when he turned to look for Shelley, realized with pain that he wasn't there, had been drawn away from the world, was out of sight and reach and rotting under stony earth. The mass thinned into a line, guided perfectly into place by the perimeter and approach lights, and men set as markers, standing up from the holes in which they had been hidden to beckon and point. Mokhtar had an accurate map of guard-posts and pickets, all details vouched for by Algerians who worked at the base. By giving away such secrets, they needn't fear for their jobs, for there would be more work when the attack was over.

Hundreds of men, some in uniform, some in Moslem dress, a few in European clothes, picked their way between the stones in silence, the smell of spice and cleanliness flowing in the wind. The night blackened, no moon. The commonplace bothered him, gravel in his sandals, ants and lice biting. He never bargained for a mass attack. Was it a raid merely, or a Dien Bien Phu?

They flattened for cover and went forward, a thousand deadly lizards closing towards the northern edge of the airfield. They passed under the tall posts of the approach lights, half sawn through, whose bulbs glowed steadily, as if to say that beyond this point lay the darkness of the heart, and that all who went there must leave the passport of their soul, and if there was a quick retreat, there would be no collecting it on your way out.

Clandestine wire-cutters had cleared gaps, through which *ferka* after *ferka* found a way. As guerrillas, they had gradually amalgamated into an army whose discipline was pooled like a spiritual experience. He watched and felt it. There had been no drill practice to make cohesion instinctive. A movement of social intelligence went through all of them, and he hoped such a valuable lesson was not only possible in preparation for an act of war. Beyond their darkness the sky was blue with light. East of the aerodrome spread the European quarter and the oasis. In the confines people were still walking, the curfew not yet down. Frank felt himself at the end of an enormously wide tunnel, along which he had staggered for hundreds of miles. An outlet into the land of dreams at last lay in front, which was about to be destroyed – or some of it, or none of it. The glow on the sky was a sheltering roof that lured them on. It was the first time he'd been waiting to attack with so many others, with a feeling of being an empty shell whose weight he could not carry, of having nothing to lose but wanting even less than ever to lose it.

Huge explosions came from villages east of the main agglomeration, shaking the ground under them. While all attention and, it was hoped, some reinforcements began moving in that direction and towards skirmishing in the south, the main force went in from the north. Openings were still being laid in the barbed wire. Heavy machine-gun bursts came from the outskirts of the town. The line spread beyond the wire, and he seemed to be on his own. Dust was blown by a strengthening wind, and grenades weighed him down. A hundred yards on was a sandbagged post and wireless hut, and beyond planes were silhouetted in their dispersal points by the airfield lights, which for some reason had not been shut off. The ground vibrated from exploding shells or bombs, he could not tell which, but he was running, now in a group, too close, too close, the gap in them elsewhere, choking from dust. Someone fell, and he went against the continual buzzing as if his head were jerking at invisible telegraph wires. He was alone again, running diagonally between two defence posts. He was not alone: bodies flattened by the wire were busy at it, as if that were all they would have to contend with. It seemed dreamily slow. He worked his way along and ran back towards one of the posts from the rear, unhooked a grenade, took out the loop, and fell flat to do the counting. Above the gunfire someone was sobbing. He was impatient to get through the wire, but hugged the bomb. He had no desire to stand up and let go, wanted to lay his head on it like a pillow and fall asleep. The world inside would splinter and come to rest. He would be in the desert, and out of it for ever.

He leapt up and threw, no time to drop before the crack of dawn and dusk, daylight and night, and blue-orange flashes bumping over him. Stones and dust shivered and fell, and he ran on all fours, then bent low and stumbling over bodies that gave to his weight. Alone once more, he saw how organization bred chaos and loneliness. He stood up, almost bursting from his own sobs. He was full of fear at suddenly not knowing what to do. It lasted a moment. Smoke and danger spilled out of the sky. You could smell it in the dust, and in the resin of shattered posts. Shadows filled a gap in the wire, and firing from the rear diminished. The airfield was lit in every detail.

A hand of great strength pulled at both legs, threw him with a crash on to the stones. The air was on fire, and he covered his head with folded arms. There was no sky left, nor light. He did not know how long he lay there, but similar earthquakes erupted all around, and he was riding a sea of stones, explosions punctuating the continuous wind and wirehowl that lay at the root of his bruised ears. He seemed to have been down for hours, then staggered towards the ineradicable noise. The group he had been with was nowhere to be seen.

At the twin-engined plane he unhooked two grenades and planted one to explode at each huge wheel. He ran to another and did the same. Blinding light opened in a split second as fighter-planes farther on the airfield fell like collapsing beds into a heap of fire and dust, then burst into flames. His own planes exploded, one an old Dakota so full of petrol that a column of smoke roped over it, and he ran back towards the wire, screaming at the shock of heat.

To see such priceless and beautiful machinery burning brought a feeling of shame. It was obscene to destroy engines by these shorthand sadistic explosions after so much effort and precision went into making them. To pulverize machinery would have been a pain to his manhood, except that these planes were used to hunt and burn them out. His hair was singed, face blackened by smoke. There was time to smile at his reflections, sentimental mixed feelings that never lead to vacillation because what you wanted to do was always stronger than what you felt about it. Through the smoke there was one last plane intact, and he ran towards it. He tied a length of string to his unpinned grenade and threw it up and over the cockpit, where it hung, and he unwound the string and laid a heavy stone on it, so that the bomb would stay high and do the work of two.

A black cloud lifted, gave a great push as he ran between burning huts. Others were turning back to the wire, shadows in the distance emerging from the smoke. Exploding bombs forced them to the ground. Frank ran on. There weren't enough to meet the counter-attack. Some were trying, bullets spitting around him. He waited for them to come through the gap in the wire. Mokhtar ordered a halt to their firing. The approach lights of the airfield had been destroyed, leaving patches of light and darkness according to how far they were from the fires. A huge transport-plane overhead that had been trying to land now turned south when rifle-fire struck it from the hills. Houses were burning in the European district. A great roll of wire burst into the air.

Retreating shadows melted into the cover of smoke and flames, some showing their backs, while the better-trained flattened and moved only when the wish rather than necessity took them. Mokhtar saw him and came over. 'We leave,' he said. 'Too many counter-attacks. We can't hold them.' Bombs from their own mortars fell in front.

They ran over the fallen posts, split and flayed by dynamite, wire, and glass underfoot. 'Where are they?'

'They've gone back,' said Mokhtar. They lay behind rocks. Frank emptied a magazine at encroaching figures who, he thought, might be Germans from the Foreign Legion, so sent off another clip for Stalingrad. They rushed across an open space and sun-fires behind made them hard targets, but several fell and they drifted away. Mokhtar gathered survivors and drove them through the safe ground of a gully. Frank caught a final view of the airfield burning, burning planes, light-beams, threading smoke, corpses, and wasted wire.

They climbed. Frank was lighter of ammunition and grenades, but felt like a lead man going up, impossible to lift himself. Shells exploded from the town, and small arms fire rippled overhead.

'Are we the last out?'

'Absolutely. Except the wounded,' – who were still shooting or being slaughtered. 'Both,' Mokhtar said. 'And the dead are being killed again.' Planes had taken off to drop flares over the hills in front.

CHAPTER TWENTY

THE horizon of obvious retreat was lit up green and blue. Night no longer existed. They turned east instead of north, the burning town in view all night. Bonfires had been started on the hillsides and peaks while the attack was still going on, and now they became white and orange under the flares, a warning to keep away from the direction they burned in. Helicopters were machine-gunning around their flames. A tongue of napalm licked up a mountainside, a sudden pictorial manifestation that made him shiver with horror. From white, it turned red, rose into a column of deep orange, shooting a smoke-pillar through the greenish light of the flare that preceded it. Handley should be here to paint this, Frank thought, though maybe it would be better for him and all concerned if he imagined it, otherwise such confrontation might burn out the spirit of his genius. It's enough to destroy any painter, though I'd like Handley to see it, because he's the only one I can think of whom it might not ruin.

They joined others, walking as quickly along the ravine as they dared without slipping twenty feet into the dried river-bed below. Most had guns, but no ammunition. A few had unused grenades swinging from their belts. Frank had a clip of thirty rounds. Mokhtar, who carried a revolver and a long sheathed knife, grunted and hounded, pushed them along, threatening to kill any who dropped behind, and Frank preferred being on his own in the belief that he would have a better chance of getting clear. The effort of each step was too intense, and for the first time he felt no automatic urge to go on and on and increase the rate of his advance. His only desire was to slow it and stop, drag behind and separate from the others. But he kept on because safety still lay with numbers. Four months had taken the guts out of him. Perhaps tonight would be the worst, and all would be well if he could pull himself along by the light of each star, drag into the fire of another day. Fortunately, there was the insistent sparkling cold to beat at night that tried to get a grip on you, pierce through despair and sharpen your marrowless bones. The mixture of sensations – climate, terrain, and the terrors of your own soul – made you walk. Mountainous shapes ahead, shadows, noise of planes passing that could not see them, frightened him. When they stopped he shivered. A sliding stone caused his hands to shake, made him wish for brandy and cigarettes, tea and food. But there was nothing – from now on walking through emptiness and touching the last emptiness in yourself. How long, how long? There was no sense in hoping to get out, looking beyond it to another state, because this was life, all there was, the vast dark area of the end that wanted you to die before letting you free from it. It encircled him, and to be encircled was to be blind.

By day they hid. He crawled along the rancid rocky oven of the earth. The sun festered on to his grey hair and blackening skin. He spent days on his belly. He was a snake. He lost his mind. The file of soldiers made a feeler from the laager of lorries, and winding up the hill passed a dozen yards away, noise and stone chips dancing around. One of the others, farther up the slope, stood and fired. He was shot dead, and the patrol carried two of their own wounded down the hill. He lay still, nursing himself on the rockbed of his cunning. In the darkness of the night he saw mirages of the day, visions of snow-mountains that Shelley had passed on to him. Glacier peaks were forested with pine and spruce, and there were green fields on the lower slopes, huts and scattered houses, cattle, camels, and mud dwellings, lower and lower, descending to scorching saltflat and sand and the immense grey stone of the wilderness, and finally to the endless ocean of sand-dunes. He ate live scorpions, scooped mud, went back to the beginning of creation. By the seashore of the desert, in sand-cliffs, were tunnels that he lived in, tunnels lined with white bricks, and he walked among them. An explosion would come, because Algerians wandering by the surf mimed out a warning. In one of the cool corridors he waited, wondering if the tunnels would collapse and bring eggtimer sand pouring down on him to suffocation. He stood up and listened, waited. From the bowels of these brick-lined tunnels came a muffled roar, and the walls he looked at shook, but stayed intact and safe. Somewhere below, that he would never reach or visualize, the air had grown into combustible gas and had exploded, shaken the deepest foundations of his life and vision, opened the hiding-places of himself and all that his heart had never thought of to desire, and all that he had always been too terrified to face or wish for.

There was no jungle in this universe. Above the sand was flinty wilderness, and higher still the meadows began. Then out of the forest spread the land of eternal snow, up to the final great peaks, the land of the abominable Wendigo, the primal layers from his underground Alhambra to the mountains of the sky and snow where the soul could sometimes go now that the galleries had reverberated to this deepset mysterious explosion that spoke to him from all the sounding places of the walls. He stood, waiting for the sand to burst through the small white bricks, stayed calm and terrified as if he were in a dream, while the grey blades of outside sunlight moved like a windmill round and round over his eyes. The only sound was the hiss of the sea, the metallic surf lazily striking the brilliant sand. Between him and the beach a tree was burning, and while he stood in the same position he saw white flames rolling over it, shaking out smells of bay-leaf and juniper, lemon and rosemary. White phosphorous was burning on its foliage, and he was pleased because the spectacle seemed to wear off his fear and awe of the explosion far underground. The tree burned but did not die, glowed and lit up the sea-beach when the sun fell.

He stayed buried, paralysed, unable to look up at the burning sun. There was no urine left in him, and he pulled roots from the earth to stop the flesh of his two jaws meeting. I'm going to die, he thought. I can't go on. He was alone, forgot when he had parted from or lost the others, stood at the entrance to his brick-lined burrow, and no one came in nor even near it. The sea was an ugly steel-flat torment edging the yellow sand and reflecting the sun's heat at him with bleak ferocity.

When he sensed that the world beyond his closed lids had turned black, and felt the night air chafing him, he stood up again. To save rummaging into his haversack for a compass he selected the Pointers of Ursa Minor and kept the dim North Star to his left. Eyes opened and accustomed to the dark, he was at the head of a wide valley, low hills on either side. Smokeless, and without lights or fire. In the clarity of his mind he speculated on how many sins one had to commit before reaching the kingdom of heaven, how many good people abandon who had come to lean on you more heavily for support than you realized in your mal-formed desire to be free of them. Your life depended on people who needed you. Nancy and the children, Myra and their child, Shelley and the girl he had left in Barcelona prison – he had abandoned them to help people whom he wanted to need him, but who, in reality, had learned well enough how to help themselves, a break with settled fate in order to control the circumstances of his own life.

He walked, feeling only the rub at his feet of grit and dust. Even the ubiquitous dog-jackal no longer broke its heart in the interstellar spaces of the night. He plodded through an unlit silence, in no hurry any more to do fifteen or twenty miles before rest. No one was on the road, no stragglers from the attack. He seemed too far north, accord-ing to Mokhtar, but remembering many glimpses of Shel-ley's map (more clear and familiar now than the cycling map he had used as a youth around Nottingham), he kept his track parallel to the mountains, and in a few days he would go up and over them till sooner or later he reached the Kabylie mountains which backed on to the Algerian coast. He was on his own, in no man's land and no man's army, felt clear-brained and energetic, and as he walked he did not think of fighting again except to decide that he was armed against friend or foe, which thought gave him not only freedom (to say it aloud) but also an affirmation of life that he was determined to hold on to. Without Mokhtar's group, he was exposed to friend and enemy alike, though if he weren't knifed or shot by unsuspecting friends he could always show the FLN identity card given him in the Monts des Ksours. Three weeks east-north-east would get him into Tunisia, and he was tempted to go there, but he wasn't in that sort of mood yet, still wanted to try his arm in the area of main fighting to the north. The purpose that had led him here raged more clearly under his vacillations of selfish desire. The tree had burned off its foliage, but the tree was even hardier, and ready to grow again. By Tunis he could reach London in a month, but he was not yet drawn to that other section of his heart. As much as to see Myra and the child, he craved in the bursting heat of the day to go back to Nottingham and visit his children. The catastrophic act of leaving them struck full force, and he wept in the night, saying not yet to himself, not yet.

The bottle was full, warm, and slightly salt, and he sat down to uncork it. He smoked a cigarette, carefully lit and hooded in the middle of the night, took off his sandals and rubbed his feet free of grit. They were tough, and he wasn't bothered by soreness, saw himself walking barefoot, for when these sandals were gone he might not find more. He had no fear of the wilderness. There was food in his pack, and he could last a few days even without. He had Algerian money, mostly coin, which might help if he met nomads, or got into an oasis one night. But there was no need to set himself spiralling on the course of desperation. He wanted no plans, especially those that might lead him astray or to disaster. He would respect patience and instinct and so be helped by them.

During the walk he enumerated the contents of his knapsack. There were biscuits and chickpeas, chocolate and sardines, dried figs and a mush of lentils. There was a map which Shelley had taken from the back pocket of a guidebook, and annotated against other maps, as well as a compass, binoculars, pencils, and notebook. The watch was in his pocket because the strap had rotted some weeks ago. He had fifty cigarettes, matches, and an unworn shirt for use when the one on his back fell off in shreds. There was a three-pronged clasp-knife, an oil-soaked rag and pull-through, and a small screwdriver. This traveller's bric-a-brac took little enough space, but to it was added a water-bottle, a light machine-gun, and one thirty-round clip of ammunition. Of the three passports, he had kept only the British one, in order to back up his story if he were captured.

Walking alone at midnight hammered schemes into the head, inebriation of hope that softened the brain and bled even the blood-poison out of you, that acid protection of borderline health that kept you alert and visionary under the stars, and cool under the sun. There's two of us, he muttered. There's Frank and there's Dawley, and we'll look after each other, so that neither of us will come to harm. The left hand must look to what the right hand does, and both can lash out for the benefit of each other, all for one and one for all. You're a one-man circus, but whatever you do you can't retrace your steps or go back into the imperative-negative blackout of the past for reasons of ease and sentimentality. Walking backwards is as evil as writing your name backwards, an exercise in weak-minded satanic self-destruction. He felt the black web of the blackest spider shaking before him, its fabric beckoning when he turned towards it, as if death were really and readily stalking and had taken the place of his own backward glance. He had never felt the weight of evil so close, and this time when he considered himself on a great mission of good.

He turned again, but whatever lurked in his wake was there no longer. It fitted too well perhaps to the tune of his own footsteps and the midnight rock-shadows shifting across his eyes, and he became confused and blinded on swinging quickly to try and catch a glimpse of him or it. The wilderness is full of ghosts. Everyone comes here when they die, or when life has ripped the bowels out of them. If an atom-bomb drops the shadows will rush in million upon million to choke the living, suffocate those who elected to come here.

Whoever pursued him (or dogged him, for there could be no purpose in ever catching up) wandered through the dream-Arabian deserts of his own mind, in those villages where he sketched the depraved inhabitants of his secret landscapes. All houses were crumbling and all people old, or eaten by the vices of their ancestors which kept the pretty mouths of their daughters half-open and their eyes large. Even the hills on which their villages stood were falling to sand and ruin. This pilgrim who sketched his own world and followed him through black night and bright day played a mouth organ, and his best drawing was an auto-portrait of a lonely, thin, long-haired, half-young, pain-racked figure with a meagre wallet on his back, and a vine-stick in hand, making his way across a plain, the eternal pilgrim, poet-painter, still endeavouring to escape the packed tormenting dissidence within himself, to find another pilgrim with the symptoms of the same disease and totally infect him.

You could not hide among the rocks and wait in ambush for him, because he was as cunning as you would ever be. In any case, you do not meet your pursuer when hundreds of miles of wilderness are spread around. And if during the day he caught you up while you slept, then he could do you no harm, for anyone was entitled to share your dreams and get what they could out of them, and put what they could into them. No matter how long he follows me, he thought, and I expect he'll stick close behind for a while, he'll get little enough to eat or drink on this thin leg of the trip.

He walked beyond dawn. Pokers were laid over the shoul-ders of the mountains as if the sun were handing out knighthoods that would last only one day. They were pale orange, about to merge with each other as the bloody middle pulled itself up among them. He crawled across the map at half an inch a day, soon to turn north and head for the mountains. In a pool of water he saw his walnut face, and the sun burned as if to draw a deeper hue out before finally releasing him.

His legs would not stop walking, and he let them have their way. They would run his soul into the ground. There were no shadows in the daytime except his own, the two of them going along pleasantly together. The sky was empty except for a few birds wheeling some way ahead, but he went on in a state of total alertness, looking for any movement in the flanking hills, and listening for the first cat-purr of aircraft or lorry-engines.

The valley widened, hills far away. In the middle of the plain a few birds gyrated above a black mound, angrily trying to make a foothold among the mass of birds already there. He threw stones, and a score of humpbacked hawks rushed into the sky, so huge and many that he thought they might attack him. One by one they swooped down again at the camel carcass, wings wide but perfectly still before the feet touched down. He stood some yards away and watched, fascinated at this manifestation of natural activity. They tore and scraped deep into the open flank of the dead animal, with many sharp swipes exchanged among themselves as they fought to close in on more tender regions. He walked near and they ignored him, as if no danger could threaten the ranks of their hunched backs set against him. Triumphant and all-conquering, they indulged in a rite peculiar to themselves rather than a common and horrible meal. They fed as if, after a great and valiant effort, they had dragged the camel from the track while it still walked. He threw another stone, but when they did not move, he passed and walked on, hoping that soon he would catch up the people and the caravan to which the dead animal had belonged.

He found a sheltering rock where the valley narrowed, rested where there was shade. He never completely slept, haunted by the thought of fire, the dread of a sudden-opening bomb that would come on like a furnace and burn him into the rocks where he lay. There was nowhere for him to run, but he hoped to hear the warning of the engine and get one last look at life before it happened or, if there was still time, roll into a position where he would not be seen. Dawn was the hour to look for a hiding-place, but he had for once ignored this necessary caution. He didn't know why. There was no hurry, and it was unwise to let exultance carry you beyond the pitch of mere tiredness, to the insomnia of exhaustion when the shallow sleep hardly brought back your energy. In rest you withdrew from the world, closed your eyes, in sleep but not of it, bound by innumerable steel threads to the stones that ultimately refreshed you enough for another long span of the wilderness.

It was impossible to edge right out of the sun, and his legs and feet seemed too close to a fire. He slept with head covered by his arms, locked in a fever of sweat and darkness.

A cool breeze opened over his legs, shadow and wind, as if he lay under a tree and the leaves rustled. A bayonet scratched the length of his clothes, grazing his skin, tugged as if to pull him from the rock. The shade had gone. He dreaded to see on opening his eyes that he had been caught. His senses swam in an ocean of darkness, then gathered together, separated and became suddenly clear. Reaching to the gun, he was surprised at the steel touch, gripped it hard and opened the safety-catch. Hearing no voice, he expected the bayonet or knife to go right into him. They were not standing close by, but perhaps lying flat a few feet away, watching, waiting for the moment of his greatest hope before striking so as to get the most amusement out of his death. The shadow came again, a rustling of palm-leaves. They were playing with him. He heard a soft noise, like an arm coming to rest.

Opening his eyes, a huge black vulture sat a yard away, hooded, unmoving, yellow and black eyes beamed on him. It seemed all set to sit there for months, though patience could not describe the fixed gaze. Its eyes were as inhuman as its feet, head, drawn-back wings, part of the expressionless whole, two coloured stones someone had thrown at it that had stuck right in and been used from then on as eyes, when instinct would have done just as well, because it looked as if it had no need to see.

He moved his leg, horrified but not frightened, wanting to kill the bird. The blue-black, glossy feathers were unreal, shining in the sun as if they were wet. When he stood up, a ripple went across one of its eyes, and he stared into them as if they were daring him to push down their impossible wall that blocked him from a world he should know about, to horizons of heaven and hell beyond the scattered horrors of the plain that he was already familiar with and only wanted to defeat and forget.

It was the middle of the afternoon and he had slept a few hours out of the day. The buzzard must have lost its glut from the camel, and set off through the scorching bileless sky to find more flesh. A line of others sat along the bottom of the valley like blackened tree-stumps that had burned down years ago, whose ash had been utterly blown away. The one nearest lessened in size, and he levelled his gun. To shoot that head would show nothing beyond the wall of merciless unfathomable eye. Within the eye was a desert brain that craved food from a desert that had none. Its life was a miracle, and if it hated anything it was only the earth from which it could get so little food, and this hatred was a javelin for nosing out the dying, whose digested flesh would let them fly eternally through this hell-sky and sometimes perch on the baking land. If he shot it, would they tear the dead bird to pieces? Or will they gang up on me? They lived on the mountains to the north and roamed over thin forests and wilderness, hunting and haunting all flesh and blood from their endless province of space between sky and earth.

He walked slowly, gun levelled, not wanting to waste a bullet, or send the noise of its death far enough to bring worse depredators on him. It was a pity; plucked and roasted it would make good food, tough but filling, though the smoke of cooking might also give him away. It was well-protected, he thought, by the hard laws of the world – passing out of its gaze and continuing his journey.

From a range of higher ground he saw the buzzards squatting where he had slept, as if still waiting for the last crack of life to leave him before coming on to where he was now. Their numbers had increased, holding a meeting perhaps on why they had permitted him to escape, discussing bad tactics and better measures for next time. Two people were walking through them, and a cloud went into the air like large flakes of burnt paper. He was disturbed at being followed, when all he wanted was to climb away from the track and rest, instead of walking on through the wide open day. The sharp beak had torn skin from his arm, and gave an intense ache. He poured water on, which burned as if it were acid. Then he drained the bottle, which did not filter through to his thirst.

When the first breeze of dusk wakened against him he saw a well in the distance surrounded by tents and camels. He hoped he had left his pursuers far enough behind to stop and get water for his bottle. The heat of his shirt, which did not normally bother him, now began to torment as if it were actually on fire, afflicting his whole body with an intolerable fever.

A thin drum-rhythm sounded. There were trees by the well, the shadows of their branches marked on tent roofs. Faint ropes of smoke curled towards clear sky, and the crazy fluting notes of a *raita* chipped the air and mixed with the pattering voice of the drum. The enchanted sound of alert and graceful music in the middle of war and wilderness emphasized how isolated and alone he was, and that he no longer felt any emotion or loss when he speculated on people who formed a great part of his life. The rope that held him to them was burned free. He could not remember how many weeks and months he'd been away. All disturbing memories had withdrawn beyond some horizon he'd left far behind or passed unnoticed in the night. Each broad day was an island that he crossed, and so was each night, and he felt that without injury from war or nature, the desert was a healthy place for one to live in, with a little food and water now and again. Optimism was arrowed into his veins, a love of life in the continuous beauty of light and air, and emptiness that was quiet enough for thought and sufficiently wide to suck out all weariness.

Children came to watch him: a boy in a ragged robe, and a *mèche* of hair sprouting from a shaved head that made the skull seem too big. He stared, while the girl smiled. The men and women from the crumbling wall of the well were looking at three ragged performers between the tents. He unclipped his bottle, and stood to watch, all of them now silently waiting. The music came faster. An old man played the *raita*, scarred and bitten legs coming below his rags, feet slightly moving to the sound of his own music. A clout had been twisted around his skull, and he was staring into the sky but away from the sun, with a smile of tenderness that hoped for some sort of reward. Frank thought he was blind.

Camels tied to the trees were searching the length of their tethers for roots. A boy threw stones to drive them back into the shade. They nuzzled and pawed the ground. The music caught his blood and he forgot his thirst and fever. The second performer wore a long, patched robe, had a white face, and reddish or hennaed hair. He did nothing except move his head from side to side and look scornfully at those gathered to watch, presenting a demonic aspect of thin wide lips and a long chin covered with a grey beard, and a scanty moustache with a gap under his nose where it would not grow. At his feet lay a damp sackbag, something moving inside as if striving to shift with the music.

No one spoke. They watched glumly. The third member was a lugubrious young man who played the drum. Black curly hair came from under his embroidered skull-cap, and his dress was a long dark robe with odd buttons down the front. He played his single stick as if disliking the inspired rhythm it produced, his intelligent face made sensitive because of his distaste for the job he was doing, as if between sessions or on the move he escaped such a life by dreaming over some tattered but unimportant book.

Drum and *raita* dominated the silence and finally deepened it, each tap-note soaring sharply. Frank gained strength from their fluency, forgot his fever till the whole world he saw pressed close and gentle against his eyes. The white-faced, red-haired man softened his scornful look for a moment, then reinforced it and stared towards the mountains as if his eyes would cut a way through while the music, in spite of its faster beat, never lost the fluid racing lines of its rhythm. Yet it remained graceful and weak, pipe and drum trying their uttermost to become powerful rather than merely hypnotic. The old man's body curved, but the youth with the drum stood with hunched shoulders and tapped out quicker rhythms with just as much ease as at the slower beats of the beginning, his look of impotence growing, as if his performance had gone on long enough and the time had come to end it. Yet the speed increased, when Frank thought it impossible. The audience seemed to be waiting for a revelation. To Frank all those in the desert looked haggard and exhausted, worn-out and noble, as if about to wake from sleep. Whether working or resting, this common quality linked every face and lost itself deep beneath the skin, shaping the bones, steeping their eyes in it and giving them the pathetic dignity of people struggling to visualize their place in a world of food and water which was continually denied them.

Palm branches flipped and rustled in the wind, grit whirling around their feet and faces. Drum and pipe notes jumped on every grain and dragged it to earth, because no one was disturbed by it. The white-faced man of the three resumed his look of disgust, his lips curling, as if ready to give them up as lost and vanish for ever into the orange-tinted hills. As if on second thoughts he bent down to the filthy sack at his feet and moved his hand around inside, a look of green, glistening fear on his face. The old man with the flute weaved more violently, veins humped on his tobacco-coloured temples, as if about to faint or fall to the ground and still go on with his thin, wild music. The man bending down at the sack suddenly sprang up, holding a live snake.

The crowd drew back in fear from this man possessed of power and talents beyond the limits of their lives, holding a weapon that could strike them but not him. Perhaps they hoped he'd lost sight of them, so they stood still, and from his expression of phosphorous rage he certainly saw no one, the pupils of his small eyes shifting in bile, mouth open and moving to insensate music. The snake held them, spade-head and fangs fixed by the neck as it coiled round his arm to fight the demonic grip. But it was impotent against such strength and he smiled in a way that set the audience laughing – which he took as a signal for the real battle to begin.

He roared from his wide-open mouth, long and grating,

as if he would destroy his own throat. A shade of fear passed over him. The strong snake lashed around the sinews of his bare arm, a loathsome scene that Frank stayed and stared at and felt the deep blackness opening below all sense and thought, his whole world collapsing as if he were about to drop into the cold black water, back into primeval slime that lay beyond the coast of horror. The real island was the truthful inner night that only truth could show you, and only truth lead you safely away from. His bowels turned to water, his brain to ice.

Palm branches swayed. Nothing obtruded. He stared at the madman turned savage who held up the snake and fought, mocking it to do its worst, bringing it closer to his open mouth as if to spit on it, then spun it round, stunning it against the air. In such an elemental contest, he could not sympathize either with man or snake. Its force pierced all stomachs and pinned them into awe. Both knew absolutely what they were involved in, a common image proclaimed under a life-and-death struggle. Frank felt a desire to empty his gun at the three men and end their show. Yet looking at it had cured his fever, left no pain from his scrapes and scratches. His blood flowed marvellously free in its proper circuits, so he let go of his gun, thinking to save his rage and ammunition for the purpose first rationally intended.

The snake's head, dazzlingly coloured, a large desert asp, worked farther from the grip of his manic fist, turned to plant its scorching fangs in the soft armflesh. Perhaps he was immune to its poison, Frank thought, a man of so much snaky bile bursting to mingle with the sweet venom of the snake, so that if the snake bit him it had an equal chance of dying. They became one animal, set on introvert destruction, the reptile an arm of his arm trying to kill the rest of the body even if it died itself. It turned the man into a monster, and as the fight went on between the man determined not to be bitten and the snake not to be strangled, it became a fight for sanity among the scattering notes of insane music, the man and the snake one normal sane creature locked in a dream-battle of reality that by some dread fluke the world had at last given him to watch, as if looking at himself in some great mirror that stretched from earth to sky, across beautifully painted scenery, and showing a reflection of himself set there by his own eyes.

He forgot everything. The snake relaxed, its life almost squeezed out. The skin on the man's face was yellow, bones stretching as if he and the snake might after all die together. Their scene was a door, an exit and entrance, but Frank longed for it to be over, for he and all people to be released and set back to normal life – if such a thing were ever possible while this day that had been unlike any other lasted.

The snake revived, but the man was quicker, used his other hand to grip it halfway along the body while the thin whip of its tail caressed his wrist. He had mastered it at last, and Frank felt a wave of joy, shared the feelings of those around who grunted and smiled at the man's feat. He felt thirsty again, thinking the show was finished. But the music weaved with more intensity, as if something else was yet to come. The victory had seemed too easy, carried the disappointment of a false dawn while the real day had still to be witnessed.

The *raita* fledged up its notes as if scattering feathers into the air, followed by drumbeats set on the impossible job of chasing them, and dragging them back to earth. The white-faced man held the snake, limp and pliable, not yet dead, gripped it with two hands near the neck.

A groan broke from everyone. With eyes closed, he was biting the snake at the neck, ripping into its flesh. The music stopped, the youth turned away, but the old man looked on, shaking as if ready to fall, but his face gentle and smiling at the victory helped by the exertions of his music. The snake-head was in his mouth, its body thrashing helplessly while his knife-teeth tore at it. As he bit on the snake the wound in Frank's arm burst into excruciating pain, the same ache as before only increased to such a pitch that he roared out. The wound burned, the air grew black, but he fought for consciousness. At his cry, other men shouted as if they too had old wounds that came back to life at the sight of the snake eaten in its final convulsions of life.

He forced himself to the horror, dying with the snake yet killing it himself, legs shaking, jaws locked. The man was swallowing pieces of the snake, eating it alive. Where had they come from, this sect from the bowels of the white and livid earth? His eyes were closed, stomach expanding under his rags, falling in, pushing out again, an unleashed madness devouring the earth's own snakes.

There was a movement behind, two newcomers approaching the outer fringe of the audience. They had been watching for some time, and one of them broke through with a revolver lifted, and Frank saw Mokhtar fire shot after shot into the body of the man who was eating the snake. He fell, writhing and spitting, flesh and blood pouring from his mouth and wounds. Mokhtar shouted at the others, a wild rational rage in his words, and they began to move. The dusk was blood red, colouring the wilderness all around as they attended to water and fires. The air before Frank went black. His eyes were pressed into his head, and he fell to the earth, raving in his fever that had returned with devastating fire.

Soil closed around him. The sun vanished, taking away consciousness, and all pictures out of his mind. He burned in the grey ash-bed of the night, he crawled towards water to escape the cares of the world, using the last remnants of mole-like strength after he fell. Mokhtar and Idris dragged him to a tent. Opening his eyes, he saw nothing. They closed, driven by fear into beneficent blackness.

He was moved with the caravan to the nearest village, the turbulent camelback journey distorting his black sleep. Lemon-rind was rubbed round his mouth, and he fought eyeless against water dripping over his teeth. He was tied on, a blanket over him, where he would drink his own sweat, rave, and freeze. The village was by a spring in the mountains, with tree groves nearby, and a wall of cliff banking him off against the north.

PART THREE

CHAPTER TWENTY-ONE

His impulse was to get out of Lincolnshire, break camp and flee like some nomad chief who feels the approach of an almighty force that will sweep him away. To lose such a painting was a disaster, the thieving of his life's soul, a base robbery of his best work that barred a desperate groping to achieve something in life.

He walked up and down all night, in his studio and then around the house. A trip to London always brought bad luck, stirred the cauldron of fate, cut all guidelines and distorted his compass-bearings. And yet, he decided, it wasn't the time to flee, for he slowly realized with the coming of dawn that whenever he thought about abandoning everything he was on the point of solving whatever bothered him. A revelation was at hand. Standing far down under his studio window, by the old tree which leaned so close that it was continually lopped to give more light, he looked over the fence and across the field, towards the wood where, a fortnight ago, he had seen someone sniping him with field-glasses. It was such a facile explanation to all his troubles that it must be true. He lit another cigar. London hadn't been entirely unlucky, merely confusing. He'd been in love with her for longer than he'd imagined, but their love-making only emphasized the unholy fact that she felt nothing comparable for him and never could, because she still hankered after Frank Dawley who had vanished months ago into Algeria on a bout of misguided and cranky idealism. If I leave Lincolnshire where do I go, with a wife and seven children, a dog, two cars and two caravans, and a brace of *au pair* girls? You don't often hear of a flat to let in London with a car-park attached. He looked up at the stars for some time, before realizing there weren't any, I'm too old for baling out. Forty-three is the pineapple age, sweet and upright. Yet maybe I'd get young again if I blew all this up. The bourgeois trap is a long one, a tunnel without end, a burrow. You went into it though, and forgot your dynamite. Nobody lured you. I'm not trying to get out. I'm leaving nobody. I'm not that sort. I'm not at the end of my tether. But I don't have ideals to help me off the hook and as an excuse to bolt.

A long tartan dressing-gown was drawn tightly around him, each hand lost in large sleeve folds and resting on the kitchen table. He was perfectly still, and when Enid entered she thought he was sleeping in that position. But his light-brown eyes were open, gazing at empty air. Water rattled in the kettle. 'Haven't you slept?'

He didn't look round. 'Why do I only crave what I've lost? A man should want more out of his life than that.'

'What else is there though, except to want what you haven't got?'

'I want both,' he said, smiling faintly to reflect the ice-old bitterness. 'What you haven't yet got is what you lost. They're the same thing, let's face it. God forgive me for getting all mystical, but when I look at those fields near the coast after a day of rain in the summer, and when it's beginning to clear up about seven, and they go all soft and distinct under the sun reddening through cloud – then I begin to want what I haven't yet got, and realize it's something that I lost in the days when I was half-conscious and didn't know I had anything to lose. In those days, I was king of myself and knew exactly what I wanted, which turned out to be this. I wish it weren't true that I had everything a person is supposed to want, that I wasn't in a position a left-handed person would give his left arm to be in. Even though I know I've got such a lot more work to do, I know that my life and all I'll damn well do is a failure. If I didn't have this lump of cold water always in my stomach maybe I'd never do these paintings that make me feel such a failure.'

Whenever he was in this rare mood of self-questioning and self-pity she felt full of love towards him. Yet at the same time she was afraid, knowing from experience that it was inevitably followed by a terrible frenetic bust-up.

'You've always known your work is good, or you wouldn't have done it.'

He took the coffee-grinder from her, turned the handle slowly. 'Good, bad, what difference does it make? It doesn't rip the despair out of my guts.'

'You're a successful artist,' she said, knowing that he sometimes liked to hear her say this.

'There's no such thing. You can be a successful shop-keeper or football player or film-maker or critic, but you can never be a successful artist. As soon as you succeed you fail.'

She made the coffee, ran a skin of butter over some bread. He wolfed it, famished after no sleep. 'Something must have got under your skin in London,' she said.

'I bumped into Russell Jones.'

'So that was it. I wondered how you'd hurt your hand. You were stupid enough to hit him!'

'Even my own wife doesn't know how noble I am, so I'm bound to cut my throat one day. I was going to hit him, it's true. But I resisted, hit the wall instead. There are some people you just can't crack open. He was terrified, the little worm, and that was enough for me. I just wanted to see whether he was human after all. There's a successful man for you. They get terrified at the wrong things.'

'And you're so nervous you won't even call the police to find out who stole your picture.'

'I'll get it back without that.'

She knew it was something worse than losing a picture, which would bring out his rage, but not this hopeless despair. 'Did you see this Myra, in London?'

'Frank Dawley's woman? I bumped into her at a party, had dinner with her and Greensleaves the night before last. I asked her to come back here and stay with us for a few days but she wouldn't.'

'A pity. We could do with a bit of company. I get fed up, seeing nobody week after week. We don't even have to make ends meet any more. That at least took my mind off it.'

'If we don't get that picture back we might have to

219

struggle again soon enough. I have a pretty good idea who did the job, but I'm not saying yet.'

The *au pair* girls shuffled in, sluttish and dreamily beautiful, sat down and waited for Enid to serve them coffee. He leaned back and laughed. 'I had a letter last week from somebody who asked me what was wrong with the world, so I wrote back and said what do you think I am, a writer? If I could tell them that I wouldn't be painting. And if I knew what was wrong with the world I'd know what was wrong with myself, and if I knew that I'd know how to put both right.' He had that look of a short-sighted man whenever he sat at the table trying to clarify his thoughts. At the moment they eluded him, not because he wasn't capable of clarity but because he was tired. Clarity only came as inspiration, unasked and unexpected, as a pleasure when it fitted into a scheme and enabled him to build some huge edifice beamed through with its light.

The girls went upstairs and plugged in the vacuum-cleaners, motor-noise whirring and shaking through the house. Mandy came in wearing her dressing-gown, sleepy and petulant, which made her face chubbier and pale as wax. She sat at the table as if never intending to leave it. 'It's about time you were down,' Handley said.

'Do you expect me to stay in bed when those vacuum-cleaners are going like pneumatic drills outside my door? You only got that sort out of pure bloody spite.'

'Your eyes will look like three-coloured chrysanthemums if you talk to me like that,' he said, bending close. 'There are only two things that will get you from that stinking bed of a morning. One's noise, and the other's hunger. You could live off your puppy-fat for a week, so noise is the only hope. You wouldn't think so though to see the fat little chuff scoffing away.'

'What can you expect?' she said. 'I'm pregnant.'

Handley looked horrified, while Enid stayed calmly at the sink. When crisis or bad news broke, his feeling and expression matched perfectly, which was the one time he could guarantee that it would. 'Again?' he said. 'I hope you aren't playing any more tricks.'

'It's only the second time,' she said. 'And I'm nineteen, anyway.'

'Oh,' he said. 'Nineteen. It's not the modern generation that's at fault. They can't be that bad. It's just my daughter. I suppose it was that picture-stealing vampire called Ralph again?'

'It wasn't his the first time.'

'I'm reeling,' he said. 'Don't tell me any more. You said you wanted to marry that apostle of spineless determination, remember, last year?' He looked into the impenetrability of her pretty face. 'Who the hell was it, then, eh? Tell me that. Oh, what the hell do I want to know for? It doesn't matter.'

She stood up and brushed her wide-flounced housecoat by him, head in the air, which in any case came to below his chin, and walked up to the sink to empty her coffee slops before refilling the cup. 'I don't suppose it does interest you. But if you want to know who it was the first time, it was that friend you brought here early last year, when there was deep snow everywhere.'

Uncle John walked in, shaved and fully dressed, wearing his best dark suit with small golden links showing below the cuffs. Handley greeted him: 'I'm glad there's one good soul in the house who isn't hellbent on doing me evil.'

'You exaggerate, Albert. But it's a pity we have to wait for the millennium to arrive before we learn to live amicably together. Isn't it, Mandy?' Enid plugged open a tin of fruit-juice and set it before him with a dish of cornflakes and a jug of cream. She then turned to the stove to fry egg and sausages, because he was the only one in the house who wanted the full gamut of breakfast – after his prison camp experiences. 'Why don't you tell him Mandy?' John said. 'He burst into my room first – looking for the toilet. I scared him away at gun-point. Then I suspect he found it, and as I came out to see what was happening in the hall, you were talking to him – and pulled him into your room, where he stayed about ten minutes. That, I suppose, was enough.' He spooned up his cornflakes. 'Wasn't it?'

'You're the only person I can stand in this house, Uncle

John, but you see too much,' she said, disgruntled at not being able to tell her own story.

Albert sat as if sand were being poured down his back. 'Frank Dawley?'

'I didn't even know his name. He left me three pounds ten.'

'You're lying,' he said, a weird smile, hands shaking.

She stood up, afraid of him. 'I wasn't pregnant then, but I was when he left. Poor Ralph got the blame.'

'It couldn't have been Frank,' he said.

'Albert!' Enid shouted, the loaded frying-pan half towards the table. 'Sit down. Don't touch her.' With her free hand she brought a heavy crash against Mandy's cheek. 'Get out, you.'

'My best friend!' Handley moaned. 'My best bloody friend does such a thing!'

'At that time,' Enid said, 'he was only a stray boozing companion you'd picked up.'

'I saw him,' Mandy sobbed, 'and knew he was a man. I'll never forget him. Why did he have to go off like that and never want to see me again?' John ate his eggs and sausages in amiable silence with himself, as if in a transport café with a wild fight going on. But he absorbed each painful word stinging his heart, the tears bleeding into him.

Mandy sobbed in agony, and Handley stood up. 'Why didn't you tell me? If you don't speak, how do we know. I wouldn't have talked you into having an abortion if I'd known it was Frank's. I'd have got hold of the bastard, made him get a divorce, and you'd have been married by now with another kid on the way.' The idea almost cheered him up. Life wasn't a series of ups and downs: with this family it was a roller-coaster that never stopped.

Richard came in, black hair uncombed, shirt and trousers thrown on. 'If only it would rain. At least then there'd be some noise outside the house as well.'

'Don't you start,' Handley said. 'I'm beginning to feel ringed. Do you or Adam know anything about that picture that was stolen from my studio the night before last?' No one did. Albert stood, his face pale and packed tight with ancestral rage: 'There'll be a bleeding holocaust in this family if you don't all set to and find it. I keep you in luxury and bone idleness month after month – which is fair enough I suppose because you're my family, *the* family, the sacred bloody Christian Western civilized family that rots the foundations of any free and human spirit – so the least you can do is rally round when somebody like me who is an artist and as it so happens the breadwinner is attacked, and do something about it. Get your curved pipe, Richard, put on your deerstalker and take out Eric Bloodaxe. John will lend you his magnifying glass. Comb the county till you find it.'

Richard chewed at a roll and butter. 'Talk sense, father. Adam and I were up half the night printing leaflets about American intervention in Vietnam. Last month's batch were handed out around Scunthorpe steelworks, and at the Raleigh in Nottingham. Next week we do Birmingham and Leicester. That's more important than finding your painting.'

John had come to marmalade and toast: 'I know who it was, Albert.'

'So do I, John. Let's see if we tally.'

'I saw that young man Ralph in the house the night before last, at four-thirty in the morning. I was at the radio getting news from Algeria. The FLN attacked a French base in the south.'

'How did they go on?'

'It failed. A shambles. The French are pursuing the guerrillas, as well as mopping up at another place. Then I went across to the bathroom and saw him.'

'So it failed,' Handley said, sweating. 'Poor old Frank. He must have been in on it. Why didn't you call Richard and Adam and have the young bastard thrown out? He's the one I suspected.'

John wiped his hands on the napkin. 'I thought he was staying with Mandy. I didn't want to break up something ineffably tender.'

'You needn't have bothered,' Mandy said. 'I sometimes think you're just a dirty old man, Uncle John. I slept as

223

pure as driven snow. You must believe me, father.'

'I do,' he said. 'Richard, get the text together about French tortures in Algeria. Call it: The Rights of Man: This Wicked Oppression Must Stop Now. Have a French version done as well so that we can send some to Paris. They're cracking up, so we can help them on a bit.'

'What about a letter to the press, signed by you?'

'You know I never do that. If I dabbled in politics, they'd say I was forgetting my place, and that would upset them. They'd never take me seriously again. Let's be realistic, and anonymous – for the time being. John, keep on to Algeria for me, will you?'

He took out a cigarette, and Albert flashed a lighter under it. 'I've broken their codes. They're pounding the guerrillas, but they're worried, because there's still plenty of trouble in the north, which they want to give the appearance of holding in check because of the talks going on.'

'Get me a report on it, then. Adam will find you the maps. There are quite a few of us interested in Frank Dawley's fate, not to mention the lives of those brave Algerians fighting for their freedom. Things are getting too complex for me. Oh, for the simple days that never existed. Richard, tell Adam to sort out his burglar's tools, because he's going on a little job. Mandy can draw us a plan of the house, because I'm sure she's been to Ralph's bedroom often enough.'

Mandy fetched the morning paper, and locked herself behind it. 'I'm finished with him,' she said, 'if he's got that painting.'

'I wish you'd all come down for breakfast together,' Enid said, as Adam walked in.

'Sorry, Mother. I only want a cup of tea.'

'We made coffee.'

'Coffee, then.' He dropped a pile of letters: 'Post, Father.'

Bills, printed matter, income-tax demands, begging letters, a copy of Elgar's *Enigma Variations* from an admirer, and a letter with a Boston postmark, which he opened at once. He'd been hoping for one from Myra, to say she'd decided to come after all, or that she wanted to see him again in London, or that she was in trouble – any word and he would have abandoned everything and gone to her. What moral obligation had he now not to betray Frank when he had made his own daughter pregnant and caused so much trouble? And yet, and yet, one should go to Algeria and save him if he weren't dead already and the sun hadn't dried up his brain and blood. How tragic and exciting life becomes when it loses its blind simplicity at last!

He stood up and glared at the shivering paper. To be angry while seated was ignominious. On your feet it was more dignified, did not allow your raging twisted anger to lock itself like a piranha in your bent torso.

'Listen to this,' he said. ' "If you give me your daughter's hand in marriage I will send it back safe and sound. But if you make one squeak about it to anyone beyond your family, I will cut it into little strips, and then into little squares, and mix it up with ..." ' He couldn't finish, threw it to Richard who read it to the end.

For the first time that morning, probably for years, there was awe and silence at the breakfast-table. 'You see the sort of people I have to deal with?'

'It's all Frank Dawley's fault,' Mandy said, letting her newspaper fall. 'I'd never have taken up with Ralph if ...'

Albert turned on her. 'Don't be so bloody cracked. Let's not try finding people to blame. It's too late for that. What I want is to get the painting, and see that Ralph lying face down in a brook with the back of his head blown off. Not that I'm vindictive, but I just don't think he should be allowed to live, the great big corpse-faced loon, frightening the life out of me with such a letter. He even signs it. I could get him put inside for ten years. I'll teach him to steal art treasures. What are you blubbering about again?'

'You heard,' Mandy said. 'I said I was pregnant. And whose baby do you think it is? Now you want to get him ten years in gaol. Don't you ever think of anybody but yourself? I've yet to meet somebody in this world who doesn't. I know that much. I could starve or wither for all you care.' Uncle John, a flicker in his left eyelid, sat with hands pressed together on the table, as if fixing them into position before bringing them to pray.

The sea roared in Handley's head, waves flowing by a lighthouse flashing at the approach to some great empty ocean he dreaded drowning in. 'I want to take action,' he said from narrow tormented lips, 'but there's always something to hem me in. That child can rot in your womb, but I'll get my picture back.' John, unable to bear any more, walked from the room saying he preferred to listen out for Algeria.

'Don't say anything you'll regret, Albert,' Enid said, laying the tea-towel back on its rail.

'Regret? Is it possible to open my trap and not say something that you lot wouldn't like to cut my tongue out for?' He rushed to Mandy and put his arms around her. 'Mandy, my love, don't cry. I'm sentimental; I can't stand anybody crying. He won't get ten years, I'll see to that. Adam will sharpen his burglar's kit, and we'll get it back without any trouble, I promise. Don't cry. I wouldn't do anything to hurt you.'

Enid passed her a Kleenex, and more coffee. Mandy sat down at the table: 'It's not that. It's just that all the men I get in with do such stupid things. It's my own fault really.'

'That's a matter of opinion,' Handley said. 'But don't let's have any guilt. We've got enough trouble without that. Thank God we're not Christians. All I want is to get that painting. I was working well, but it's put a full-stop on me. I shan't do another for months.'

'I'll get it back,' said Mandy, 'all on my own. I'm the only one who can.'

'No fear. He'd chop you up as well. He's a homicidal suicidal maniac. He's too pale for me. I never did trust pale people.'

'He doesn't sleep enough,' Mandy said, 'that's all. But I'll bring it back, I promise.'

'I'm sure she will,' Enid said. 'Then we can forget about it and get back to normal life.'

Handley wondered whether this was a threat or a promise, but he agreed. 'All right. And if you do it,

I'll buy you that new Mini you've been wanting. But you'd better work on it straight away, otherwise me. Adam, Richard, and Uncle John will go and pay him a visit, and if we do we'll leave his old man's farm a smoking ruin. If he thinks he's going to commit the crime of the century and get away with it he's mistaken.'

'I wish I didn't come from parents who were working-class,' Mandy said. 'What's the point of being so violent?'

Handley, calmer now, lit his after-breakfast cigar. 'If you came from any other class he'd be inside already. I'm treating him like a human being. I'll just punch him up.'

Richard and Adam went off to their various subversive tasks. Mandy grabbed his hand to kiss it, and he dragged it away: 'What the hell are you trying to do?'

'You're our lord and master, aren't you?'

'I'll kick your arse,' he said. 'Whose side are you on, anyway?'

'Suicide,' she laughed, and went upstairs to dress.

'If there's anybody in this family who's likely to drive me off my head,' he raved, 'it's that fat little trollop. I'd walk out if I thought it would do any harm, but I know it won't, so I might as well stay.'

'If I hear another word out of your mouth today,' Enid said, 'I'll be the one to go. Get up to your studio and give us a rest. If one of your paintings had been stolen a couple of years ago when you were raffling them off at a shilling a ticket – couldn't even give them away in fact – you wouldn't have bothered about it.'

CHAPTER TWENTY-TWO

THE summer woods were thick and green, odours of broken elderberry stalks and a rabbit spinning across the clearing when he stood still a few minutes. He could tolerate the day only when he walked in the woods, abandoned the heavy sun and thunderous air, and whirled his stick through a bank of mildewed bluebells. Such cool shade was invigorating after sleepless days and nights. He'd left the house quite early, loth to be there when Handley's black Rambler purred through yesterday's mud and his family ranged forth to recover the painting and do him injury in the process. Handley was nothing if not impetuous. All the complexities that might make him stop and ponder went into his paintings, and such a man could not have it both ways. On the other hand he was dangerous when you did something to make him think he could, and that force and subtlety would combine to make a whole man of him.

He sat on a fallen tree-trunk and lit his pipe, agreeably at peace with the world whenever he could stop thinking. Usually this wasn't necessary, but the hole he had cut in the middle of Handley's painting blew an even larger hole in his tranquillity. He was a surgeon, a murderer, and a vandal. The trouble about such decisive action was that it made him question himself, and therefore settled nothing. His mother this morning had nagged him about Mandy, and forbidden him to see her, a promise that seemed unreal except to make him realize how much he was in absolute conflict with his parents, and would therefore end up doing all they wanted him to do. They would wait, and give him everything he craved or even mentioned, which was the modern technique of parents who, far from being modern, wanted an even more traditional response from an only child. Parents lived a long time, and they could wait, wait till you were thirty, forty, fifty, or even dead, and only come to crisis-point in such patience if for some reason you were sent to prison. By making no positive decision they bred in their children equal disabilities and so ruined them for life. From prison they might disown you, and set you free, though there was always a chance that they'd forgive you, in which case you might as well hang yourself, for you'd lost, and for ever. One could always go away, but then there'd be no anguish of the just, and all in life would lose its value. He'd tried it, discovered that being their son it was impossible to exist without this problem, and that they'd got him until they chose to let go – when he had his own children in a similar grip.

Pipe-smoke cleared the gnats away, but made him cough. By the time you ask yourself what you want out of life, you know already. He needed a house, land, income, book-lined idleness, and love for the rest of his days, to achieve which he would scheme against friends and enemies, and shatter his dream of peace and idleness to such an extent that he'd be sick at the advent of it.

Wind ruffled the treetops. Summer in England was his favourite season, and he wanted a continuation of it for ever and ever, short nights and long variable days. A twig cracked, and two arms closed around his neck. He cried out and jerked free, pipe spilled in the bracken.

'Does my love frighten you so much?' Mandy said. 'It's not going to kill you.'

'How did you find me?'

'Your father pointed this way. I went in ever decreasing circles till I – got you.'

He found his pipe, and smiled. 'I love you. I'm sorry I jumped.'

'It's understandable,' she said. 'I love you too. I really do.' They stood a few feet away, looking at different parts of the wood, he the centre, she towards the edge.

'How are things at home?'

'Wild,' she answered. 'If I don't get out of that zoo soon I'll have cubs.'

'Sit down,' he said. 'This wood belongs to my father. If I'd known you were coming I'd have brought some armchairs out, and a cocktail cabinet. What's the matter then?'

'The old man's as sick as a dog. He lost a painting and blames it on poor Uncle John. As if he'd steal anything. He really is losing his grip.'

He was amused at this unexpected suspicion. 'Did he get my letter?'

'Look,' she said after a silence, 'if you've been writing stupid letters again asking for my hand in marriage I'll do my nut. You know how crazy the last one drove him. It may be your little kick, but he doesn't dig that sort of stuff. It's county crap. If you want to marry me we can do it any time you like, and you know it.'

They sat by the tree. 'True,' he said. 'But I have my mother to deal with first. If only we could be born without families.'

'We'd starve to death,' she said. 'Where's the painting?'

'In my room.'

'Let's get it.' She took his arm, twigs and bushes pressing her. 'I know why you did it, but we must get Uncle John out of trouble.'

If Handley didn't suspect and hadn't received his letter (maybe that vicious bulldog gobbled it up), then there was little point in keeping it. And if, as Mandy said, he wouldn't object to them getting married there was even less reason – except for the gaping hole in the middle.

'I knew it was you,' she said. 'But there are times when Dad's brain doesn't work fast enough. He hasn't cottoned on yet. He's moaning in bed, covered in hot-water bottles and waiting for the doctor. Thinks he caught flu in London.'

Ralph's father, a tall amiable man wearing an old jacket and a limp felt hat, was shovelling pigshit into a dumper truck. Mandy smiled and greeted him. 'I can't shake hands, my dear. If you both want a job you can help me clean this up.'

The humid heavy air drove the stench up her nostrils. 'Perhaps one day,' she said. 'Ralph borrowed my father's latest painting and I've come for it back. He's getting an exhibition ready for the autumn, otherwise he wouldn't bother.'

'I'll help you later,' Ralph said sheepishly, no intention of doing so. His father knew it also, and smiled sadly. Spilsby was a humanist, a man who believes one gets wise with age, and that everyone else does also. He was often disappointed in this respect, but never admitted it, otherwise he would not have been a humanist. 'Mother's in town,' he said. 'Gone to get those curtains.'

'Mandy and I love each other, Father. We want to get married.'

He leaned his spade against the barn. 'Want to? What a way to treat a girl! Speak like a man, Ralph, and say that you must!'

Mandy smiled, huddled close. 'I'm pregnant.'

'So, you'd like to get married,' he muttered. 'We must have a drink.' They walked into a parlour furnished with antique chairs and tables and a richly embroidered sofa, but with excruciatingly garish lampshades hanging from wallbrackets. Spilsby poured three glasses of brandy, and hoped they'd be happy. Mandy's throat drew hers in with one graceful slide. Then she kissed Ralph modestly on the cheek, and shook hands with his father. Ralph shifted from one foot to the other, as if his unpredictable courage had tricked him into a situation he was now rather afraid of. 'I imagine you'll both be well looked after,' Spilsby said. 'We'll have to have a long talk with your parents, Mandy, before anything can be settled.'

'It is settled,' she said, pouring a second glass of brandy and drinking it down. 'I'm in the family way,' she said, helping herself to a third, fulfilling her simple and effective philosophy of: If you want it, take it.

Spilsby put the bottle back in the cupboard. 'Of course it is, my dear. But there are always details. Did I hear you say you were pregnant?'

'You did, really.'

'Really?'

'Really. Aren't I, Ralph?'

'Really?' asked Ralph. 'Are you sure?'

'Yes, really. Really really.'

'Really?' said Spilsby.

Ralph was reeling, his face white. It was the first time he'd heard about it, thinking at first it was one of her flippant jokes. 'Well, yes,' he said to his father, not knowing whether he ought to stand by her like a man, or back up her stupid joke.

'Perhaps you'd better wait until your mother comes back before we talk about your engagement.'

Mandy saw him turning nasty if they stayed ten more minutes. 'I want that painting for my father,' she said. 'He's got the gallery man coming at twelve from London. I'd love to meet your wife, Mr Spilsby. Maybe I'll call tomorrow.'

They went up to Ralph's room. He'd been dreading this,

though no one could say he lived by dread alone, which might have explained his continual jaundice and the liverish twitch that sometimes controlled his mouth. She went unsteadily to his bed, and lay on it, head resting on the spreadout palm of her hand, hair draped like a waterfall over the pillow: 'Aren't you going to get me a drink?'

He stood far off, to keep her tempting beauty in full view, and yet stay safe from it. 'You've had three already. Are you really pregnant?'

'Don't start that again.'

'Are you?' he shouted, fists clenched. 'Are you?'

'I might be,' she smiled. 'I'm very late. I'll fall down those stairs if I don't have some black coffee. I suppose he sits up half the night making that brandy in the barn. He'll break the last of his three-star bottles one day and nobody'll be fooled anymore. It got me drunk too quickly to be any good. It's ratbane and acid. I'll get the customs and excise on to him. It got me right at the back of the head, here. Something's inside, eating me away. Right here. Feel it?'

'I get that,' he said, a hand on her neck. 'Is it like a lot of ants crawling about?'

'That's it. You are sensitive, after all. I suppose that's your idea of sympathy. If somebody told you he had cancer you'd say you had it as well, then expect *him* to feel better by feeling sorry for you.' She pointed to a huge roll standing in the opposite corner. 'Is that the painting?'

'Are you pregnant, or aren't you?'

'Of course I am,' she cried, 'till my period starts. What does it matter anyway? We're engaged, aren't we? I hope you don't expect me to get that great canvas on a bus. They'll have to tie it on top.'

'I'll drive you home,' he said. 'But I won't be able to stay for lunch or anything.'

With such a weight on his shoulder he seemed relaxed to her, more fitted for life than she had ever seen him. He was unaware of raindrops falling between the house and Land-Rover. 'When we're married,' she said, 'maybe we should go to Canada.'

He slid the logroll of the painting in. 'Why Canada?'

'You might like it there.'

'A good place to bring up children,' he said, searching for his key. He backed out, to find his way blocked in the yard by his mother's powder-blue Morris Traveller.

Mrs Spilsby unfolded from the door of her car. Her husband rushed over from his work. 'We have a visitor, dear.'

'Ralph,' she cried, 'where are you going?'

'To take Mandy home.'

She came around for a better view. 'Who?'

'Mandy,' Mandy said, her large eyes staring. Wind flipped raindrops across her face.

'What are you taking from the house? There, in the car?' She was almost Ralph's height, her hair broken in its rolled shape by a brown hat. She pulled off her gloves as if about to drag the canvas out into the yard. She was short-sighted, but didn't wear glasses even when driving. 'Is it a carpet?'

'Won't anybody tell me who she is?' Mandy said.

Spilsby was red-faced. 'It's my wife.'

'I'm pleased to meet you,' Mandy said, offering her hand. She ignored it. 'Take that carpet back.'

'It's a painting of my father's. Ralph borrowed it one dark night from his studio.'

'This is my carpet, and you're stealing it. You belong to a notorious and thieving family.'

'Mandy and I are engaged to be married,' Ralph told her.

'Leave that canvas alone. Your son stole it, not me.'

'Engaged?'

'I'm afraid it seems like it,' her husband said.

Mandy held the door-handle of the Land-Rover, wanting to get away as soon as possible. 'You'd better be careful if you're going to be my mother-in-law. I'll be the one that's marrying into thieves, and it's lucky your son wasn't put away for five years for nicking that painting. My father sent me to get it back, instead of the police. Or my brothers would have come with guns. There's no messing around in our family.'

233

Mrs Spilsby let go of the painting: 'You're a vicious little liar.'

'It's not true,' Spilsby said. 'It can't be.'

'We love each other,' Mandy said, tears of rage in her eyes. 'And nobody'll stop us getting married.'

Ralph's peculiar misery made him smile 'Come on, Mandy.'

'I'll get the authorities on to this,' his mother shouted.

'Who the hell are they?' Mandy wanted to know. 'You'll get the ground ripped from under you.'

'You're a disgraceful little baggage,' she cried. 'I've heard all about you. You'll never marry my son.'

'I won't, if you're not careful. You're a nasty-tempered, dirty-minded, interfering old bag. And I'm not going to put up with it.'

Mrs Spilsby rushed towards her with uplifted hand: 'I'll thrash you, I'll . . .'

Her husband held her. 'She's pregnant,' Ralph said.

She swung round. 'What? Oh my God!'

Mandy took the starting-handle from the Land-Rover and held it high with both hands: 'Don't let that stop you. Come on, try and thrash me, you domineering bitch. Your sort can't frighten me. I'll flatten you.'

Ralph pushed her into the car, got in the other side and sped out of the gate. 'I'll have him put away,' his mother was shouting, and Spilsby's condolences were scraped by engine-noise.

They drove in silence, until Mandy laughed. 'Whether you marry me or not,' she said, lighting a cigarette, 'you'd better get away from her.' A lane turned towards green hills, sun and rain mixing on the high crestline. 'You're twenty-five,' she said. 'How much longer will you put up with it?'

'I'll get away,' he said, 'when I'm ready. If your father says so we can be married in a fortnight.'

'He'll say yes. I would have killed her.'

'It's a good job you didn't. It's weird though. I've never felt like the son of my parents. Either they were born burned-out or I was.'

'I expect you all were,' she said. 'Still, most other people are.'

He drove up the mud lane to Handley's house. Binoculars were trained on the car when it entered the village. It disappeared under the tunnel of leafy trees, then came out at the turning, spitting mud and twigs from its tyres. Handley, dressed now, pale and tight-lipped, went down to greet them.

'I'll carry it into the hall,' Ralph said, his heart on fire. 'But first I'll turn the car round.'

Mandy selected a dry patch of ground and climbed out: 'Don't be afraid. He'll welcome you with open arms to get his painting back.' And she would have her heart's desire of a new red Mini, and Ralph after all had unknowingly set off the action which led to it.

'I have to see someone in Boston,' he said, ankle-deep in cold mud, 'otherwise I'd stay.'

Handley stood at the door. 'If you drop it you're a dead man.' Eric Bloodaxe licked Ralph's hand, which so enraged Albert that he came from the doorway and kicked him between the jaws, sending him back into the kennel without a growl of protest.

They trod silently upstairs to the studio. He remembered Mandy saying Handley was prostrate and ill, but he seemed all right at the moment, albeit silent and grumpy.

'Let's open it,' Albert said when they were inside, 'and see those pretty games of noughts-and-crosses you've been playing.'

Ralph turned to run, but Handley's scissor legs reached the studio door and slammed it shut. He spun the key in the lock: 'Let's be grown up, shall we? I want to see how vicious respectable people can behave. Unroll it.'

Ralph opened a heavy penknife. 'Put that back in your pocket,' Handley said. 'I don't want any last minute suicide sabotage. Undo them with your fingers.' They watched. If it weren't perfect Mandy saw her beautiful spruce car sinking into the quicksands. While knots and string were being undone, Handley lit a cigar and poured out a brandy. He was going to give Ralph one, but drew the bottle back until he saw the painting.

It seemed in perfect condition. Globes of sweat stood on Ralph's face and his hands trembled. Mandy gasped when the painting lay flat. A hole had been cut neatly in the centre, meticulously measured, as if Ralph had wanted to contribute something to the total effect, a few inches in diameter, small compared to the whole area, but a hole nevertheless, through which all other details of the colourful and complex design seemed intent on flowing. If looked at long enough it hypnotized and psychically unsettled one, and appeared as if all the intricacies of Albert's art had been born through it.

Something stopped him flying at Ralph across his sea of creation. They pored over it like ghosts, midday lights on, Handley noting the few threads of canvas sticking out loosely from the generally neat edges of the perfect circle. He had violated his painting, gouged out its eye with diabolical patience and delight.

'So you think you've done for me?' he said, with a faint smile.

Ralph stood up to his full height, a man who always used his courage at the wrong time. 'No, I don't. But you deserved it. What else could I do to make you feel ashamed of the way you treated Mandy last year?'

'What's he talking about?' Handley said.

'I don't know,' Mandy wept, her red Mini vanishing. 'What did you do it for? How stupid can you get? What's the point of it?'

He was stunned by sudden regret, wary at the sight of Handley who didn't seem as upset as he ought to be.

'You want my daughter's hand in marriage, do you? Is that it? And you want a new Mini, do you? Well, you can have her for your wife with a bullet-hole right through her. And you can have a new car with a grenade-hole through it. Get out of my sight, both of you. Don't let me see you again.'

Ralph unlocked the door and went down the stairs.

'I'm not budging,' Mandy cried, 'unless I get the car.'

'Aren't you? Do you want to go flying out of that sky-light window like batman there?'

'I got the painting back. Now I want that car.'

He took out his wallet, and wrote a cheque for three hundred pounds.

'It costs six hundred,' she grumbled.

'You think I'm buying it cash?' he said. 'Get it on the never-never, then we'll never pay for it. Now get out.'

She kissed him. He called her back. 'Tell your mam I've got the painting, and that it's all right. And be careful on the roads.'

The sun went and came in again between pale blue water clouds. Fresh air hit him from an open window that he couldn't yet lock after Ralph's little job. He'd get Mandy to hem the painting round the hole. Maybe a patch would be possible. The green man of the tree shook its leaves and rustled. He couldn't imagine leaving Lincolnshire, but lack of imagination was the state in which he committed his most decisive actions. The new record caught his eye, and he put it on the gramophone thinking it might relax him before going down for dinner.

Elgar's Nimrod music was so sweet that he loathed it, yet listened to its long mellow pre-womb Edwardian English dirge as if playing before an impassable wall that the spirit of the music was too gutless to climb and cross, weaving out the soothing sounds of glorious resignation, the peculiar self-satisfied English pipe-smoking resignation that engenders viciousness and sadism if it goes on too long. It showed him the corrupt rotten soul of the English played out of a burning stillborn heart. He understood its suffering: such music lacked the messianic human love of great work, locked as it was on an island where no armies have moved or revolutions swayed for hundreds of years and where liberty has no meaning any more. Elgar had his hands in its entrails all right, writing music while his country rotted – not the *Enigma Variations*, but the *Enema Variations*, more like it.

He lifted the needle and slid the record back into its case, thinking he might give it to Ralph as a wedding-present. He reset the painting against the wall, flush on the biggest easel. Cancer is the sum of their unrealized ideals, the festering nation that hasn't got rid of its king or queen recently. He stood back and surveyed the hole, the eye, the magic eye, the third eye and only eye, not my left or my right but my middle and best, straight from Tibet by P & O packet-boat. I'll hem it round and paint it blue, and leave it like that, Albert Handley's third eye looking out on this world of yours, with no one looking in on mine.

CHAPTER TWENTY-THREE

SHE pulled up tufts of grass that grew from the borders of the path, and where she had worked already was clearly defined, but beyond, where she had not, only a thin uneven trail led between two apple-trees to the back fence. It was slow work, without purpose if there were more important things to do – which there were not. What had frightened her into sending Handley away? Was it fear of being deflected from her course of waiting for Frank to come back? From that sort of war she might wait ten years, then discover he'd died at the beginning. Or she might know nothing at all. Nevertheless, she could wait. She was fond of Handley, and to say she had sent him off out of fear was merely a way of gratuitously attacking her resolution, so she changed her reason to one of self-preservation in order to be more truthful and feel better.

After lunch she put Mark in his carrycot and wedged it in the back of the car. He was a fat pale baby, anything but placid, and objected to the movement and noise. Her father, seventy-five years old, was ill with a stomach-ache that wouldn't leave him, and on warm days he lay in the garden on a special bedchair reading the *Jewish Chronicle* and shouting in rich Yiddish at the black tom from next door who stalked across his lawn after the birds.

Mark roared, but she couldn't turn to him, being on the outside lane of the motorway and overtaking a line of cars at seventy miles an hour. The right-hand blinker flashed as she raced along in her new MG. A car from the middle lane suddenly set itself to swing out in front of her. She pressed the horn, and braked sharply. A ripple went through all lanes of traffic, and the ash of panic filled her mouth as she thought of Mark behind. She skidded, but stayed in control, and the car that had tried to join her lane slid back, allowing her to accelerate and roar by. Mark was no longer crying, mollified by the common danger. The only answer to English traffic, she thought, was to get a bigger car, which was safer because it tended to frighten the souped-up souls in their fast sardine-tins. The driver had been a young girl in a red Mini, now on the outer lane but a quarter of a mile behind.

Her mother came to the car and picked up Mark even before saying hello to her daughter. Myra smiled. Anyone over twelve was valueless to her mother, had to be looked after and deferred to perhaps, but lacked that spark of life in their eyes to say that they were still growing. 'How's father?' Myra asked, struggling to get out the empty cot.

'He's asleep right now,' she said. 'What a lovely baby. He's like you, you know. I suppose he gets his blue eyes from your grandfather, because George's eyes were brown, weren't they?'

She took off her coat in the hall, and Mark was already in the kitchen and propped in a high chair kept specially for him. The house smelled of the same floor-polish and moth-balls, carpet-cleaner and paint, and places where dust wanted to settle but had never been allowed, as when she was a young girl rushing in from school to get out of the hat and uniform she loathed before going to meet friends.

The baby, whatever her own feelings, loved his grand-mother, and never came so much alive as when he was at her house. To her, he was George's child, and she only knew of Frank Dawley through vague stories from Pam, much of it speculation because Pam didn't know much either, Myra thought, pleased at how secretive she'd been. Mrs Zimmerman made a bowl of cereal and mashed a banana in it. 'He won't be hungry,' Myra said. 'It isn't his feeding time yet.'

'Of course he's hungry. Look how fat and beautiful he is. They're always hungry at his age. Don't think I don't know.

I've had three of my own, so I should. And I looked after Pam's four when Harry left her and she went to get him back.'

'That was rather shameless of her,' said Myra. 'I always thought she'd had more pride.'

'He came back, didn't he?'

'And look how ecstatically happy they are.'

'That's not the point. The children are better for it. Your father and I were wondering the other day when you are going to get married again. It would make us very happy, you know, especially if you found someone who understood you a bit better. I know you weren't very happy with George, but we never said anything.'

'That's true, you didn't, though I don't know what you could have said that wouldn't have made it worse. But I've no intention of rearranging my life just yet.'

'I know you went to Morocco with another man just after George died, but since you parted from each other perhaps you ought to get someone else, if only for the baby's sake.'

'*Get* someone?' she smiled, hardly covering her irritation. 'We don't live in a slave supermarket.' Yet it was no use being angry. Their two worlds simply could not meet. Mark, with wide smiles and an arm waving, devoured each spoon of food before him. He was happy, relaxed, and lively here, whereas it had the opposite effect on her. If she fed him at this time he could have rejected it, but here, with the inane cuckooing ministrations of her mother, he puffed and blowed and gulped endearingly. 'Thank goodness you have such a good child,' she said. 'And such fair hair. Go on, darling, eat, eat! You melt the ice in your grandmother's heart. None of Pam's were like him. He's so knowing. He knows me, don't you? And what about grandfather, then? You see, he's looking for him. He is. You see it? Only seven months old. Eat. Go on, eat! Of course he'll eat it all up, won't you? No, he's certainly not like any of Pam's. They were never like this at his age.' A baby in front of her, no matter what its faults, was better in every way than any other far-off baby no matter what its virtues. 'And to think you waited so long before having one. You should get married again and have a few more. You can't think how much pleasure that would give, and not only to me and your father. You make such a good mother. Look how marvellous he is!'

She was beginning to stifle. It was midsummer, and the central heating seemed to be full on. She didn't feel she made such an ideal mother. Practical, conscientious, loving perhaps, but did that make you a real parent? There was no need to shape a career out of it, though she often felt that Mark might benefit by having a man around, and only time and her own passions could take care of that.

'Do you have any news of George's book?' her mother asked, taking a huge cake out of the cupboard, a sight that sent a stab of indigestion to Myra's heart, though she would enjoy eating it when offered a piece.

'It's being reprinted. I forgot to tell you in my letter. I got two hundred pounds in the post this morning.'

'Poor George,' said her mother, 'that he can't spend it.'

'It's over a year now,' Myra said. 'Such a stupid accident. It was unforgivable to do a thing like that. Mark was never George's baby, you know. It came from the man he tried to kill, Frank Dawley. We were going away together.'

'It never said that in the papers,' she said sadly, sitting down.

'I didn't exactly tell lies, but I kept everything as simple as possible. No one saw the accident.'

'Dreadful,' she said. 'It's a wonder you weren't killed. And look at him, beautiful Mark, he didn't suffer from it, thank goodness. None of you did, really.'

Her father came in, a frail old man with white hair and luminous eyes. He looked older every time she saw him, more brittle and fragile. His hair, always clipped close to his skull, had in the last few months been allowed to grow long, and instead of the sharp expression that had made him successful in business, his face had softened and become more noble. She had always loved him because he'd never posed the same threat as her mother, whom Myra dreaded turning into as she got older. He'd understood her rebellion, in the light of his own which he had generously and good-humouredly suppressed, realizing that no matter how far she strayed from them, the cord of affection would never snap if he permitted her to do more or less as she liked. He had been wise and accurate, always too grown up to fall back on the heavy father-culture that had been perpetrated against him as a young man. He'd recently taken to ordering Yiddish novels from New York, and reading Hebrew again, and this made his wife glad, for it brought him closer to her, but it also made her weep, because it seemed as if he were preparing for the end of his life.

There was an air of doom about the house, which Myra remembered as a young girl. And yet it was cheerful enough. Surely the subtle spiritual organism of a baby would be able to detect it if it really existed, and here he was, laughing happily. Maybe it was in her rather than the house. Her father laughed too: 'He is a little devil. I'll have a piece of that cake, Gladys.'

They drank lemon-tea amid self-generating chatter, levity that would have embarrassed her if she hadn't been fond of them. When you get old, life becomes less serious, she thought. Having thrown off their worries they made it seem like the prime of life. One had to think up something like that in order not to feel sorry for them.

Her father promised to come out to the country soon. 'I'll dig your garden when my aches have gone.' He piled so much sugar on to the slice of lemon that it capsized and sank, then floated up to the surface for more.

'One breath of a sparrow would blow you over,' his wife said.

His eyes glittered, then sparked out, like a rocket on its highest curve. He opened them. 'This pain gets sharp at times. Maybe some cake will settle it. If your stomach plays up, give it some food to work on.'

Myra stopped him giving a slab to Mark. 'He's still too young, father.'

Mark rattled his spoon and mug in a fine din, as if to say it wasn't true, and he'd eat all the cake they gave him. 'You can see that mouth shaping up already,' he joked. 'He'll be a difficult man to live with. I don't like the way that down-ward curve settles in when he's not smiling.'

'Don't give him a bad character before he's actually got one,' she said. He bent over his tea, scooped out a spoonful and blew it cool, then put it towards Mark's lips, who jumped up and down at the suspense of its slow approach.

'Make sure it's not too hot, dear.'

'Don't be a fool,' he snapped, 'by thinking I'm one.'

'Forgive me for speaking,' she said.

Myra smiled. Mark was waiting for it like a cat for an unsuspecting bird to come close before leaping. His large blue eyes were settled, as if they threw extra light on to the spoon. He took it, and an expression of uncertainty creased his cheeks.

'He doesn't like it.'

'Be quiet!'

He did. He waved for more.

'What a boy!' he cried. 'A real Russian, the way he takes to his tea.' There was colour in the old man's cheeks, and he stood without thinking of his stick. Myra knew that no-thing could bother him at such a time. She saw there'd be somewhere safe to leave Mark if she wanted to go away, or be on her own for a while. It was comforting to know. She'd always cut herself from her parents' orbit, and now realized how hard it had made her life. To stick in the same district, like Pam, had great advantages, for you and your parents alike, and she felt the dangerous lure of giving in and living close by, the life of a widow with one child who would maybe marry again into a state of eternal satisfaction from where you could laugh at things that happen to other people and feel superior because they don't bother you. If you were part of a married couple living off each other's spiritual fat and too busy ever to need anything from others, you turned narrow and blind to the rest of the world. It was a blessed and innocent state of self-induced death, protection and lethargy more than love, yet always an attraction to someone who rebelled against it so strongly. Fortunately, she thought, I am not the sort who could ever consider it. But the draw was so strong and real that the desire she felt to give into it almost frightened her with its sexual intensity. She had only to come home, how- ever, to kill such an idea. The temptation she needed, but not the fulfilment.

For two hours they played with the baby, and then she wanted to go home, to get away before she stifled – or stayed for a week. The grip of ease was on her, and that was a sure mark that she must be off. Tomorrow they would quarrel, or she would be bored. It was better for them to go on liking each other than that she should stay.

'Come again,' they said, as she wrapped Mark in his shawl. 'We love having you both.'

'I enjoy it as well,' she admitted. 'I'll see you next week, and phone you on Friday night.' They stood by the front gate, her car moving from the kerb and gliding up the road, hidden by the Humber which her mother still drove.

Back at the house she telephoned Albert Handley to say she'd like to come to Lincolnshire – if it were still possible. It was a month since they'd seen each other, and she spoke of her visit as a break from her loneliness at the house, not particularly as a means of seeing him. 'Don't bring your car,' he said. 'I'll send Richard for you. You'll enjoy the journey that way. If he takes the route I tell him to you'll see so much beauty in this clapped-out country it'll make your heart race.'

'When shall I come?' – hoping he'd say soon.

'When can you be ready? Make it at ten in the morning. You can? Richard will set out at four o'clock, and be there in plenty of time. No, it's all right. He'll be glad to. Loves being sent on errands in the Rambler, and you're perfectly safe with him. Not a better driver anywhere. A very cool lad. Don't let him charm you, though. No news, I suppose? Oh well, don't worry – just wait. It'll be all right in the end.'

'Is there anything I can bring?'

'Only yourself, and Mark. I'd come and get you myself, except that I'm doing a painting I can't leave. If I left the house while I'm working my heart would drop out. So I'll see you about three tomorrow, right? Right.' He went off quickly, as if some menace were advancing on him at the

244

other end, and she sat down to wonder how convenient her visit would be. Beyond the jollity of the telephone line she picked up trouble, then doubted her sharp senses, because it could have been the automatic feedback of her own low spirits after the few hours at her parents.

She had been buzzed by the same red Mini on the way back, and this time got a better look at the girl driver, with long fair hair and snubbed nose, an attractive fleshy face until it turned and the delectable lips shaped vile words through the greenhouse windows, and continued for half a minute while they were dead level at seventy miles an hour with only a few feet between them. Myra thought they wouldn't forget each other's face for a long time, each so vividly seen. Her own expression had been one of steady concentration, coolly observing the masterpiece of dumb obscenity from such a good-looking girl.

CHAPTER TWENTY-FOUR

THE house was quiet for a few weeks, everyone locked in their various occupations. Handley painted and prepared for his exhibition, brooded on Myra, and the diabolical brewing up of disturbance whose root-cause one could never find when things appeared peaceful. He wanted to write to Myra, phone her, but always drew back at the last moment, because work was stronger than love. He painted in shirt-sleeves, skylight open with the coming of summer, intent on blocking out white squares and oblongs with his demanding visions.

Mandy left three weeks ago, as soon as the red Mini had been delivered. She'd sent picture-postcards from various rest-stations on the Mi showing dramatic views from bridges, and wide-angle shots of complex entrance points – the eighth wonder of the world that crumbled under the mild frosts of winter. She'd headed for Nottingham and Leicester and had been three weeks going up and down the motorway, day and night, non-stop, nothing else, spending a fortune on petrol. He'd sent Adam to get her off, but Adam came back white-faced and shattered saying how many times he'd been near to cremation or manglement trying to hedge her into a service station and get her to listen to reason. She had no driving licence either, though judging by her skill at the wheel she had no need of one. Albert calculated that if she'd driven up and down the M1 since setting off with the car she'd already done over twenty thousand miles and slashed the car's value by two-thirds, so the company wouldn't find it worth their while taking it back when they realized that no more payments on the hire-purchase would be forthcoming. He at least expected her to come crying home for a new set of tyres.

John had his tea at four-thirty precisely, brought in on a large tray by one of the *au pair* girls. With a prolonged eye-giving smile as she walked from the door to his desk she set down a huge pot of tea, plate of bread and butter, ham and pork pie, jam and cakes. His only other meal was breakfast, and the occasional celebration-dinner.

He sat at his radio-set at certain hours of the day and night, impeccably dressed because he could never forget the rags of his prison-camp days, filling faint-lined limp-covered school exercise-books with messages which he filed away sadly when the vital link of his existence stayed unexplained, and when various reports on Algeria or Laos had been culled from them and passed on to Handley or his sons. His benevolent heart, tuned in to the waywardness of the world, made him the conscience and nerve-centre of the family, and they respected his knowledge, age, past sufferings, malarial fits, and occasional epileptic violences, or his inexplicable choler at the sudden appearance of strangers who threatened his ordered life and whose stench of the jungle threw his delicate psychic balance out of true. Family turmoil was as much as his frail spiritual condition could stand. He had no wish to see the outside world, and this isolation had so far been his only way of learning to understand it again. And by thus pulling himself back from the precipice of disintegration he also became able to understand himself.

His amiable and highly educated presence had dominated the Handley household for longer than most of them could remember. He had educated Richard and Adam from the age of five in the romance and ethics of revolution, in the mechanics of insurrection. Being Handley's children, born in chaos and brought up to fend for themselves, they had been willing learners, less likely to repudiate the teachings of a kind uncle than if the same laws had been poured out by their father. He had also passed on to them his saintly amiability, though this was sided with Handley's strength and ruthlessness, and so gave a peculiar breadth of character that was unlikely to weaken with age. John's library was a unique collection of War Office manuals, police instruction books on the handling of demonstrations, French tomes on the psychology of masses and crowds, German and Russian texts on street-fighting and revolution. His favourite words were from the Book of Joel: 'Beat your ploughshares into swords, and your pruning hooks into spears: let the weak say, I am strong.'

He switched off his high-powered receiver, laid down his earphones, and passed an hour eating, and idly looking through his notebook: 'Turn your back on politics,' it said. 'Politics have nothing to do with Revolution. And civil disobedience is useless unless its principles are stiffened by the backbone of Revolution.' On another page: 'The American rocket and bomber bases must be treated as were German bases in occupied France during the war. Adopt the attitudes of the French Resistance to the Nazis. And not only the land of the bases, but also the land of the fox-hunters must come under the hammer. The police, the armed forces, civil defence personnel are an army of occupation. Those who join their ranks are traitors. Those who sit on jury service are traitors. Those who hold state secrets and do not try to divulge them to an enemy or to make them public knowledge are also traitors.' He read more: 'The people, by acquiescing to the possibility of nuclear war are giving in to their own death-wish, since they have allowed themselves to be diverted from their ability to become large in spirit and carry out a revolution. The ruling class prefer this death-wish to permeate and operate rather than that the will to revolution should develop. That is presumably what they mean by being better dead than Red. They are already dead. But are they dead beyond the powers of resurrection?'

'All the time one must be ready. All through life one must educate and train oneself for the Revolution, imagine it in all its detail and in a thousand permutations. One must breathe and live for the Revolution, because a revolution is a mystical occurrence as much as something which is brought about and controlled by organization. It is a healthy state of mind. The perfect and ordered world around one can crumble in a week, and one must be ready to step in and stoke up the fires of destruction in order that you may build when they have gone out – but not until.'

'A revolution is not an impossible pipe-dream in this small old-fashioned country. One must make a career of helping to bring about the Revolution in face of the imponderable forces of inanition. This modern world could become prehistoric and half-empty in four flat minutes, and until that time the only political philosophy will be that of Positive Nihilism.'

He pursed his thin lips between cups of tea, smiled at his sense of humour. Revolution must become a religion, civil war a religious war. Ideological was a poor word for it and didn't state the case well enough. A man who died for a political cause was a deeply religious man, though one should not ask too closely who his god was.

Tea finished, he lit a cigarette and sat back with the restfulness of sanity and good health, laying aside the turned-up papers of his notes. Flies landed and took off from the vertical landing-grounds of the window-panes above rows of books, but he saw no reason to kill them and still their engines. They flew where warm sun heated the glass, summer bluebottles at liberty to annoy him with their touch and noise, thoughtless and helpless innocents feeding from the effluvia of the rotten earth or refuelling on his jam-stained spoon. Flame crawled up the matchstick, and he let it fall into his wastepaper-basket. Worn-out carbon-paper soaked in thousands of words twisted under invisible heat. He should douse the fire out, but wondered how much the flame would eat before he grew afraid and leapt on it. Every man who owned a pen, shoes, a slice of bread, was an enemy of the Revolution he envisaged, if he did not consider that it also belonged to someone else. Everything on your back, feet, in your mouth was common property. There was to be no ownership whatsoever, and no state to distribute it, either. Your house was everyone's house, provided everyone's house was your house. Abolish private property, and you abolished privacy, for who would want privacy if they had no property. Privacy is piracy. The prime sin of the world was the ability and opportunity to possess, to have and to hold till the heart grew cold and became an object from which all evil sprang. Privacy was the root of compounded malice and evil. The only time privacy was essential was in order to preach all this, but even then you had no right to such privacy for long, even to the extent of owning a wastepaper-basket that was about to catch fire.

He opened the window, and bluebottles flew out, then picked up two dusters and lifted the basket at arm's length before sending it down the side of the house like a missile to repel invisible invaders. It landed by a blackcurrant-bush, that did not take fire, though the noise brought forth frenzied growls from Eric Bloodaxe around the corner.

His hands shook, unable to plug in the earphones, so he listened from the loudspeaker instead. Signals fell over themselves to get at him, each with a different pitch and music. Fifteen years had gone by since he came to this house, and though he was wiser and steadier in the heart, he seemed no older, felt in fact more full of vigour and youth than he ever had.

He stood by the open window looking down at the charred basket and flakes of paper leaping in the wind. Sweat glistened below brown calm eyes that gazed beyond the garden at fields rising and falling towards knots of wood and coppice. At first it had repelled him, that vegetable charnel-house of the earth. Distance chilled him, space horrified. All he had wanted was four walls, the self-imposed limits of his own world. Yet without reason he thought of getting out, going on some journey to a place where he could put his so-far wasted life to some ultimate use. Perhaps the impulse now set on him was what he had waited for all along, began as a vague but irresistible restlessness that unconsciously clarified itself while he continued his normal life and only occasionally brooded on it. The calamity of his existence came upon him as he stood by the window, the enormous gap of full consciousness that now gave back a promise of his native strength.

Hands under control, he switched off the radio, disconnected himself from the exterior telegraphic signals of common affairs and business scything and chipping and pulsing through the air, and pondered on the various world situations to decide in which direction he must go.

CHAPTER TWENTY-FIVE

HALFWAY across England they stood in a layby hoping for some fresh air, but all they got was a petrol reek whose rainbow stains beautifully coloured the road. 'It's foul,' said Myra. 'How long can one go on living in it?'

'Get a mile up one of these side-lanes and it's sweet enough,' said Richard. 'I'll take a detour in Lincolnshire, and the air will be so clear you'll faint. It'll cut you in two. I like living in cities, though. I'm kinky for factory-smoke and petrol-fumes and plenty of machine-noise. I love it. It's blood and gold-dust to me. Two years I spent in Leicester working in a factory were the best of my life. Factories, power stations, machines – that's all that matters. When I look up and see a four-engined jet sliding across the sky I want to go and see my best girlfriend. I think of love.'

They drove on, and he continued talking. 'I hitch-hiked to Cornwall last November to have a look around. Father thought of moving there, heard of a house, and wanted me to look at it. On the way back I got a lift and reached Oxford late at night, and I went into a place for some coffee. A group of students were standing at the counter, and when I went up they made sneering remarks about scholarship boys. I was amused. It was rather a nice experience to be taken for an undergraduate. The more roles I have in life the better.'

His head was held back slightly, as if to see more of the road. He had dark curly hair, and a long rather sharp nose that gave a piercing distant gaze to his eyes. 'I drank my coffee, and singled out the ringleader. When he left I followed him, and caught him up as he turned off the main street. I became all the working-class scholarship boys rolled into one, and had an idea that this young blood or whatever they call themselves shouldn't be allowed to get away with it. I'm a man of ideas, and sometimes they're so strong that I'm forced into action.' He laughed, reached a straight piece of road and overtook a lorry that had slowed him down for the last half-hour. 'If I act from bravado or boredom and not out of an idea it's usually a fiasco. So I have to be careful.'

'What kind of an idea?'

'Well, while talking to you just now I was wondering whether man can benefit from having his soul laid bare. It makes him hate himself so much that he's going to destroy himself because he can't stand it. He'll lose all confidence, and that's bad. Nevertheless, he's got to learn to live with his own soul, with the depths of his own real and far-out soul, though sometimes I think he'd rather die than do it. That person who made the stupid remarks about scholarship boys didn't have the human vision to have a soul. I tried to talk to him and make him listen to me, but he didn't like it, so to defend myself I sunk my boots into him. His social hatred wasn't enough for him to do much about it when it came to the crunch. It was all very silly, really. I don't suppose for one minute it helped him to think next time before opening his trap. From then on, when I got a lift in a car or lorry I told them I was a student from Oxford. You've no idea how easy it made things. I did it as an experiment, and it worked so well I kept it up. I got so good at it I nearly vomited one day, and that ended it.'

'You're almost as bad as your father.'

'That would really worry me. Father has great talent, but he's ruthless, unscrupulous, over-generous when he feels like it, and being an artist his thoughts are totally disorganized. There are times when I actually have a great liking for him, even though he is my father. I nearly flattened him two years ago when he lifted his fist to my mother, but there were no ill-feelings about it. He wouldn't have forgiven me if I hadn't stopped him. Some silly quarrel or other.'

'About money, I suppose,' she said, 'in those days. You were all terribly poor, weren't you?'

'That's true. But they never argued about money, never. It was always about the children, or about his ideas as an artist, or – well, anything. They loved each other so much that everything was important enough to quarrel about, bitterly and violently at times. They had their hell, we had ours, so there was nothing to reproach them with. It was all out of love, you see – and still is. Father was determined never to go out to work, and Mother was determined never to let him. That was the whole basis of their happiness, so how could they quarrel about money? Their mutual agreement about what they would never disagree about saw them through. I often marvelled at it, as soon as I began to understand. I suppose we had a perfect childhood, really, having Father at home all the time, like any sons of the idle rich, and we never actually went hungry, thanks to all his tricks. He used to write begging letters, and say that when he was famous he'd get them published, and call the book: *The Collected Begging Letters of Albert Handley, R.A.* But he won't, of course. Now he says he'll save them in case we ever get poor again.'

To Myra he was an intelligent young man who, being so young, was a complete mystery until he explained himself. It was one of her faults that she rarely understood or sympathized with those whose ages differed from her own. She drew Mark up to show him the road. Passing cars were clocked on his senses by a wave of his arms. He was in a peaceful and interested mood as the car funnelled through green landscape. Now and again the colic struck, and out came the rose-hip syrup, but travelling usually soothed his blood, as if he were already setting his gypsy eyes at the open road and thinking to search the world for his father. It calmed her also to be on the move, disencumbered from the house and all petty thoughts.

They were well on into the flat fen zones, the holland drains of the country. The air was different from any other part of England, with its smell of sun and water. Seabirds hovered over green and yellow fields, slipped across loam and worried at the tractors. A red Mini stood by a gate, barely parked off the road, and a girl leaned on it looking blankly at any traffic that passed. The bonnet of her car was up, but she did not wave.

'I know that attitude of troublesome despair that bodes ill for all and sundry,' Richard said. The car stopped smoothly, shot into reverse and drew up by the Mini's side. He wound down the window, shouting: 'Are you back from running in the M1?'

'Drop dead,' Mandy called, tear-marks on her face. 'It took you long enough to find me.'

'I wasn't looking for you, love,' he said, 'I'm sorry to say. Had a breakdown?'

She smiled, as if to give him canker. 'No, I'm smelling petrol. It sends me.'

'Maybe the good wold wind'll blow your bad mood away. This is Myra Bassingfield.' Myra recognized her, the terror of the motorway for the last three weeks, the angel at the wheel who had buzzed her and whom she had passed at seventy miles an hour. They didn't shake hands. 'She's coming home,' Richard said, 'to stay a while. A friend of father's.'

'Another one to feed,' Mandy said. 'That makes twelve of us.'

'Thirteen,' Richard laughed. 'There's a baby inside.'

'Is it father's?' she asked. 'I'll never know how many brothers and sisters I've really got. It's a horrible life.'

'He's not your brother,' Myra said. 'And don't be afraid for your food.'

'You'll walk back if you're not careful,' Richard said. Myra offered a cigarette, and wrung a thanks from her. 'I'm broke, flat broke. No fags and not even the price of a cup of tea, nor the money to phone a garage. There's enough petrol in my tank to get home, but that's about all, except that the bloody thing won't start. Nearly six hundred pounds of brand-new British rubbish.'

'You've knocked it to death,' he said. She went sulkily into the Rambler, found some sandwiches in the glove-box and pulled them apart in a few seconds. Richard tried the Mini for ignition faults, fuel failure, and mechanical defects, but could not start it. 'We'll lift it on to my luggage rack, and carry it home like that.'

'You only want to humiliate me,' Mandy cried. Black rings of exhaustion made her eyes look bigger, big enough, Myra thought, to send any man mad. She had in fact hoped for a romantic rescue by some stranger, but much to her disgust no one had stopped. 'We'd never get up the lane with it on your luggage rack because the tree branches are too low.'

'Well,' said Richard, smiling at her show of dignity, 'we'll just have to tow you. It's only forty miles, and we can leave it at Stopes's Garage.' He uncoiled a rope and attached it to both cars. 'I'm frightened,' she said. 'I don't know how to drive on tow.'

'Just watch the brakes,' he said. 'I won't go over thirty.'

'Lend me some money and tell the next garage to send a breakdown truck. Then I'll see you as soon as it's fixed.' He caught the glint in her eyes. If he lent her ten pounds and the car was mended there was no telling where she would head for next. He was afraid to let her go without a week's rest, for there was a desperate look in eyes as if, because of the breakdown, she couldn't wait to get back on the road and plough into it. If she came home the house would stop worrying.

Myra offered to drive. 'You can stay in with Richard, and look after Mark.'

Mandy looked fiercely at her, then at Richard. 'All right. But if anybody scratches it, I'll do my nut.'

'I'll take care,' Myra smiled.

'You didn't buy the bloody car,' Richard said, tired of her irrational stubbornness, 'so shut up.' At a wave from Myra he cruised along the road.

The Rambler, having discarded the Mini, made its way up the muddy lane, lush branches and nettles as high as a man clawing its sides as if to welcome their black panther back. Handley came out in shirt-sleeves to greet them, glad of an excuse not to work for a few days. He hoped to go for walks with Myra, or take her by car to the coast, or to the various high-spots of the county so that they could talk about many things. Enid would come too, of course, and a gay party would be made up.

Myra admired the caravans, the compound, the house. 'Did he look after you well?' Handley asked.

'Perfectly,' she said, feeling tired. 'We drove Mandy the last forty miles, which made it merrier. Her car had broken down.'

'Where is she?' he snapped, then remembered that it wouldn't be polite to break the month's peace while Myra was here. 'I've something to say to her.'

'In the car,' Richard said. 'The Mini's being fixed. Nothing serious.'

'I hope not. That's our second car.' Handley looked thinner, browner, as if he were much of the day out of doors. But she also found him more open and nervous than during his time in London, as if gripped by continual worry and irritation. 'Mandy! Come out of there.'

She sat up on the back seat, winding down the window. 'I'm not. Tell Mam to throw me some sheets in. I want to sleep here.'

'Don't be daft,' Handley said. 'It's nothing to be ashamed of. We all have breakdowns some time or other.'

But they could not persuade her, and went into the house, Handley carrying Myra's case, while Richard followed with the baby. Enid had set out a cold lunch in the kitchen, of ham and cheese, cold fried fish and chicken, wine, beer, and tea, and many kinds of bread. She met them at the door, wearing a beige woollen jersey-dress in which to shake hands. She was fair and tall, and Myra was impressed by her broad eyes and narrow smooth-skinned face, and an expression of passion and intelligence marking the curve of her lips. Here, she thought, is a woman who says yes to everything because there is nothing left to say no to. 'I had a very good trip,' she answered, 'in such a superb car.'

Albert smiled with pleasure. 'Yes, it's not a bad old bus,' and took her coat.

'It's his favourite toy,' Enid said. 'He'd be lost without it.' Myra imagined so. They were immediately like two sisters trying to put the only man present in his place. He should have expected it, rather than bank on a society of equals, all pally and sexless until he made his grab, then appallingly and deliciously willing. He poured four tots of brandy: 'Here's to a peaceful and pleasant stay. We'll have a bite now, and leave the banquet till tonight.'

'I'll have to see to Mark soon,' Myra said.

Handley downed his brandy. 'Don't think about him. Helen will do that. She's capable – be fourteen next birthday. I wouldn't mind a pint of muscatel and a T-bone steak.'

Enid lifted a thick sheet of sweet ham on to a slice of bread: 'London's ruined you, I think.'

'My imagination ruined me before ever I got to London.'

Enid watched Myra watching him and told herself that they had been to bed together. When, she did not know, but surmised there must have been some opportunity between tragedies. Yet it couldn't have been serious if Albert invited her to stay in the house. He had done it on her once or twice, she suspected, but had been painstakingly discreet. She didn't really mind what he did, as long as he didn't commit the ultimate foolishness of leaving her. She was convinced he would never do that, yet had to guard against it nevertheless. If he had brought this Myra to the house with any idea of fornication she would make a public announcement of her pregnancy – which the doctor had told her about only that morning. That would put a stop to it. And if he hadn't, he would go into raptures at the news, as all men should, and as Albert had often enough for it to become a reflex action of cheer and jollity that led to a total blackout of drunkenness when the terrible truth went finally into his middle.

He poured tumblers of Bordeaux claret, little sensing what he was in for. Myra, who had a headache, preferred tea, while Richard, with a ton of dust in his throat, downed the glass and asked for more. 'I don't lag behind when there's wine flowing like water – which is rare enough.'

'It may be rare,' Handley said wryly, 'but I owe the wine-merchant three hundred pounds, which makes about five hundred bottles of steam in the last few months. I drink beer much of the time, so if we aren't careful this family will be wiped out by cirrhosis of the liver.'

'I found an empty crate in the caravan yesterday,' said Enid, 'which I suppose Maria and Catalina scoffed.'

'I'll put a stop to it,' Handley said, corking the bottles.

'What about Mandy?' Richard said. 'She'll die of hunger.'

Enid pulled a tray from beside the sink, set down food and a cup of tea, then walked across the yard in the thin showering of rain. When she slid it through the car-window Mandy pulled it in greedily and began to eat. 'Thanks, Ma. I'll come to the kitchen as soon as they've finished at the trough.'

'If you don't,' Enid said, 'I'll pull you out and give you a good hiding. We can't have you upsetting everything with your tantrums.'

She showed Myra her room, next to Uncle John's. It was carpeted from wall to wall, and in the middle was a low three-quarter divan with a white cotton bedspread touching the ash-blue carpet on all sides. A small chest of drawers painted yellow stood under the curtainless window. The walls were white, and facing the bed hung an early picture of Handley's. It lacked the quality of his present work yet was easily recognizable. A small shed stood in the middle of a wood, with a slanting wall of red fire drawing towards it. She thought it might be rather terrifying to wake up from a nightmare and have it as the first sight of the real world.

'It's a beautiful room,' she said, thinking it the apotheosis of colourful spartan negativism. She sat on the only chair, a thin cushion spread over the seat whose centre had broken through. Enid was curious: 'Have you known Albert long?'

'Just over a year. I was introduced at the opening of his exhibition, by a friend of mine, Frank Dawley.'

Enid opened the window. 'This room hasn't been aired since it was painted. Richard will close them all when he brings your baby up. Have you ever been to bed with Albert?' The house had turned quiet, though the weather was roughening outside. Maybe it would grow calm with the new moon, which would be full tonight. Myra stood, and Enid noted her figure, a great deal younger than her own, yet not much better for all that. 'I'd better leave,' Myra said.

Enid laughed. 'No, really, don't do that. As soon as I saw you I knew we were going to be friends. The thought just popped into my mind, and I asked it.'

'Why didn't you ask Albert?'

'I'd never get a straight answer. He doesn't know the meaning of the truth, and never has. I wouldn't want it, either, not in those details. Men and women can have secrets from each other, but not women.'

Myra liked her dignity and hard charm. Her presence explained much about Albert, because it seemed that with any other women he would have appeared smaller. 'I did go to bed with him once. We weren't in love, but neither of us could resist it. I'm in love with Frank Dawley, who gave me my child.'

Enid knew that Albert downstairs must be wondering what they were talking about, and that soon he would start pouring brandy down his throat or throwing chairs around, knowing it was about him. 'Men are such babies,' she said.

It seemed a banal remark, not worthy of her. Maybe she hadn't known a man well enough yet. 'I didn't come up here to be with Albert on those terms. I'm not as stupid as that. Just to get out of my house for a few days.'

'Albert told me,' Enid said, believing her. 'We were think-ing of going to the seaside tomorrow in the Rambler. Not long ago poor Albert used to walk there, twenty miles, and take some drawings that he hoped to sell on the seafront for a few shillings each. I often wonder how many there are stuck on people's walls in Nottingham, or forgotten in drawers somewhere. Still, it kept him fit. He hasn't succumbed to the soft life yet.'

'I don't think he will,' said Myra. Mark was crying downstairs.

She took Myra's hand: 'I'm glad you came. Now that we've been honest we can really be friends.'

Mark sat quiet and smiling on Handley's knee, who snapped his fingers and pushed out his tongue, winked and made popping noises with his mouth as if he were the father. Thirteen-year-old Helen begged to take him out. She was slightly built for her age, her face the same colour as Albert's and similar to Handley in feature, with long black hair falling in ringlets down her back. Her great heroine was Mandy, and she followed her tantrums and victories as if all her body breath was needed to keep the glow of admiration in her eyes. Handley gave Mark to her, who enjoyed being passed around, and let her take him out. 'Will he be all right?' Myra asked.

'Forget the little blue-eyed Dawley,' he said. 'They'll feed, cuddle, and worship him at the caravan. Helen will see to him. He can play with Rachel, as well. She's our three-year-old. We've got them to suit all ages.' Paul who was twelve sat in a corner surrounded by a thousand parts of some plastic construction set, unwilling to break off and talk. 'He won a scholarship last year and got taken on at the local grammar school. The others were just as intelligent, but they never passed that pernicious test, I suppose because I was too broke at the time for them to be considered. Still, John took care of their education, taught them all sorts of useful arts like tactics and bomb-making. That reminds me, you'd better set his tea out. It's nearly half-past four. I'll go up and see how he is.'

The eyes of the radio were dim, its face of fifty dials cold and blue-black. John lay on his bed, shirt open at the neck, and gazing at the white ceiling. 'No work today?'

'None,' said John. 'I'm pondering.'

'Am I disturbing you?'

He sat up. 'Not at all. I've been thinking for some weeks, Albert, that my world is too small. I've outlived this room, and am wondering what to do, what for example would be the right course to take compatible with the way I've spent my time here. It must be something in tune with it, because the fifteen years ought to be given some meaning.'

'I can see that,' Albert said, 'but it should come right from your heart, if it comes at all.'

John sat at his table, stacking the scattered logbooks into some sort of order. 'You're right, Albert. It's good to have a brother who understands me so well. I'll never forget what you've done for me. You gave me back my life.'

Albert gripped his hand. 'Don't overestimate it, John. You suffered, and I understood. It went right into my own bones. I wondered if you'd like tea downstairs today. Myra's come to stay a few days with us. I mentioned her once, the woman of Frank Dawley who went off to Algeria last January and hasn't been heard of since. Her life depends on him, but I'm beginning to think she's given up hope, which is a pity. She's the sort of person whose spirit withers without hope. She's got his baby, too. It'd be easier I suppose if she had a telegram to say he'd been killed, but she never will, not from a guerrilla war. You either come back, or you disappear. He chose that sort of war, though no woman chooses to get left behind.'

'If he went into the country through Morocco,' John said, 'and if he's not dead yet, he must be somewhere in the Kabylie mountains. Last time we talked about him I looked at the map. He'd go to where there was most fighting, naturally, though the distance is so great that it would be a feat even in peacetime to reach the Grande Kabylie from southern Morocco on foot. There's too much desert and wilderness.'

'How much?' Handley asked.

'Could be over eight hundred miles. You can't go a straight line over open country. Too dangerous. And zig-zags could double it.'

'Sixteen hundred?'

'In the summer. A hundred and forty in the sun. No water. Nothing to eat. Hunted. She may be right.' He looked sad, as if he'd spent days wearing himself out over it.

'I've never thought about it in this realistic way,' Handley said. 'She has, obviously.'

'You swim in the ocean of your paintings,' said John. 'It doesn't excuse you, but it exonerates you.'

'I don't think it does,' Handley said, his eyes glittering.

He switched on the radio, its panel lighting up. 'I can hear anything on this, messages never sent, morse that forces my hands to write words that stick like hot needles in my guts. If you want to stay alive and see trouble, stick close to the devil, and maybe Dawley is all right after all. And if you get killed you're still the winner, because you know nothing any more about the trouble you were in. When the devil betrays you there's no pain attached to it. Limbo is worse torment than hell, because there's always a hope that hell will be destroyed, shocked and shaken from within, broken down on all sides by the foces of torment and despair. What is the message I was waiting for, but never came? Well, it was written down in block capitals, and said: AN INSURRECTION BEGAN IN HELL THIS MORNING. GOD AND THE DEVIL WERE TAKEN OUT HAND-IN-HAND AND SHOT. THEY WERE SOBBING AND COMMISERATING LIKE TWO PANSIES. ALL SUFFERING HAS BEEN STOPPED BY DECREE. THOSE WHO CONTINUE SUFFERING UNNECESSARILY WILL BE SENTENCED AS COUNTER-REVOLUTIONARIES.'

'Stopped by decree until further notice,' Handley said.

'For ever,' John said firmly. 'Otherwise why should one wait so long. Isn't fifteen years a long time to hope for such a telegram?'

'What about heaven? Did the revolution strike there as well?'

'Heaven does not exist. Never did, except perhaps as an abandoned suburb. God may have a villa there but he commutes every day to hell. Men were led to believe that heaven existed after death in order that they wouldn't be

261

moved to seek it on earth, and so destroy the flimsy social order in which they lived. In the twentieth century they've started, quite rightly, to seek it. When hell is destroyed, build heaven in its place, until neither exists. There is no room for them. People were persuaded that hell existed after death so that they would not try to create it on earth. But that never stopped them, so all we need is to build the most perfect earth possible without the help of such concepts and balances. Most people exist in ways that would qualify them for a certificate saying that they live in hell – men, women, and children who are all innocent, but who in their sublime naivety and sense of justice get hold of guns and join the rebellion. Your friend Frank Dawley is fighting in Algeria from the sickness of false pride, and in one way is as guilty as the French he is fighting against – though if he is still alive he probably qualifies for innocence because of his experience in suffering.'

'Frank's no idealist,' Handley said, 'but a workman who saw the futility of his life and used his energy to try and lift others out of their suffering. He's on the right side, in spite of his using the revolution as a spiritual quest, like most of us. Revolution is the only remaining road of spiritual advance. I'm not on it, but I know it is. I don't mean the revolution of those middle-class English Marxists who live in Hampstead or the juiciest of Home Counties, because at the first sniff of civil strife they'd join the government militia or run to hide in the nearest police station. Frank Dawley isn't one of these and never could be. What I'm talking about is the common quest for spiritual energy that you get from the idea of revolution.'

John went down for tea, and Myra had gone upstairs to sleep off her tiredness and headache. She lay down, her case not yet unpacked, wondering why she had come to this house. Though feeling some affinity to the more tender aspects of Handley and his art, she seemed nervous and raw among his family, while hoping she did not show it. But it was right that she had come, for there had been nothing else to do.

Her glasses lay off and open on the bedside table staring

at the window, while she stared at the opposite wall. Her unaided eyes saw things more clearly than they used to, and she would either get a less powerful pair or perhaps go without them altogether. Yet they made her alert in the morning if she still felt sleepy, increased her range of hearing, and helped her to judge people better with her glasses on – in general more able to deal with the world. When among people you liked but did not know why, and could not ask the cool question as to why you were there, a higher reason obviously existed for your presence with them, that you could not understand at the moment, but that would be illuminated later during the greater confusion of being alone.

She drifted into pleasant oblivion, but got up after an hour and washed her face. Mark was being fed in the infants' caravan, and was glad to see her when she came in. But he soon clamoured once more for Helen, so she went outside. It was cooler and quieter along the lane she had ascended in the car that morning with Mandy sobbing beside her. The mud had not yet dried in the wind, and well-patterned car-treads were printed on it by a delivery-van coming up in response to a panic-call for more drink and food. She looked directly up at the sky through thick leaves that turned black against the broken glass of the blue, then climbed the steep bank, pulling herself up by stumps and branches, blue blouse and skirt merging into them. A wide field of stubble fell through the slit of sky, a well-marked footpath only a few inches wide cutting it diagonally across and spearing a small wood at its far-off tip.

Heavy clouds piled above the trees. It was an unnatural feeling, being so alone, without the baby, without Frank, and out of her own house, so far away from narrow ties and preoccupations of normal base-life. She felt better than at home. In the wood a man was plucking leaves from a bush and putting them to his lips. She had entered by a broken fence, so self-absorbed that her footsteps made no noise in the thick grass.

He bit at some of the leaves, took them away from his mouth so that they fluttered to the ground. He walked to

263

the nearest tree and clipped off a piece of bark. He flaked it to dust, and smiled. The humid summer had eaten it through. The lazy call of a bird made him look up nervously. There was something tender and pathetic about him, and so no cruelty in secretly observing him. He broke a stick and smelled the white disfigured joint. She wondered where she'd seen the face before, or of whom it reminded her. Lines of pain creased his forehead at what he had done, and he straightened the stick and put it in the grass as if intending to come back later and bury it. What unease remained in his expression was caused by some vital disillusionment that his sensibility had taken years to overcome. The marks of the first great inhuman betrayal were still in the lines around his eyes, and would stay till he died because they had become a permanent part of his features. She made no noise, but he turned and they recognized each other, never having met before.

'You must be Myra,' he said. 'Albert told me about you.'

'You're John. He told me about you, too.'

'I recognized you by your hair and eyes.'

'He must have described me well,' she said. 'He's a painter, of course.'

'It's not that. It's that air of being alone in the world that you carry about with you. I like to meet people who can't conceal what they are, and what ails them. It's very touching and refreshing. I hope you don't mind me saying so?'

'No,' she said. 'Albert told me you never left the house.'

He took out a cigarette, and gave her one. 'This is my first time in fifteen years. You are the first person I've met. I suppose you thought I was someone just escaped from a lunatic asylum. I was just renewing my contact with vegetation, trees, and grass. It was very painful, until I knew someone was watching me, and I saw it was you.'

She noted how similar his voice was to Albert's, but without the demonic edge of assertion. 'I came to stay a few days,' she said.

'I know. I was to meet you at tea, but didn't. It's better this way.' They went through the wood, John in front to clear the way. Reaching another field they walked side by side. 'So neither of us know the way,' she laughed. 'But I don't suppose we'll get lost.'

'I read your husband's book,' he said. 'He must have been a profound and unhappy man. Those who write so lovingly and understandingly about the earth are really only happy when they become part of it. That may sound cruel, but it's an observation I couldn't help making as I read it. It must be a great success, because that sort of earthly love has an appeal for many people in this country.'

'The critics approved,' she said, not wanting to talk about it. He sensed this, and they walked a few minutes in silence. He pulled up a handful of grass. 'Albert and Enid saved my life.'

'I know.'

'I'm glad you do. They've had hard lives, but found the love to save mine and not boast of it. I'm beginning to wonder what I can do to make my resurrection and their sacrifice worth while. I can't continue to live at ease with myself and do nothing for the rest of my life.'

She waved away a cloud of thunderflies attracted by the sweat on her forehead. 'I'd like to sit down for a moment.'

'Of course. I don't suppose you have any news?'

'Nothing.'

'You must forgive me, but that question was only a clumsy way of getting on to the subject. I've thought a good deal about him.'

'I didn't realize you knew Frank.'

'Albert told me. Of all the people I've heard about and haven't met he fascinates me the most.' They walked two more fields and back in the direction of the house. Wheat was high in one, and the path through the middle was hidden by close high stalks, so they went by the hedge, bending when it arched towards the wheat. He walked with nimble assurance for a man who hadn't been beyond the house and garden in so many years, stepping quickly on any small patch of earth to avoid bending dozens of delicate rods. 'I'd like to meet him,' he added, 'one day.'

'I hope you do. I'm sure he'd like to meet you.' He opened

a gate for her to pass. 'There's only one way I can ever see him,' he said, if he isn't dead already, he thought. And neither of them talked any more before reaching the house.

Ralph was not unwelcome at The Gallery, which was the most one could say about his appearances there. Handley, being unable to obliterate him, had to forgive him for the desecration of his painting which, in its precision and black thought, had been almost German, which pained him since his forgiveness meant that Ralph would now be able to marry Mandy. He wanted no micrometered nightmares eating into his favourite daughter, yet what could you do if you didn't intend to marry her yourself, except give her away with a good smile?

The question had been: Where was Mandy? Ralph looked at Handley with worry and loathing and disbelief when he said she'd departed for the battlefields of the M1 with the single-mindedness of an eleven-year-old girl in France from a bourgeois family during the war who'd set out with home-made bombs to join the Resistance. Ralph suspected Handley of having sent her away, hidden her until his passion was iced over.

He called every day to see if she had returned, and now found her locked in the Rambler and refusing to come out, playing patience on one of the lunch trays.

'Mandy,' he shouted, 'please let's go for a walk. I haven't seen you for a month.'

'That's no reason,' she said, letting down the window, 'but I will soon. I can wait. I don't want to miss the big dinner, though. You seen the booze-chariots going up and down? Dad will get bombed-out, gutter-drunk. He's got his new bird up here. And Uncle John's gone over the fields. Things are a bit upsetting, so I'm sticking around for the fun. Are you invited?'

'I think so; your father mumbled something before pushing me aside.'

'You'll really see us in action.'

He'd heard this last phrase from his mother before leaving the house. 'You're going *there* again! Have you ever seen such a family in action?' She was trying day by day to wear him down, but the guilt he felt after wrecking Handley's painting had given him so much strength that he'd be able to resist her for years if necessary. It set him up with great self-assurance, which made her give up the loony-bin as a last resort for the dark and twisting path he had chosen, deciding that since he seemed strong again, more normal means of persuasion would be necessary.

He leaned by the car, looking in and down on her. 'I think I know you all well enough by now.'

'You think our bark is worse than our bite?'

'It may be. Come out and give me a kiss. You can't stay cooped up all the time.'

'I feel safe in here. I've got the spare key in my pocket, and might take it into my head to light off, back to the motorway. With a powerful car like this I could show some of those rotten Minis where to get off, and leave a few wrecks smouldering on the hard shoulder! It weighs nearly two tons and does a hundred and twenty, the best thing Dad ever bought with his money. So don't keep on about me coming out. What have I got to come out for? I've got all I want in here. Yeh, if people keep chipping their tinny faces in at me like rabbits I'll slide off for another month's fun.'

He stood back, appalled by her recklessness. Yet it was exactly this tendency that attracted him, Mandy being the only girl he knew who could threaten to crack open his mother's skull with a starting-handle, which proved that she had more than a fair share for both of them. It was fortunate that she was a woman, and Mandy, and he felt that the sooner they were married the better. 'It's getting dark,' he said.

'When it does I'll switch on the light.'

Handley was wisely leaving her alone, and so would Ralph, if only his feet would carry his heart away. He saw Myra come in through the gate with Uncle John, and wondered who she was. They went into the house without a greeting.

'Give me your hand,' Mandy said.

He rested it on the half-opened window, and she kissed the back of it, pressed her lips against the padded flesh, and spread his fingers wide. His face reddened, and a burning pleasure stirred him. 'I love you,' he said. 'Come for a walk and don't torment me so.'

'I can't. My legs ache.'

'After all that sitting down and driving?'

To keep insisting would annoy her, whereas to stay quiet would at least prolong this charming tenderness. 'I love you, too,' she muttered, grinding her teeth into one of his fingers.

His yell of pain snapped at the whole house. 'You bitch!'

Mark was startled by its savagery and began to cry. Helen stood at the caravan door, black hair spread and eyes indignant. 'Can't you be quiet? There's a baby in here. Why don't you do your courting somewhere else?'

Ralph got into his Land-Rover and bumped down the lane, while Mandy indulged in a new game of patience. He couldn't take any more. It was impossible. Only Eric Blood-axe was fond of him at that house, howled when he strode through the gate. Blood slid silently from his finger, went round the steering wheel and fell between his legs on to the floor covered with muddy sacks, not in actual fact a bad wound, but jumping so that it was hard to keep his grip. I'm not an old man, he thought, hanging around her for this sort of welcome which she must have nursed in her bloody little mind after three weeks on the road. He shot the junction beyond the village and almost caught the back fender of Miss Bigwell's A40. Another story for Mother. It's lucky I didn't have an accident. Maybe I wouldn't be so ready to go back to Mandy if I had. He turned the car, and stopped in the village to buy a newspaper as an excuse for having left The Gallery in such a hurry. Then he went back up the lane, licked and welcomed by the thick green leaves. He also wanted to see them in action at their banquet that night.

CHAPTER TWENTY-SIX

Eight champagne-glasses had been stacked on the dining-room table, one base inside each bowl, making a tall slim tower that reached almost to the ceiling.

The long room was set between hall and kitchen, plainly whitewashed, with two large uncurtained windows on one side, and an empty wrought-iron fireplace on the other. The floor was bare planks, for Handley even in his affluence thought that carpets would somehow spoil it, liking to have at least one room where he could hear himself walk in bare feet. A ship's oak table, bought at a sale in Louth, ran down the middle. A huge eighteenth-century dresser lined the top wall, covered and hung with dinner and tea services. The only other furniture was eight chairs around the table, at which eight people sat.

'It's the first real party I've had in this house,' said Handley, taking up a bottle, 'and I've had money for over a year.' He was sprucely dressed in a charcoal-grey suit, and a white silk shirt with a light-blue rather broad clotted tie going into his waistcoat. 'So I don't want to see any murders at the end of it.'

Enid stood a candle on a shelf so that he could blow it out with champagne-corks. 'I channel my aggression,' he said, 'on to unfeeling inanimate objects from now on, eh, Ralph?'

Ralph smiled, less formally knotted, an arm strongly around Mandy who looked demure and luscious in that state, her warm eyes fixed on the bottle gripped by her father. He slowly untwisted the wire and removed the cage from over the cork. Light was gloaming outside, softening the fields and wolds, dimming the room, until the row of tall candles were lit along the middle of the table.

Tradesman's vans had been rumbling all day through the slush laden with fish, meat, and drink. They were eager to serve Handley in the vain hope of getting paid. The fact that he had money made him even worse at paying. If he had money he wanted to spend it, not shell it out on food that he'd already got on credit. So in order to make him pay they supplied more and more, fought for his custom because he spent so freely. But he did not pay, and it was difficult to dun him while still spending. If they dun, buy, for if you start to pay they become insolent. 'It's a good thing I'm not living in a depressed area,' Handley said to Enid, 'or they'd string me up from the nearest lamp-post. Luckily it's a good posh county with a long tradition of this sort of thing. I don't think I'll move, after all, at least not until they rumble me.'

Thumb pressed against the cork, the other hand turned the bottle in its palm. 'We've a few things to celebrate tonight.' he said, 'but I dare say we shan't know what till we come to them.' The smell of roasting meat floated from the kitchen. 'We're welcoming Myra, for one thing. For another, we're celebrating Mandy's engagement. Ralph's parents should be here, but they didn't answer the invitation, though they might still come. Then of course there's Frank Dawley, lest we forget.' He levelled the bottleneck towards the candle-flame, the room quiet but for his own pattering voice. 'And John is coming from his own world and back into ours, which might make a difference to somebody.'

The cork bulleted sharply out, left the candlewick smoking and flameless, but not waiting to see where it went Handley held the foaming bottlemouth over the topmost glass which was filled, overfilled, spilled into the one below, then overflowed and levelled up to the rim of the one underneath that, filling and spilling in the manner of a baroque fountain right down to the bottom glass. The second cork sent a sharp neat crack down the mirror above the mantel-shelf so that it seemed in danger of falling in two. 'Seven years' bad luck,' Enid cried, taking plates of olives and anchovies from Maria and setting them along the edge of the table.

Handley laughed. 'We've had them already.' Each took a glass from the fountain, so that it ceased to exist. A great thirst gripped them after the heavy and troubled day. Six bottles went in the hour before dinner. Handley laced the first draught with Courvoisier and lit a cigar so that he could draw breath between each mouthful. 'Don't you feel guilty at such luxury?' Adam said mischievously, 'when there's so much shortage in the world?' Handley's forceful laugh startled Richard and Myra from their quiet conversation by the window. John poured another glass for Mandy, who was anxious to wet her lips again because the dry wine seemed incapable of salving her thirst as it should. She grew light at heart and kissed her lover, which doused all his desire for more drink. Handley looked at them, a momentary glare, not knowing whether to envy Mandy's freedom or his future son-in-law's luck. He turned to Adam: 'In some countries cigars are fourpence each, and champagne half-a-crown a bottle. It's a luxury to us because the country needs bombs and napalm to rain down on the Frank Dawleys of the world – or his equivalent in all sorts of countries. Every glass of this stuff means a bullet for them. Every packet of fags a workman smokes means the same. We're all guilty if you like, but pour me some more, then it stops being guilt and becomes blame, and I can drown both with booze till it's not too bad to bear.'

'I just wanted to know how you felt,' said Adam, a sudden disturbing note in his voice. He looked faunlike in the candle-shadows, curly hair and straight short nose, small teeth showing when he spoke and faced his father.

'Do you want a private talk?' Handley said, pouring more drink.

Adam put the rim of his glass under the same bottle: 'I want to say it now.'

'Go on, then.' There was silence, as everyone waited for him to get up courage. Mandy giggled, and Handley snapped at her to shut up.

'I'm tired of feeling guilty,' Adam said. 'The weight's become too much for me these last few months. Every time I eat cornflakes or smoke a cigarette I'm tortured by doubt and guilt. I'm not so strong as you, or John, or Richard.'

'I'm used to carrying weaklings on my back,' Handley said. 'Let's get on with the booze, then the grub'll come quicker.'

'That's not the point,' Adam said with persistence and courage.

'What have you done?' Handley wanted to know.

With a great effort he said: 'I joined the Young Conservatives last night.'

Mandy laughed, and Ralph cheered. Handley's cigar dropped. 'It won't burn the floor,' he said, as Enid rushed to pick it up. 'Is that all? O God our help in ages rotten past, with no hope for tomorrow. I could have understood it when we were poor, but not now that we're rich. What's the girl's name?'

'Wendy Bonser.'

'Bonser's daughter? Some girl. So one of my family is marrying into the landed gentry? Do you love her?'

'Passionately, Father.'

'That's a start, anyway. We send you off, and we welcome you back. Thank God I'm an artist, or you'd have broken my heart. I can stand anything. I even sent my eldest son to theological college, so you haven't really shocked me.'

'Yes, you thought it was a good thing in those days,' said Richard.

'Don't you start. Our Cuthbert was a brilliant Sunday-school student. He had that superior smile of asceticism ticking away on his clock ever since he was a kid. He'd have been Jesus Christ if he'd been born one thousand nine hundred and sixty years ago. If the vicar hadn't taken an interest in him he'd still have been here, poncing and sponging like the rest of you. Well, here's to Adam and Wendy, and a long life to everybody.'

At the head of the table, he uncorked a bottle-forest of Bordeaux red and white. Mandy was on his left, and Myra to his right. At the opposite end sat Enid. Adam was subdued, felt snubbed by his father who had not created a row and thrown him out. He sat to the right of Enid, and Ralph was on her left. In the middle and facing each other were Richard and Uncle John. Soup vanished quickly, followed by braised herring, the pride of Dogger Bank. It was a great feast, though the mechanics of chewing did not so far permit any of them to say it aloud.

Waiting for the next course Handley stood up, a glittery restlessness in his eyes. Eight candles were lit down the middle of the table, a flare-line leading to Enid at the other end through a maze of wine-bottles, bread rolls, and platters. He took off his jacket, tall and slim in his waistcoat, shirt-sleeves fastened by a pair of gold cufflinks. The character of each face prospered in candle-shadow. All were beautiful, Myra thought, their talk more fluid now that the first hunger-pangs had gone. They'd all made concessions, given up some of their lives to be here. Mandy returned from the motorway, John pulled out of his ethereal solitude, Myra travelled from her own rooted house, Ralph dodged his parental curse, Adam left the charms of his newly-found heiress, Richard gave his pamphlets and maps a rest, Enid relaxed her chatelaine role of mother and manager, and Handley descended from his forest-bound swamp-coloured studio. His dark leanness glared at them. The established order of lunacy, family, and idealism shook the length of its barbed rope and dragged them in smiling to eat and talk, the subtle uniting captivity of organized deadness. But no, he thought, not with us. We're different because it's cold and bare outside, being set on an island between the North Sea and the Atlantic, bashed at by waves from east and west. Just a little dinner-party for family and friends. Is this what I've starved for as an artist all my life? As long as I'm still working, I suppose it is.

He smiled, but not for happiness or because he was amused. A smile covered a multitude of sins, not one of them original. 'Are all your glasses filled to the brim, even Mandy's? I'm wanting each of you to make a toast to the first thing that comes into your mind – anything, as long as it's revealing.'

'It's a bad game,' Enid said, assembling the plates. 'Either it doesn't work, or it causes trouble.'

He drank. 'Don't stab me in the back. It isn't a game. It's a way of thinking and drinking at the same time. There's no significance attached to it. How could there be with simple passionate people like us?'

A chair scraped as John stood up. 'Here's my toast, to the

273

war, the great hundred years' war against imperialism and the established order, class war, civil war, dark and light war, the eternal conflict of them against us and us against them, whether it's taking place underground as at the moment (except in a few choice spots of the world) or whether it's breaking around us now in this twilit haven of peace. May such a war go on to the victory and hope of the bitter end.'

They cheered, and he stood, bald, erect, matching a stern face with subtle and gentle eyes. He wore a dark blue suit with the faintest of pin-stripes running down the cloth, a red tie at his shirt and a white rose in his buttonhole. He looked at them and spoke slowly, smiling as if knowing they would never take him seriously, long thin fingers of his left hand deliberately turning a glass, the other behind his back. Not all cheered, though the general noise was loud enough to spur him on. Myra and Ralph had kept silent, but Adam, in spite of his recent conversion, approved out of family loyalty and his special regard for Uncle John. 'And I also propose,' he continued, 'a toast to a long journey I'm shortly to embark on, and about which I hope to say more later.'

They drank, but stayed quiet, puzzled by his last sentence. Was he going to leave them to a world without Uncle John? He lit a cigarette, and sat down on seeing Maria and Catalina enter with the platter of roast beef, a great haunch carried between them as if it were a dead man on a shutter. They set it before Handley who was on his feet saying: 'My toast is to art, to art, do you hear? And to the war that goes on till the bitter end. We'll leave the other toasts for later,' he added, picking up knife and steel to carve, and brushing aside their cheers as if they might infect the meat. There was silence during beef, fried marrow, and boiled potatoes. Small flat salads of sliced Lincolnshire cucumbers sat between each two plates. Myra admired the cooking and organization that had gone into the meal, qualities she had tried to instil into the village women of the WI in those far-off days when George was alive and she was a prominent talker at their meetings. She congratulated her, and everyone threw in their agreement. Handley leaned close, a darkening flush to his face. 'Glad you came, love?'

She nodded, and he said: 'Do you still love me?' Mandy listened, a smouldering cigarette between her fingers as she forked up the beef. Myra saw how irresponsible he was. 'I didn't come to hear this,' she said, loud enough for Mandy though not for Enid. 'I'm fond of you, and nothing else.'

But Enid saw what was happening, having taken a small portion, and finished already, breaking off knobs and beads of candle-wax from the nearest stick and putting them back in the flames. John rescued Myra by asking about Morocco. Had she been as far south as the Tafilalet, or gone through to Colomb-Bechar in Algeria? And if so, what was the landscape like? What months of the year had she been there? His questions implied so much more knowledge on his part than she had gleaned from her few months' stay that she wondered if he had been to the country while hoodwinking everyone for a month that he had stayed in his room.

Richard and Adam sat side by side with mutual expressions of misery and betrayal. 'Why did you do it?' said Richard. 'You must be on a secret mission for Uncle John, who wants you to join them and find out about their strength and organization. What else could it be?' He didn't look at him, but spoke straight in front at the wavering candle-flame.

Handley stood with his glass high: 'We'll have a toast from Mandy before she passes out.'

'Get crocked,' she said. 'I can swamp down as much as anybody.' She pushed away her plate of meatscraps and cigarette-ends, and lifted her empty glass for Handley to fill. Adam fetched in another armful of bottles and began to uncork them. 'Here's my toast,' said Mandy, 'to the racing-car my good sweet father is going to get me as soon as the Mini's worn out. Then I can go to Germany for a run on the autobahns. They're hundreds of miles long.' Her eyes moistened as she looked around, then slid back all her wine.

'I have bad news for you,' he said thickly. 'That Mini you

twisted my arm for hasn't had a penny paid on it, apart from the deposit. They'll be here in a few weeks to pull it from under you.'

'If I get a sports car in part-exchange, it won't cost all that much.'

'You'd better enjoy that Mini while you can,' he said. Their two voices were joined in a deadly duel, as if the loser would be shot dead and vanquished, pushed unsung into the earth.

'I'm going to sell it,' she said, 'and put the money as down-payment on a sports.'

'You'll end up in jail,' he said.

'You will. You signed the guarantee.'

There was silence, while they stared at each other. Then Handley smiled and sat down, calling that those who wanted second helpings should push their plates along. While waiting for his to be filled Ralph made a toast, hands trembling and eyes averted, wanting to say: 'A curse on this house.' But it would stamp him as melodramatic, and they would roll his sanity in the mud. He had been their football for too long, but would get his revenge when he married Mandy, when they'd think twice about sending a son-in-law to prison. He looked at Handley whose eyebeams blazed across waiting for him to speak. Or would they? They might see it as a neat way of unloading him and at the same time striking a blow at his parents, who had not answered his invitation so as to injure their own son. You couldn't jump off that spinning family roundabout without spilling your jelly brains in the dust. He held up his glass: 'In all sincerity, I drink to Mandy.'

She was on her feet. 'Oh no, you don't. Why do you want to show me up? Can't anybody leave me in peace?'

'It's a perfectly acceptable toast,' said her father. 'A bit wet, maybe. But here's to the happy couple, the gentleman-farmer and his lady wife, Ralph and Mandy. I know they're going to be very happy because they came into the world at the right time.'

Mandy resumed her chain-smoking. Even with a box of matches nearby she lit a fresh cigarette from the tiny end of the one just used. Handley swallowed and spoke: 'I'd like to drink to this house, this Jerusalem-on-the-Wolds where I've spent twenty years. But I'm thinking of leaving it soon, packing us all off down south.'

'That's the first I knew,' Enid said, flushed. 'It's my house, anyway, and I've no intention of moving. You were born in Leicester, but I belong to Lincolnshire.'

He took a scrap of newspaper from his pocket. 'How's this for a good buy? Listen: "Converted Thames dredger moored off Gravesend. A lovely home. Vast. On two floors. Seven bedrooms, three reception rooms, L-shaped bridge, cloaks, hall, and two bathrooms" – not counting the rather large spare one outside! "Running water and gas central heating. Garden on shore. A snip at eight thousand pounds." That's for me, captain of a boat that never sailed and never will. My beautiful family squatting in the bilges. Garbage disposal through the portholes. If life get too hard you scuttle it and swim away like a rat.'

Enid fetched a huge cartwheel of cherry-dotted cake, carved out portions and sent them around the table. 'So you're getting into that sort of mood are you? Wanderlust and family hate? Well, it won't do you much good tonight, because I'm not going to put up with it. I've a little announcement, but it can wait until I do a little toasting of my own.'

He poured liberal glasses of muscatel. Myra wondered when they would get up and murder each other, but considered they were too open and violent for that. Anything so quick and merciful would be against the rules. A warm white flash swept across the room, and Richard lowered his camera. 'Yes,' Handley said, 'it is a historic occasion. Pin us down forever so that we can look back on it as a great gathering. Make an album and call it *The Family*. It's bound to sell well.' He held Myra's hand and kissed it. A score of bottles had been emptied. 'The cake's good,' he said. He took Mandy's hand also, but she dragged it away: 'Not until I get my sports car.'

Pots of coffee were set out, sweets, brandy, cigars, bowls of fruit, cheese, and more salad. The candles were burning low, flames shaking into cups of fat. John fetched fresh ones, walked along the table fixing them in.

'What are you going to drink to?' Handley said.

Myra hadn't thought about it, but stood up. He filled her brandy glass. Should it be Mark first, and then Frank? Or because Frank was in danger maybe the toast would do him more good, for Mark was safely asleep in the caravan. 'To Frank Dawley,' she said, 'and to his son. To Albert's painting, Mandy's happiness, Enid's marvellous supper. To John's liberation, Richard's dedication, and Adam's vacillation. All one can do here is drink to everyone.' The camera drenched her in white phosphorus. All light blinded you, never showed the way. Only in the dark were you able to see, by keeping daylight as a far-off memory to guide you at the utmost pitch of blackness.

'Put that camera away,' Albert said. She sat down, but could not see. The candles wouldn't emerge from the flashing shadows and refocus. She felt tired and dejected because she did not know what she was doing here. She felt part of them, a mute appendage of their mad society, yet as if she had no right to accept it. Yet her reason for being here was that in their noise and violence and madness they seemed nearer to Frank Dawley than she ever was, even though she'd lived with him and had his child. It helped in the sacred act of recollection, for it was hard to pull him back from the haze and fire of the desert, see his eyes and body in the specific action of walking, eating, drinking, talking to friends. This was difficult not through lack of imagination but because he was still alive. If he had died she would see him with greater clarity. George was complete in every nuance whenever he came to mind because he was no longer on this earth, while Frank was indistinct because he didn't so much want her to remember him as be with him.

'Toasts are meaningless,' Richard said, 'so here's to all things of meaning. You have to persuade yourself that life has some significance otherwise you sink into the morass of the living dead. When you've persuaded yourself that your life has meaning it is your duty to help the living dead.'

'Well put,' Handley said. 'I couldn't have said fairer than that myself.'

'I wouldn't have wanted to.' Adam stood up. Since announcing his conversion, and predilection for Wendy Bonser, he appeared more urbane, effete, and supercilious. 'Here's to true love, and England, and, oh, all right then, Father, I drink also to the war against imperialism and the established order etcetera-etcetera.' In view of this addendum there seemed little hope of winning him back to the more robust ways of the family. His pale blue tie had a nonchalant wave in it. He sipped his brandy, rather than threw it back in the good old Handley style that he'd followed till now. They drank with him nevertheless, for he was still their son and brother. In the world of the family it was sin now, pay later, whenever you have time, because we can wait, and your dying breath will smudge the mirror that the last member of it holds in front of your mouth. He sat down, uneasy at such a thought, and reached for the cigar-box.

Ralph leaned over for an approving light at the same candle. 'Nobody loves it more than me,' Handley said, 'but I don't like it very much.'

'We'd all of us do the place more good,' Adam retorted, 'if we at least liked it. Any love for England in this room is destructive sentimentality. All love is destruction, that I'll allow, but I *like* this country as well.'

Uncle John stood, cigarette still smoking, and sipped at his glass of muscatel. Brandy and cigars he'd never taken to. He spoke quietly, so that they had to listen. 'In talking about love, and like, and England, you are losing a sense of proportion, Adam. We are no longer living in England, but in the world. It may be difficult to accept. In fact it took me fifteen years in a cell padded by my own thick thoughts to disentangle the tentacles of octopus England and discover that I belonged to the world. I'm forty-five years of age, not twenty. Many young people nowadays know it instinctively, are born with it, though I'm afraid that most do not. The world is one country, topographically speaking, divided by a system of seas and rivers and mountains. Those who say they love England are only in love with their childhood and youth, and those who stay in love with it go immature into the grave. Love of country is a fatal infatuation, especially to those whom you make your enemies.' His eyes glittered, and the aura of gentleness shifted to one side. 'It may take an act of cosmic violence to unite the world. We hope not. But it will certainly need innumerable civil wars and revolutions before the world can agree to become united. We are at the beginning of the hundred years' war, a series of sporadic conflicts under which the world as we know it will disintegrate. At one of these, in Algeria, we have a mutual friend who set out to take part in it. Some of you know him, all of you except Ralph have met him in one way or another. He came to this house once, and left marks on various people. I drove him from my den and solitude at the point of a gun, because in those days my sanity turned to insanity when it was disturbed. My senses have now recovered their power and sense of proportion. Nine months ago Frank Dawley went to Algeria and hasn't been heard of since. Anyone who takes on that task is helping in some unrewarded, idealistic, mystical way to bring about the unification of the world. In the future they may become the new yet unacknowledged saints, men who went into the desert, fasted by necessity, fought by conviction, and died by faith. A man who values his life at nothing, and whose belief in something good becomes everything to him, is a religious man. All great changes towards materialism and socialism are brought about by religious men. For a truly religious man the light can never fail, and if universalism becomes a religion and socialism is the way we have chosen to bring it about then even the mistakes and tragedies of socialism have to become acceptable. That fact alone is a severe test on a man's faith, on his sense of spiritual quest, but the greater the test on his faith the greater his faith becomes. I imagine it is unfashionable to confuse religion with politics, but such a steel-like mixture is necessary if we are to fight not only our opponents but also sometimes the system we are using. To make religion politics, and politics religion, is the only way we can use our faith, and at the same time keep it, and not be dragged down by a defeat of the spirit. Religious faith sharpens the bayonets of a political system. The desert wind blows hot and cold, is covered by light and darkness, yet always exists around your feet. It has taken me fifteen years to get back a sound mind and formulate my faith, and now that it is accomplished, I'm going to leave the love and protection of my brother and this house and go on a journey. I don't know how long I shall be away, or even if I shall ever come back, but I think it is fitting that someone from this family should make it his mission to go to Algeria, find Frank Dawley and help him, or bring him back if he is no longer fit for the fight. That will be my task, so my final toast is that we should drink to that journey, and to Frank Dawley who has already made it. After I've prepared myself and worked out the details I shall set off. You cannot sit thinking in a room all your life. Sooner or later you have to step outside and act.'

Handley did not drink with him. 'You can't do it, John.'

'Is my brother going to fail me?' he smiled.

'It's not a matter of failing. I'll never do that. But you've made your life good and whole again. You can't throw it away. It'd be a fool's errand.' He stopped, had a sense of betraying Myra who might, he thought with horror as he sat down, think he did not want John to go to Algeria and bring back Frank because he was too selfishly in love with her.

'I shall go to Algiers,' John said, 'get into the Kabylie Mountains, and some way or other join up with the FLN. Richard can print my papers on his press. I shall be a foreign but sympathetic journalist, and I shall find Frank Dawley, because I don't imagine many Englishmen are involved in their fight. Do you want me to go, Myra?'

The questioned seemed unreal, buoyed up on the hot air of shimmering candles, cigar-smoke, and wine smells. So did her answer: 'Yes,' she said.

'Why not?' Adam stood in such a hurry he upset his glass. 'John's going on a personal quest to help Myra by finding Dawley with whom she is in love. It's no revolutionary idealistic project he's indulging in, but an old-fashioned romantic search.'

'There's a bit in it for everybody,' Handley observed. It was strange, the first toast that meant anything left them embarrassed and antagonistic. No tree burned in a swamp of indifference, for the miasma around it could not catch fire, and water would suck out the flames. John would be taking the soul out of the house. 'You belong with us. Think it over for a few months.'

'I belong where I want to go,' he said. 'It's decided, so why don't we bless it, the whole family, by drinking to it?'

'You're going over the bloody precipice,' Handley said, 'so be careful. We're all part of you, and don't want you to take us with you. Most of all, I don't want to lose a brother. Dawley's a young man: he'll survive.'

'It's not a question of survival. Such a word is unworthy of you, Albert. Which of us here will survive?'

Myra stood up and walked outside, through the hall and into the garden. Their shouts could not bring her back. Had they no consideration for her feelings? Frank would laugh at such a party, such sentiments. It was indelicate of John to connect her with his breaking away from the house. He was noble in his intentions, but being noble left its scattering of hurt people. He could have talked about it rationally to her alone, or to Albert, but this set-piece drama before everyone made it trivial and embarrassing. Yet why should the contemplation of a noble deed be dragged into the mud? She should fall on her knees and thank him, wish him godspeed and all success in wanting to find her lover at the war. Sickness was smeared across her heart. A noise of shouting and smashing glass came from the house.

She went in immediately, and they were crowded around John, laughing and happy. Enid was setting more candles along the table. John was embracing them, shaking them all by the hand. Myra did not lie at his feet, but she kissed him, and said she would stay at the house until he left on his mission.

CHAPTER TWENTY-SEVEN

Moonlight was pouring into her room. She could not sleep. No one could, on that side of the house. Its white glow shone at the walls and bed, masked her face as she put on her dressing-gown and sat by the window. Moonlight made streets across the room, and she stood to walk in its winding grey alleyways. Clouds shifted them, dissolving her city. At one corner she saw Frank, luminous and ash-grey, grey stubble on his chin, eyes empty as moonlight. He stood between two cartshafts of illumination, grinning because he felt he should not be there. It was not the moon he wanted, neither its face nor light. She was afraid of him, as she was of all people when she did not know what they wanted. Maybe he knew. If you were doing what you wanted, there was no need to know what it was that you wanted. One way or another, the sun and moon burned you up. What else were you born for? Certainly not to complain, only to know. He came forward, and she cried out as if the apparition would scorch her lips. He was the stake she would burn at, and she drew away.

Mark cried in his cot, alarmed at her vision, and she soothed him for fear he would waken the house. It was a momentary dream, and he slipped back into peace. To ask what she wanted from life was a wild and irresponsible question that she was unable to answer while Frank was missing from it. In London she once saw him walking along Oxford Street, and ran after him through packs of shopping people. An insane rush of hope pushed her along, yet when the man turned out to be someone else she was glad. If it had been Frank how would he have explained being in England and not back with her and their son? No excuse would have been good enough.

In spite of her body-and-soul ache to see him again maybe she did not want to until he had utterly purged himself of all desire to trek away from reality. Solitude had taught her to mistrust men's ideals, especially those realized at her own desolation of spirit. She loathed her meanness but acknowledged it. To abandon Frank was a thought impossible to set in motion. She believed, but could not act. You could not act until you ceased to care. You didn't act upon your own ideals. Other people did that, without deciding to do so. You made your ideals known, spun forth the message of love and brotherhood and war, but going out to forge and prove helped no one but hurt many. You split open the body and mind, let the sensibility and love fruitlessly pour over the desert sands, and in the end the damage was greater to yourself than even to the one you love. Man was not big enough for such a combined operation. Even Uncle John knew this, and would only leave on a mission of rescue rather than a jaunt of idealism, as Adam had been sharp enough to see. Frank will only succeed in what he wants to do if he dies at it. Perhaps that was why she did not want him to come back, because to look on a broken man for the rest of one's life would be heartbreaking for her. If he came back he would be crippled, so she cried with bitter tears that there was no point in him doing so. When you abandon the moon, and walk too near the sun, your eyes are burned and blinded. The moon is gentler than the sun, might kill you slowly in the end or send you mad, but it doesn't burn you up in one great flash when you step within the limit of its power. Why couldn't she have told him this before he went? The transition was gradual, he would not have listened, and the moon confuses, weakens, does not allow the steel pivot of reason to be inserted. The moon demands that you be subtle, and subtlety does not work with someone enamoured of a scheme of the sun. He had to go. You had to let him, and the solitude his absence leaves teaches you to distrust men's ideals and the harsh, rational ideas of the sun.

She sat by the window, the metal-grey moonlight pouring over her. People walked up and down the stairs, restless, looking for tea or cigarettes, or a final drink. Only John's room was silent where he slept profoundly, she thought, exhausted by his intense and unremitting preparations for the long journey south, his own pathetic surrender to the hard time of the sun. It was a warm, full-mooned night, and the house smelled of food, drink, and tobacco. She came back from the lavatory, and saw Handley walking up with a tray of bottles. He wore trousers and collarless striped shirt, stepped along in bare white feet. 'Come to the studio,' he said softly, 'and I'll show you my painting.'

She was about to say no, not wanting to be alone with him, but walked up behind, will-less because she did not want to be alone with herself. Enid was there, in any case, smoking a cigarette. The studio seemed unnaturally tidy compared to the disorder of the dining room. Windows and skylight were open, but it was nevertheless hot from too much lighting.

'Sit down,' Enid said, a warm smile for her. 'This is the hottest part of the house in summer, yet far from the maddening crowd. We're thinking of building another house soon, two miles away, so that we can leave this one to the tribe. I'll take the bus here every day to see if they're all right, just as if I'm going to work.'

He poured brandy, water, slipped in ice, and passed it around. 'I'll show you this painting now that the light's right for it.' A large cloth fell from a five feet by eight canvas standing on two boxes by the far wall. Sky took up some of it, a band of eggshell blue and grey smudges along the top, then came trees, valleys, the earth, animals, and men, which loaded the greater area of the picture. Near the bottom was a band of soil, the thick chocolate skin of the crust, and finally a line of jet black where the depth of his consciousness had been reached.

'It looks as if it's coming to get me,' Enid said. Handley explained that it was supposed to. What was the use of a painting if it didn't get you by the scruff of the neck and pull you into either bathroom or jungle and show you things you'd never seen because you'd been afraid you might like the horror of them? It did the same to him, but he smashed them to bits on the anvil of his mind and re-arranged them on canvas so that it could do the same to others. Myra noticed a small hole in the middle of the painting: 'What's that for? Was it torn out?'

'That's another story,' he said. 'The ideal place for this

picture to be hanged is between two trees, so that the closer you get to it the more you see through this hole into reality. It's what I called Albert Handley's Third Eye, the theme and keynote of my exhibition. It would work if you set it up at a window in the middle of a city and saw the slums and factories through it, or if it was physically possible you could hang it across a main road and while looking at the picture and wondering what the hole was for, a bus comes running through and blacks you out for dead. It's the third eye that's as plain as all piss-water but which nobody sees, the third eye of dream and reality that looks at you through the territory of my painting.' He picked up small pieces of canvas, fitting them over the hole and blocking it, unable to choose one that harmonized. 'Ralph cut out the original, when he stole the painting, a prime piece of Lincolnshire witchcraft to do me an ill-turn but which only gave me a fine idea.' Over the hole he finally fixed an old photo of Uncle John as a young man in uniform, sad and raw, sepia-faced and faded, forlorn and wondering where the hell he was. Myra went forward and recognized him, dark hair showing under his service cap, his gentle eyes strengthened by the thinner and more youthful lines of his face. It fitted the picture so well that she shuddered, a heroic framework for this life-beaten man who in his resurrection was actually determined to carry out an act of heroism. They knew John would do it, or die doing it, and Handley's inspired action in using him as the eye of the third eye in this one particular painting of his soul proved his extreme and brotherly faith in him.

'You can't hate England,' Myra said passionately. 'You can't. I'm sure you don't.'

He was delighted. 'You see it, then? You really get the intention?'

'He never did hate it,' Enid said, sipping her brandy.

'We won't talk about that. It's too difficult. The last shot I fired in anger defending the maggoty homeland was at German bombers flying over the east coast to gut Nottingham in the war. After that I became an instructor. But our John in that uniform looks like somebody in 1914. There

286

were plenty of photos of that sort in our family, the only thing left of them by 1918. A photo. A million dead. Someone has to bridge the gap between the million dead and the soul of today. It's never been done. They were born of a tight-fisted nation that could not survive the loss of one million dead ripped from its cities and fields. Other countries did, and have. I'm monstrously English, frighteningly, rottenly, marvellously English. So maybe I'm Jewish. I hope so. But wasn't it fantastic that those millions didn't walk away from it all? I brooded on it last night. It stopped me from sleeping. A million dead. Two million Germans. Two million French – though some of them at least had the sense to mutiny. I wondered why so many consented to die, and came to the conclusion that it was one vast, overcivilized homosexual international holocaust, a group of nations fucking each other to death in a cosmic daisy-chain, and each dead man the spermatozoa of countless millions crushed in the uncreative death-womb of the mud. It was the earth turning in on itself, inverted sexuality. As another sixty thousand perished in the mud a general in the headquarters chateau wanked himself off in the porcelain bog. I got them all weighed up. So had a few million Russians when they refused to take part in this obscenity and voted with their feet for peace. A country only deserves love when the potential for that sort of dirtiness has passed from it. Imagine what sexual dreams the generals and presidents must have when they know that the pressing of a single button can cause such massacres. I'll paint a picture of a general masturbating with one hand, and launching rockets with the other.'

'That wouldn't be art,' said Myra.

'But it would be truth. What more do you want? I could do a series of cartoons, call 'em "The Pleasures of War" if it weren't for good old Goya. It would be a fair title, anyway. The art wouldn't be derivative, that I'd guarantee. But there's an endless fascination for me in 1914 and thereabouts. It's still in the English blood, because the artists and writers haven't taken it in yet and let it flow back to the people. Nobody's tried. Maybe they never can, and never

287

meant to. 1912: Rudolf Otto von Sachsenschloss, a twenty-year-old callow youth all down at mouth (because a sabre-scar hadn't yet healed and lifted it up to a glittering smile of strength) a reserve ensign of a Wurtemberg sharpshooters' regiment, met Lieutenant Oswald Burton of the Sherwood Foresters who was spending his leave in the Rhenish Pala-tinate complete with Baedeker guide-book, on a hiking tour of six weeks, whither he'd repaired after being blighted in love. It was a long hot summer (one of those they used to have before 1914) and the pine-smelling needlegums took flame, and fired large acres of forest. The two young men helped to fight the blaze, heroes side by side, so that they were fed and wined by grateful villagers after it was all out and over.

'The following year they meet in the Pyrenees, go up to great heights on muleback, eat their picnic meals, take champagne, brandy, and cigars to help down those delect-able patés and sausages. They swim in mountain pools, discuss great battles of the past, and drink toasts to eternal friendship.

'We now switch to Christmas 1914. Earthworks and mole-hills zigzag the fields and gentle humps of north-east France. British and German soldiers are playing football in no-man's-land, laughing and running to keep warm. Lieu-tenant Oswald Burton, thin-faced and looking thirty, goes over the parapet with revolver in hand to get them back on the afternoon of Boxing Day. There is fury and hatred in his eyes, more for his own men than the Germans. The lads from Worksop and Mansfield, Radcliffe and Lenton hate his guts as well. On the German line Oberleutenant Rudolf Otto von Sachsenschloss borrows a rifle from his batman. He is looking for a little sport. It was the British who sug-gested football. He fixed this irate English officer in his sights who is threatening his own men with a revolver. He drops the rifle and picks up field-glasses. "Mein Gott! It is Oswald." He reflects a few moments on the tragedy of war, chews a quotation from Goethe in his teeth which he finally spits out, then shrugs his shoulders and picks up the rifle again. Burton drops dead with a bullet in the middle of his forehead. No more Sherwood ale for that landowner's son. At the same moment a random shell whistles over from a drunken battery of the Royal Horse Artillery, seems to hover in the sky as if not knowing quite where to land to do most damage. Men of both sides scatter and drop. Rudolf Otto, too proud to do so, is blown to pieces. Only the football was safe: the dizzying spiral of European history took one more savage plunge into the abyss – opening the door towards the vast oozing shit-pits of Passchendaele – as the football rolled into a crater and bobbed about among nub-ends and shellcases.'

They sat at either end of the divan, Handley in a chair. 'People see everything through dark glasses. Without a third eye you are blind and lost, live in the abyss, unless you can read a book or look at a picture that can give you the use of one for an hour or so. There's neither forward time, nor backward time, only vision, and a truth of scene that could never have occurred to you.'

'You should write it in your manifesto,' Myra said.

'It's all gobbledegook. It wouldn't mean anything – except to critics, of course. It would be an act of megalomania to write it down, and an act of intellectual arrogance to try and interpret it. If people don't see it without having it explained to them (after a continual viewing of fifty-six hours, which nobody ever gets) then the painting has failed.'

Enid walked to the window. 'I certainly hope your next show is successful, because we'll be needing money by the end of the year.'

'That's your invariable reaction,' he said, 'to when I talk about my work.' Myra was ready to go back to bed. 'Downstairs at our shambles of a dinner a month ago,' Enid said, 'I never got the opportunity to make my toast.'

'Do it now,' he said, glad of a diversion from her baiting. They filled their glasses. 'Here's to my next child, then.'

He drank, but nearly choked. 'You can't be.'

Her head was held back. 'Why not? I've had six already.'

'Seven,' he said.

'Seven, then. So why can't I be pregnant again? Eight is

the figure of plenty. It often happens. I'm only forty-one. I knew I'd got seven already, but you were testing me, weren't you? There are three here, three in the caravans, and one at college training to be a priest. Have I passed? If I hadn't picked you up on it you'd never have forgiven me. Anyway, there's no mistake. I knew a month ago, but couldn't tell it to you till it hurt. I'm not an alarmist or a common trickster like Mandy. So look cheerful and drink to it. You always did before, if only with a glass of beer.'

'And so I do now,' he said, inwardly raging at her breaking the news with such intentional spite before Myra. He drank his brandy, and walked to the open window as if to heave himself over the ledge and out. But there was no point in flying, because you hit the earth and quick on a moon-night like this, plummeting through tree-branches and digging your own grave at the impact. 'Don't do it,' she mocked. 'It's got to be born and fed. And so have we.'

Myra felt a sort of appalled admiration at the cruel way they went for each other, surprised that they could take it, and still stay together. 'It won't settle your problems that easily,' he said, splashing out a large glass of soda-water and drinking it off. 'It's so damned hot in here. We must be in for a heat-wave.' Enid also felt a strange warmth in the room, that pressed against her eyes and temples like a headache. 'Give me a drink as well, and some for Myra.'

They stood by the table, as if for protection and reassurance. 'I don't like it tonight,' Albert said. 'The devil's around, or maybe it's just the bloody moon eating through my veins.'

Enid laughed. 'You're so funny when you get in this mood.'

'As long as you love me,' he said. Their hatred had gone, but Myra felt that something worse had taken its place, and wished for the hundredth time that she had not left her own house where she felt spiritually undisturbed. She preferred not to witness this sort of life while her own was so much confused.

'You're spoiled and self-indulgent,' Enid said, 'to get into such moods.'

He ignored her so successfully that she thought he might not be well. He leaned out of the window and sniffed, then turned an altered face towards them. Hot oily smoke, almost invisible yet pushing upwards like a wall, was coming from the kitchen.

He ran for the door. 'The house is on fire.'

On the floor below he pulled Ralph out of Mandy's bed, so that his thick naked figure stood tall before him. 'Quick,' Handley roared at his bleak face that even the pleasures of love had been unable to soften, 'get up to my studio and steal every painting you can lay your hands on. The house is burning down.'

Mandy ran by with a bundle of clothes. 'Get the Rambler and the caravans clear,' he shouted. Richard and Adam had been talking, and were still fully dressed. Thank God for the gift of the gab, he thought, as the three of them descended to the kitchen. The skeleton of a flaming door fell across their toes, and they drew back. Handley picked up a carpet and, using it as a shield, fell inside. Acting blindly in flame and smoke he plugged both sinks and turned on the taps, then opened the window and dived out into the mud.

Paintings were sailing out of the sky like eagles, falling on fences, bushes, into mud, and ruination of his sweat and dreams. Mandy towed both caravans at once down the over-leafed lane, those inside not knowing what peril threatened as they swayed and bumped along in the safety of their bunks. At the bottom she met a fire-engine, and by a swift efficient manoeuvre drove clear and let it through.

Richard and Adam hosed water towards the centre of the fire, but heat and smoke drew it short. He knocked the rubber pipes from their hands. 'Too late. Get out what you can.'

They ran up the stairway into his studio. Ralph who had made a rope, turned into a naked sweating demon impervious to sulphur and smoke. He hooked up boxes and bundles of papers and slid them down the still cool wall. Myra caught them, sent the rope back. Enid stacked them. Handley freed Eric Bloodaxe and tied him to the outer gate, then watched the house reddening slowly, put on its mantle of smoke so as to expire in dignified secrecy. He stored the more precious objects inside the large kennel, for a few drops of rain were scattering. The garden was littered with clothes, books, papers, bric-a-brac, furniture. A radiogram smashed to pieces on a concrete bench. It's a good job I never furnished it well, Handley thought, as fire-engines arrived and turned on the foam. Or had many possessions. The caravan idea was brighter than I thought. His limbs trembled, and he lit a cigar in order to feel more at home now that he plainly had none. 'Anybody left inside?' the fireman said. Handley pointed to the studio, still floodlit with electric light. 'There are three in there, but they'll get down by the tree.'

'Where?'

He pointed. Adam was already in the tree-top, a bundle tied to his back. Enid and Myra were carrying things to the front of the house and laying them out tidily. Hot smoke boiled as floors and roof dropped into the centre. Foam seemed to help it. Richard fought his way through crinkled char-edged leaves, and with Ralph above him they slithered through in a few seconds and fell to the ground. Handley assembled his canvases by the gate before paint on them melted.

Lurid scorching air threw them back, pushing, until they were halfway down the lane. Red of the fire mixed with red of the morning. 'What are we going to do, Albert?'

They stood with arms around each other. He'd always imagined that losing one's house by fire was a great boon to a free spirit such as himself, that he'd laugh in its face as long as no one was hurt. But this impossible child-dream seemed to have burned him completely hollow. After such a fire there was a law of silence which you could not disobey. They sat among bushes on the damp bank of the lane. He walked up again, to see house and tree vanishing in their own cocoon of destruction, eating each other up. He couldn't take his eyes from it. Even the fences were burning. A deep crumbling sound lay under the crash of great sparks. The past was burned out, and the future was unthinkable. The spoor of twenty years had gone. The whole edifice was rumbling and rendering down through an enormous mincing machine, fascinating, fantastic, frightening under the crude shock. Foam was still pouring over in a useless attempt to show willing, though Handley thought you might as well piss on it for all the good it would do. He shivered, gooseflesh patching his face and arms, teeth jumping so that his brain was drowned by the noise. He made a great effort, paced up and down till it stopped. A line of fencing collapsed, the limits of the house and its grounds merging with the fields.

'There's not much we can do, sir,' a fireman said.

Handley offered a cigar from his tin. 'It's all right.'

'Thank you, sir. A hell of a fire. I haven't seen one round here like that for a long time.' He put the cigar in his pocket: 'I'll smoke it later with my tea.' Handley walked away. The intensity was weakening, the world falling apart.

Mandy had parked the caravans on open ground by the pub. Leaving the Italian girls in charge she backed the Rambler up the lane and passed out two tea-flasks and a bottle of whisky sent by the publican. 'You're an angel,' Handley said. 'A real heroine. What a family I've got, even though the house is down.'

'They're eating beans on toast,' she said, wide-mouthed with pleasure at her father's compliment. 'They've never had such an adventure, all sitting on the caravan steps in their nightshirts. Even Mark's awake and enjoying himself.'

'It's a bit of an adventure for me as well,' he said wryly.

'The whole village is around them.' She wore slippers, and a coat over her nightdress, her long hair tied into a ponytail flashing outside. 'We can get your paintings on the back of the Rambler, Dad, and then they'll be safe. They're fixing up rooms at the pub for you lot up here.'

The whole lane was softly lit by the glow of the house. 'If anyone asks what I've done with my life I can now truthfully say that I made a fire.'

'Someone did,' Enid said, drinking tea from a paper cup. Handley passed the whisky bottle, then took a drink himself. 'But where are we going to live till we get somewhere?'

'Come down to Buckinghamshire,' Myra said. 'I've a large house, and a flat over the garage. There's room for everybody, and the caravans.'

'There's not much stuff to move,' Handley said, relishing the fact now that whisky made him feel better.

'You live near the motorway, don't you?' Mandy smiled. She seemed happy and decisive, even mulling on future pleasures, while the others were sluggish, and too wan to think about much.

'You'll get no time for that,' said Handley. 'We'll be busy for the next month or two. We need a new burrow, but we can't park on Myra. We don't want to ruin more lives than necessary.'

'You can, and stay as long as you like,' she said, knowing that Frank would like such a thing. If John found him and they both came back, so much the better. She hadn't seen John – no one had.

'Mark's all right,' Handley said, at her terror. 'Is that it?'

She fell into Enid's arms, holding on, shuddering. They had forgotten him. No one had shouted his name. In saving the paintings they'd lost him out of their lives. She whispered his name to Enid.

'Where's John, then?' Enid cried to them all. 'Don't look so dumbfounded, where is he?'

Mandy screamed, and led a frenzied stumbling run towards the smoking walls of the house. It was almost day on the hill-top, grey clouds rolling high. The firemen pulled Handley back. 'What is it? You're all out, aren't you?'

Handley fought free, a demon running to the charred walls. 'My brother!' he screamed. 'John! John!' He was thrown back, slung on to the soil and cinders, the scorching clinkers of his ruin. He crawled away groaning. Enid and Myra lifted him up, a terrible wrenching misery possessing them all. 'Did anybody see him?' Richard cried. 'We'd have seen him or heard something. He couldn't have been in there.'

'Nobody could have died like that. He didn't even shout.'

'It's not true,' Enid said. 'I can't believe it. He must have gone somewhere.'

At that moment he was standing on the platform at Louth station with two packed suitcases and a briefcase by his side, waiting for the first train to London. He flicked his lighter, and lit a cigarette with the sharp white flame.

PART FOUR

CHAPTER TWENTY-EIGHT

THE woman came in and set down his tray of chickpeas and mutton, dates, and sheep's milk. He was craven and blind with hunger, but would vomit if he touched it. The smell of real food tormented him. He scooped something from the first dish. The woman smiled, and shuffled out. Those who visited him did not wear veils. Being sick, he was inhuman, or a child. The elder woman had a sleek plump face, thick lips, and brown eyes that looked with a smile at every dish to see if he had eaten. Ragged trousers showed under her skirts, drawn in tight to her brown calves. There were gold teeth in her mouth. She wore a kerchief on her head. He ignored her out of physical weakness. The fatigue of observing these small points forced his eyes to close. She had three daughters, one who was sixteen, slim, pallid, and consumptive, the first one out as if her role of leading the other and the first shock of world air had been too much for her, wilting the forceful spirit and turning it in on its own weakness. She never smiled, but burned her way by him smelling of spice as she picked up his slops or the colourless camelhair blanket that had fallen on the floor. She was white and gaunt – finished. He'd known a girl once who worked in a tobacco factory and one day went to a sanatorium never to be seen again. She had the same impermanent, brittle, stern expression. Her breath went straight to heaven, they said. The mother bullied her, but only enough to prove to the girl that she wasn't ill enough to die. To stop bullying would frighten her. The girl was taller than her mother by a foot.

He was a casualty, kaput, unable to stand or eat, suspended above every sensation he'd ever known, and wondering whether he'd been left here to die. The world was divided into those who lived with their mouths open, and those who went with them closed. You saw the latter all over the place, the permanent open-mouths who were naive and unselfquestioning, the gums of all countries, John and Audrey Gum hand-in-hand in a corner of the sunless snug with never a care in the world or a word between them. He'd known many, but never for more than a few minutes at a time. He closed his mouth.

His watch had gone, and he never felt anyone take it. It was an act of mercy to be relieved of time, hours of revolution, days of sickness, weeks of hope. In this house all comers offered a hand to be shaken, whether they knew you already or not, as if you had just met in the middle of a wilderness, even though you'd touched hands a dozen times before with a smile and only a shade of recognition. It needed many greetings to establish friendship. What use was a watch among such people? No acquaintance is ever finally made, no friendship killed unless you die of wounds or your liver dries up. They brought him lemon syrup every time he opened his eyes. The consumptive girl poured yellow thick fluid into a cup and filled it with water from a beige earthen jar. He gulped it halfway and she refilled it. Another great swallow and in poured more water until the syrup lost all taste. The well was deep, the water good, not even reminding him of the buckets that dragged it up. She belonged to people who lived before the invention of the smile. It never distorted her thin face and pale straight lips. She would not touch him or get too close, or let her gaudy cinnamon-smelling dress swing near. He smiled out of weakness because he could not talk, having come back along a tunnel towards daylight and now hanging on to the solid ledge at the entrance as if he were made of straw and had no strength, clinging till he became solid and his force returned so that he could crawl away over the level and open earth.

He was naked under the blankets, and as far as he knew owned nothing except twenty-four hours of half-sleep every day. He was a landed and spiritual proprietor of sleep, owning sleep, all of it, forests and gardens of sleep, and the will to occupy a million square miles of wilderness, to descend from the tree of fire to the nether zones of ice and guts, down into twisting tripes and corridors of graven dream. It was nothing but memory, pure vicious iridescent memory, the primal slime of the past and his parents' past waiting to pull him in by neck and leg, hair and teeth, into the heat of midday and the sweat of the afternoon pall.

The hour before dawn was deceptively cool, when he felt he could stand up and walk out of the house, holding on to its outer wall perhaps, then by stick and guile make his way across the hills. He would be discovered and shot down, or the sun would shake him into leaf and powder. He lay like a hollow stone. Weakness made him panic, as if that were the permanent and final state of his life till death caught him secretly while fast sleep. The one escape seemed to get up and walk, crawl, either live or die, but not trough down into this panic wash of debility. For a time it made him loathe people, every fit person he saw coming into this room. But beneath his weakness he knew that this was wrong, that he should not run out and die alone, and that behind his tissue and spiritual inanition was a faint determination to survive. There was nothing to do but wait, drink the vile and bitter herbs, the dust-coated pills brought from God knew where and at what cost, and hope that the trick of life would work. He put his thumb on a large red ant to squash it, but it bit his flesh before he could find the force to press down. The earthen walls were bare, blemished in spite of the planing effect of use, breath, and smoke. The smell of kerosene and burning oil came in at dusk from the next room, filtering around the edges of sacking hung in the archway. All he wanted was to drink and sleep, but no water would douse his fever, and no sleep refill his veins with desire and strength.

Pamphlets and papers in French were put beside him on the floor by these women who were fiercer at heart and even more revolutionary than the men. But he wasn't bored at the endless days drifting by, not even by the thought that he might be a burden on those who looked after him. He seemed to be taking weeks of their priceless hospitality, but only ten days went by before he began to wake from his illness and notice his room and the people who cared for him.

One of the leaflets he picked up, yellow paper and large

pockmarked print, described the big attack he had taken part in, telling how it came as an astonishing surprise to the enemy who, being so far south and in such open country, had always considered themselves safe. Frank could not understand how they had been taken unawares. Drawing towards the town on the previous days and nights all had seemed confused and obvious. Those who had taken part were referred to as 'heroic soldiers' – *'Les heroïques soldats luttant contre le légionnaire et le mercenaire, les combattants loyaux luttant contre le napalm...'* – who had destroyed seven transport-planes and damaged ten others, and caused heavy losses to the enemy. The country was denuded, so no one had thought to suspect or look. The beige flat-topped hills towards the town and oasis had crawled with hundreds of men, brown and olive patches that from the air may have appeared like clumps of alfalfa grass or vegetation that a chance shower had drawn up from the baking flats. No plane had flown over low enough, and no binoculars from road or outposts had penetrated the sage-green and purple hills. They lay in their private ovens for the common good, the Algerian *Moudjahid* risking a day-time death-trap in order to spring down at dusk and do with rifles and grenades what should only in all sanity be attempted with mortars and artillery. The planes went up like jellyfish laden with gasoline, white lights bursting the crab-exterior of wings and wheels. The vague scuffling under a vast umbrella of stars and noise portrayed nothing glorious, but the leaflet turned it into an inspired strike for independence, and it needed no poet to put such phrases together, but only the experience of having been part of it for the fine words to dominate your fibres for ever.

He could claim no share of glory, because he was exhausted and sick, and because he had so far survived. Dozens had been left behind, out of the oven and into death, and scores more had been killed in the organized *rattisages* of subsequent days. The hunt was always on, and any time the sackcloth might be pushed aside and show the automatic rifle of some para or legionnaire. He was old enough to know that he could worry about that when it happened. Eyes burned through an inch of grey stubble hiding his emaciation. A shirt of white and charcoal stripes had just been given him, loose and with long sleeves, and his khaki shirt and trousers lay newly-washed on the floor ready for when he was able to get up one night and walk away.

The air was close, and smells hung thick from his morning ablutions. A cock scraped out its cry beyond walls and doors where a blue-white sun smothered the hills. By thinking of it, he could feel it, and the fear of it no longer daunted or pushed him back into sleep as a defence against the recollection of something dangerous. He wanted to leave at no matter what risk. A scorpion lay flat and literate on the wall, an alphabetic insect shaping itself in the first clear letter of the world, grey lines with grey callipers and an aerial sting-tail which looked as if it came from a big family and was a long way from home. He reached for some paper and crushed it before it had time to kill itself. It was an easy enemy, that you could see. Its twin-brother had turned into a globe of sweat, and broke into a run down his face. The greatest heat, when you were lying in bed, came at five in the afternoon, with the sun on its first slow pull away from your part of the earth, collected humours of the day falling into its track, and an intense pitch of fiery dampness turning his shirt into a foul dishrag without one muscle moving.

He read the papers, eyes close in the dim light. In earlier campaigns Azrou had been burned, Nahra flattened, the people of Laghouat wiped out. Massacre and destruction had been poured on to them, oil into flames by the self-conscious madmen of Europe, gaolers and bullies and scum-soldiers who perpetrated atrocities they would never mention to their grandchildren who would sit on their knees when they became kindly old men. They indulged in frenetic cruelties of 'pacification', they humiliated, exploited, butchered wherever they went. Behind them came the technicians and tillers of soil, roadmakers and administrators, idealists who did even dirtier work because they believed it was good, or were glad to have a career and servants they would never have achieved in their own country. But after a hundred and twenty years the Algerians had finally risen, and would not be put down. He found his friends proud and competent, dedicated and amiable, endlessly suffering and brave. 'Le Moudjahid! he is the soldier of the FLN, the political militant, the contact-man, the shepherd, the herdsman, the schoolchildren who go on strike in Algiers and Oran, the man who fights by sabotage, the student who joins the men in the hills, the man or woman who hands out leaflets, the poorest peasant who, with his wife and family, can only suffer and hope. The Moudjahid is the combined effort of a whole people guided by the FLN and having but one idea: the independence of their country.

'The Moudjahid is the one who cuts telegraph-wires, derails a train, burns down the house of the colonialist farmer. Every peaceful means to free ourselves from colonialism has been tried, and all that is left is to take up arms in order to recover liberty and independence. The Moudjahid is in the mountains and valleys; in every town and village he is the heroic soldier fighting against the mercenary and the legionnaire. Our wounded bleed to death or succumb under torture, perish by arbitrary justice, die protecting women and orphans. But the virtues and moral worth of the freedom-fighter are an indivisible part of the Algerian Revolution. Such qualities will lead us to victory, because true dignity and spiritual greatness are the first attributes of this fight without mercy, this fight to the death in which nevertheless we must not lose our sense of humanity, so that in the future we can remember our sufferings and in so doing recover our tenderness, affection, and sensibility in order to build a free and democratic country for the people.

'The occupying powers have tried to divide the Algerian people among themselves, separate brother from brother, but they can never succeed. The people are united and determined to triumph in this war of liberation. Our people will confound and defeat the enemy: they are the creative force, the inspiration and faith of our fight. The secret of our success resides in the support of the people. The Moud-

jahid is a citizen-soldier face to face with a conscript who does not wish to die for something in which he has no belief. The *Moudjahid* has a social duty, and a clean conscience, and though he is willing to die for these ideals, the fear and thought of death never for a moment enters into his soul.

'Small groups yesterday have become a regular army today, developing a power of offensive, gathering their war material, and improving their tactical skill. Faced with an enemy bent on genocide the Algerian army has rapidly reorganized. The *Moudjahid* in uniform operates in the mountains and wilderness. The *Moussebelines* – those without uniform – operate in the towns and villages, accomplish their missions in the streets, in cafés, cinemas, on the roads, in public gardens. They hunt down informers and torturers. They destroy police stations and guard-posts. They transport guns and ammunition, hide and look after the wounded, act as guides and liaison runners, report on the movements of the enemy. They draw the enemy into ambushes, form scout guards around our halting-places. The enemy cannot sleep or rest. He can never remain calm, or forget that we are there. Faced with the young and old, people of the towns, peasants of the countryside, students, and workmen, all those who make up the FLN the enemy has the whole country against him. The colonialist hordes continue their savage repressions against unarmed people, their extortions and pillage, and remain a devastating force. But they will be met by the serene courage of the Algerian *Moudjahid*. In combat he always stays within the limits of the laws of war. He must respect the human being, the plants and crops, animals of the field and all those works necessary to the wellbeing of the population. As well as fighting the enemy he must assist the people for whom he is fighting. He must help them in their misery and hunger, ignorance and illiteracy.'

Daylight was hot, darkness was hot. He could move, read, think. When the girl came in, he asked for water: '*Fish 'andukum môya?*'

'*Aho el-môya*' – giving him a cupsized earthbowl of warm liquid. He spread it over his face. Using the lid of a small tin for a mirror he pulled his razor painfully up and down the long bristles. She watched from the doorway, arms folded at waist level. The face in the tin was distant and indistinct, as if behind a waterfall, but the image gave him the assurance to shave by touch and not butcher himself. The more he scraped the more polished seemed the tin. With the bristles off, matted over the surface of the water like iron filings, his face was smaller but not so bony as he'd thought it would be. He expected her to smile but she didn't, so his ego was satisfied by not being pandered to. Her feet made no noise, and only her clothes moved when she took up the water and went. Love came with two faces, usually that of the great destroyer, rage and maggot-fire hiding behind the smile of the all-embracing womb of sweetness that tried to get you. Love destroyed your will, the soft evil old-fashioned swooning love that one had read and been told about, that froze the bowels and cooked the heart, the two-way facing foxy tearabout let loose in you by some far back ancestral parcel of yourself trying to do you in at the crucial moment or turning-point of your life. It was a sort of love you had to say goodbye to, drop dead to, get off my back love to, without losing your decency and self-respect, and your responsibility to others. Sweat poured out of you like thought; thought was salt and sweat in contradistinction to snot and shit. Blood wasn't thought, but disaster, and he'd seen enough spilled and splashed, grey and yellow flesh flashing maggoty under the sun and inking the rocks, death-pits and treegallows, scorched teeth and blancoed bone to last forever. The love all knew about was zither strings on which your enemies played, the love of evil that they got you to stave off by the way you spent your money, the whole sticktwisted righthanded idealism of love me and nothing more, love your father, mother, sweetheart, wife, children, country, king, and soil, the sky turned blind when it laughed behind your back, a black patch over the H-bomb mushroom exploding while you groped in the dark and called it love, romantic semantic schizoid psychic

306

platonic tectonic bucolic rancid fervid fetid bubonic love, the love that locks you deep in the dungeon of your putrescent silted soul. Swim up like a fish to the red-hot sands of the desert and set off through your own death towards life. It's a gamble in which no one wins but which those who take may win through, though at the moment he didn't see how he'd ever get beyond this cellar under the sky.

If he asked himself what was to be done, the only answer that came without thought and therefore truly was to stand up, to walk, to leave the tunnel of malaise and fight to the pinhead spotlight of sickness, resume his trek over rubble and sand and get to the mountains and maybe catch another glimpse of the sea before he croaked. If the dead love, the rotten love, the western love pulled out of you there was nothing left, except to lie for weeks in a hole in the ground hugging the bit of life still somehow tucked under your skin. What you had left, at this low pitch, was the will to get on your legs and move your arms to fight or build, walk, march, kill if anybody tried to stop you doing these things. When the foul and useless love you had been conditioned to accept by a finished and rotten society dead in its tracks had died, and you knew that to love only one person out of all others in the world, and be yourself loved by someone else out of all the others in the world was wrong in every sense, then you began to experience a new warmth of life, a responsible manifold feeling towards all others and not just one. The love of one was the love of death and of the devil. The love of all was a respect for creation. You could not love only one person in the desert, because if you did you and everyone would perish. There was a love in which the phallus dominated all else, the boss and operating member tyrannizing over everything you did or wanted to do. The other love was controlled by the hands that helped, taught, built and if necessary fought. The phallus could not be ignored, but neither could it be allowed to dominate, for such a dominion was destruction leading you to the sinkpots and gutters of the earth, dropping you and everyone through to the cloacae of oblivion. You came a long way to find simple truths, too far on foot over the earth, too far into the labyrinthine depths of your own flesh and blood, and yet never far enough, never to the extreme limits that the spirit can endure. No one else can live for you, neither the servants nor the telly nor books, nor any yarnspinner back and blighted from the fantastic pot-zones of heaven and earth. You had to go yourself, right in, right down, through the eye of a needle and into many mansions, queer street and rotton row, shit creek and blind alley. No one could go for you or do for you. The light burned in your forehead and shone right in front, and if the earth and coal fell it fell on you, with no one to blame but yourself and nothing to lose but yourself. Only your own skull was crushed, your own light stamped out, and since you didn't know anything about it nothing would hereafter matter.

The silent cinnamon glow of this tall young woman walking in and out day after day put her softly withdrawing life into him, a spirit and blood transfusion taking place with neither of them knowing it until it was too late. Towards the end, after Mokhtar had spoken about arrangements to get him to the base zones of the Kabylie Mountains, and when he was walking round the room ten and fifty times a day to build the fibres back into his legs, he sensed the decline of her strength, though she did not walk more slowly or breathe heavily and with pain. She lived on by gentleness and will, but her eyes grew lighter, burned intensely when they were turned away from his, and he looked at them before she realized he had seen her. They were grey-green, small and almost closed, as if to see better in the dim light and save what life remained in them.

He stamped on his love for her. He held her hand a moment on the night he went away. Her fingers were thin and cold, and she muttered something in Arabic in reply to his few words of French. He felt that neither had understood the other's speech, and did not need to.

CHAPTER TWENTY-NINE

Sand blew against the back of his head, hot grains stinging through his hair. Hat in hand, he walked along, for the moment unarmed, feet scuffling away the last two hundred miles to mountains and sea. Thin, grit-choked alfalfa grass stretched all around and up to the heights which now had trees on them. He was glad that the hot wind was coming from behind. Walking into it, the black mood would have sent him mad. They had been three days on the march, a guide in front and a *Moudjahid* soldier behind so that he began to feel like a prisoner. 'You are going away,' Mokhtar said. 'Snow for the winter, perhaps a sea-cruise to Egypt. Everything is arranged along the route. No more fighting.'

'Let the desert bloom,' he said, pissing on the sand, 'and lizards drown in it.' The heat of life was diminishing as they sat down to eat, three points of a well-spaced triangle, mobile rag-bundles resting before dusk and a few more miles into darkness. The triangle was deformed by surrounding huge rocks, and when the thin plane whistle was heard they hugged the ground and spread grey cloaks over themselves to become part of the outcrop and invisible. His moving shadow marked out the land, patterning much of it, robbing the sun as he walked of direct touches of the earth. He took his shadow with him, he in a straight line as it slowly shifted round all points of the compass. At night as he lay it was held down firmly so that it wouldn't walk away unawares and leave him naked and incomplete. He was no longer on the run, out to escape from others and himself. Yet he felt particularly insignificant under the great sky.

Another ten days and, if he didn't perish from bullets or napalm, he would be in the mountains. He was feeling his way towards some new phase at last, but could not fix clearly in his mind what it was because he felt no guarantee of getting there. He went on without hope, but with strength and intent matching together. Thought played no great part in his plan. The only way he could prove to himself that he was alive was to become dead. They moved, met nomads at dawn, ate beans and mutton, chickpeas and crackling bread, figs and dates. They drank tea. Dawn was like dusk: rose, rose, O Rose thou art sick. He watched it settling on the next range of flowing green-armed hills. Which Rose was that? Poor Rose. What disease did she have, this female day you walked across. Who could tell, till the sun came up? If she was sick, she was sick, and that was that. She'd either get better or get dead. He'd been dead, and proved he was alive – to himself. Each day began this way, the day that might on a whim change back into dusk and die like the night. A breath of wind came, rose turning to sunflower-yellow, warming a little out of the sun's nostrils. Far off on his left-hand was the way they were going, and it seemed no great pull to him. He picked up a stone, weighed it and let it drop. He spat on it, the smell of his night-sweat wafting around him. The guide blew his snot, and knelt on the ground in the same direction. Yet he wanted to go on, to reach the bitter fighting of the north. He had not quite died. He felt cheated. The world owed him a death, hadn't yet paid its debt to him. He was clear, free, easier than he'd ever been, but wasn't there another land still to be crossed? He was a believer as only an unbeliever could be, a believer in the materialist future who found his life hard after a mere few days out of the soft, warm acid-bath of death. The sun was shining and the wind was light, walking was effortless, but the familiar weight had not returned to his heart. Belief in the future one-way track of the world was not heavy enough. He did not feel serious or grim, and the great horizon made fun of his new uneasiness concerning it.

They hid among the rocks while a man on a donkey went by wearing a ragged striped shirt and baggy pantaloons. No one was trusted, not even friends. When face and limbs were pressed on to the earth, he felt more responsibility to the ideas he was trekking and fighting for. Pepperdust, crushed insects, salt stone and grass-juice were eating his own spit and sweat. The soldier passed him a half-smoked cigarette, and after a few draws he slid it back. A large white bird with black wingtips and yellow beak flew low, perched on a rock for a closer look, then lifted vertically as if yanked on an invisible wire. He did not like such birds, buzzards who were slaves to rotting flesh, chained to the dying, and the wounded who staggered along. They were part of the earth yet not of it, preying on it and waiting to taste flesh spiced by the spirit that had seasoned it. They reminded him of people who fed gluttonously off the meat and salt of the earth, who breathed in death as their spiritual seasoning and indulged in glamourized flights to heaven that made them feel superior and safe, and were set apart from struggle and a real knowledge of machinery and bread. From above they saw a pall of smoke drifting beautifully, but from below a tree was on fire with tortured trunk and writhing leaves, cellophane flames spreading and bursting towards cooler air. On the ground you walk away to get out of range, not fly towards it for a better view. Smoke blinds, but flame burns off a layer of your flesh, frightens you into awe when its blackened ruin smoulders and the mooncircle of ash is all that's left. Buzzards fly towards free meat and dreams, romance unstriven for and found in far off paradisial places – not crawled towards with sweat and effort, bloody feet, scabs, burning eyes, black nostrils.

In the wilderness you threw stones at such birds – and never hit them. Eyes looked, and their beaks cremated you. When you died they devoured your dead meat, divided it among a tribe, flew off with you in their several bellies towards the sun. It seemed like a bad wish fulfilled, going away from the earth. Maybe the bird would fall dead over the sea and your flesh sink back to the fishes. Perhaps a soldier shot them through the belly and so you were killed twice in the same way – the worms getting you in the end. Your flesh was at many mercies, but perhaps it was immortal after it was dead.

A village was clear of the French, and they entered in the afternoon. Small brown donkeys stood in the shadows of crumbling houses. He walked slowly. A middle-aged man in flowing white, with a thin face and sardonic mouth led them through a flock of long-haired black and white goats.

Sheep and mules were mixing freely by a well. They could not stay. A French column was coming from the east, and women and children were walking mutely to the hills they had just left. After eating, Frank strolled among the houses. He was offered tea, which he accepted. A twelve-year-old girl with no hands waved her stumps and asked for money. He laid a coin on the red withered skin of her wrist. She smiled from a long, rather fleshy face that seemed to have no settled features, as if she had just come out of a bitter snowstorm and was still cold from it.

They hadn't slept for two days, treading over miles of ground where the land was comparatively quiet. A Peugeot station-wagon took them a pre-arranged fifty kilometres along a straight narrow road. The land was dead flat, scrub, stones, half sand, and barren. They ran quickly when the Peugeot stopped, hid in a water-course while a convoy went by. The Frenchman who had driven the car and whose white face had not spoken one word talked to military police. Frank watched through binoculars, saw him resume his journey in safety.

The mountains were close, foothills of thirst and sun lifting to a purple crestline of five thousand feet. The girl's face haunted him. Her stumps fitted into the sockets of his eyes and blocked out the stars. His face streamed salt as he crouched low in the blinding heat. He craved the mountains. Food and comfort had no meaning, but he wanted to climb vast slopes and crawl through woods, get nearer to the cooling sky. The last scorching will of the desert was on him, a final flash so intense it made him wonder how he could ever have walked into it. But he considered that a man has to go into a place where the sun burns and wind chastens, where no other lives can feed off your own and where you reach the desert of your soul, of yourself, where the wind and sand can smother the immediate emotions of unsolvable chaos living with you and that you live with, and where the wind can reveal areas of yourself that had lain dormant. To survive it means that you want to live, which hadn't been so certain before. Solitude sings to you, real truths, real lies, and real songs of which there are few because they are real and not false. Having the largeness of spirit to try and change the pattern of your suffering you grow in the desert, for when suffering increases you understand the causes better. The immense space against which you pit yourself intimidates you yet increases vision. By showing such great areas of land and spirit you see that this vast emptiness will soon be filled with more than the turmoiled minor emptinesses of before. The stumps of the girl's arms tormented him, the flesh still hot and burning under his eyes. He hoped she had been born that way, so that he could blame nature and not man, and laugh at his misspent tears. If God existed, you could curse until your lungs burst, but you couldn't weep at what He did.

The last of the desert was burning under his feet. They weaved among upcrops of grey rock, stepped between fields of flint-teeth that looked as if they had been dropped by great metallic dragons that had turned vegetarian at the sight of green and distant mountains. A range of glistening salt-hills intervened, silver humps and hollows baking in their own utter barrenness. The pack burned scabs into his sweating spine where flesh had healed to tenderness during the long sickness and rest. Pain could be cut off, ignored by all senses subdued, and separated by the incessant walk that numbed everything but his private theatre of recollection, giving continual performance against colourful and fabulous backdrops of imperishable outdated scenery that he couldn't help noticing because it changed so slowly. The saline undulations they walked over for days would have been insupportable if the high ranges of the Tell Atlas had not pushed their shadows closer every time he woke up.

Pine-cones cracked in unendurable heat. They went for miles on knees and belly. He wanted to think of Myra, but could not keep her image in focus. It was almost as if he never expected to see her again. She and the child lived in a far-off other world, and at the moment he could make no bridges to connect the two. They had taken ten days to get over the first range of mountains – up six thousand feet, and twenty miles on. They joined a column which travelled by day and night, or tried to. This was a base area, a safe zone, but there were more bombs and rockets than ever before. Planes were always overhead, blasting the hillsides with noise on one run, scourging it with flame and smoke on the quick return, like two strokes of a painter's brush, said Djemal, a sixteen-year-old youth walking behind who had run away from the Lycée in Constantine a year ago to join the *Moudjahid*. He sang songs about the people of Algeria marching to victory against their colonialist oppressors, whistled the Marseillaise softly before curling himself in the foetal position and going to sleep at whatever time they stopped. On waking he looked like a baby in the womb of leaves and bushes, about to be born complete with uniform and rifle, razor-knife and bombs. It was as if the older men who were more silent had given him what remained of their ardent spirit for safe-keeping till the perils were over. Frank was cleaning his new Czech rifle, and Djemal wanted to know why he had come to Algeria, a question he forced himself to ask in order to make sure he had guessed the right answer.

For a while Frank had nothing to say. It was hard. It seemed as if he had been born in Algeria, and that the question was irrelevant. When they stopped in villages the people now automatically spoke to him in Arabic, as if he could be no other than one of them. But he now felt himself a middle-aged man looked up to by a youth, and he must provide an answer. 'I came to help people who needed help,' he said, 'and to help myself. When you help others, you also do good to yourself. It began when I drove a lorry-load of guns over the Moroccan border, and stayed to take part in the struggle.'

Djemal laughed. 'It's strange, nevertheless. You must be a communist.'

'I might be,' Frank said. 'But the one certain thing is that I belong to the FLN, because I have an identity-card in my pocket to say so.'

'I'm a communist,' said Djemal. 'After the war we are going to build a new Algeria – right from the bottom, because the country is ruined except for airfields and roads.

There'll be so much work that no one will be idle. We'll build houses and factories and hospitals, schools, and places where our workers can take holidays. We shall construct a great African country.'

A tremor passed under the ground. They were near once more to civilization, with its sensations of fear and the desire to run from the danger of exploding chemicals. They lay all day watching a sparsely wooded hillside burn across the valley. No one was hiding there. It was meant for them, hidden by smoke from their own trap, a screen no helicopter could penetrate. It blocked out the sun and they choked through handkerchiefs and rag saturated by precious water. You didn't think of the future for fear something in the present took away your capability of ever thinking back on it from a future beyond that. Another rippling explosion gave him a gothic gut-ache. A dead and withered branch fell among them, scattering cedar-cones. Would they now turn to this hill? They were forty in all, caught on the periphery of the base zone and brushing the outskirts of a French brigade. Without reason the beast could send up a ten-man claw in their direction, then call in the planes when it came back mangled.

They took advantage of the smoke and moved on, their formations the shape of eight-pointed Moslem stars drifting between the trees, until precision was lost and they merely followed the vanguards, though still widely spread. They crossed a track and began to climb. Looking from higher up, the smoke became a shifting bank of dull green, a new forest grown and suspended above the one burned out. The setting sun tinted it purple at the diffusing borders. Staves of flame showed beneath, spiked up by new explosions. They had moved out before the trap closed. An hour later they would have fried and died under it. 'How did they know?'

'Some French soldier passed on the news,' said Djemal. 'It often happens. A lot have come over to our side, even officers. They see we are winning, or that we cannot lose.' He remembered the man who had ridden them along a dangerous road in his Peugeot, his white fearful face and small grey eyes not turned to them during the whole length of it, as if he didn't want even friends to recognize him. Meeting him on the street he might seem a typical reactionary *colon*: presumably the military police took him for such when they stopped him, setting his fear down to the fact that he had come over perilous ground where he might have been sniped at from one of the riverbeds flanking the road. 'Sometimes we are caught in *their* traps, and the Gardens of Paradise become pits and sheets of fire. We turn into hares – but spread in the right direction. You must always know which way to run, how to pull out in swift order.'

They were doing so now. There were cedar-forests on the mountainside, and it was cool and windy among them, refreshing after the sun and sand-ovens of the south. They crossed a track at five thousand feet, then lay down for a rest between bomb-smoke and darkness. A few lights cringed on the foothills, almost red. The evening was clear, strange, neither cloud nor smoke anywhere. There would be no tea for them, either. The sky was purple, hills iron-rust, totally silent. His eyes still ran from the smoke. Immediately after wiping them he could see. Then they were filled again. He ached, even in his blood, though his bones did not feel the roots and rocks under him. The great Djurdjura mountains across the flatlands turned dark like a wall, white sparks above fixed in the ice age of the sky. Beyond would be the sea, white foam and blue waves, ships, and a different freedom from the one he had now, a picture that he did not want to imagine until he could taste the salt air that leapt from it.

Out of one's confusion comes the greatest strength, if you give in with patience to that confusion and know that some day you will find more meaning in it than you could ever get out of order. No one could see them. Not aeroplanes, nor even helicopters ten feet above the ground. The mats were the same colour as the earth, and they were lying in graves among bones and dust, fighting for life from oddments of the long (and not so long) dead. He spied out the track, too absorbed to notice the sun burning his hair. Like Switzerland, they said the French had continually said, these great inaccessible mountains, craggy and wooded, soon to be snowed up for the winter. But it was like Algeria, because it was like Algeria, and in Algeria, and in no other country on earth, Djemal said before he died. The ambush had taken place far over the valley by a white-walled red-roofed farm. An old man sat outside, a statue of rags with nothing good about him except his hearing, which was phenomenal. He detected a convoy coming along the road, and warned everyone. They took up rifles and revolvers, and spread over the countryside. There were eucalyptus trees at the back of the farm, and olives dotted down the hill. The convoy stopped, and a gun was unlimbered. They fired. A tree before the farm burst into flames. Then the house went up and the old man vanished in smoke and ruin. They relimbered and went on. Arbitrary law was the rule – which was called war. A boulder blocked their way. The officer got down from the lorry and was shot dead, a bullet out of cedar trees. Only one shot, though two dozen laid the ambush. The soldiers fired, at nothing. They spread out. They came back. They went on, taking the dead officer with them. A few minutes later planes flew over, and Djemal was the only casualty.

Go forward, go back, circle, stop, run. Sharp-angle retreat. Flank march. Attack. Wait. Scuffle. Retreat. Do nothing for three days. Go forward. You can always go back if that's where the advantage lies. Grave-stones bake, and bushes that can't get out of the sun wilt also in silent torment. Great mountain flanks rise across the valley, sheer walls of rusty stone in places, or ash-grey, or banked with olive-woods that seem, through the merging, enlarging, isolating power of the binoculars to be almost as dense and one shade lighter than jungle. Waiting, you isolate faces and scenery in the mind by the wielding of imaginary binoculars, superimposed over the real and dangerous detail that never escapes the eyes. The imaginary lens of discretion shifts at will across the legendary escarpments of memory, over the top, beyond farther valleys and into other countries, where your own particular republic lies – height, distance, and dense undergrowth removed from the common reality of the half-blind world but which, with one sudden pull of the will, floods in and becomes your real self staring you in the eyes. It is a dangerous exercise – at the moment – because it obliterates the valley and road you have been set there to watch. But he can't help thinking of his own children abandoned so blithely three years ago. If life becomes the progression of a more or less straight line you are poorer in spirit at the end than you were at the beginning when you first thought it easiest to live your life in that way. To turn back, zigzag, go in circles, demands courage but produces understanding.

From this spur of land both approaches to the village were controlled by heavy machine-guns, and were sealed off from the other world, first point of a star screening the battalion headquarters. If I were attacking I wouldn't come along the roads, neither from east nor west, the obvious ways which are easy to defend, but over the high mountains which shoot above it to north and south, and which nobody could be expected to climb. That's our obvious way of retreat. You're only on the side of history if you think of and do the impossible. If they come against us, we get more of them; if they send a patrol first to mask the main force, we get the patrol, if they send planes over they don't see us. They can send planes on random off-chance bombing but we've been through that before. You can't lose a war like this, you can only die, which is better than in previous wars when you did both.

The village is compact and crawls up a hill – like all important villages. Olive and fruit terraces fall away on three sides. People live here, but silently. The tin-rattle of goat and sheep bells still sounds round about, but you hardly ever see them. The days are hot in the sun, bring flies and midges out, living off the smell of donkey-shit and steaming pungent straw in a stone shed nearby. It was a long way from the camels of the sand-dunes nine months ago, when the taut skin of the camels reminded him of the oldest preserved body in the world that he'd seen in the British

Museum. The camels had died at the same time, great barrel-humps of bodies in a stonehenge circle, with no sign of what had happened to the people on them. He saw the first oasis after the sand, beige and blue houses on a hill surrounded by a deep-green palm-forest.

A rattling well-chain rapidly unfolds on its wheel, and the bucket smacks hard into water below, all sounds distant yet clear in this alpine silence. The bucket is hauled up twenty times a day, water in abundance, real life at last. He tasted it, cold and earth-fresh, and the stones round about smell of it in the sun for a few minutes.

The arrow is a liar, the straight line a lure and a trick. The lifeline on the palm of the hand may be straight and definite enough, forcefully curving through the landscape of cuts and callouses, scars and dust, but to circle and go back when necessary is still part of that life arrow, the straight line in the sky that you may look for but never see, but which is always over you. He wondered what geometry had to do with life, despicable shorthand that lopped it off and hemmed it in. See that road at which my optic sights are laid? A mortar-bomb would find its own trajectory, follow the setting it was on. The drifting and subtle decorations of arabesques are equally part of the true spirit. Days were meaningless, counted as units of time. Distances and directions were null and never to be considered.

He dug both elbows into the stones and pulled himself from the grave. Numerous insects clipped and hustled about the grey light. He staggered as if to fall, the air not weight enough to hold him, leaned against a rock which still had the warmth of day in it and let his piss stream down. It grew chilly, and he searched for the bush where he'd left his blanket. The sky was so white it needed a long stare before making out the lacy network of stars. The sudden pale flush of them sweeping above the blue-ashy precipices of the Djurdjura swung him somehow back to his Lincolnshire night-wanderings when living there with Pat, the pale expanding autumn sky above the worlds met with on his long solitary walks. He smelled the grass and hedges, wavering leaf-smoke and the farm-mould at the end of a lane. He stood still from his walk in order to recall it more clearly, not so much in a mood of loving recollection but out of curiosity to see whether it would come back totally. It did not, almost faded, until he thought of Handley and his brood who, he didn't doubt, still lived in the rambling and rickety house he'd once visited. He remembered an exquisite encounter with his fair plump daughter, and the odd meeting at revolver-point with someone called John, a mad pensioned-off brother who dreamed of controlling God and the world by radio. He thought of them as if they were part of his own family, and had such a forceful strange desire to be among them again that he seemed to be out of Algeria and danger and almost on his way there. He was disappointed, when his vision dropped, to find it was neither true nor possible. He wanted to see everyone – Nancy and the children, Myra and his child, the Handleys, even Pat who had gone back to her husband. After being so long in the desert he felt he could live at ease with them all as one big tribe.

He speculated on it, traipsing the valley five miles to get food and a space to sleep in. The wind buffeted between great pinnacles to the north. It was cold and damp, altering the spirit of the seasons, an equinox breaking towards winter, rough seas, and snow. But it was still light and comforting under the common moon, and his regular foot-steps were strong even to himself, in spite of hunger chewing around the hollows of his stomach. He thought of Handley scoffing food in the Greek Street restaurant, as he had with himself and Teddy Greensleaves the last time he saw them both. Maybe Handley lived in a flat now on Park Lane, and his kids instead of poaching went out at night emptying parking-meters. He suddenly felt human at re-calling something he had never given up, the life you could not step out of because it stalked you as a shadow even along this Algerian upland valley with the moon on its trees and the path he walked.

A rabbit with upstuck ears flopped out of his track, startled him by the feverish zigzag of its grip on survival. It didn't even have to know when to run, but shot away from its own ripe ruin when the mood of the earth shook it, all nerves and no reason, all fear and no civilized lunacy to stand and fight or find out what the tremors signified. As for them, they starfished at the threat of bombs, but never ran as bleak engines overhead shed noise and planed the hair's-breadth off their backs.

The thought of it stirred him to walk more quickly and his shadow caught up with a voice he recognized. He offered Makhlouf a cigarette, who shivered when he stopped to take a light also. 'There'll be frost and snow soon,' Frank said.

Makhlouf held his hand, smiled over the lighter flame. 'Every autumn I think we'll be in Algiers before the snow comes, with cigarettes and coffee, bread and newspapers.'

They walked on. 'It's warmer on the coast.'

'But I don't think so this year. We'll stay in the hills. Frostbite and pneumonia.'

'It's my first time in this *wilayet*,' Frank told him.

'They say you're going out.'

'You have enough men, I suppose,' Frank said. 'It's only guns you want. I can understand it.'

'You brought us guns. But we need men as well – everyone.' Makhlouf had received a terrible mouth wound, though his lips had grown back into a not altogether unhandsome shape. But his sentences of French came strangely out, sounds not tallying with the movement of his lips, like a speaker in some badly dubbed film. His wound had healed, but he nearly died from pleurisy, and he now roamed the hills like a spectre, thin and active with whatever company would have him. He rattled, rather than breathed, and the shape of his mouth was solidified in the form of an ironic, almost cynical grin – as if put on to apologize for the noise his breathing made. Whoever slept near him and woke in the night, which happened often when broken by exhaustion, heard the weird hollow rhythm of it. Makhlouf knew of this and slept apart, the grin still with him and varying with the intensity of his noise. He was tenacious, quick-witted, and strong, and used these virtues to defeat a concerted move to keep him in some safe rest area. He was a survivor of the Battle of Algiers, and had been a casual labourer on the docks most of his life. Under the red beret of a French paratrooper he'd killed in the Aurès Mountains, his head was completely shaved, a faint grey covering to his skullskin. 'They'll get you out,' he said. 'I heard them talking about it down at the post.'

He kicked a stone as he walked. 'They don't trust me,' Frank said, 'after so long.'

Makhlouf laughed. 'You've done enough. They want you to go overseas, and tell people about our struggle.'

'No one would listen to me.'

'They don't trust anyone,' Makhlouf said. 'Why should they? They don't need to. If anything goes wrong, a bullet is the only answer. A quick one. Life is simple.'

It was, until you thought about it. Then it became a derangement of the senses. It was all right as you waited, hidden, ready to kill, kept your mind drilled on war and politics, but even this was working less and less, the derangement staying uppermost as if he were losing his nerve. They were right to boot him out, no matter what reason was put on it.

It was cold, and twenty slept huddled in one small room. Even Makhlouf's rattle of life was welcome since it helped to keep them united, like the low purr of a worn-out fan evenly dispersing the spice and sweatfumes of suffocation. Walls shook with thunder, sounding far beyond the outside, yet sharp enough to penetrate his sleep. It made him uneasy, would stop him remembering his dreams. Orange flashes bumped against his eyelids, turning the blue walls grey. He rolled over and straightened his legs, pushing the bottom of another's feet. The small space held them in two rows, and Frank, now awake, noted how close he was to the black and red Kabylie blanket drawn half across the door. The spout of a Bren-gun pushed it to the wall, and a guard filled the space with his body and shouts.

Frank knocked a stump of candle down, pushed from behind by others struggling to get free. A giant handful of earth hit him in the face, and a body fell on to him, rolled sideways and stood up. He staggered and ran to the trees. Blazing branches fell across the house. The inside chains of himself pulled and strained, but he gripped a sharp stone in the palm of his hand as he lay on the ground to stop the chain snapping and leaving him to finally disintegrate. 'Paratroops have landed where we were yesterday,' Makhlouf said. 'Artillery, planes – everything.' The light in his eyes seemed to be choking him. A green flare shaped out the grove and all their faces, a circle looking in on itself. The bank of a gully descended, and he wondered whether they would stay on the hill-top, or pull out. A radio-telephone sparked. This was one attack they didn't get word of. He fought his way from sleep, not entirely wanting to wake up and face the reality of something that did not seem quite real any more.

A cold grey light was let into the valley, streaks of violet beyond veils of dust and smoke. He slithered, hanging to bushes to break a direct fall. The hill-top flamed outwards, shaking gusts of soil and air on to them. A man rolled free, stricken by shrapnel, going down in a ball so quickly that one of his boots flew off. The grey tooth-like crags beyond spewed mist. *'Bouclage,'* Makhlouf shouted, *'ou rattisage?'* They seemed to be part of the crumbling cliff. Thorns ripped into his clothes. The tail of a chameleon flickered down among the rubble. LMGs opened up on the hill-top. They reached the *oued* bottom and found markers to guide them along its course, a climbing flank march to the spur they had just left. Frank heard the noise of the Sikorsky helicopter and flattened with the others. Three passed over, slicing smoke and air to drop another platoon on the hill. The FLN had set fire to the trees with kerosene so that the helicopters hovered helplessly above unable to put down reinforcements the paras had called for. Dull thumping of grenades spanned the distance, but nothing could be seen except black and yellow smoke. White phosphorus spewed out of the pudding. A straggle of mortar-bombs fell across their retreat, bending and fusing the cedar-trees on fire. Helicopters had dropped grenades into the smoke and came clacking back over them. They lay in a forced rest for ten minutes. Any lifting head would have been blasted by their own guns if it gave the company away. Discipline was strict and not without rage. His face was in the soil, and the taste on his parched mouth forced him back to the past as hunger pulls a pig to its empty trough. But the trough seemed to have filled up, and his recollection was so sharp that it stung him to pain and happiness, so that he thought he had stopped living. Any future misfortune must stem from such periods when you did not know what was happening in the present – unless you jerked out of it to smash back the dragons of memory that only emerged from their lair to destroy you.

Makhlouf pulled his arm. They moved away from the *oued* and went up between the thickening trees, scouts ahead and behind. They passed through a former village, a collection of charred places, bits of rag and paper, where the paras had been three weeks ago. The men had fled, but all women and children were caught in their net. They walked quickly in silence, one village out of thousands. What did memories matter when something like this blotted them clean away and sent in its place a catastrophe that would be remembered for ever? Everything living had been shot down.

Smoke to the south-east rose up slantwise as if to avoid the sun. Shame at this picture of massacre made him want to die, to never get out, to kill his uttermost and perish here. Those who saw it were robbed of their manhood, never able to face women and children again without remembering what they had been powerless to prevent. Did it shrivel the souls of those men who acted in this way? He didn't think so. German Nazis from the Foreign Legion had set up torture-houses in Algiers, trained others in the same game. Yet thousands of Germans had also deserted. The Algerians didn't like them, but took them carefully to the frontiers on an arduous trek of repatriation. The Germans handed over weapons and ammunition as the price of their ticket to friendly soil. Tell the world about our struggle when you get out, the FLN officers said, and some Germans organized arms traffic, sent money to collecting-

points in Paris. A few of the deserting legionnaires –
Italians, Germans, Yugoslavs – changed their minds in
Tunis and Rabat, and came back over great and perilous
wasteland routes to rejoin the FLN.

They lay on a hilltop, hidden among stones and gorse, a
ferka of thirty men with twenty rifles, three LMGs and a
mortar. Warmth spread through cloud and sweated them
like a Turkish bath, became a knife-edged autumn sun.
There'd been no water for a day, and then only a few hand-
cups of green slime that he'd preferred not to look at. He
could only croak, impossible to converse with Makhlouf, so
looked with care and interest between the bushes and
across open ground of the uplands. It was hot and silent, a
smell of stones and sweat, and of cedar bark rising out of
thick forest. Faint notes of a cowbell came from a far-off
meadow. They expected nothing, yet had never waited
when nothing came.

Helicopters, 'those putrid horseflies of pacification with
ten maggot-murderers in each body' – to quote a leaflet he
had just read – passed over now and again, and they collectively willed one to descend on impulse. It was a good land-
ing-ground, uneven but tenable, as perfect as one could
allow if they weren't to suspect a trick.

Flies and midges hounded them, touched eyes, walked up
nostrils, bit lips, but such torments were set apart from his
patience. Five hours passed, and at times he almost slept. It
was an inviting hilltop to occupy, pacify, fortify, employ as
watchpost or base from which to send out patrols. Lost and
isolated, it looked as if no soldier's boot had ever stepped on
it. To sleep meant chaos and death, sudden fire and nightmare, so his eyes stayed open, unseen slits between flesh-
puffed bites he'd thought himself immune to after a year
in Africa. In the Kabylie Mountains they bred more fiercely
than in the south, venom his blood could not yet absorb
without pain.

They were ordered by radio to keep their position all
night, sweat out dreams on to thorn and gravel. Biting mist
hurt into his marrow. The greatest fight during the cross-

ings of successive wilderness had not been with the French, but to keep up with the physical tenacity of people around him who had come to the FLN because they could no longer bear to be treated like dogs, who had lost friends and families in endless and unendurable massacres, and who had reasoned that the only place for them was under the green and white flag. Bitterness and idealism toughened them even more than the previous hard life.

A green light near the coast lost itself in cloud, finding the one free hole to heaven, and good luck to it. Man-arsed sparks would disintegrate, unseen cold dust falling back to earth after they had lit up some poor bastards for a hail of bullets and phosphorus. Springs in his eyes snapped open when he tried with great effort to sleep.

Insects flung their last bites before being banked down by snow. He could smell it. Over six thousand feet up, it was ready to float on to them, hail in by crosswinds. What if some bull-brain mulling over a map in Legion headquarters should spot the subtly formed contours of their hill and decide to pacify it in the morning, to attack from landward on all sides and destroy their fondest hope of a godsent ambush. It was a game of psychic hide-and-seek, of pulverizing the rectitude of Lambert gridlines on the map one by one. An attack would chase them down from the hills like frightened stallions into the flaring waves of the sea.

He sweated, began to see more in the world than the next tree, the oncoming rock, the ragcap in front. Gates of fire and chaos fell on him. Unable to sleep, he wanted to get up and make for the nearest barrage or deathpost, through darkness into the blackest night of all. He gripped hard so as not to let go, a sharp stone and the magazine of his rifle, the pack of bombs and ammunition between bare feet. Chafing fleas were armed with minute hooks, power, and virulence that for months his flesh had resisted or brushed off as to unimportant to kick against. Another rash of lights went up, green lace flickering along the pale-blue undergut of cloud. A low rumble of guns or thunder followed. An attack at night was rare. After the vicious scrambles of the day you either slept at the backend of exhaustion or, more often, moved elsewhere in an endless game of musical chairs that, going on long enough, was designed to paralyse the less arabesque mind of the adversary. He imagined it would be difficult for a man who had commanded or been involved in this kind of revolutionary war to take over in peacetime, to set a raw and idealistic country along the line of material progress and development, especially one just out of complete and utter ruin. Maybe a man stored up the sort of energy and talent that would let him make a good job of it.

Moonlight flaked on surrounding pinnacles, tall fingers, rockhands, light-grey fists and knucklebones, a frightening sight, blue flames and limbs of panic ready to rush down from the highest peaks like overpowering ghosts and finish off all contenders whether they were guilty or innocent. The machine and metal of his gun squashed such terror, pushed fear into locked cupboards from which it would not emerge until or unless the age of machinery was destroyed. A gun saved him from the despair of not being able to distinguish good from bad, ghost from reality, day from night. In normal life maybe he would not need it, but now he did, in this eternal insanity of move and countermove. Its clean hard metal and machine-shaped wood set him apart from trees and rocks, and told him on which side of them he stood, even though other machines and metal were trying to destroy him unless he could take cover and sufficiently hide among those same trees and rocks.

Metal and living wood fused in him as he fell asleep.

When madness ended, sanity began. Thirst, fleas, hunger, and midges pulled away with the magic scene of a helicopter gliding towards them up the valley.

It hovered over clear but bumpy land, looking for the softest point to set down its wheels. Cloud had lifted, woods and lesser hills below had lost their smoky purple of the morning, lay flat and green, hillocks and ridges waving away to the next upshoot of high peaks. LMGs were sighted on the door, rifles and the mortar set for intervening space. The expected monster looked fragile and vulnerable. His vacillation and fear had vanished in an hour's sleep.

The pilot took care but suspected nothing. Guns swept the ground but they lay with iron control, hidden. The first soldiers came out skilfully, throwing themselves to the ground at great speed. He would have heard the thumps they made, but four were caught in mid-flight by the first bursts, and fell dead or wounded. Six others fired from under the helicopter's belly, then moved forward. Frank lined his sights at the petrol-tank, sent his magazine into it.

Shouts and gunfire shut off engine-noise. His second magazine went for the cockpit, calmly manipulating trigger and bolt as if on piecework at his old job in the engineering factory, but still as always keeping up the quality of articles sent out. Nightmare had gone, and a workshop of calmness and order closed around him. Mortar smoke flashed along open ground. He fired on fixed sights, unmoving elbow dug painfully in.

The helicopter sagged. A whistle blew and he wanted to laugh at the out-of-place, half-time sound of it. His mouth was full of coffee-grounds, accumulated bile-dust of day after day passed in the unnatural forced drive of exhaustion. He existed for a moment in emptiness, a human spent cartridge suddenly without senses. He shook it off, recalling his love of life and power of endurance. Two men nearby slumped over their benches as if they had worked too hard, or as if bent in shock at some mistake in their pay-packets. Another screamed in rage and pain because the machine seemed to have packed up on him.

Noise died as smoke cleared. He reloaded, senses sharp, danger always in silence and emptiness. A paratrooper stood up and rushed forward, arm swinging back, a brave fellow with nothing to live for. Frank fired three times, and as the man folded the missile curved towards them, slow, gentle, and sure. Bullets cracked through the explosion. Warm dust and flesh threw him sideways. The *aarif* stood and shouted orders, and Frank unhooked his grenades. The engine roared back into dominance, and the machine tried to lift, blades driving smoke in a large circle.

The *aarif* knelt, and two men near him went down. An LMG trained on the cockpit spat whole magazines away. Frank ran and hurled three bombs. None reached the machine, hid it from view of every gunner. He swore, and hugged the ground, disappointed at not hearing the final rending smash-up. Someone ran over him thinking he was dead, and leapt across open ground in front. He clipped on his last magazine, and followed.

A fist of light threw him back, hot smoke boiling in as the helicopter exploded. He crawled away, a terrible ache in his shoulder.

They withdrew from blackening fire and carnage, a beacon-signal for French reinforcements. Nothing remained that needed assistance, but it would draw them nevertheless, and they had to move speedily down, after fighting into the flames to collect arms and ammunition.

In the forest they were five men less, but they had rifles and machine-guns for another dozen. In such an army there were always more men than guns. Frank could barely carry his own. The fight had taken twenty minutes of their lives, and he felt the accumulation of twenty days travail tearing him apart. He kept up with their running, Makhlouf at his side wherever possible on the narrow track.

Feet shook as he followed the rough steep steps of a cliff face, fifty metres' drop over the tops of cedars, corpse-grey backbones and poisonous dark-green cauliflowers and a midday pullulating heat pulling him dizzily down towards them. A continuous high-pitched note humming through the back of his head made it difficult to keep his eyes open. He saw Makhlouf in front, in startling three-dimension, swaying along under a load of guns and pouches, and a spare beret like a red ear hanging from his pocket. The soft clarity of his movement was like an exceptionally marvellous painting come to life. Beyond him were others, blurred in dull brown going down through the trees. Only the nearest man was in focus, and he had no voice, no sounds penetrating his ears as roundedly as Makhlouf did his eyesight. He was black from the fire, sooted and corked, and all were unrecognizable one from another by face or race, united in moving quickly along a rocky valley, a track devoid of trees.

Helicopter-engines muttered, homing on to the smoking chaos they had fled from. They ate half-cooked beans, and supped from a few tins of condensed milk, which gave energy but choked him with thirst. His shoulder burned, but there was no blood. To touch it would be putting a hand into the fire. Both hand and fire lodged in his one body, but longed to stay apart, to widen the gap until it disintegrated out of pain and life.

CHAPTER THIRTY

JOHN HANDLEY boarded the steamship *El Djezair* at Palma, carrying his own luggage, and dressed in a pale grey suit. It was the end of September. The sky was hazy along the line of Majorcan mountains, but clear blue over the pinnacles and buttresses of the cathedral. The boat funnel was already churning, and a tree of smoke shadowed the baking sunclean quay. 'Yes sir, she's my baby' pounded from the bar radio, and a group of people were handclapping its rhythm as a steward showed him to a plastic deckchair along the port side of the boat. Smells of food and fuel oil permeated everywhere.

He stood at the bar with a bottle of lager, toasting himself in his brother's style: 'Here's the sky on your head!' After backpedalling from the quay, the ship steamed slowly into the widening bay. In ten hours he would land in Algeria, but his purpose was muted after many delays in Paris, time spent establishing FLN contacts whose addresses had been given him by Richard. At last he had been accepted by them, and received a *laissez-passer* from the FLN Provisional Government.

Tunes being played were composed at the time the ship was built, he thought, the jogtrot of the French *colons* from the twenties and thirties. Studying their faces, he saw that it was all finished for them, that the dance of gaiety covered brave despair which their flushed and half-cheerful faces would not admit to. A Frenchman danced with his wife, half young and half carefree, dark and good-looking, but her expression was growing towards that of raddled anxiety, of the soon to be dispossessed. He did not imagine it. The boat reeked of racial venom that the blue sea could not wash away. The Algerians of tourist class kept apart, less noisy at their separate tables. John had read and heard enough in Paris to know why. It was a boat whose passengers showed neither joy nor anticipation for the end of their journey, as if they would not stay long in the place they were going to.

In the dining room an elaborate and stultifying four-course meal was served, and John saw how scrupulously and tactfully the stewards had assigned places at table so that no Moslem sat with Europeans. Facing him was a Spaniard with a business in Algiers, who wanted to know why an Englishman should visit Algeria at this stage of its history. He would do much better to come in a couple of years when the rebels had been finished off. He scoffed at the idea of John being a tourist. What was there to see, in any case? He'd lived there forty years, and there was nothing, nothing now but filth and laziness, barren mountains and sand, and a handful of rebels causing trouble. Algerian riff-raff who had undone all the good of civilization. 'And as for the people, they'll cut your throat if you go beyond the suburbs of Algiers.'

'I won't let that worry me,' said John, standing up to go back on deck. His ineffable middle-aged gentleness worried the Spaniard, who stood by him later at the rail. John would have preferred an overnight journey, for there was nothing to see except the occasional steamer passing from east to west. The bar was closed after coffee, and people wandered up and down, or dozed on deck chairs as the boat rattled its way across the sea he had last sailed on coming from Singapore in 1945.

'You mustn't go beyond Algiers,' the Spaniard repeated. 'I thought a million French troops had made the country safe at last?' John said, wanting to get rid of him and study his maps in peace. Richard had procured a thick packet of large-scale survey maps for him, of areas where fighting was heaviest, and of zones said to be already liberated by the FLN.

'It will never be safe for *us*, not with ten million troops.'

John pitied him, yet wished he did not exist. The man was frightened, and because John was not, saw a danger of losing the protection that his fear gave him. If everyone were afraid they could at least learn how to feel safe. Those who were not tainted with fear were traitors, saboteurs, or innocent foreigners who did not realize what was at stake. They weren't pulling their weight, and detracted from the collective fear needed to give vital energy for the defence. And because John was an outsider of Spanish-Algerine felt as if the finger of the world were pointing at his insecurity and guilt. John asked what business he had in Algeria, and he replied that he owned a farm near Algiers, and a block of flats in the town. He was sixty-five, and if he lost both, he would starve. 'So you see, we can't leave.'

'To lose all,' John said, turning from water racing by to set his grey eyes fully on the man, 'is to become free. When you own nothing then you can live. Your eyes only open when you have nothing. Your spirit will flower. Ever after, you can share the fulness of your heart with others. If ever you lose everything' – he took a small card from his wallet, his name and the address of Albert's non-existent Lincolnshire house written on it – 'come to me here, so that I can willingly share all I have with you' – he grasped the shocked man's lapel with a gaze that burned into his eyes and in some way frightened him. 'There'll be a camp-bed in my room, and food on my tray.' The Spaniard sweated, thanked him, and went quickly to his deckchair where he tried to sleep for the rest of the journey and keep out of this madman's way.

John stood alone and during his musing remembered the fire he had started in the kitchen on the night of his departure, and smiled in the hope that it had succeeded in consuming the destructive pride of the family. If not, he would try again when he got back. If so, they would live in tents and caravans, and prosper under the hardship, pride gone, comrades once more.

Approaching Algiers the air was sultry, yet on top deck, exposed to the wind, it became damp and penetrating. Sailors were hoisting signal-flags, which shot out on the lap of the wind when the string was pulled. The coast to the east merged with heavy air and cloud that no stiff breeze could shift. An oil-tanker was waiting to enter the roads. Trying to penetrate the bad visibility with field glasses he half discerned distant peaks of the Kabylie Mountains.

After a fortnight in the sombre humidity of downtown Algiers John gave a taxi-driver twenty-five English pounds and was driven to the nearest FLN roadblock in the Kabylie Mountains. After many detours he arrived there at five in the afternoon, having taken all day to do the hundred miles, and been shot at several times by Algerian militiamen. His papers were checked at the roadblock, and the major said they had organized a tour for him, to see a hospital, schools, and training camps, and that it might also be possible for him to interview prisoners.

John nodded, wise and of few words. 'Are there any Englishmen fighting for your cause?'

The major did not know. 'Some English deserters came over to us from the Foreign Legion, but I believe they were repatriated through Tunisia. All deserters can choose repatriation, and most of them do.'

Two orderlies struggled up the hillside with his suitcase, camera, field-glasses, and haversack. For a fortnight he was guided about the hills, seeing the black and blighted circle of one doomed village after another, the marks of massacre, endless graves. He was shown an improvised arms factory, and caves in which grenades were made out of milk-tins. He watched a napalm attack by French planes on Algerian Nationalist positions, a distant upsurge of boiling nightmarish colour that brought the spread of childhood horrors bursting out of his mind. He lost balance, held a tree branch to stop the sight of collapsing trees spinning him to the ground. Even when the earth had settled down to the steady work of burning itself to death, he heard from within it the thump and scatternoise of fighting, and remembered his own short-lived term as a soldier. He calmly scanned the hills and boulders while the major pointed to landmarks of the trap now drawing in more French forces. He took John's hand. The vantage-point was no longer safe, and they had to run.

He saw the prisoners next day, young men of twenty in their camouflaged commando suits. They were ragged, weary, hungry, though not particularly disgruntled, and stood in line between the trees. John chose the man who looked most dispirited and asked why he had been taking part in this war. 'I don't know,' he said. 'I'm a conscript.'

'Did you like fighting?'

'No.' He was tall, sandy-haired, and had a raw unhealed scar down his left cheek.

'Where do you come from?'

'Auxerre.'

'What do you want to do now?'

'Nothing. Go home.'

'If you get home,' John said, 'will you tell others about what's happening here?'

'Perhaps. It's terrible. I don't know.' John reflected that it was beyond the resources of the Algerian Nationalists to indoctrinate each of the million Frenchmen set against them in this way, should they be sent in the tracks of those already captured.

He saw children gathered outside a hut and being taught to read by a young man from the city. The remnants of a European suit showed how recently a change of heart had sent him to this bleak wilderness. John had often come across groups of such dispossessed infants, grazing between trees like flocks of half-starved goats yet guarded by an adult who negotiated food for them and tried to see that none actually died. They were fed on a priority scale, which sometimes meant as much nutriment as in normal conditions. As far as possible they were kept under the green umbrella of wooded areas, for in the open any flicker of movement would be blasted from the air. Cut off from house, parents, or village they ran and fought in the sunlight, rolled in autumn leaves, slept in outside *djellabas*. 'The children are cared for as much as our soldiers,' his guide told him. 'They are the future citizens of Algeria.' He had learned good English at the Lycée in Constantine, had not in fact wanted to take to the hills, because he had enough pro-French, middle-class ambition to get control one day of his father's transport agency. But his brother was arrested – by mistake as far as he knew – and died while in the hands of the paras. There was no decision to make. Life became simple. At the first attack he was wounded in the leg and permanently lamed, and so he became a teacher and shepherd of orphan children, spent his night whenever there was a lamp or candle reading the French text of *Kapital*. He was well read in all matter concerning revolution, including the phase of government when the war was over. John made him a present of his fountain-pen, and a street-map of London.

'Here,' said the major, 'is our hospital.' Nets and camouflage-cloths were spread high and flapping between the trees. Huge poles had been rigged where trunks were sparse. John looked for huts or tents, motor-cars perhaps. 'It was,' said the major, 'one of the best hospitals in the *wilayet*. Before moving it here we used to put out red cross signs but they were machine-gunned. Now our wounded can be looked after in secret. We occasionally spread red crosses where nothing exists just to test their panache, and we are never disappointed to see bombs and napalm raining down.'

They entered between two bushes. John thought the path would lead to an encampment, but steps descended under his feet and feeble lamps flickered along the narrow tunnel. Fumes mixed with damp earth, caused him to cough and wonder what it was like being carried down with shrapnel or a bullet in the lungs, and the thought brought tears to his eyes. The mutual cruelties of the world mauled his senses, and at such times the justness of the cause being fought for did not help his manhood to face these realities. It was easy and comforting and necessary to believe certain things and fight for them, but to see what suffering took place during the transformation of the social order (or one part of it) was enough to break the heart.

The tunnel turned at right-angles, and then again sharply, for soldiers had been known to advance into such places preceded by flamethrowers, and such an intricate entrance was better for picking off the machinist before he came into the central ward, gave time for the lightly wounded to escape by an emergency exit.

He stood ten minutes in the dark. Wounded men were lying on the floor wrapped in greatcoats and ragged blankets. Damp petrol fumes made even John join in the coughing, and as he walked between them the disinfectant stench brought him close to retching. He could see clearly, and those sitting up showed gaunt faces, olive-wax features wondering who this man was from another world, who found it so warm that he paused to force out the peg-buttons of his skeepskin coat. The major explained that a doctor and three nurses looked after the hospital. Once the wounded reached it there were few deaths, but fatalities were common between battleground and casualty station. They had still not solved this kind of problem. The rules of Red Cross protection were hardly refined enough to help in such a struggle, but perhaps they would be so when this type of war became more general. John wanted him to finish before asking the question he made at each stop, but at the end of the row, following his own intense scrutiny of every face and revealed feature, he saw Frank Dawley resting with his back against the rocky wall. His eyes opened, and were set in a dull stare.

The black earth stank, the reek of months or years, of petrol and wound odours, palliasses soaking in urine and excrement. His hopes, when he'd imagined it would end like this, had been nightmares, sweat-rivers and black seas desolate under the light of a slaughter-moon, a sickle-back sweeping along the rim of the earth. Any man who came down to this must count it as a certain end in his life, the point at which only death or resurrection could occur. The major talked on, and it seemed to John that the top of the ladder in guerrilla warfare was the gift of an easy and authoritative tongue, with little way to go before it led to a government post.

His eyes closed for a moment. They were hemmed in by grey bristles that spread over the pallow-eyed face. John took out his wallet, and gave him the letter from Myra which contained a photo of her and the child. 'This is the man you were looking for?' the major said.

'Who are you?' Frank asked, taking the envelope.

The doctor was a young man of twenty-five who had not finished medical school. 'He was brought in a fortnight ago, and is ready to be discharged. His papers are in order for repatriation – out by the coast.'

'When?'

He laughed. 'We don't know.'

'My name is John Handley,' he said. 'I'm Albert's brother. I've been sent here to look for you.'

Those who could walk were allowed into the fresh air, stood at the entrance waiting for eyes to focus on humps of rock and twisted tree-pillars. 'I made up my mind to come and find you,' he said, hand on his arm. 'It was so easy that I still can't believe I've done it. A month ago I was in Lincolnshire with Albert and Myra, and all the brood.'

Frank smoked one of his smooth well-packed steel-tasting cigarettes. 'You may not find it so easy to get back.'

'Has this life made you pessimistic?'

'Not at all. But I know what is involved. The Yugoslav ships don't have a regular schedule, and often they can't get in at all. French warships go up and down playing guns and searchlights on the coast. We may wait months.' He wondered whether anyone but John could have discovered him in this way, and at the same time talk so blithely about getting out. He'd only seen him for thirty seconds two years ago, at Albert's house in Lincolnshire when he'd inadvertently strayed into his room while looking for the lavatory. John, sending morse at his radio-set, had picked up a huge revolver and threatened to blow his brains into the wall if he didn't clear out. 'I left my passport at the last place in Morocco,' Frank said, 'but it followed me by FLN courier. There's more organization here than you imagine. I suppose it looks like one big slice of chaos with everything so worn-down and shabby, but it works better than any so-called civilized town.'

John was amused by his defensiveness. They walked some way from the hospital, sat on a spur of land looking into a valley. 'Did you bring any books with you?' Frank was eager to set his eyes again on print that could be immediately understood, wanted for a while to restrict his world to clear shapes and lines of letters that would liberate his mind into the sort of pictures he chose to make from them. 'My luggage should catch me up tomorrow,' John said. 'There are one or two things you might like.'

'The fact is,' Dawley said, 'I feel at home here. I'm a part of this country. I've learned to exist in it. I don't know that I want to leave just yet.'

'You don't have much choice. They're sending you away.'

'That's true. I'll have to go. I wouldn't want to hinder them. They're all right, in spite of what they've had to do at times.'

'And you helped them, I think.'

'I wanted to. What else could I do? A friend of mine died, an American. When I get out I must write to his father, even though they loathed each other. I must write to his girlfriend as well.'

'Did you want to die?'

Frank laughed. 'You're bringing the wrong values in. That was always an irrelevant question.'

'Still, I'm asking it.'

The sight of John, his clothes, speech, manner, face, and body with the air of externalized living still on them made him hungry. The sparse diet he had grown used to seemed not enough at the apparition of this man newly-arrived from the outside world. He had a wild craving for food, for pork, cheese, sugar, cake. The desire went through his whole body and he laughed aloud at this strongest material sensation he'd had for months. He mentioned it to John.

'I suppose that answers my question. It's a good sign.'

'I don't believe in signs. It'll pass, this unnatural unnecessary hunger. I'd like to stay here with these people, right to the end. I believe in their cause. I've been with them so long that it's mine as well. There's nothing false about it any more.'

'It's also mine,' said John, 'though I needn't say it. But I came here to find you, and to see that you got safely back to England. Myra wants to see you. She's never known in the last year whether you were dead or not. She's grieving for you.'

'I tried to send a letter,' said Frank. 'I thought she might have stopped caring. Yet I never did, really. You can never be sure of these things. The morning I left her in Tangier was a dream I was always trying to get back to. I managed it only when I was most desolate and disembodied. I must see her soon, or I will die completely. It's funny, but I was strong before you came, but now I feel as if I'm caving in. I'm human again, weak. No, it's all right, John. Don't despair! I always was, but I kept it down. It was always a fight, for me. I've never been half so strong as I think I am. But I feel strong in realizing that. I want to go away for a while, because I know that a rest from this will never weaken me towards it.'

He lit another cigarette. 'Myra wants to see you. We all do.'

'I'm busy here. I love Myra, but I believe in what we are trying to do in this country. How can a person be in love, and fight, and still be sane? Don't you have to give up one or the other? Can any dedicated man, even a poet, say, claim to be in love with someone while he is writing his verses? Still, maybe you don't have to believe that love is dead to draw enough strength to fight for a cause you believe in. Otherwise you're not a whole man. I can get out of here for a while to see Myra, and then come back quite easily if I want to, or go to another war like this. There'll be plenty in my lifetime.'

'You seem determined.'

'But this one will soon be finished. France can't go on. I can't understand why you came out to look for me, John.'

'I wanted to see what kind of a man you were. The glimpse I had of you when you came into my room by mistake wasn't enough. I frightened you off with a gun then. I don't think I could do the same now.'

'So you won't tell me?'

Both were silent. Explosions vibrated through the cold black night. 'You know,' John said at last, 'we don't want you to perish out here.'

'Perish! What language. It's good to be talking English again. But how can one perish? You mean die. What does dying mean? I once knew a man who had cancer six times but didn't die. Each time he went right to the point of death, and then became completely cured – by the guiding hand of his own spirit, as far as anybody knew. He went down from fifteen stones to five. Worked in our shop at the factory, and we got fed up visiting him and having collections for a wreath. He developed antibodies when close to pegging out, then his weight shot up to normal for another few years. Nothing could get him, but everything had a try. He even had TB as a young man. Then syphilis between two bouts of cancer. Lost the use of his kidneys once. In the end, when he was nearly sixty, he got run over by a loaded furniture-van. I don't suppose he could stand old age. So don't talk to me about perishing or death. Why should I worry about that when I'm not yet thirty?'

CHAPTER THIRTY-ONE

HALF-A-DOZEN grey-haired donkeys as small as dogs were strung along the footpath laden heavily with baskets of mortar-shells, cartridge-belts, food, and oil. A roll of cloud that hid the great drop below looked firm and solid, as if any legs that lost foothold or balance would not be let down by it. They ascended towards more wet cloud, then crossed a plateau so deep in snow that the donkeys, led by an old man, were barely visible.

'It seems we forgot our skis,' John said, hurrying after

them. 'But never mind. Perhaps we'll come back one day for winter sports.' Frank had made an overcoat from his only blanket, cut arm-gaps and head-hole and drawn it around him with a length of rope. John had at first insisted he take his sheepskin coat.

'You need it more than me,' Frank said.

'I'd be honoured if you take it, though.' There was a glint of compassion and self-sacrifice in John's eyes that irritated him, a blackmailing mothering solicitousness that smouldered like a lamp about to tip over and ignite. It was an English attempt at dominance that he had not met from anyone in Algeria, a final feeble wish to make contact with another human being by the only means left to him, which in this case would mean John sickening from exposure. He felt sorry for him, but would not give in. 'I'm warm enough, thanks. I've toughened up a bit this last year.'

'Really,' said John, hurriedly taking it off. 'I shan't need it.' His sharp face was thinned by the fires that burned in him, giving the temporary impression that he could cross Siberia naked and survive.

'If I faint from hunger,' Frank said, 'I might ask you for a loan of it, but not now.' He swung his own blanket-overcoat around himself and drew in the rope. John had thrown away his suitcase and fitted the remains of his belongings into a copious but lightweight pack in which he still carried his loaded service revolver. He levelled this at Frank: 'Take my coat,' he cried. 'Take my coat. You need it more than I do.' His hand shook, and he rubbed sweat from his face.

Frank snatched the gun. 'You should give this to somebody who has better use for it.' But he laughed at the argument and gave it him back, and John put it into the pocket. 'You wear it the first week,' Frank said, 'And I'll wear it the second – if you still want us to share it.'

'We'll be on the ship in three days.'

'That's what they say. It'll be more like three or four weeks.'

Saturated by snow up to the waist they followed the track of the donkeys. John had learned enough to know that Frank was looked on with special favour by the FLN. He was not one of the thousands of Germans who deserted in such numbers from the Foreign Legion merely to be repatriated back to the cushier life of the economic miracle in the hope that their war crimes had been forgotten. Dawley had actually driven a huge cargo of arms from Morocco south of the Monice Line, and stayed on to fight with them.

'You can stuff personal comfort,' Frank said at that night's resting-place, 'as far as I'm concerned. Black bread or white bread, it makes no difference to me, as long as I can think on it and move on it.'

The northern slopes of the Grande Kabylie, well-covered with cork and olive-trees, ran sharply down towards the sea. Frank and John Handley shared a cave with other soldiers. They entered through a maze of thorn-bushes – though the area was completely free of the enemy – into a space large enough to stand up in, a hideout running twenty feet back into the hillside. A farther compartment which burrowed out at an angle was used as a storeroom for food, arms, and ammunition. They walked down towards the sea, but were turned back by Sten-armed FLN pickets.

Winter mist that spread along the coast gave Frank sore guts and rheumatism. White chops foamed on the sea, and passing ships were invisible though their hooters sounded – lost, melancholy, but determined at any cost to make tracks away from this inhospitable and stricken coast. He didn't blame them, wishing he could also leave it, in his present mood. 'I'd like to live on a ship, John, be the only passenger on a large cargo-boat that goes around the world, on every route and eventually to all parts of it. I'd have a cabin and part of the deck to myself, and would see all regions of the earth from the ship: Spitzbergen, Macassar, Valparaiso, Odessa, Yokohama, New York, Socotra, Buenos Aires, Singapore, Sydney, Archangel, Java. I'd never go ashore again, but I would see people. That ship would be a bit of everything, monastery, brothel, zoo, office, hotel, floating beer-hall, workshop. Lots of people would pass through it. Yet no, as soon as people start coming into it the idea loses its attraction. I'd like to be a hermit-figure on that ship. In the end I'd want to die at sea, dropped into the warm tropical tin-opened ocean. How's that for the end of the world, John? You never expected me to say such things, and I suppose it all comes from the miserable moth-eaten all-consuming past, and meeting someone like yourself who has just come out of it, and is trying to show me my place in it again. Such pipe-dreams have to be put in their place, pulled and stamped on if you can't burn them while they're still inside. And if you want to fight against the extinction of your better self you've got to scorch out the sort of past that can only give you such paltry and hollow pipe-dreams when you're at the end of your tether for a day or two. Plough the past under the rubble, and sow the best sea-salt in it – that's the only thing to do.'

They waited for the ship to come. Myra's letter had dropped to pieces, soaked and creased to extinction, and he left the remains of it in the hollow bowl of an olive-tree. It was a simple letter, giving news of Mark, wanting him to come back, and hoping he was alive and well. But it was warmly written, and he longed to see her and his son. He also wanted to visit Nottingham to find Nancy and his two other children. The only thing out of your past that was ineradicable was children. After three years he had a blind and painful yearning to see them again and help them, somehow wanted to live where they could all be close to him, an insane proposition that haunted him on this wild, saturating, and hungry coast while he waited for some boat to take him off it.

On waking in the morning he climbed to a lookout rock and scanned the sea with John's binoculars, hoping for some spectacular scene to fill his eyes – other than the usual files of men and donkeys. Perhaps one dawn I'll see a huge P & O liner stranded on the rocks below. Or maybe I'd wake in the night, startled by the grinding noise of its collision, then by hordes of destitute Algerians streaming by the cave intent on loot, and materials for the army. And I would go out and join them, walk down to the great liner and help them strip it of its luxury for their subsistence against the all-beating elements.

During the long days of waiting they talked little, considering how much each had to say, as if saving the flood of it for the safety of Lincolnshire. He hoped the storm would let go its fury, for he wanted to cross on a leaden calm. The prospect of gliding along over a great watery placidity attracted him after the torment and turbulence of the last year. Or perhaps it's my only hope of a rest, he thought, before the greater confusion to come. What right had anybody got to a peaceful life?

'Does Albert know you've come out here?' he asked, on a walk they took together through the drizzling mist.

'The less I talk, the more I do. I only discuss what I'm not going to do. But on this occasion we were all having dinner, including Myra, and I did tell them I was coming here.'

'What did he say?'

'That I was a fool. But I felt sufficiently in control of myself to agree with them, and still set off.'

'Don't you think you were lucky to find me?'

'I believe in fate. I was fated to.'

'You just happened to meet me.'

'Fate.' John snapped out the word, like a saw going through wood.

'Suit yourself.'

'Albert will judge when we get back.'

He smiled, careful to make it compassionate should John take it into his occasionally muddled and paranoid head to snatch at the revolver bulging under his torn and stained coat. 'I might be more inclined to talk about it in Lincolnshire,' Frank said. 'Let's hope we get through that black sea. We might be in for months of gales. Makhlouf told me it was sometimes like this all winter.'

After dark he couldn't sleep. It was still raining, a night laden with blackness. John slept in the shelter wrapped in coat and blanket, oblivious to the chill, stretched out straight and peaceful as if still in his army bed in England. It seemed that nothing could trouble his sleep, and Frank envied such animal-like capacity for indulging in it. He himself had lost it, being on his way out, while John took to slumber as if he might be here for good, which made Frank superstitiously wonder whether or not he'd ever feel the deck of a good steamer under his feet.

The sea was boiling up, as if the devil would make tea with it. Stretch out your arm with a kettle on the end and it would get snapped off. The wind was a mad steamroller, could push down trees, throw a helicopter against a cliff-face like so much spit. It roared along the coast and over the sea out of control, dangerous because of the night, crushing stars and pine-cones – though ships were moving through it. The roar was so great he expected boulders to be thrown up into the forest. The ship must attack the storm if it is not to be smashed itself. It sets out on an offensive against nature in which survival is a great victory. From a fish in water he would become a ship if and when he left Algeria, set out on his fight against the all-conditioning soul-moulding world. To fight was the only way to combat extinction, to mount the totality of his mind and body against annihilation by the sedate and backward sliding world. Yet he felt, in his agony of suspense, and the infinite postponement of getting away, in the tormented state of mind at being forced to leave and yet not wanting to, that for him complete victory was impossible because he had not been tempered in the true steel of the materialist world. In fact just plain victory was out of the question. You can conceivably break through the enemy lines, but you die on the barbed wire. Or, at most, you cut out your enclave in no-man's-land, and hold off all comers, friend and enemy alike, until you have dug galleries and catacombs in which to work out your ideas to the bitter end. The conception of wide-open spaces beyond the bloody lines of battle and death is only a dream, valuable only for drawing you into the conflict in the first place. But it is a conflict in which neither armistice nor surrender is ever possible to contemplate.

The storm lessened, and one night a boat waited offshore in the mist. Men were grunting by with loads on their backs. The moist hills rolled behind them. He stood outside and an FLN officer shone a torch in his face. 'You go down in an hour, at two o'clock.'

Back in the cave he took papers from a briefcase. 'Both of you.' They crouched. He counted ten one-thousand-franc notes. 'This is your pay, a thousand francs a month. Please sign here.'

Seven pounds ten for a year. He'd expected nothing, but that was what the ordinary FLN soldier received. Then he gave it back. 'Keep it, for the cause.'

They embraced. 'We won't forget what you've done for us,' the officer said. 'Tell everyone how we fight for our liberty. A guide is waiting for you outside. Here is your *laissez-passer*. You have plenty of time to get down.'

It was six hundred feet and three kilometres to the sea. Baked within and sweating outside, he hauled up his pack, and they set off for the rocks. He felt lean and nimble, not turning to see whether John was lagging behind. His arms were bars of steel, currents of energy running in to keep them working. Young lambs bleated from under carob-trees. How had they survived? It's a wonder God didn't turn in his grave at what was perpetrated in this war. He could no longer think of it. Such things would come to him later. They trotted the brown wet soil, filtering between trees, the last bouts of wind knocking into them, thorns ripping at his ragged slacks as if to send him out naked. The full moon was half-hidden, clear, then obscured, and plain again.

John fell, and he turned to help. 'Keep it up. We'll soon be on the boat.'

He was gasping as if his chest-wall would splinter. 'Leave me if I can't keep on. Leave me alone.'

Frank could not believe that the boat and a certain sort of liberation was so close. Their party descended steeply, no path to be seen, an occasional smoothness under the feet if they didn't look down too often or anxiously. 'I won't leave you,' Frank said, 'not even if you throw an epileptic fit. Come on, get up.' He took his belongings, heard him panting behind, and followed the vague shadow of the guide waiting below.

The sea made no recognizable noise, and the wind had become part of their breath with its soft hissing. The rain-grit lifted but showed nothing, then came down again. He felt himself going quickly to the edge, towards some endless sudden drop of the land. On waking as a child he stood on the bed, still in his dream, and walked to the edge, fell off into his world of wakefulness – and a broken ankle. You stopped falling, and there was no broken drop that the body could not take nor the soul catch up with though badly jarred. When they rested he felt the power of John's set eyes wildly against him. 'Let's smoke,' he said 'Shield everything.'

'The sky won't see it,' John smiled. 'Its black eyes are shut tight tonight.'

'They'd better be. Your fags will just about last till we hit Gibraltar – or wherever it is we're dropped. I'll take you out to a meal – by way of thanks and gratitude for your having come all this way to get me back safe and sound.' It was impossible that they'd ever reach anywhere, except the stony ground of this bleak coast, in a thousand gobbet-pieces after the French warships blasted.

John threw down his unlit cigarette, stood and looked around as if the bars of the world were shutting in on him. He ran back up the hill, springing and zigzagging like a mad goat, stones and soil scuffling from under his feet, scattering at Frank who chased him. He ran to the left, a shallow outflanking move that soon set him in front. He leapt from a treebase and brought him down. John foamed and kicked, but Frank fixed his limbs and bones tight. A rattle shook his throat: 'Let me go! Let me go!'

'Where?' cried Frank. 'Where? Where do you want to go?' Did he want to crawl back into the desert like Jesus Christ? He was too old. He'd die, and it couldn't be allowed, for Albert's sake, for everybody's sake. A black chilling emptiness spread through Frank at this unexpected bar to their departure, shrivelling his will, denuding every field in his world of hope and desire. He neither wanted to get on the ship nor go back to the war. His spirit sank into a pit of emptiness. Despair tightened his stomach as if it would never let go. Yet somehow he kept his hard physical controlling grip on John as if he were some animal he had to vanquish. He felt the revolver under his hand and took it from him, feeling an impulse not to use it on John, but to kill himself.

'Where do you want to go?' he asked again. 'Tell me, you madman. Maybe I'll learn something.'

'Leave me. I want to stand up. I won't run.'

'Stop struggling, then.' But he heaved and pushed, and Frank's strength was breaking under it. 'Do you hear?' He took the revolver away from his own mouth. It was something he could not do. If he wanted to die, and at that moment he had suffered enough to find it possible, then he would go on living and kill himself that way. The gun was pressed against the wild beast that lay under John's heart. 'If you try to run again,' Frank said, 'I'll shoot you, and get rid of you for good and all. One false move and you've got all that you ever wished for all rolled up into one big wish. Do you understand?'

He nodded.

'Go in front of me. We're almost at the beach. If I kill you no questions will be asked. Stand up and walk.'

Head down, John staggered towards the shore. For some reason Frank exulted, thought of his entry into Algeria when he had driven Shelley Jones forward at the point of a Sten-gun. Foam splashed on to the black rocks, sent curving lines up the gravel.

There was a cat on the beach, a small cat sitting by the rocks, hard to see because of its grey and white stripes. He had never seen a cat on a beach before. He found a stone shaped exactly like. an egg and threw it at the sea. He imagined throwing real eggs into the sea, a black insult, like pelting life with life, a holy pagan waste, a madman's defiance, potlash, eggs into the salt sea, a negative backward turning motion that you could not do.

They climbed on board the motor-launch, subdued and quiet, and set off through thickening mist towards the ship.

PART FIVE

CHAPTER THIRTY-TWO

A COLD orange fireball of dawn split up the semi-detached houses on the southern outskirts of Paris. Frosty clothes-lines and lights in the unseeing windows, and the smooth whining eardrum-click of the train swaying along under its own track-lights, and the short no-man's-land permanently laid between the dead-still established lives and the moving caravan of those who never stopped, registered on John's glazed eyes and ears. A woman walked the corridor with an enormous borzoi hound, and smiled at him, the obvious oblivious Englishman, bald, well-shaved, and already dressed. It is dangerous to lean out of the window. He stood firm, even to a sudden sway, underfoot vibrations well controlled. Dawn was the time he felt so guilty at being on earth that he could face anything from breakfast to self-annihilation. The terrors of light and night met each other at daybreak – in dreams if you were still in bed. Either way you could not escape. Standing in a train you smiled at the reflection of your own face as the train swept under a bridge, a face going so quickly by that there was no time to take a gun and blast the glass that kept you from its actual yellowing flesh. The revolutionary struggle is also a spiritual struggle. He and Frank were in agreement, and both were right. Energy, Imagination, and Intelligence were to replace the autocratic triumvirate of Inertia, Stagnation, and Reaction. The *coup d'état* called for a parachute-drop, fireball surgery, and he wondered whether the creeping takeover of guerrilla warfare were enough. He needed like everyone to set the forces of liberation against his own heart and soul, the consciousness that controlled him, ambush the laws he lived by, mine and blow up all preconceptions, erode them away if they were too strong, retreat only to prepare further stratagems against these ancient enemies of a new and resurgent spirit, make all one's life a protracted war against the flesh-built habits and indulgences of yourself. It is a method of ceasing to live under water, of eventually reaching higher consciousness where energy, intelligence and imagination can be used for the benefit of oneself and other people. Not yet fifty, he felt too old to go on living. It wasn't a matter of age so much as being worn out in a struggle he should never have started and undertaken, maintained through false hope and stale pride and the softening idealism of the congenitally demented. The animal talent and human bravado had been given to his brother Albert – the imagination, energy, and intelligence which he used for his work. The instinct to survive was good and necessary, but never enough, without the paraphernalia of self-assurance pushing you upstream at every lock and difficult weir. Lack of self-assurance was the basis of all illness that gave you the golden trinity of consumption, syphilis, and cancer – or whatever three reigning death-monarchs happened to be on hand for those who denied themselves the life-force in any particular era. Lacking the spirit of force and fire you called on death to do its worst, and if you didn't lack enough assurance for death to take up the call with avidity, it might be necessary to do the job yourself if you could stand the pain and poison of a razor's-edge life after years and years of it.

He boarded a bus outside the station and rode across Paris, the wide cobbled avenues and boulevards coming to life, layered by exhaust petrol from Peugeot and Renault, Ondine and Simca. He read metal names on passing bonnets, smelt the drift of coffee and smoky frost under the wide open blue sky of cold northern Paris.

At the Gare du Nord he checked in his luggage and walked over the boulevard. His greying border of hair needed clipping, and he wanted the civilized barber's perfume to float around him in place of petrol and dust. Dawley had gone to London by plane, indulged in the luxury of a cheap night-flight, for he wanted to see Myra and his son, and visit his wife and children in Nottingham. On landing at Gibraltar he had craved pork, but the first big chop had laid him up sick for three days in the Queen's Hotel, cursing all the vile trichinoid pigs of Spain while retching into the chamberpot. John had said goodbye to him at the airport, then taken the ferry across to Algeciras. The idea of travelling by air was the one genuine fear left in his life, and though he valued it for that reason, he could not bring himself to give in and overcome it. He had, in any case, a strong premonition that whatever plane he flew in would crash, fall like an ironfisted boulder out of the sky as soon as everyone inside had been long enough there to feel safe and on their way. So he would not travel by that method with Dawley, his one last desire in the world being to see him safe back to England, delivered into the place where he would do the most damage and complete the work of revenge that John had dreamed of for twenty years, that his own soul had sweated and rotted over, and that his own body had never in any way been able to carry out. But Dawley was a man who had not suffered in the way John had. Those who can't forget anything cannot learn anything and are unable to improve their lives or carry out their deepest wishes. But Dawley had been hard enough to undergo a baptism of fire in a real revolutionary war. His course was set, his strength gauged, his determination focused. He had no label, but his purpose was such that the safety of such a precious cargo could not be jeopardized. Even superstition must be used to guard him to his final destination.

The train going across nothern France, towards a country he loved but never wanted to see again, seemed like a new home to him, a place he would like to settle down in on condition that it never stopped. He talked to a young man who had been teaching English in Madrid. A pale face, threadbare jacket, and long hair made it seem a parsimonious living he had made. He was not glad to be going back to England, he said, hated the food, expense of wine and cigarettes, dourness and compliance of the people, weather, dirt, hard life and dogshit, ravelled up in his own tautologies and complaints. 'Not that I dislike England,' he went on. 'I'm sure I'll enjoy it as long as I can feel like a tourist. When that feeling stops I'll have to swim the Channel, get back to sanity and the mainland.'

John's eyes blazed, and the man grew silent, reaching for a bottle of Fundador brandy from one of his kitbags. He offered a drink, but John refused. Words went through John's mind, insistent bangings at the back of his head so that he did not know whether or not he was breaking the sound-barrier and the person opposite was able to hear what he was saying. The country he was born in had, in the final throes of imperial rottenness, sent him to Malaya to fight for the retention of greedy mercantile piracy that he had no heart for and could never believe in. He had seen men starved and tortured to death – human, pathetic, mercy-pleading men – for wicked principles, a policy of grab-all and keep-all by the free use of men's backs and blood. Since there was such base evil on all sides what was the use of surviving? And yet, around him during his imprisonment had been those who looked on with patience and cunning, waiting to assume the noble privilege of their own government and destiny. The soft-brained words blazed through him, circling at great speed the nearer he got to the coast. He let the window down for a fullblast smell of the sea, saw the open landscape billowing towards clifftops and a moving rash of white birds mute above the inexorable tread of the train.

He went to the door and opened it, held it from swinging out by the strength of his wiry suit-covered arm. As for England, he thought of its ageless and gentle countryside, mellow people with smooth and matey lives, and the ingrown spite of a failed and debased empire. Casual days without intelligence or equality, an octopus sinking back in clouds of inkiness and sloth, fobbed off by dreams and nostalgia for its vanishing manacled days. After all, one could see it at last, the English were an island people who had once been thrown into temporary greatness by a hundred-year bout of energy. They were insular plain-speakers once more who muddled through by clan and hierarchy, the eternal mean categorization of a rattled élite, and a dead bourgeoisie, and the people who knew their place because they had taken into their systems the poison of centuries from this so-called élite, and into their bodies the self-

bones of degradation – except for the chosen few who were buried under the common mass. They stared such poison in the face as they flopped before telly or radio every evening after eight hours of labour which they at least enjoyed more though they would never admit it. They were all in all a good people, safe on their island, pottering around in rundown factories and protected farms. Frank had faith and patience, and did not believe any of this, and for him who had these qualities it need not be true with such devastating force that struck at John. Many people in the country had twentieth-century brains and energy but were held under by the eternal sub-strata of hierarchical soil-souled England. They didn't even know how to pull themselves up by their own bootlaces, because they were made of silk and gold-tipped and might snap if yanked too hard. The soul of indoctrinated England was sprayed at the people every night like deadly insecticide, spew created by intellectual semi-demi-masterminds in the form of advertisements and songs of yesteryear, and those were the days, and these you have loved, and scrapbook for this and that, and as you were, and this is how you are as others see us, and O'Grady says, as you were then exactly and nothing more, and you'll never be any different because that is how God made this right-little-tight-little offshore island and you should be proud of its past greatnesses.

He managed to close the door, sweat shining on his face. The train drew into the town and towards docks. Tonight he would be talking to Albert, Enid, Richard, Adam, Ralph, Mandy, Myra, and perhaps even Frank if he was back already from Nottingham. He had neither sent nor received news since leaving two months ago, so was anxious to get the late train for Lincolnshire and bask in their congratulations for a great job safely done.

Yet when the ship crept out of Calais he considered staying in London for a few days. The delights of the wolds, and of his family, seemed as empty and unacceptable as the rest of the world. He did not even want to see Frank. There was no hurry, unless you lacked confidence and did not believe in what you were hurrying towards. He stood on the top deck of the ship, case at his feet, alone. A strong cold wind that rocked it among the waves buffeted him and played weird tunes in the aerial wires. Morse sang from the radio-operator's cabin telling of gale-warnings and rising seas, the incoming weather of the final world in a language he understood. The last word was weather, elemental weather fearful to ships ploughing the white-green waves, a ship that bucked and furrowed, engines burning underneath it all.

The gullshit cliffs loomed out of drizzle and mist, sending a pain of hopeless love through him. England, he thought, if only you could begin again from nakedness, become a green infant born from the soil and salt sea, put a coat of all colours on your back of all colours, and start in intelligence and gentleness, but without me, without me.

He opened his suitcase on a wooden bench and hastily searched through it. Under the clothes lay stacks of loose papers in foolscap sheets, years of radio-logs compiled in his Lincolnshire room out of loneliness, a tenacious persistence in taking down radio-messages from a thousand sources in the hope of finding and hearing and recording for himself and everyone a message from some non-existent God or god-like fountain beyond all the layers of the stars that might contain the precious message of life that would fill him with energy, imagination, and intelligence.

As the hundreds of sheets of paper covered with his neat writing scattered like birds and snowflakes and dead leaves over the arms of the harbour that the ship now entered John's hand gripped the butt of his long guarded and loaded revolver. Forgive me, Lord; I know what I am doing. He opened his mouth wide, as if to shout at the pampered disputatious gulls of Dover and tell them to watch out for what was coming. Placing the barrel of the gun well inside, he tilted it to what he hoped in his final lucid moment was the correct angle, and pulled the trigger. The nearest gulls wheeled away sharply at the noise, and the humble abrasive boat-siren announced that he was home at last.

CHAPTER THIRTY-THREE

'WHERE have *you* been?' Nancy demanded, as if he'd gone to the pub for some fags and come back two hours after the dinner had burned to a cinder. She stood aside so that he could set his suitcase in the hall. 'The bad penny turned up again.'

'How are you, love?' he said, kissing her.

'I'm all right. What the bleddy-hell was you doing all this time? How are you?'

'Going around Algeria. I'm fine, fit enough. Won't you make me some tea?' She'd altered in thirty months, a few lines by the side of her hazel eyes, oval face paler – though everyone seemed pale in this country.

'You've got a cheek,' she cried, 'leaving me all this time and then walking back in here as large as life and asking for a cup of tea.'

'You didn't expect me to crawl in, did you, and sup at the dog-bowl?'

She was trembling with surprise and anger, but managed to get the kettle under the tap and on the stove. 'Why didn't you send a telegram at least?'

'You might have thought I was dead or something. I don't like to frighten people.'

'I suppose you wanted to see who I was living with?'

He noticed a uniform tunic hanging on the wall. 'You live with who you like. I left *you*.'

'You can hardly deny that.'

'I don't want to.'

She set out two cups. 'Do you want some cheese on toast?'

'Please.'

'I'm not living with anybody, except the kids, if you want to know. One bloody man's enough in my life, especially if his name happens to be Frank Dawley.'

He pointed to the tunic. 'Who's is that? Where are the kids?'

'The third degree. That tunic's mine. I work on the buses, and I'm due on the afternoon shift in an hour. The kids are at school and when they finish they go to Mary's for their tea. Then she comes and puts them to bed, so they're fast asleep by the time I get home at eleven.' She sliced dried-up mousetrap cheese on to toasted Miracle Bread and slid it back under the grill.

'You look smart,' he said, 'in that shirt and skirt.'

'I had to earn some money. I'd rather be independent than rely on a rotter like you.'

He embraced and kissed her. 'It didn't do either of us any harm.'

She snapped away. 'The toast'll burn. You do look altered, though, I must say. You've got less meat on you. And your hair's gone grey. Did you have a lot to put up with out there?'

'Not more than I could manage.'

'So it seems. But still, you look in the prime as well.'

'I had to get to it some time. Phone up the bus depot and tell them you've got flu.'

'Pull up your chair and eat this. You make impossible demands on me.'

'I don't want you to dislike me, that's why.'

They sat at the small kitchen table. Nancy drank tea. 'I can't dislike you, though that's what you deserve.'

'Is it? It's not. You've never been out of my mind, you and the kids. In the tightest spots in Algeria, when I was close to being killed a dozen times – I don't suppose you believe it – but you were all in my mind, you and others. I had to go out there for the sake of people like us, as well as to do what I could for the Algerians – all equally. I'll tell you something about it soon. I'm not sentimental, but I couldn't have kept up that sort of life for long if I hadn't thought about certain people, good people whom I'd see again when it was over and if I got out of it.'

She looked at him, and their hands touched on the table. 'Don't let your toast get cold. You'd have wolfed that down at one time, without me telling you,' she said. 'I believe what you're saying. But it's been hard for us here. I'm not complaining though. I'm just telling you.'

'I know, love, I know.'

'But I won't give up my job,' she said. 'Whether you've come back or not I'm going to stay independent. That's one thing I believe in. If a man can be, a woman has a right to be. Nobody can take that from me any more.'

He stood to hang up his coat, then finished his meal. 'Have you got four pennies for the phone?' she asked.

Alone he wandered into the living room. It was roughly tidy, the children's toys swept into a corner. There was a new television set, and a transistor radio on the windowsill. The stair-carpet was badly worn. In their bedroom his record-player was closed up and wedged between the wardrobe and the wall, with a cardboard box of his books secured by string and set on top. On the dressing-table was a photo of himself taken three years ago, when he was twenty-seven, sporting his best suit and looking grim but youthful, a tight squat unopened face when compared to the grey middle-aged visage facing him in the mirror. Nearby was another photo, of a plain mannish sort of woman he did not know, with: 'To Nancy, affectionately from Laura' scrawled along the bottom. He assumed it to be some pal of hers from the bus depot – as if there weren't enough men: though maybe not if they nipped off to Algeria and such places. The window looked on the untended plot of housing-estate garden, barren and frozen under the bitter haze of winter.

He went down and sat in the kitchen, poured himself another cup of tea, then ate an apple. He had come back out of friendliness to Nancy, and to see the children, and did not know what would come after this. He had undergone the discomfort of travel and war in order to obliterate and avoid the greater discomfort of life at home, she thought. But if that was so, why should he come back when the journey was finished? The truth was that for him it would never be ended.

She walked in, reddened by the cold air outside.

'OK?' he asked.

'Just for today. I don't like to let them down.'

'Are you glad to see me back?'

'You're a stranger to me. I never expected to see you

again. But the kids haven't stopped asking for you, so they'll be glad.'

'That's one thing.'

She smiled. 'Of course I'm happy to see you, you damn fool.'

'I hoped you might be. You can't kid me.' Not that he would stay long, but he had gifts, and perhaps plans for them all. 'Nobody ever leaves for good,' he said, 'unless they kick the bucket somewhere.'

In the living room he emptied the scuttle on to the dying fire, moved coal around with the heel of his shoe, which he drew back to the carpet when a cloud of white smoke shrouded it. He remembered how he had left her two summers ago, packed and walked out one Saturday afternoon with few words, only the feeling of an unexploded bomb inside and the simple stark message that he had to go. His silence and her bitterness corroded all communication, so that the parting was inevitable and somehow too easy.

He sat by her on the sofa, drawn close to the flames. 'You'll have to tell me about Algeria,' she said. 'It must have been interesting doing something you'd always talked about. You are lucky. But I suppose you have lots of plans.'

'Some,' he said.

'Do they include me? I'm not begging, don't think that, but I just want to know.'

'They'll have to, I think. I'm glad the kids are all right.'

'They're fine.' Simon was seven and Janet eight, and he saw a photo of them above the fire, augmented shadows of the smaller bodies he'd known yelling for first turn on his knee when back from work. He kissed her. Something had to take place before they could enter the sea of conversation both felt boiling inside and unable to break loose. 'Let's go up to bed, until they get back from their tea.'

She stood. 'You won't go for a few days though, will you? I'm glad you're back for a while, anyway. Give me a few minutes, then follow me up.'

He didn't wait for the bus, but made his own way to Myra's from the station. He had grown accustomed to walking, finding the cross-country tracks and going from A to B in a straight line. It felt like a game he'd bought in a shop, a one-inch map from the bookstall and off he went on a seven-mile jaunt of mild English Trackopoly. Winter time, sludge on the footpaths – go back six squares; leave luggage at station – go forward ten. The space was small, but there was no one to run from yet, no need for lying low in copse or wood. Yet he was singling out patches of forest for the assembly of ambush groups, hideouts for murder gangs, secret routes for lone assassins, areas for concealing arms and food dumps, rearguard defence lines. At the edge of the town a car stopped and a man's hand waved to give him a lift. 'No thanks,' he shouted. 'I'm walking for my health.' But the cold made his various scar-wounds ache, and he sat on stile or gate now and again for a smoke.

It was hard to believe all this rich land was his, that it belonged to him and everybody else. It was a good thought, yet false, though if anyone had tried to scare him from the footpath now, saying he was on private property and had no right there, he would have murdered them in a light-hearted revolutionary way, counting him the first casualty in his own personal war of national liberation. He cut a yew stick and walked along, musing on Handley's surprise and maybe pleasure when he visited him next week in Lincoln-shire. He'd come down that morning from Nottingham on the train, after spending a week with Nancy.

A woman rode along an intersecting path on a bicycle. She wore a blue mackintosh, and a knitted hat was pulled over her ears. On a special seat behind sat a young child, comfortably tied in, looking up and around at blackbirds crossing a field as his mother pedalled along, her body bent for more leverage. Frank stood and shouted after her. She rode on. By the farm was a large compound of pigs, the sun glistening on their pink backs. He called again, and started to run, but she hadn't heard. The rasping sound of a machine-saw came from a close-by wood, and the lazy noise of a jet-engine filled the momentary space when it stopped, echoing high beyond the low hills. She had come from Wingham direction and was heaving along a flat unfenced cart-track, wobbling slightly to avoid ruts. There was a brown field to one side and a green one on the other, and she went towards Parkwell by her own short cut.

He stopped running, but gave a final shout 'Myra!' She came to a paved lane, and pedalled out of sight. His mountain eyes were mystified by damp fields. He had lost his desert certainty, and the split-second assurance of wide-open spaces. The calamity of narrowness made him doubt that it had been Myra. The longer you look the less convinced you are, because that which needs looking at for a long time is most open to doubt. The clear winter vision baffled him, and he walked on along the path, hoping he would find her at home. He'd telephoned from the station but had been answered by some childish shuddering idiot who said that Dad had gone to the funeral at Dover. She'd obviously changed her telephone number from the one two years ago.

He walked into the village street of thatched houses, and bus-shelter opposite shops and grey stone church, remembering his injuries when her husband had tried to kill them both. In the side-garden of her house were two large caravans, and the once impeccable lawn had been trodden into bare earth. A four-year-old girl in duffle-coat and pixie-hood smiled as he walked along the path. He recognized Myra's old car standing beside a red Mini and a new M.G. A dark-haired girl came down the caravan steps and gave the younger one a glass of milk.

By the garage door was a pram in which a baby slept, a boy stowed under the blanket and windshield hood. He bent close and stared at him. The Italian girl pulled at his arm: 'Here, what the bloody-'ell you think you are doing? Who are you?'

'Whose baby's this?'

She saw his smile. 'You like children?'

'Yes. Is it Myra's?'

'That's all right.'

'It is?'

'Yes.'

'He's my son, then.'

362

'My God! You never seen him before?'

He slept. 'I'll wake him later.'

'He's a good baby,' she said. 'A very good boy.'

Twelve-year-old Paul stood by the back door, pulling the triggers of a double-barrelled shotgun. While Frank was wondering where he'd seen him before, Mandy came from the kitchen and pushed her brother outside: 'If you want to play soldiers with that thing go up the back garden. It's a jungle enough for you to hide in. Hello,' she said, recognizing Frank, 'where did you jump from?'

'I came to see Myra. What are you doing here?'

'Living. You'll be unlucky. She went to Dover yesterday with Dad, to see about Uncle John's funeral.'

'Uncle John? Which Uncle John?'

She stared at him. 'Uncle John. I don't suppose you knew. He blew his brains out. What few he had. Those who blow their brains out never had any to blow out. But by the time they know it they're dead.'

They walked into the kitchen, Mandy weeping: 'This is the fifth damn time I've cried today. I can't stop. Poor Uncle John!'

'Sit down,' he said. 'Don't get upset.' It seemed like a premeditated Handley-drama faked for his arrival.

'I can't help it,' she said. 'What else is there to do?' No blinds were drawn, or black suits being aired, but then, the Handleys never went in for things like that. Had it really been a joke, they would have.

'What are you talking about?' he demanded. 'Why are you all at Myra's?' He felt as if he'd walked into a nightmare and dream all thrown into one. Sun shot through the window over the checked linoleum tablecloth. He leaned on the washing-machine.

'Back in Lincolnshire the house burned down, so we all came to live at Myra's. I don't know why. We aren't short of cash. Dad just wanted to, so maybe he was knocking on with her. At least that's what Mam threw at him when they were quarrelling one night.'

He shook her: 'For Christ's sake, tell me what happened to John.'

'Take your cowing hands off me, or I'll let fly. How should I know? He left on the night of the fire, and we still don't know if he had anything to do with that little disaster, to look for you in Algeria. It seems he found you. Then the other day a copper knocked at the door. Dad started trembling like a leaf, till he remembered he was rich. Next thing we knew he was ready to shoot off to Dover with Myra. Mam though it was an elaborate trick for a dirty weekend, and went with them as well – so don't look so blue. Dad phoned this morning to say John had shot himself. They left me looking after the place, with a hundred mouths to feed. I'm married now, made it six weeks ago with the world's most genuine zombie. There'll be another little zombie in the world soon.'

He was back in Handley-land, where a manic non-stop gift of the claptrap reigned over all residents and comers. 'Why did he shoot himself?' he asked.

'Pardon me,' she said. 'God isn't back from lunch yet. But I'll be sure to ask him though when he comes in. I expect John had had enough. Or maybe he thought he hadn't had anything. He was always strange, apart from epilepsy. But he was so sweet and kind. Oh, don't worry, I shan't bawl again. I can see it troubles you.'

'It's the cause of it that disturbs me, not your crying. I can't believe it, though. I said goodbye to him at Gibraltar airport. He wouldn't come on the plane because he didn't like flying. It might crash, and he'd get killed, he said. Maybe he though he might be tempted to do it during the flight. He was in a hurry to get away from me because I kept pressing him to come on the plane, and I suppose he thought he might give in.'

'You didn't try hard enough,' she said. 'He must have tried a bloody sight harder when he went out there to find you.'

'I didn't ask him to come for me,' he said.

'You were glad to see him, I'll bet.'

He hadn't been, but this wasn't the time to say it. 'When is Albert due back?'

'Late tonight. He'll go again for the inquest, I suppose.

364

He's broken up about it. Sounded terrible on the phone. Sleep here if you like. There's room in the flat.'

'My luggage is at the station. I thought I might have to stay in town.'

'Fetch it in the Mini, and buy a gallon of petrol on the way. If you've got no money tell 'em to put it on our account. Everybody does. We owe hundreds round here already. It's a good job we left Lincolnshire, with the creditors closing in. I thought when I got married I'd stop living like a bandit, but Ralph's mother cut him off without a penny, and so we're still part of the worm-eaten ship.'

The regular thump-thump of a machine sounded from upstairs like a heavy loom or treadle worked by hand. 'That's Richard,' she said, 'and Adam at the printing-press. They turn out loads of stuff, send it every day all over the country. This house is the middle of the spider's web of revolution, and it's costing us the earth. Dad paints more than he used to, and earns more money, but it'll ruin him in the end.' Her oval heavily-lidded eyes speculated on a future she wanted, and wasn't sure that she wouldn't yet get before she was twenty – with less than a year to go. 'My heart's set on a simple life,' she said. 'Ralph and I would be happy if we could get a small house right away from here, where we could live in peace.'

Late that night the Ford Rambler drew up on the road outside. Handley, Myra, and Enid came into the kitchen breathing smoke and frost.

Frank stood up. The picture of the day had altered, switched into complete indifference now that they were home. It had turned him from his own house with Nancy and the children packed off to school, through train corridors and a walk across countryside, to this establishment full of weird and fateful people. He saw it on their faces as they came in and he looked around.

Myra noticed a strange man in her house, another friend of Albert's perhaps who had dropped by on his travels – either one of the family, or a recent painter acquaintance up from London. Handley, mouth down, took off his fur hat, and overcoat that reached his ankles. Enid pushed by him and put the kettle on, the tips of her long blonde hair brushing Frank's shirt. The silence was bruising them, a strange quiet bout of recognition and surprise, and all wanting to speak and break it. Myra had taken off her glasses getting out of the car, resting her eyes by not forcing them to see clearly. Here was a different person, this man with an olive skin stretched over the bones of his face, a scar below his left ear, a face without a smile and not willing at the moment to say much. She thought how possible it would have been to pass him on the street – except for the eyes, which she would have noted in any man. The grey eyes looked at her, bringing no humour from the wilderness of his travels, and no mercy in the love he had pulled back with them. They were not the eyes he had gone away with, for the lustre was no longer there, the light had drawn back into the depths, shining on to the interior acres of his thought rather than too much and too shallowly on the outer world as it had done before. He stood more alone than anyone else in the room, though that may have been because her love was enveloping him and ready once more to attempt possession. But not entirely. He was alone, stronger, so that with such eyes and rendered features he would stay that way, the one controller of his own mind and actions. He had gone away with the idea of destroying his love and her love. But the cinders and dead ash had brought him back just the same. He wasn't powerful enough to wreck anyone's love, not even his own, and this knowledge had kept her thinking of him every day, wanting to talk to him, touch him, her visions all the more immediate because she had never been entirely convinced that he would come back. She'd had a hundred premonitions of his death, seen him so many scattered lumps of clay, tortured, hanged, shot, dead of hunger and thirst, wandering insane with his senses spread broadcast by hot sandy winds of the summer desert.

She smiled and went to him, hands touching. As I grow older I know better how to be young. She felt the flooding emotions of passionate love on seeing him again. Handley's forehead creased, but he smiled nevertheless. 'Let's drink to *your* safe return, anyway.'

'I'm sorry about John,' he said. 'I'll tell you about it. But there was nothing I could do. Nothing. I thought that once we got out of Algeria he'd be all right.'

'I know,' Handley said. 'You don't have to say it. I tried for over fifteen years, and failed. I softened his life, worked for him, nursed him, and yet, all the time at the back of my mind was the dread of this happening. It was always there, nagging and tormenting. I knew it over the years, a panther behind his face waiting to spring. My own brother does a thing like this, and the wickedest thought I have is: Why didn't he do it at the beginning instead of wasting his life for another fifteen years? That's wrong. If he had, none of us would have been there thinking about our own rich lives yet to be lived. I was the only one who tried to stop him when he first proposed going to Algeria. I should have locked him up: barred his window and fastened his door with wood. And yet, what *can* you do? What bloody right have you finally got to settle a man's life when he's set firm on his own way?'

He poured glasses of whisky for them all. Frank looked at Myra. Being in love, he remembered telling himself on the plane from Gibraltar, to fight down his rising emotion at the thought of seeing her again, is a state of paralysis and death. You can't act when you are in love, or do anything, unless the woman is willing to follow you anywhere, which is not love. Love and passion combined make the pleasantest form of suicide, yet here he was, more in love with Myra than he'd ever been with any other woman. It was strange, falling in love with a woman who already had your child.

'Have you seen Mark?' she asked.

'I was playing with him. He's a beauty.'

Handley laughed. 'There'll be a few more soon. Enid's having one – her last, I should think. And Mandy's having her first. Let's drink to them all!'

CHAPTER THIRTY-FOUR

TAKING a flashlight he walked to the large studio hut which
Handley had erected at the end of the garden. Permanent
heaters had been installed, and warmth and the smell of
paint, the comforting reek of turps and glue met him as he
came in out of the frost. He found the light-switches, and
closed the door. The fantastic colour-cathedral of Handley's
life covered every wooden wall, so that it was like being in
another man's stomach, seeing with his eyes, smothered by
his entire vision. He must be a machine to turn out so
much. It was a wonder his arms had strength, never mind
the imagination. If Mandy's idea was right, John had tried
to burn all this when he set fire to the house in Lincolnshire, before setting off for Algeria to pluck him from the
raging fires of civil war. Even the Handleys needed their
legends, since anarchy was not enough.

He sat by one of the large tables and smoked a cigarette.
Of all places on the compound this was the quietest. Only
faint waves of shouting penetrated from the inhabited
areas. Albert had done well to place himself here. The
house, the caravans, the flat above the garage, all were
eruptions of strife and metallic noise that only subsided for
a few hours of darkness each night. He sometimes longed
for the silence and danger of the desert. Eric Bloodaxe,
that blue-blooded bulldog that held some corner of affection in Handley's twisted heart, howled balefully over the
roofs of the village.

John had been buried a fortnight. The inquest said he'd
committed suicide while of unsound mind. No other verdict
was possible. The lumpen-bourgeoisie demanded it. It had
to be suicide if they were to keep their confidence and survive. The idea of actually choosing death in opposition to
the best of all possible lives that they offered was alien to
them. Well, they would keep it until it was ripped away
from them by machine-guns and Molotov cocktails. The
one infallible answer was always violence, violence, and still
more violence. In Algeria it was already succeeding in what

it set out to do. It couldn't fail, provided it was prolonged and violent enough. If the sky starts to fall in, pull down the stars as well. When you are surrounded by a ring of fire and can't get out, all you can do is learn to jump. While learning to jump the fire goes out. You are free. Once free, burn every bush till there are no bushes left, till even the ash burns again to ash and the soil itself jumps into flame. Destruction appalls them. They are terrified of losing their property. The scorched-earth policy is the one sure answer to such endless indoctrination, and to defeat the easy power that they have. Threaten the fourth dimension of civil war, the end-all of life from which renewed life can spring more quickly than if no destruction had taken place.

This outpost-compound had its armoury of Sten-guns, rifles and shotguns. Handley had seen to that, stowed them under the garage floor from where they were taken out for a ritual pull-through and polish every week. There were stores of food, petrol, and John's radio transceivers which Richard and Adam knew how to work. Even while poor they had been prepared, though no one knew precisely for what, with the possible exception of Richard. Certainly no one could accuse Handley of thinking himself to death, since he considered he needed no philosophical justification for what he thought and did. They had left the atavistic age of being content merely to live for the moment, and had entered the era of wanting to survive, which no one else seemed to have done, apart from the government and all its offices, which was only to be expected. Handley couldn't work unless such supplies and equipment were close by. His spirit would be paralysed, hands crippled, brain sedated, eyes bandaged. They meant freedom to him, expansion, gave stature and a final sense of self-respect in face of the impending bourgeois atomic juggernaut. On their side they had the Bomb, and if he didn't have a gun or two on his he would curl up and die at the vast injustice of it. He could only marvel at the fact that he'd fallen in with such a talented and bandit crew, *franc-tireurs* of the atomic and conformist age. Yet Frank considered that one had to be careful not to get rounded up in the incipient disorder of their lives, and to avoid this the community would have to be worked on, given security and direction in both social and military spheres. Handley was happy to let it run itself, to stagger from debt to debt and scandal to broiling set-to, but Frank and Adam talked of forming a permanent council to guide things in a more organized way. Frank thought they should begin immediately, but Adam, being a Handley, knew the ways of the family somewhat better, and so suggested that the present way of life went on until social and moral disintegration set in, at which point a permanent council would almost form itself with everyone's automatic and grateful consent. There matters stood. And there, Frank saw, they might stay for a long time yet.

The door opened, and Handley came in. 'I knew I'd find you here.' He opened a cupboard and poured brandy. 'I don't suppose you had much of this among the Moslems.'

'I didn't need it, somehow. Where's Myra?'

'Feeding Mark. She'll be in in a bit, as soon as he's hit the sweet pillow. How do you like the community now? You've been here a fortnight.'

'I'm part of it, it seems.'

'You are.' They smoked cigars, ash falling unnoticed. Handley was recovering from the shock and emptiness of his brother's death, his mental landscape no longer swamped and intolerably burdened by it. He had breathed it fully in and knew that he had to work and live without John for the rest of his life. There had been no black sign on the house, for it was never one of the Handley colours. 'I'm opposed to it,' he had said, 'in clothes, flags, food, excrement, and paintings.' But his love was too brotherly for him to forget his grief at this futile unnecessary suicide. Yet no spark had gone out of him, no lustre drained from his eyes. He seemed as energetic, abusive, and lively as ever. He had worn his cap and topcoat to get from the house to the studio, always considerate of his health where the weather was concerned, and when he felt particularly well.

'Am I stopping you from working?' Frank asked.

'Nobody ever did that. I can slap paint on, whoever's around, as long as they don't mind a blob now and again in

370

the left eye. Did you talk to Myra about bringing Nancy and kids here?'

'She agreed. I must go to Nottingham soon and collect them. They'll take a bit of persuading, but I think I can manage it.'

'We'll fit in,' Handley said. 'It'll make twenty of us, including Eric Bloodaxe. Twenty-one souls if Cuthbert comes back. I'll have a few things to say to him though when he does. He's bound to. Getting thrown out of that cushy theological college and about to be ordained. To think a son of mine could have been criminal enough to be so stupid! Still, if we get a bit overcrowded we'll put up tents. Do a few of 'em good, a life under canvas. Or we can build a bungalow between here and the house, and a few can sleep in the Rambler. We could get hundreds in our little community, come to think of it. We'll call it the Villa Back-to-Back if we want to give it a continental flourish. It'll be so small and high, the whole packed lot, that if we sling a wall around it we'll have a genuine medieval city on our hands. As for transport we could turn into a mobile column at a pinch, with three cars and two caravans. Send the Mini and four people ahead as a spearheading scout car with the quick-firing pulverine mounted on top, then the Rambler pulling the heavy caravan with five in each, and us poring over the map-tables, then the last eight in the light caravan, and the rest in the Morris as a rearguard. At night we'd form a laager in some layby and pitch tents. Still, I don't see that being necessary for a while, though it's as well to bear it in mind. Might be a way to have a continental holiday. Let my lot loose at the heart of Germany and they'd surrender in two minutes, though don't ask me who.'

'You're the only one of us all who never seems to change,' said Frank light-heartedly.

Handley slung his cigar into the bin: 'I did my altering while you were in crappy-nappies. My first deep breath took me to the age of thirty or so, then I changed into the low dumps till I was thirty-six, when I switched gear into mainstream. Now I keep the black ship going to hell, all sails flapping, panache, and spinnakers taut as drums and pointing across my cold uncharted sea. It's not that simple, but it's a way of putting it, Frank, my old lad. We'll be having the big reunion dinner tonight, so I'll go and see how the organization's going on. Don't get too drunk on my three-star plonk.'

He went out, coughing through the icy mist. The compound seemed unnaturally quiet as soon as the door fell to, an unnerving impossible silence as he sat in the dim light listening to it. He didn't know at the moment for how long he would be able to immerse himself in the Handley roundabout. But the stillness matched the temporary peace of his life long enough for him to make decisions out of the deeper quietness of his heart.

He stopped thinking while the noise stayed far away, switched off all lights but one and sat in his own dusk, smoking ruminatively. He had the nagging uncomfortable feeling of being a member of society once more, even though it was composed solely of Handleys. But the thought that perhaps he had only exchanged one form of guerrilla band for another made him feel more optimistic.

Myra came in. 'Mark's asleep at last. His teeth give him a lot of trouble.'

'He'll know how to bite on life, then!'

She sat by him. 'Do you really approve of me giving my place to Albert and his family?'

'It's your house,' he said.

'Don't evade the question.'

'Their house burned down. You gave them yours.'

'But Albert has enough money to buy another. In any case, I do consider it to be your house as well.'

'If it had been I should have done the same.'

'The village is already up in arms. Nobody talks to me at the shop any more, and I can't have anything to do with the Womens' Institute even if I wanted to. They complain every day to the police about noise and litter.'

'Does it bother you?'

'No. Mrs Harrod even stopped coming.'

'There are enough of the Handleys to make up a labour force. The *au pair* girls like it here because it's nearer to

London. You don't mind me bringing Nancy and the kids down, then?'

She said she did not. 'As long as they fit in, the more the better. I suppose I look on it as a sociological experiment, or I would if I didn't like it so much.'

'You do a lot of work,' he said, 'catering and caring for everyone. It must be like running a hostel.'

'Most of it runs itself. I think it's what I always wanted to do. I have you, so I feel happy at last. I'm fond of everyone who lives here.'

'I hope you like Nancy.'

'I don't see why I shouldn't. I hope she likes me.'

'I think she will.'

'Adam says you are going to collaborate on a book about your experiences in Algeria.'

'Yes. I write it all down, then he'll advise me on the finer points of style. I suppose he'll actually rewrite it. We'll become a literate community in spite of ourselves, a hotbed of books and conspiracy. Richard has many other ingenious plans, all sorts of stunts and tricks of sabotage. The Handleys are so mad and wild that no one would suspect them of intelligent planning.' He stood up: 'Let's go over to the house and see about the big dinner.'

CHAPTER THIRTY-FIVE

HE was blinded by a combination of strip-lighting, table-lamps, ordinary bulbs, and candles, that turned the room into a chamber of dazzling incandescent clarity, with such light pushing to the limits of all-white walls that there seemed to be smoke in the air, though no one had yet lit a cigarette. The dozen of Handley's paintings spaced around the walls could only be seen as grey and metallic – unless one came in for a special show during light day. The house had turned into far more of a Handleydrome than his former Lincolnshire residence had ever been able to.

Bottles of Yugoslav Riesling stood along the table, and

each person's name was written on the back of a photo of Uncle John. Handley stood up from the head of the table and moved two chairs down to the left. 'It's got to stop,' he said in a loud voice. 'There's to be no top of the table any more. Let's kick off in the right way. If there's one thing I can't stand it's an ordered life. Put the cards in your pockets and sit where you like. And if you're forming factions already before I have time to wipe my nose, then on your own heads be it.'

There was a muted irritation at this deliberate displacement of seats, which gradually eased however as the first line of bottles wavered and disappeared. The main course was rabbit stew and rice, and the bottles of Riesling gave way to a stolid line of Nuits St Georges. Enid, in a thoughtless moment, had put Schubert's quintet on the record-player, but reasonably low so that everyone could talk against it. Adam stood up, his glass dark red to the brim, and his mouth full. His elfish face was sad because Wendy Bonser had long since fallen out of love with him. Unable to stand the voices at the Conservative Club he had mimicked several of them brilliantly at the bar one night and been thrown bodily out. He was now deeply back in the family, more subversive than he'd ever been. 'Let's drink to living off the land. The dozen rabbits that make up this stew were caught the night before last by Richard and me, with the help of our twelve-year-old apprentice Paul. Of course, we were well-trained in traditional Lincolnshire poaching by our assiduous dad, and we have now transferred our skills to Buckinghamshire.'

'You're boasting,' cried Mandy. 'You're drunk already. Sit down.'

Ralph had not spoken to anyone for days. In fact Richard thought he hadn't opened his mouth since joining the Handley family except to push food and drink into it, but couldn't be sure because he'd never been close enough until tonight. He now broke silence and stood up, leaned over the table supported by ten springy outspread fingers, dark hair splayed, face heavy and pale as he glared at them all: 'You're thieves. You can't even keep your exploits

374

quiet. You just want to embarrass Myra, and me.'

'If you back me up again,' Mandy called, 'I'll blind you.
Nobody has a right to back me up. I can defend myself.' He
sat down, and though not a man of excessive weight the
chair almost cracked under him at the ponderousness of his
smashed ego. He drained his glass at one long throatslide,
and smiled to stop himself going mad and running amok.

'We have a certain mission in this village,' Richard said,
facing his brother who now sat down. 'Believe it or not,
Ralph, we're going to civilize it. I don't suppose you know
what that word means. For example when we came here
there was a notice tacked up outside the village pub which
said: NO DIDACOIS. NO GYPSIES. We found it repulsive in its
racialist smear. Well, it was down the first night. They put
it up again. In fact it goes up and down half-a-dozen times,
but they no longer have it there now. We're planning to
have some of our gypsy friends go in, and if they don't get
served it's war on that pub. Oh no, we're not going to complain to the Civil Liberties Council. Nothing like that for
us. Nobody's going to get us on that bourgeois treadmill.
That pub will go into the ground with everybody in it if it
doesn't serve all comers. So will a few pubs in neighbouring
villages, as well. That's just one of our minor campaigns.
Now, about the ethics of poaching rabbits ...'

Myra smiled. On her property they were safe, it was their
'base zone', and nothing from the outside world could move
them. She was joined to them by her respect for Albert's
painting, and by an inexplicable fondness for the whole
following. Her grief at the suicide of his brother (whose
death she connected with his expedition to a civil war to
bring back the father of her child) also welded her to this
family. She lived in a compound where no relationships
seemed fixed, and where no one temperament was like
another. The final test and complication would be the
arrival of Nancy and her children – whenever Frank chose
to bring them in.

As for money, she had cleared twenty thousand pounds
from the share-out of her father's will, even after the death
duties had been lopped off, and such a mountainous sum,

375

invested on Handley's advice in a London Borough Council, was accumulating interest for them all, an abundance of reserves that would hold them up for a long time. She was buying two fields near the village, satisfying her own desire to own more land, on which they could build, use it for picnics, or put it to any use that the community might decide on.

She looked at Frank across the table. He smiled. He was like a man back from famine rather than war, a traveller who had been to the magic circles of the moon and fought with the demonic apotheosis of evil till the bones went white within him and had suffered more than his soul had the capacity to take, as if he had been robbed of the ability to love, and had taken on the incurable sickness of compassion. His eyes were edged with chaos, and a strength that thrilled and frightened her. He was the man who was leaving the demanding sphere of the moon and entering the machine-age pull and energy of the sun, a man halfway there but who had been through the worst fire of getting free, and was now where it seemed that little could stop him making the great change of the world, though no one was to know yet what the cost would be.

Enid grew angrier the more Richard expatiated on the political significance of poaching. 'Sit down,' she said, when he came to the end. To break in before would be to tread on a holy theme of the Handley way of life. 'I only believe in poaching if we're too poor to buy food, and at the moment we're not.'

'That's contrary to our policy of living off the land,' Handley said quietly.

'If I want any rabbits I can buy them at the Co-op,' she said. 'I never ask you to steal them for me.'

'Death to all shopkeepers!' cried Adam.

'I don't see why we should be driven out of this village,' she said.

'Let them try,' said Richard. 'We can hold them off for weeks.'

Only Handley and Enid were on their feet, the normal end of any upheaval, it seemed, in whatever house they occupied. Frank did not see how their community could exist for long under this internal tension. But he grew to see that because of such upheavals – which were, after all, merely the Handley method of debate and consensus – it could go on for ever. And if he could not stand it he could always remove himself to a land where the bonfires of insurrection had burst into reddening flame, to lead or follow against the dark forces of whoever governed.

'I suppose,' Handley said to Enid, 'that you're getting latched on to your usual neurotic dream of wanting an ideal place to live and die in, where you are on totally unrealistic terms with the people, and are unselfconsciously hobnobbing with the local gentry? I don't have to ask where Mandy gets her death-wish from. All these ideas ought to be chased from the brains of such grown-up people. You can't live at peace with the world. Not this world which won't ever let you live at peace with it except on its own impossible strait-jacket terms. We're not that sort of gang, family, tribe, or whatever you like to call us. The world hasn't got to be only lived in, because even if you keep yourself at a distance it will corrupt and destroy you by forcing you to keep your distance, but it has to be continually attacked, raided, sabotaged, marauded, plundered, insulted, and spat on. It's not the sort of place you can walk around with your head cocked back in bollocky-eyed disdain and splendour, because even the birds of the air which they've trained and which had been trained without meaning to be, will go peep-peep and shit in your eye. You only make your mark and set up your score by giving no quarter either within or beyond the law. The village may not be ours by day, but it will be by night. We can't at the moment melt in among the people like fish in water but after a few years the situation may be different.'

While he was speaking the lounge door opened, and a tall burly young man wearing a cap and overcoat stood a little inside the room. Handley noticed him but went on talking. The man slowly opened his overcoat at the food-heat, and took off his cap. He wore a black shirt, and the white reversed dog-collar of a priest. His face was sensitive though

377

overfed. He had a long narrow nose and thin expressive lips, and curly fair hair that fell over his forehead and the depth of his brow. He could have been any age between twenty and forty. Listening at first with respect and attention in what may have been a habitual expression, his lips slowly took on the shape of contempt that finally was exactly duplicated on Handley's face when he stopped talking and looked at him for a moment. That, thought Frank, must be Cuthbert.

Handley was determined to finish: 'But we can forgive Enid balking at some of our activities, because she is basically a noble and gentle soul who can't throw out her past because she's still living in it. And as for Ralph, he should be ashamed of himself. His family are rich Lincolnshire loam-farmers who plundered their tenants and workers for decades, and when he shows a bit of individuality his pain-in-the-heart of a mother pitches him out without even a strip of field to use as a necktie or arserag. And as for Mandy she's just got the same belly-yearnings as her mother, combined with my pitch of obstinacy, which she's perverted to her own sybaritic use.'

'You're talking like a madman,' Enid cried. 'In a few years you'll be in jail and we'll be destitute. You'll soon be as crazy and epileptic as John whom we sheltered and kept alive for so many years unless you get back to your painting and stop all this nonsense.'

Cuthbert broke in, shouting through his smile: 'Well, well, I can see the old matrimonial death-grapple is still going on. Call it a community, call it what you like, but I can smell it a mile off for what it is. I come home and what do I find? The same old gluttons at the pig-trough. What you want around here is a bit of plain speaking!'

Enid's back had been to the door, and only now did she notice his presence. She turned and smiled at her favourite and eldest son. 'We didn't expect you till next week, Cuthbert. How are you, my love?'

He ignored her. 'Aren't you going to welcome your firstborn, Dad?'

'Sit down and get some stew,' Handley said, grim-lipped.

'Maybe it'll stop your mouth up.' Cuthbert was the perfect blend of his parents, in that you could not distinctly see either of them mirrored in his features, though at the same time you knew he could be none other than their son. Enid set him a place, and Maria brought a plate of stew. Richard, not too willingly, poured his wine. Frank sensed that the equilibrium of the house had been permanently displaced by his arrival.

'I've got news for you, Dad,' Cuthbert said between food. 'I've been thinking that with everybody's permission I'd like to stay here, because I've nowhere to go since leaving college. I hope nobody minds.'

'You're welcome,' Handley said, 'as long as you fit in like the rest of us. There's plenty of work to do. We all earn our own keep.'

'Give him time,' Enid said indignantly. 'He's only just stepped through that door.'

'And he can step right out of it again if there's any trouble or disruption. He had the best bloody prospects in the world, of becoming an ordained priest in the Church-of-rotten-England, and he spoils it all through lust and greed, and I suspect a bit of simony and black mass thrown in. He could have infiltrated right into the middle of the enemy's juiciest pie. What a chance gone to dust and ashes. It gives me the knee-ache to think of it.'

Cuthbert stepped up by his chair, kicked a couple of bottles aside and blew a candle out with the flap of his trousers. He stood full height on the table, his head bending slightly under the smooth chalk of the ceiling. With a deliberate gesture he ripped off his priestly white collar, so that only his black shirt remained. 'In coming here I chose freedom. Do you hear, father? FREEDOM! I've had enough of being your germ in a sealed train steering for the heart of the imperial poxeaten church. I resented being used by you, and used by them, which is what it amounted to. By intermittent intelligence, continual fawning, and eternal hypocrisy I nearly got stuffed into that pit of frayed hymnbooks and incensed cassockrags that you intended me for. But I'd rather risk my life than my spirit. I was beginning to like it, and if I'd stayed another month I'd have been so genuinely deep in it that you'd have lost all control of me. That's what I call a crisis of conscience: getting out before you are too far in. I can't lead a double life. I had to come back here so as to stay loyal to you and the family. It's all right for you, Dad. You think it's easy to live six lives at once, because you're an artist, but me, I'm not an artist. I'm honest, and can't stand having my guts corroded by playing false-face to something as corrupt as the Church of England. Oh no, not me. I can be treacherous to a cause which has been genuinely set up to help a large section of hapless mankind get out of its awful sufferings, and all that stuff. Find me a *good* cause to rip open like a rat from the inside, that I can believe in from the bottom of my heart, and I'll enjoy no finer work destroying it. Then I'll show you what skill and patience I've got in me, so that even you would pat me on the back – father.'

Handley had, for reasons of family solidarity and to put on a show of love and understanding in front of Frank and Myra, been rehearsing a few lily-white phrases of a welcome-home speech, but now they flew back in his mouth and choked him purple. 'Sit down,' he commanded, standing up. 'You're the only one of all my brood who is worse than me. One day you'll steal my turps and cut my bollocks off. You're the sort who in the Middle Ages would have taken a quiverful of poisoned arrows to the top of a brand-new cathedral built to the glory of God and picked off his friends first and his enemies second. Still, welcome back, Cuthbert. I think no one will object to such a valuable sackbag of assets joining our community. There was never much of "hear all, see all, say nought" about our Cuthbert – was there, Cuthbert? So I'm sure his time with the trainee clergy has been an admirable exercise in self-restraint. And when he does open his mouth nobody can accuse him of having a concentrated epigrammatic idiosyncratic style either. So before we get down to a night of drinking, talking, knifing, remembering John, and cracking nuts, I'm going to have the last ceremonial word, as an artist always should. We'll found this community as a memorial to my

380

brother John, and to his life, such as you all know it was. There should be enough money to keep this project going, but if there isn't then we'll have to find ways of getting it. England's a rich country still, so I don't see why it shouldn't support us while we're trying to bring it crashing down. And if ever it does crash we'll be able to fend for ourselves, because some of us will be running it. And if it's beyond a state when it can be run at all, by anybody, then we'll still keep alive, because chaos is very conducive when it comes to the likes of us living off the land.'

Cuthbert turned his eyes from one member of the family to another, and to those who were strangers to him. Frank saw him, and burned his look away. Introductions would come later, but there were no smiles between them.

'We all have our pledges,' Handley went on. 'Mine is to keep painting, to open the furnace-ovens and pull out the steel, work till I go mad or drop dead, to keep my patience and courage even when I can't do a stroke for weeks, to work cheap and sell to the highest bidder. My labour and long hours cost nothing, is so dirt-cheap that it's free where art is concerned, and in the end I place no money-value on what I turn out. But I know what it is worth to others, and I also know that my heart is never willing to sell it. But it's no use creeping into a corner to have a quiet cry when Teddy Greensleaves takes half a dozen canvases away on a tumbril cart to their doom in his gallery, though I know that when they go a few more gobbets of irreplaceable flesh have been snapped off my backbone. And so all I can do is have bad dreams, and carry on painting – as long as the rest of you work with me.'

Cuthbert stood up with tears on his cheeks, and a glass in his hand. 'We'll drink to that, Dad. We'll drink to that. And to Uncle John. And to Mother, and all of you.'

Everyone gathered around, including Ralph. Handley looked at them all with obvious distrust, but concealed love, then smiled sardonically and put an arm around Cuthbert. Frank was bemused, saw many weeks, even years of invigorating chaos ahead, of great ideas, and great work, and to this only he lifted his glass.

This is the second part of a trilogy, of which The Death of William Posters *is the first.*

A SELECTION OF
POPULAR READING IN PAN